3–

Dear Reader,

Those wonderful Yarbro men are back—this time it's Wyatt, down on his luck after a lifetime of rustling and robbing trains, and determined to make a fresh start with Sarah Tamlin, the spirited banker's daughter and a woman with a past.

I also wanted to write today to tell you about a special group of people with whom I've recently become involved. It is The Humane Society of the United States (HSUS), specifically their Pets for Life program.

The Pets for Life program is one of the best ways to help your local shelter—that is to help keep animals out of shelters in the first place. Something as basic as keeping a collar and tag on your pet all the time, so if he gets out and gets lost, he can be returned home. Being a responsible pet owner. Spaying or neutering your pet. And not giving up when things don't go perfectly. If your dog digs in the yard, or your cat scratches the furniture, know that these are problems that can be addressed. You can find all the information about these common problems—and many others—at www.petsforlife.org. This campaign is focused on keeping pets and their people together for a lifetime.

As many of you know, my own household includes two dogs, two cats and four horses, so this is a cause that is near and dear to my heart. I hope you'll get involved along with me.

May you be blessed.
With love,

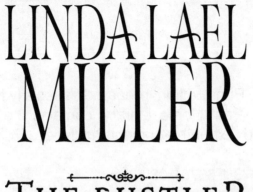

LINDA LAEL MILLER

THE RUSTLER

A Stone Creek Novel

**Doubleday Large Print
Home Library Edition**

HQN™

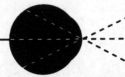

This Large Print Book carries the Seal of Approval of N.A.V.H.

For Donna Hayes,
and all cowgirls everywhere.

THE RUSTLER

A Stone Creek Novel

PROLOGUE

Southern Arizona Territory
August, 1907

A RUSTLER'S MOON GLIMMERED faintly in the sky, a thin curve of light soon obscured by rain-ripe clouds. Wyatt Yarbro sat a little straighter in the saddle and raised the collar of his battered canvas coat, not so much against the threat of bad weather as the intuitive sense that things were about to head south, literally *and* figuratively. He tugged the brim of his hat lower over his eyes as the kid rode toward him, bearing the unlikely name of Billy Justice, along with a shotgun, bad skin and a contentious attitude.

Skirting the restless herd of soon-to-be-stolen cattle, Billy drew his sorrel up alongside Wyatt's paint gelding, shifted his slight frame with an easy, soft creak of old leather.

"The boys are ready," Billy said, in that lazy drawl of his. "You with us, or not?"

Inwardly, Wyatt sighed. Thunder rolled across the darkened sky, like a warning from God. *Turn your horse and ride, cowboy,* said a still, small voice deep inside him. *Go now, while the getting is good.*

His younger brother, Rowdy, was up north, in Stone Creek, and he'd offered Wyatt a place to stay. Said he could get him honest work, help him leave the outlaw life behind for good. Still, the town seemed far away, like some fairy-tale place. Wyatt was flat broke, his horse—won in a poker game in Abilene two weeks after he got out of a Texas prison—wasn't fit for the trip.

He supposed Rowdy would wire him some money, if he could swallow his pride long enough to ask, but stealing would be easier. It was the only trade he'd ever learned.

"I'm with you," Wyatt said without inflection.

Billy nodded. "Then let's make for the border."

Wyatt assessed the sky again, watched as a streak of lightning ripped it open in a jagged, golden gash. "I don't like this weather," he admitted.

Billy turned his head and spat. "You turnin' coward on me, Yarbro?" he demanded coolly.

"Ever seen a stampede, Billy?" Wyatt countered, keeping his voice quiet. Young as Mrs. Justice's boy was, Wyatt had him pegged for the sort who could draw and shoot without so much as a skip in his heartbeat or a catch in his breath.

The cattle, more than five hundred of them, roiled in the gulch below like water at the base of a high falls, swirling in on each other in dusty, bawling eddies of hide and horns.

"Nope," Billy said, his tone blithe. Wyatt knew the kid was probably planning to gun him down from behind as soon as they'd delivered the herd and collected the loot. He wasn't afraid of a pockmarked whelp, even a cold-eyed one like Billy, but the charge in the air itself made his nerves claw and scramble under his skin.

"Let's get this done," Wyatt answered, and rode in closer to the herd.

The wind picked up, howling over the bare Arizona desert like a banshee on the prowl for fresh corpses, but the gang, six of them in all, got the critters moving in a southerly direction. Wyatt watched Billy and his four riders even more closely than the cattle, making sure none of them had a clear shot at his back.

They funneled the herd through a narrow wash, raising dust so dense that Wyatt pulled his bandanna up over his nose and mouth and blinked to clear his eyes.

He thought about his brother as he rode. Rowdy, a former member of the infamous Yarbro gang, just as he was, had managed to set his feet on the straight and narrow path. He'd changed his ways, gotten himself a pardon, and now he not only had a wife and a new baby, he wore a star on his vest.

Despite the brewing storm, and his own uneasy feelings, Wyatt grinned wryly behind his bandanna. Rowdy, the erstwhile train robber, a lawman. That just proved what he'd always known: life was unpredictable as hell. Right when a man thought he had it all worked out in his brain, it would twist like a rattler striking from the wood pile.

Wyatt had never known any other way of living than holding up trains. Neither had Rowdy, until they pinned a badge on him and made him marshal of Stone Creek, Arizona. Soon after that, Rowdy had met and married a schoolmarm named Lark Morgan.

While he envied Rowdy a little— what would it be like to settle down with a good woman and a community of friends?—Wyatt wasn't entirely convinced the change would stick. Once an outlaw, always an outlaw, as Pappy used to say.

And Pappy had been in a position to know.

Wyatt felt a mingling of irritation and sorrow as he thought of his father. If he'd been standing over the old man's grave at that moment, he wouldn't have known whether to weep or spit on the headstone.

He was debating the virtues of one approach over the other when a second bolt of lightning struck, this time in the center of the herd. Eerie light illuminated the whole scene—the terrified cattle and the other men stood out in sharp relief against the darkness for a long, bluish-gold moment—and then all hell broke loose, exploding in every direction like dynamite tossed into a campfire.

Wyatt's horse reared, shrieking with panic, and nearly threw him.

He caught the scent of scorched flesh. Cattle bellowed in fear, and the other riders scattered, fleeing for their lives.

The paint gelding wheeled in the midst of hoof-pounding chaos, and though he fought to stay in the saddle, Wyatt found himself rushing headlong for the ground. The wind knocked out of him by the fall, he lay there in the dirt, blinded by dust, and waited to be trampled to death.

Cattle pounded past him, shaking the earth itself.

He didn't know where his horse was—he couldn't see anything—but he supposed the poor critter was already dead. If the horns hadn't gotten old Reb, the hooves would have.

Wyatt managed to roll onto his belly, raise himself onto his hands and knees. It was a shame he wasn't going to survive the stampede, because it would have made a hell of a story.

The cattle continued to rush past him, spilling around some shadowy barrier. Amazed at his own calm—the whole thing might have been a yarn spun by some old geezer in a saloon—Wyatt felt his way forward and came up against the side of a dead steer. Ducking low, he felt the sharp edge of a hoof brush his right shoulder, but the crushing pain he'd expected never came.

He huddled close to the dead cow and waited it out, praying his horse hadn't suffered. Reb was a good old cayuse, deserving of green pastures and peace. He should have died with fresh grass between his teeth, not in the middle of a stampede.

Lightning lit up the landscape again, and then again, and Wyatt saw more dead cattle around him. He began to think he might make it after all, but he didn't catch a glimpse of Billy or the others, and he was still fretting for the horse.

Gradually, after what seemed like the better part of a politician's oration at a Fourth-of-July picnic, the din subsided and the ground stopped quaking.

Breathing slowly and deeply, Wyatt waited another few moments before daring to get to his feet. Eyes full of dirt, he wiped his face hard with the bandanna, then threw it aside.

He gave a low whistle, more out of habit than any hope that Reb would come.

But he did. The gelding nudged Wyatt between the shoulder blades, nearly knocking him off his feet, and nickered companionably.

Overjoyed, figuring he must be imagining things, Wyatt turned.

And there was Reb, reins dangling, bleeding where a horn had nicked him on the right side, and coated in red Arizona dust.

His heart swelling in his throat, Wyatt swung up into the saddle.

Pistol shots punctured intermittent rumblings of thunder, now distant, like the cattle.

Maybe Billy and his gang were trying to turn the herd.

Maybe a posse was making its presence known.

One way or the other, Wyatt Yarbro had seen the light.

He reined Reb to the north and made for Stone Creek.

CHAPTER ONE

IT MIGHT HAVE BEEN the suffocating heat that had Miss Sarah Tamlin thinking of perdition—though of course three days of endless sermons had to be a factor—and how she'd almost certainly wind up there one day, as she pounded out the wheezing refrain of "Shall We Gather at the River" for a sweltering congregation. Seated at an organ hauled into Brother Hickey's big revival tent in the bed of a buckboard, Sarah endured, perspiring, longing to fan herself with her sheet music or brush away the damp tendrils of hair clinging to the sides of her neck.

Every year in August, sure as the hay harvest, Brother Hickey and his roustabouts descended on the community like a circus without animals or parades, erected a canvas sanctuary on the grassy banks of Stone Creek, and set about saving the heathen from certain damnation.

A portion of the congregation seemed to deem it necessary to get saved on an annual basis. There wasn't much to do in a place the size of Stone Creek, after all, and with no doubts about the fate of their immortal souls weighing on their minds, folks would be free to enjoy the picnic that always followed the preaching.

Sarah forced the last few notes of the old hymn through the organ pipes and sighed with relief. The air was heavy and still—a baby gave a brief, fretful squall—and then, remarkably, a breeze swept through the gathering, as soft and cool as the breath of heaven itself.

Startled, Sarah looked up from the cracked and yellowed keys of Brother Hickey's well-traveled organ, over the turned heads of the salvation-seekers, and saw a man standing at the back of the tent. Tall and clean-shaven, with dark hair and eyes, he carried a dusty round-brimmed hat in one hand. His clothes were trail-worn, and the holster riding low on his right hip, gunslinger fashion, was empty. A grin tilted a corner of his mouth slightly upward.

Brother Hickey, moving behind his portable pulpit, which jolted over country roads and cattle trails right alongside the organ, cleared his throat and opened his Bible. "Have you come to be saved, stranger?" he boomed, employing his preacher voice.

The dark-haired man took a few steps forward. He moved with an easy grace, and for the space of a skipped heartbeat, Sarah wondered if he was some avenging angel, sent to put a stop to the show. "No, sir," he said. "I don't reckon I have." His gaze strayed to Sarah, sitting there in the back of that buckboard, her best calico dress soaked under the armpits. The grin widened to a fleeting smile, as if he somehow knew the stays of her corset were stabbing the underside of her left breast, and all her other secrets, as well. A smile that imprinted itself on some sweet and wholly uncharted place inside her. "That was fine music, ma'am," he told her directly. "I hope there'll be more of it."

Then, affably apologetic for disrupting the proceedings, he sat down next to Marshal Yarbro, who was grinning, and the two of them bumped shoulders.

Brother Hickey lifted his hands heavenward, closed his eyes in earnest and silent prayer, and then slammed a fist down onto the pulpit. Everybody jumped, Sarah noticed, except for the marshal and the stranger sitting beside him.

"Now is the day of Salvation!" Brother Hickey thundered, his copious white whiskers quavering. "Sinners, come forward and be bathed in the Blood of the Lamb!"

Several people rose and approached the makeshift altar, though most of the repenting had been done at previous services. There was dear old Mrs. Elsdon, who'd probably never committed an actual sin, two or three ladies of ill repute from Jolene Bell's saloon, brothel and bathhouse, though Miss Bell herself was noticeably absent, a handful of cowpunchers from Sam O'Ballivan's ranch, mostly likely hoping to speed things along so the picnic could get underway.

If Sarah hadn't been staring at the stranger, she'd have been amused. The revival was in its third and final day, and by now, even the most pious were ready to socialize over fried chicken and apple pie. The children were restless, longing to chase each other under the shady oak trees, wade in the creek, and make noise.

The praying and the saving went on for a long time, but at last Brother Hickey was through gathering in the lost sheep. He signaled Sarah, and she arranged her fingers on the keyboard, tried to put the dark-haired visitor out of her mind, and played a thunderous rendition of "What a Friend We Have in Jesus."

As soon as she struck the final chord, the benches emptied and the stampede began.

Sarah sat still on the hard stool in front of the organ, almost faint with relief, her eyes closed. It was over for another year. As soon as everyone had left the tent, she would climb down from the bed of the wagon, slip out the back way, and make her way home. She kept a jar of tea cooling in the springhouse, and when she'd drunk her fill, she'd strip, stuff her corset into the stove, and take a sponge bath.

"Miss? It *is* 'Miss,' isn't it?"

Sarah opened her eyes, saw the stranger standing right beside the buckboard, looking up at her. Again, she felt it, a peculiar jolting sensation that brought a blush to her cheeks, as though he'd read her thoughts and even imagined her shut away in her bedroom, naked, sluicing her flesh with water from a basin. She resisted a humiliating urge to smooth her hair, sit up straighter. "Yes," she said stiffly.

"Wyatt Yarbro," the man said, putting out a hand.

Sarah hesitated, then took it, though tentatively. His fingers were strong, calloused, and cool as the breeze he'd blown in on. "Sarah Tamlin," she allowed, feeling foolish and much younger than her twenty-seven years.

"Would you like some help getting down from there?"

Short of lifting her skirts and leaping to the sawdust floor, as she would normally have done, Sarah had no graceful options. "All right," she replied shyly. Then she climbed into the buckboard seat, careful not to let her ankles show, and Wyatt Yarbro put his hands on her waist and lifted her down. She stood looking up at him, stunned by the effect of his touch. Light-headed, she swayed slightly, and he steadied her.

His eyes were a deep brown, and they glinted with mischief and something else, too—some private, deep-seated sorrow. "I reckon it would be a sight cooler outside, under those oak trees alongside the creek," he said.

Sarah merely nodded. Let herself be escorted out of the revival tent on Mr. Yarbro's arm, in front of God and everybody.

Rowdy approached as Wyatt reclaimed his pistol from the table set aside for the purpose, his old yellow dog, Pardner, at his heels, and tipped his hat to Sarah.

"I didn't see Mrs. Yarbro in the congregation," Sarah said. She liked Lark, a former schoolteacher who'd stirred up quite a scandal when she took up with the marshal.

"The baby's getting teeth, and it makes him fractious," Rowdy replied. "They'll be along later, when the heat lets up." He turned slightly, gave Wyatt an affectionate slap on the shoulder. "I'd introduce my brother properly," he added, "but it seems you've already made his acquaintance."

"I'm the good-looking one," Wyatt said.

Just then, Fiona Harvey showed up, holding a plate piled high with fried chicken, potato salad and apple crumble. Fiona, who was thirty if she was a day, wanted a husband. Everybody knew that.

When and if Fiona managed to get married, Sarah would become the town spinster.

"You look hungry," Fiona told Wyatt, batting her sparse eyelashes.

Sarah, who considered Fiona a friend, simmered behind a cordial smile.

Wyatt tipped his head and flashed a grin at Fiona. "Why, thank you, ma'am," he said, accepting the plate.

Rowdy rolled his eyes, caught the expression on Sarah's face, and winked at her.

"You're welcome to come and sit with us," Fiona simpered, indicating a cluster of women sitting on a blanket under a nearby tree.

The marshal took the plate from Wyatt's

hands and gave it back to Fiona. "My brother's much obliged," he said smoothly, "but we've been expecting him, so Lark's got a big spread on the table at home."

"Thanks just the same, though," Wyatt said.

Fiona took the rebuff gracefully, said she hoped Mr. Yarbro would come back for the fireworks and the dance that would take up after sunset, and he replied that he might well do that. With a sidelong glance at Sarah, he allowed as how he enjoyed fireworks.

She blushed again, oddly flustered.

And Fiona pressed the plate into her hands. "Take this to your papa," she told Sarah. "Heaven knows, he'll appreciate a decent supper, the way you cook."

"Why, *thank you,* Fiona," Sarah said.

Wyatt and Rowdy exchanged glances, and one of them chuckled.

Fiona smiled and walked away.

"Give my regards to your father," Rowdy said, as Sarah turned to go, once again at a loss for words. The next time she saw Fiona, she'd have plenty to say, though.

"I'd better see Miss Tamlin home," Wyatt said, and before Rowdy could protest that

Lark had dinner waiting, he'd taken Sarah's arm and escorted her halfway to the road.

Since it would be rude to tell him she could get home just fine on her own, Sarah bit her lip and marched along, resigned, carrying the plate like a crown on a velvet cushion.

An old spotted horse with a long cut on its side ambled along behind them, bridle jingling, reins wrapped loosely around the saddle horn.

Sarah looked back.

"That's just Reb," Wyatt said.

"What happened to his side?"

"He had a run-in with a steer a while back. He's healing up fine, though."

Sarah wanted to ask a thousand other questions, but all of them jammed up in the back of her throat. She was sweating, her hair felt as though it would escape its pins at any moment, and she could almost feel the flames of Brother Hickey's beloved hellfire licking at her hem.

Mr. Yarbro donned his dusty hat, which made him look like a highwayman out of some dime novel. Sarah was painfully conscious of his hand, cupping her elbow, and the way he moved, with a sort of easy prowl.

"Are you really a bad cook?" he asked, visibly restraining a grin.

"Yes," Sarah admitted, with a heavy sigh.

He chuckled. "Guess that's why you're not taken," he said. "No other explanation for it, with looks like yours."

Sarah was scandalously pleased, and determined to hide the fact. She didn't think about her appearance much, given the busy life she led and her naturally practical turn of mind, but she knew she was . . . passable. Her hair was dark, and she kept it shiny with rainwater shampoos, vinegar rinses and a hundred brush strokes every night. She had good skin, strong teeth, exceedingly blue eyes and a slender but womanly figure.

For all that, she was an old maid, too plainspoken and too smart to suit most men. Most likely, Mr. Yarbro was merely dallying with her.

"My looks are in no way remarkable, Mr. Yarbro," she said, "and we both know it." She paused. Then, ever the banker's daughter, started adding things up in her brain. "Are you an outlaw, like your brother was?" she inquired bluntly.

"I used to be," he said, surprising her.

She'd expected another answer, she realized. A lie, falling easily from those expressive lips of his. Faced with the stark truth, she didn't know what to say.

Wyatt laughed and resettled his hat.

"What did you do?" Sarah asked, once she'd found her voice. They'd entered Stone Creek proper by then, passing Rowdy's office first, strolling along the sidewalk past the mercantile and her father's bank. The sun was setting, and old Mr. Shaefer was lighting the gas streetlamps, one by one.

"Robbed a train or two," Wyatt said.

"My goodness," Sarah remarked.

"You're safe with me, Miss Tamlin," he assured her, grinning again. "I've seen the error of my ways and I'm determined to take the high road, like my brother did. Are you planning to head back to the creek for the dancing and the fireworks?"

Sarah shook her head, bemused.

"Then I reckon I won't bother to, either."

So he hadn't been taken with Fiona, then. Inwardly, Sarah gave a deep sigh.

All too soon, and not nearly soon enough, they'd reached the gate in front of Sarah's house.

He opened the gate for her, stood back politely while she passed through it. When she looked over her shoulder, he touched the brim of his hat.

"Good night, Sarah Tamlin," he said. The glow of a nearby streetlamp cast his fine features into shadow. The paint horse waited politely on the sidewalk, nibbling at the leaves of Sarah's favorite peony bush.

Sarah swallowed, rattled again. "Good night, Mr. Yarbro," she replied. Then she turned and hurried along the walk, up the porch steps, into the house. When she pulled aside a lace curtain to peer out, the train robber was gone, and so was his horse.

WYATT ATE TWO PLATES full of supper, admired Lark, who was pretty, made the acquaintance of the other younger brother, Gideon, he'd nearly forgotten he had, and dandled the baby on his knee for a while. The little kid was cute, if a mite fractious in temperament. His name was Hank, and he looked just like Rowdy.

The *big* kid, Gideon, gave Wyatt a suspicious once-over and took off for the festivities down by the creek. It was full dark by then, and fireworks spread like chrysanthemums against the sky. Wyatt, Rowdy and the baby sat on the porch steps in front of Rowdy's small house, conveniently located in back of the jail, listening to the crickets, the sound of distant merriment, and the tinny tune of some saloon piano. Lark was inside, doing the things women did after they'd served a meal.

"You've done well for yourself, Rob," Wyatt said quietly, using his brother's given name. "A fine woman, a steady job, a son. I envy you a little."

Rowdy leaned back on the porch step, resting on his elbows. Silvery light from the fireworks caught in his fair hair. "No reason you can't have the same," he said.

"No reason except two years in a Texas prison," Wyatt replied. He'd told Sarah straight out that he'd robbed trains, but he hadn't mentioned the stretch behind bars. With a woman, a little honesty went a long way.

"Everybody's done things they're not proud of, Wyatt." Rowdy shifted, looked reluctant. "About Sarah—"

"What about her?" Wyatt asked, too quickly.

Rowdy considered a little longer before answering. "She works in her father's bank," he said. "Every cowpoke between here and Tucson has tried to court her, but she's having none of it. I think she's one of those—well—*career women*."

"Career women?" Wyatt echoed. During supper, he'd learned that Lark had inherited a whole railroad from her first husband, and she ran it from Stone Creek, by mail and telegram, with a baby balanced on one hip. "You mean, like your wife?"

Rowdy colored up a little. "Lark's different," he said. "Womanly."

Wyatt considered the fire he'd glimpsed in Sarah's blue eyes, her slender waist, her delectable breasts, ripe for holding in a man's hands. He imagined taking the pins from her ebony-colored hair and watching it fall to her hips in heavy, silken waves. She was "womanly" enough for him, and then some.

"I might as well tell you," he told Rowdy,

"that I intend to marry Sarah Tamlin as soon as I've got steady wages coming in."

Rowdy's mouth fell open. "Wyatt, you just *met* her. She's got a temper, and she plays poker."

Wyatt chuckled. "*Poker?* Even better!"

"She smokes cigars," Rowdy said.

"I might have to break her of that," Wyatt replied, enjoying the image of delicate little Sarah puffing on a stogy.

Rowdy thrust out a sigh. "Wyatt, what I'm trying to tell you is, she won't have you. You're an outlaw. She's a blue-blooded banker's daughter with a college education."

"And I'm not good enough for her?"

Rowdy started to protest.

"Hold on," Wyatt said, handing Hank over, since he felt a little soggy around the posterior region. "I *know* I'm not good enough for Sarah. Pappy wasn't good enough for Ma, either, but she loved him until the day she died."

Sadness flickered in Rowdy's eyes. He'd been Miranda's favorite, her boy Rob, and he was younger than Wyatt. He couldn't be expected to remember the early days, how she'd laughed and sung under her breath whenever Pappy came home from his travels.

"She wasn't happy," Rowdy said.

"She bore Pappy six sons," Wyatt reminded him. "Ma had plenty of chances to leave, Rowdy. She was a good-looking woman. Even after we were old enough to take care of ourselves, she stayed right on that farm. Why do you think she did that?"

Rowdy relaxed a little. "Ma was Ma. Sarah is Sarah. She'd never throw in with an outlaw, Wyatt. She'd figure you were after her papa's money, or out to rob his bank."

Wyatt stood, stretched. Rowdy and Lark's house was small, so he'd be sharing an empty jail cell with Gideon until he found a bunk someplace. "Where can a man get a bath in this town?" he asked.

Rowdy laughed. "We've got a real fancy tub right here in the house—hot running water, the whole works. Talk of the town. You can use that."

Wyatt didn't want to disrupt the household, and he felt shy about stripping down under the same roof with a married woman. It was an unfamiliar compunction. "I'd rather not do that," he said.

"Then I'll drag a washtub into the jail-house and you can heat water on the stove," Rowdy said, rising to his feet, the baby in the curve of his arm. "I've got some extra clothes you can wear until we get you some duds."

"Pump water will do," Wyatt said. "If it wasn't for that revival, I'd go down to the creek to bathe." He swallowed a good-size portion of his pride. "And I'll pay you back for the new rigging, Rowdy."

"I know," Rowdy answered.

An hour later, alone in the jailhouse, Wyatt poured the last bucket of water into an old tin washtub, dented and spotted with rust, peeled off his clothes, and sank into it.

It wasn't the Blood of the Lamb, but for the time being, it would do.

CHAPTER TWO

GIDEON ALMOST GOT HIMSELF SHOT, bang-
ing into the jail like he did, in the middle
of the night, with Wyatt sleep-flummoxed
and in the altogether and all. He had the
.45 cocked and aimed before he realized
where he was, and who he was dealing
with.

"Shit," Wyatt said, wrenching the thin
blanket up over himself and falling back
on his cot with a sigh of relief, the pistol
still in his right hand. "You oughtn't to bust
in on a man like that. I nearly put a bullet
in you."

Gideon slouched onto the cot opposite

Wyatt's, illuminated by a beam of moon-light straying in through the barred win-dow, and wrenched off one of his boots. "I *live* here," he said, and it was clear from his tone that he was none too pleased to be sharing his quarters. "Except when there's a prisoner, of course. Anyhow, it wouldn't have been the first time somebody put a bullet in me."

Therein lies a tale, Wyatt thought.

"Hell of a place to call home," he said, grimacing a little at the irony of the whole situation. After two years in the hoosegow, he'd ended up sleeping behind bars again. He reckoned it was God's idea of a joke. "Where do you sleep when somebody gets themselves arrested?"

"Around," Gideon said, after a long and studious pause. "I'll be heading out for col-lege pretty soon. I mean to be a Pinkerton man, or sign on as a Wells Fargo agent."

The underlying message was clear enough: *Don't go thinking I mean to be an outlaw, like you, just because we're kin.*

"Who'd have thought it," Wyatt mused, in a wry undertone, staring up at the low, shadowed ceiling of the cell. "Two of

Payton Yarbro's boys turning out to be lawmen. He must be rolling over in his grave."

The boy stripped to his skivvies and stretched out on the cot. "Pappy died fighting for what was right," he said. "What are you doing here? In Stone Creek, I mean?"

"Just looking for a place to be," Wyatt answered. He didn't expect the kid to trust him, the way Rowdy did. He and Gideon might have the same blood flowing through their veins, but in every other way, they were strangers. In fact, he kind of admired his younger brother's caution, figuring it must have come from their ma's side, since Pappy had never—to Wyatt's knowledge anyway—exhibited the trait. "Who shot you?"

"Happened at a dance," Gideon answered. "I'll tell you about it some other time." For a few minutes after that, he was quiet, except for some creaking of the old rope springs supporting his mattress as he settled his sizable frame for sleep.

The silence, though blessed to Wyatt's ears, did not endure. "I saw you walking

Sarah Tamlin home today," Gideon remarked. "And I reckon you know her father owns the Stockman's Bank."

Wyatt smiled in the darkness, though a wing of sadness brushed the back of his heart. Most likely, he'd never really know Gideon, or be known by him, since the boy was bound for some far-off place. College. It was a thing Wyatt couldn't imagine, though he'd read every book he could get his hands on. "You figure I've switched from holding up trains to robbing banks?"

"I'm just warning you, that's all. Rowdy takes his job as marshal seriously. Brother or not, if you break the law, he'll shut that door on you and turn the key. Don't think he won't."

"I appreciate your concern," Wyatt said dryly.

Another pause descended, long and awkward. The boy was brimming with questions, Wyatt knew, but asking them required some pride-swallowing.

"Tell me about the others," Gideon murmured.

"The others?" Wyatt hedged.

"You know who I mean—Nicholas and

Ethan and Levi. Pa told me their names, but not much else."

"It's late," Wyatt answered. "If you want to know more about the family history, why don't you ask Rowdy?"

"He won't talk about them."

"Maybe he's got reason, and you ought to accept that and let the matter rest."

"I've got a right to know about my own brothers, don't I?"

Again, a sigh escaped Wyatt. He cupped his hands behind his head and closed his eyes, but sleep, the delicious, dreamless refuge he'd been enjoying earlier, eluded him. "Did it ever occur to you that it might be better all around if you didn't? It isn't always so, but there's some truth in that old adage about ignorance being bliss."

"Tell me."

"Will you shut up and let me sleep if I do? I've got things to do in the morning—like find work."

"I will," Gideon agreed staunchly.

"I'm the eldest," Wyatt recited dutifully. "Nick is a year younger. He's always been a bit on the delicate side, not much for outlawing. Last I heard, he was living in Boston, writing poems and starving. By now, he's probably contracted consumption—he'd enjoy a disease like that. Then come the twins—Ethan and Levi. Levi's a little slow—and Ethan is a born killer. Rowdy is next in line, and I figure you probably know as much about him as he wants you to."

"What was he like—before?"

"Tough. Fast with a gun. Smart as hell. Not much he was ever scared of, as far as I could tell. That's how he got the nickname. Ma called him by his given name, Rob—she had a soft spot for him." Wyatt thought he heard the boy swallow hard, over there on his cot. It struck him—with a brief but hard pang—that he probably knew more about Billy Justice and the members of his gang than he did about Gideon, his own brother.

"Pappy said Ma died having me," Gideon said quietly, revealing a great deal more about himself in that one statement than he'd probably intended.

"It wasn't your fault," Wyatt said.

There was a shrug in Gideon's voice when he answered. "She'd be alive now, if it hadn't been for me," he argued.

"You can't know that for sure," Wyatt

pointed out, feeling sorry for the kid. It was a rung up the ladder, he reckoned, from feeling sorry for *himself*—he'd done enough of that in prison.

Gideon was quiet again, but just long enough for Wyatt to start hoping the palavering was over, so he could drift back into oblivion. He slept like a dead man, and rarely remembered his dreams, if he had any, and he considered that a blessing. Other men he'd known, back in Texas, hadn't been so fortunate.

"There are some things a man just has to let go of," he told Gideon.

"I reckon," Gideon agreed, but without much conviction.

Wyatt rolled onto his side, with his back to his brother, and punched down his pillow, though it was already flat, figuring his saddle would have served better. Been cleaner, too. "Good night," he said, with a yawn.

"What was she like?" Gideon asked. "Ma, I mean."

Wyatt suppressed another sigh. Stayed on his side, eyes wide-open, staring at the splintery, raw-timbered wall. "She was a fine woman," he said. "Half again too good for Pappy, that's for certain. She loved him, though."

At last, Gideon fell silent, though Wyatt knew there would be more questions, right along. With luck, they'd be ones he could answer.

THE MORNING AFTER Wyatt Yarbro walked her home from the revival picnic, Sarah overslept. She bolted awake, flustered, and scrambled out of bed, groping for her wrapper, wrenching it on, not bothering to shove her bare feet into house slippers.

"Papa?" she called, from the top of the back stairs leading down into the kitchen. *"Papa!"*

Dear God, suppose he'd wandered off again? The last time, he'd sneaked out wearing only a striped nightshirt and his best beaver top hat; she'd been lucky then, catching up to him at the corner, but Mrs. Madison, their neighbor, had witnessed the spectacle. Sarah had lied, smiling a brittle smile and explaining, perhaps too quickly, that her father had been sleepwalking lately.

The lying hadn't been the worst part, though—Sarah lied on a daily basis, to such an extent that she made notes in a ledger book in order to be consistent. No, the terrible thing had been seeing her intelligent, affable father looking so bewildered.

The back door was still locked; Sarah rushed to the front.

Ephriam Tamlin, founder, president and holder of majority shares in the Stockman's Bank, sat on the porch step, spine straight, a shotgun lying across his knees. He'd stuffed himself into a moth-eaten army uniform, Union blue.

Sarah put a hand to her heart. Drew a deep breath. "Papa," she said, careful to speak softly, so she wouldn't startle him.

"They've come, Nancy Anne," he said, without turning to look up at her. "The Rebs are here."

Sarah sat down beside him, tightening the belt of her wrapper and offering a silent prayer that no one would pass on the sidewalk and see them taking the morning air in such inappropriate garb. She reached for the shotgun, but Ephriam gripped it with strong, age-spotted hands.

"I saw their tent," Ephriam went on. "Bold as Lucifer, those Confederates. Made camp right on the banks of Stone Creek. Heaven help us all if it's Quantrill."

Sarah closed her eyes for a moment, swallowed a hard lump of misery before attempting to speak. She laid a gentle hand on the faded blue sleeve of her father's coat. "Papa," she whispered. "Look at me."

He turned, his kindly blue eyes blinking behind the thick, smudged lenses of his spectacles. This was the man who had been her rock, before and after her mother died. He'd protected her, provided for her. Helped her keep a shattering secret. Now, he looked befuddled, as though he knew he ought to be able to place her, but couldn't quite manage it.

"It's me, Papa," she said. "Sarah. And the war has been over for forty-two years."

He blinked again, rapidly now, and looked down at his ancient uniform and the shotgun resting across his lap. He was sixty-seven, too young for dementia. "I've had another spell," he said, with a look of such mortified regret that Sarah felt bruised inside.

Gently, she took the shotgun from his hands. "No harm done," she said, her voice hoarse with emotion. It probably wasn't true, of course. He'd glimpsed Brother Hickey's tent and mistaken it for a Confederate camp, and unless he'd followed the creek both ways, he must have walked right through town—dressed up in his old uniform, with the shotgun held smartly against his shoulder, like a soldier on patrol. Heaven only knew how many people had seen him, and were even now passing the word over fences and clotheslines.

"I'm sorry, Sarah," he said, looking so wretched that fresh tears scalded her eyes.

"Come inside and change," she replied, with an attempt at a reassuring smile. "I'll make breakfast, and we'll go to the bank and attend to business, just like we always do."

Ephriam nodded, rose stiffly from the step. Looked down at his uniform with a rueful shake of his head. "I'm not the man I used to be," he said sadly.

"Nonsense," Sarah said briskly, once they were inside the house and out of sight of the neighbors. She set the shotgun aside with caution and straightened his blue coat. "You're Ephriam Tamlin, head of the Stockman's Bank. Now, what would you like for breakfast?"

THE TELEGRAPH OPERATOR SHOWED up just as Rowdy, Gideon, Lark and Wyatt were finishing up their morning meal. Stood panting in the open doorway, skinny and sweating, a sheet of yellow paper clasped in one hand.

Rowdy immediately pushed back his chair and rose.

The baby, perched on Lark's lap while she spooned oatmeal into his mouth, started at the commotion, and old Pardner gave a questioning bark but didn't rise from the hooked rug next to the cookstove.

"There's been a lynching down near Haven," sputtered the little man on the threshold. He looked like a scarecrow in Sunday clothes. "Bunch of ranchers caught a couple of cattle thieves and strung 'em up. They want you to come. You and Sam O'Ballivan. I sent Zeke Reynolds out to Stone Creek Ranch with the news."

A chill trickled down Wyatt's spine. For a moment, he was out there under that rustler's moon again, in the aftermath of a storm and a stampede he'd been lucky to survive, distant shots echoing in his ears.

Rowdy snatched the telegram from the messenger's hand and scanned it a couple of times, in the way of a man who hoped it might say something different if he read it enough. Swore under his breath.

"You're not a Ranger anymore," Lark said quietly, gazing at her husband with luminous brown eyes. Her hair was fair, like Rowdy's, and shorter than most women's, just touching her shoulders. "And you're the marshal of Stone Creek, not Haven."

"If Sam goes," Rowdy told his wife, avoiding her eyes, "I'll be riding with him."

"Me, too," Gideon said.

Wyatt didn't speak, and that was a hard thing, not offering to help. If there was one place he couldn't afford to be seen in, it was that little border town, just outside of which he and Billy Justice and the boys had helped themselves to more than five hundred head of cattle.

"You're staying right here," Rowdy told Gideon, but his tone lacked conviction. Like as not, Gideon would get his way.

Meanwhile, Wyatt saw his dream of

settling down, living under his own name instead of yet another alias, marrying up with a woman like Sarah and raising kids and cattle, scatter into the air like the fluff from a dandelion head. As soon as Rowdy and Sam O'Ballivan rode out, he would, too—heading in the opposite direction.

He should have known he couldn't live in the open, like ordinary men.

Rowdy handed the telegraph operator a coin and dismissed him with a muttered "Thanks" and a distracted wave of one hand, reading the message again.

"If you're going to Haven," Lark said firmly, getting to her feet, swinging the baby onto her hip in the same motion, "so are Hank and I."

"Who's going to mind Stone Creek?" Wyatt asked, not because he cared much about the answer, but because he thought Rowdy might get suspicious if he didn't say something. "Is there a deputy?"

A slow grin broke across Rowdy's strained, thoughtful face. "Yes," he said. "I'm looking at him."

Wyatt felt hot color rush up his neck. "Me?"

Rowdy nodded. "You," he said.

At last, Wyatt stood. "I don't know anything about being a lawman," he protested, but carefully. "Until two years ago, I had a price on my head."

"So did I, at one time," Rowdy said, unfazed. He could be like an old dog mauling a soup bone when he wanted something. Changing his mind wouldn't be easy, if it was possible at all. "Turned out pinning on a badge was my salvation," he said, catching Lark's eye as she set the baby down on the rug beside the dog and moved to begin clearing the table. "That and a good woman willing to take a chance on a former train robber."

Lark blushed prettily. "If you think you're going to charm me out of going to Haven, Rowdy Yarbro," she said, "you are sadly mistaken. As soon as I've done these dishes, I mean to pack for the trip."

"Gideon will take care of the dishes," Rowdy said. He was watching Wyatt again, though, and there was something disconcerting in his eyes, an intent, measuring expression. They hadn't talked about the months between Wyatt's release and his arrival in Stone Creek—there hadn't been time. But Rowdy was a hard man to fool, and he clearly had his suspicions.

Gideon banged the dishes and cutlery around in the sink, but he didn't protest the washing-up.

"It might be better if I just moved on," Wyatt said. "I'm not cut out to uphold the law. Hell, it's all I can do to stay on the right side of it. You know that."

"Stone Creek is a quiet town," Rowdy answered easily. "Most you'd run up against would be drunken cowboys, or railroad workers whooping it up on a Saturday night."

Gideon grumbled something about getting shot at a dance, and did Rowdy call *that* quiet? But Wyatt was too focused on staring down the marshal of Stone Creek to pursue the matter right then.

"Gideon Yarbro," Lark called from the bedroom, where she could be heard opening and shutting bureau drawers, "if you break one of my good dishes slamming them around like that, I'll horsewhip you from one end of Main Street to the other!"

Exasperated, Wyatt shoved his hands into the hip pockets of his borrowed denim pants. Everything he was wearing, save his boots, pistol and gun belt—he'd left that outside out of deference to Lark—belonged to Rowdy. He sure hadn't counted on adding *a badge* to the getup. "Why is a lynching in some other town any of your concern, anyhow?" he asked.

"I wrote you about it," Rowdy said, still watching Wyatt a little too closely for his liking. "Told you what happened there."

Wyatt's mouth went dry. "I guess that particular letter didn't catch up with me," he said. He and Rowdy had written each other on and off for years, but it was a scattershot sort of thing. He'd ride into a town, stop in at the post office if there happened to be one, and inquire if there was mail for him, sent care of general delivery. Sometimes, there was. More often, there wasn't.

A month ago, he'd wound up in Tucson, and there was a letter waiting from Rowdy, full of news about Lark and the baby and his job in Stone Creek. He'd related the story of Pappy's death, and said if Wyatt wanted honest work, a friend of his named Sam O'Ballivan was always looking for cowpokes.

At the time, Wyatt had regarded that letter as a fluke of the postal system.

Now, he figured Rowdy must have figured he'd wind up in the Arizona Territory eventually, maybe looking for Pappy, and wished he'd never set foot in the post office in Tucson. Or, better yet, thrown in with the likes of Billy Justice before Rowdy offered him a fresh start.

"I can't stay, Rowdy," he said.

"You'll stay," Rowdy said.

"What makes you so damn sure?"

"That old nag of yours is practically dead on his feet. He doesn't have another long ride in him."

"He made it here, didn't he?"

Rowdy didn't seem to be listening. "I've got a spare gelding out there in the barn. You can ride him if you see the need. Name's Sugarfoot, and he'll throw you if you try to mount up on the right side."

"When it comes to riding out, one horse is as good as another," Wyatt said, but he was thinking of old Reb, the paint gelding, and how sorry he'd be to leave him behind. They'd been partners since that turn of the cards in Abilene, after all, and Wyatt would have been in a fine fix without him.

"You're a lot of things, Wyatt," Rowdy reasoned, "but a horse thief isn't among them. Especially when the horse in question belongs to me."

Wyatt scowled, said nothing. He was fresh out of arguments, at the moment. Hadn't kept up on his arguing skills, the way Rowdy had.

Rowdy saw his advantage and pressed it. "And then there's Sarah Tamlin," he said.

"What about Sarah Tamlin?" Lark asked, appearing in the bedroom doorway with a fat satchel in one hand.

Wyatt glared at Rowdy.

Rowdy merely grinned.

"She smokes cigars," Wyatt said lamely. "You told me that yourself, just yesterday. Plays poker, too. Gives a man second thoughts."

"She does *not* smoke cigars," Lark insisted.

"So it's true about the poker!" Rowdy said, in an ah-ha tone of voice.

"I wouldn't know," Lark said, with an indignant sniff.

"I heard she was a member of the Tuesday Afternoon Ladies Only Secret Poker

Society," Gideon said, looking smug. "And she's not the only one. It might surprise you who goes to those meetings."

Rowdy chuckled.

"Gideon," Lark warned.

He turned back to the sink, flushed, and scrubbed industriously at the kettle Lark had used to boil up the morning's oatmeal.

"It's just a rumor," Lark told Rowdy. "Respectable women do not play poker. *Or* smoke cigars."

"Whatever you say, dear," Rowdy replied sweetly.

Wyatt just shook his head, confounded.

"Come on," Rowdy said to him, beckoning. "I'll show you around town. Sam can swear you in when he gets here. What I do is, I count the horses in front of the saloons. If there're more than a dozen, I keep a closer eye on the place—"

Wyatt followed, since that seemed like the only thing to do.

"THERE," SAID SARAH, straightening her father's tie outside the door of his office at the bank, grateful that the place was empty at the moment. Thomas, the only teller, had gone out when they arrived. The train would be pulling in at the new depot within an hour, pausing only long enough to swap mailbags with the postmaster and take on any passengers who might be waiting on the platform—or drop off new arrivals.

It was Thomas's job, at least in part, to rush back to the bank and report to Sarah if any important visitors showed up. She was always on the lookout for unexpected stockholders.

"I'll handle things, Papa," Sarah assured her father, who had turned fretful again after breakfast. She was fairly certain he hadn't seen her stuff his army uniform behind the wooden barrel of the washing machine on the back porch, but she wasn't absolutely sure. "If someone comes in to open an account or inquire about a loan, let me do the talking. I'll say you're busy. All you have to do is sit at your desk, with your papers—if they insist on greeting you personally, I'll be careful to call them by name so you know what to—"

"Sarah." Ephriam looked pained.

"Papa, you know you forget."

Just then, the street door opened with a crash, and Thomas burst in. Plump, with a constellation of smallpox scars spilling down one side of his face, he seemed on the verge of panic.

"Sarah!" he gasped, from the threshold, one fleshy hand pressed to his chest. "It's *him*—the man in the photograph you showed me—"

Sarah's knees turned to water. "No," she said, leaning against her father for a moment. "He couldn't possibly have—"

"It's him," Thomas repeated.

"Calm down," Sarah said hastily. "Remember your asthma."

Thomas struggled to a wooden chair, in front of the window, and sat there sucking in air like a trout on a creek bank. "S-Sarah, wh-what are we going to d-do—?"

"What," Ephriam interjected, suddenly forceful, "is happening?"

Even in her agitation, Sarah felt a stab of sorrow, because she knew her father wouldn't be his old self for more than a few minutes. When the inevitable fog rolled in, shrouding his mind again, she'd miss him more keenly than ever.

"You're going to take Papa home," she told Thomas, who had begun a moderate recovery—of sorts. He wasn't sweating

quite as much as he had been when he
rushed in, and his breathing had slowed
to a slight rasp. "Go out the back way, and
stay off Main Street."

Gamely, Thomas got to his feet again.
Lumbered toward them.

When he took Ephriam's arm, though,
the old man pulled free. "Unhand me," he
said. "This is an outrage!"

Sarah's mind was racing wildly through
a series of possibilities, all of which were
disastrous, but she'd had a lot of experience dealing with imminent disaster, and
she rose to the occasion.

"Papa," she said, "poor Thomas is feeling very ill. It's his asthma, you know. If you
don't get him to Doc Venable, *quickly,* he
could—" she paused, laid a hand to her
bosom, fingers splayed, and widened her
eyes *"—perish!"*

"Great Scot," Ephriam boomed, taking
Thomas by one arm and dragging him
toward the front door, and the busy street
outside, "the man needs medical attention! There's not a moment to spare!"

Thomas cast a pitiable glance back at
Sarah.

She closed her eyes, offered a hopeless

prayer that Charles Elliott Langstreet the Third would get lost between the depot and the bank, and waited for the Apocalypse.

By the time Charles actually arrived, she was quite composed, at least outwardly, though faintly queasy and probably pale. She might have gotten through the preliminary encounter by claiming she was fighting off a case of the grippe, but as it turned out, Charles didn't come alone.

He'd brought Owen with him.

Sarah's heart lurched, caught itself like a running deer about to tumble down a steep hill. Perched on a stool behind the counter, in Thomas's usual place, a ledger open before her, she nearly swooned.

Owen.

Ten years old now, blond like his imperious father, but with his grandfather's clear, guileless blue eyes.

The floor seemed to tilt beneath the legs of Sarah's stool. She gripped the edge of the counter to steady herself.

Charles smiled, enjoying her shock. He was handsome as an archangel, sophisticated and cruel, the cherished— and only—son of a wealthy family. And he owned a thirty percent interest in the Stockman's Bank.

Owen studied her curiously. "Are you my aunt Sarah?" he asked.

Tears burned in Sarah's eyes. She managed a nod, but did not trust herself to speak. If she did, she would babble and blither, and scare the child to death.

"Surprised?" Charles asked smoothly, still watching Sarah closely, his chiseled patrician lips taking on a sly curve.

"We came all the way from Philadelphia on a train," Owen said, wide-eyed over the adventure. "I was supposed to spend the summer at school, but they sent me packing for putting a stupid girl down the laundry chute."

Sarah blinked, found her voice. "Was she hurt?" she croaked, horrified.

"No," Owen said, straightening his small shoulders. He was wearing a tweed coat and short pants, and he seemed to be sweltering. "She did the same thing to Mrs. Steenwilder's cat, so I showed her how it felt."

"The girl is fine," Charles said. "And so is the cook's cat."

"We're going to stay at the hotel," Owen

said. "Papa and me. I get to have my own room."

"Why don't you go over there right now and make sure the man we hired at the depot takes proper care of our bags?" Charles asked the little boy.

Owen nodded solemnly and left.

Sarah's heart tripped after him—she had to drag it back. Corral it in her chest, where it pounded in protest.

"Why did you bring him?" she asked.

"I couldn't leave the boy with Marjory," Charles answered. "She despises him."

Sarah squeezed her eyes shut, certain she would swoon.

"You must have known I'd come, Sarah. Someday."

She opened her eyes again, stared at him in revulsion and no little fear. He'd moved while she wasn't looking—come to stand just on the other side of the counter.

"If only because of the bank," he went on softly, reaching out to caress her cheek. "After all, I have a sizable investment to look after."

Sarah recoiled, but she still needed the stool to support her. "You've been receiving dividends every six months, as agreed," she said coldly. "I know, because I made out the drafts myself."

Charles frowned elegantly. His voice was as smooth as cream, and laced with poison. "Strange that you'd do that—given that Ephriam holds the controlling interest in this enterprise, not you."

"It's not strange at all," Sarah said, but she was quivering on the inside. "Papa is very busy. He has a lot of other responsibilities."

"All the more reason to offer my assistance," Charles replied. He paused, studied her pensively. "Still beautiful," he said. A smile quickened in his eyes, played on his mouth. "You'd like to run me off with a shotgun, wouldn't you, Sarah?" he crooned. "But that would never do. Because when I leave, I'll be taking our son with me."

CHAPTER THREE

SAM O'BALLIVAN MUST HAVE BEEN an important man, Wyatt concluded, because they held the departing train for him. He arrived driving a wagon, with a boy and a baby and a pretty woman aboard, a string of horses traveling alongside, led by a couple of ranch hands. While all the baggage and mounts were loaded into railroad cars, Lark and Sam's wife chattered like a couple of magpies on a clothesline.

Rowdy made the introductions, and Sam and Wyatt shook hands, standing there beside the tracks, the locomotive still pumping gusts of white steam. Sam was a big man, clear-eyed and broad-shouldered, with an air of authority about him. He not only owned the biggest ranch within miles of Stone Creek, he was an Arizona Ranger, which was the main reason he and Rowdy had been summoned to Haven.

"I hear you're a fair hand with horses and cattle," Sam said, in his deep, quiet voice.

The statement gave Wyatt a bit of a start, until he realized Sam was talking about ranch work, not rustling. "I can manage a herd, all right," Wyatt confirmed.

Sam gave a spare smile. His gaze penetrated deep, like Rowdy's, and it was unsettling. "I'm looking for a range foreman," the rancher said. "Job comes with a cabin and meals in the bunkhouse kitchen. Fifty dollars a month. Would you be interested?"

Rowdy must have seen that Wyatt was surprised by the offer, given that he was a stranger to O'Ballivan, because he explained right away. "I told Sam all about you."

"All of it?" Wyatt asked, searching his brother's face.

"I know you did some time down in Texas," Sam said.

Wyatt stole a glance at the pretty woman laughing and comparing babies with Lark a few yards away. A tall boy stood nearby, waiting impatiently to board the train. "And that doesn't bother you? Having a jailbird on your place, with your family there and all?"

"Rowdy's willing to vouch for you," Sam said. "That's good enough for me."

Wyatt looked at Rowdy with new respect. What would it be like to be trusted like that?

"I figure we ought to appoint Wyatt deputy marshal," Rowdy said. "Being the mayor of Stone Creek, you'd have to swear him in."

Sam nodded, but he was still looking deep enough to see things Wyatt didn't want to reveal. "Do you swear to uphold the duties of deputy marshal?" he asked.

"Yes," Wyatt heard himself say.

Rowdy handed him his badge just as Gideon showed up, a pair of bulging saddlebags over one shoulder, the old yellow dog padding along behind him.

"Pardner's going, too," Gideon said, apparently braced for an objection.

Nobody raised one.

Inside the locomotive, the engineer blew the whistle.

"Guess we'd better get going," Rowdy said, with a grin. "The train's got a schedule to keep."

With that, there was some hand-shaking, and some fare-thee-wells, then the whole crowd of them boarded, even the yellow dog. Wyatt stood there, Rowdy's star-shaped badge heavy in his left hand, and wondered how he'd gotten himself into this situation. It was all well and good to figure on running for it before Sam and Rowdy caught up to what was left of the Justice gang and learned that he, Wyatt, had ridden with the sorry outfit. The trouble was, except for stealing one of his brother's horses, a thing Rowdy had rightly guessed he could not do, and taking to the trail, he didn't have any choice but to stay right there in Stone Creek.

Hell, he might as well just shut himself up behind the cell door over there in the jailhouse right now and be done with it.

He watched, feeling a strange combination of misery and anticipation, as the train
pulled out of the depot onto a curved spur,
Stone Creek being at present the end of
the line, and snaked itself around to chug
off in the other direction. Steam billowed
from the smokestack as it picked up speed.

When he turned to walk away, he almost
collided with a small boy in knee pants and
a woolen coat.

The kid's gaze fastened on Rowdy's star
as Wyatt pinned it to his shirt.

"You the law around here?" the boy
asked, squinting against the bright August
sun as he looked up at Wyatt.

"For the moment," Wyatt said.

"Owen Langstreet," the child replied,
putting out a small hand with manly solemnity. "I got expelled from school for throwing a girl named Sally Weekins down the
laundry chute. Not that you can arrest me
or anything, Sheriff—?"

"Name's Wyatt Yarbro," Wyatt told young
Mr. Langstreet, "and I'm not the sheriff.
That's an elected office, one to a county.
Reckon my proper title is 'deputy marshal.'
Why would you go and dump somebody
down a laundry chute?"

"It's a long story," Owen answered. "She didn't get hurt, and you can't arrest me for it, anyhow. It happened in Philadelphia, and that's outside your jurisdiction."

Wyatt frowned. "How old are you?"

"Ten," Owen said.

"I'd have pegged you for at least forty." Wyatt started back for the main part of town, one street over, figuring he ought to walk around and look like he was marshaling. He wasn't looking forward to going back to the jail; it would be a lonely place, with nobody else around.

"There probably aren't any laundry chutes in Stone Creek," Owen went on, scrambling to keep up. "Papa says it's a one-horse, shit-heel town in the middle of nowhere. Even the *hotel* only has two stories. *And* no elevator."

"That so?" Wyatt replied. The kid talked like a brat, using swear words and bragging about poking a girl down a chute, but there was something engaging about him, too. He wasn't pestering Wyatt out of devilment; he wanted somebody to talk to.

Wyatt knew the feeling.

"He's going to take Aunt Sarah's bank away from her," Owen said.

Wyatt stopped cold, looked down at the kid, frowning. "What?"

"Papa says there's something rotten in Denmark."

"Just who is your papa, anyhow?"

"His name is Charles Langstreet the Third," Owen replied matter-of-factly. "You've heard of him, haven't you?"

"Can't say as I have," Wyatt admitted, setting his course for the Stockman's Bank, though he had no business there, without a dime to his name. If Sarah was around, he'd tell her he was Rowdy's deputy now, out making his normal rounds. It made sense for a lawman to keep an eye on the local bank, didn't it?

"He's very rich," Owen said. "I'm going to have to make my own way when I grow up, though. Mother said so. I needn't plan on getting one nickel of the Langstreet fortune, since I'm a bastard."

As concerned as he was about Sarah, and the fact that some yahoo called Charles Langstreet the Third was evidently plotting to relieve her of the Stockman's Bank, Wyatt stopped again and looked down at Owen. "Your *mother* called you a bastard?"

Owen nodded, unfazed. "It means—"

"I know what it means," Wyatt interrupted. "Does this papa of yours know you're running loose in a cow town, all by yourself?"

"I'm not by myself," Owen reasoned. "I'm with you. And you're a deputy. What could happen to me when you're here?"

"The *point* is," Wyatt continued, walking again, "he doesn't know you're with me, now does he?"

"He knows everything," Owen said, with certainty. "He's very clever. People tip their hats to him and call him 'sir.'"

"Do they, now?"

The bank was in sight now, and Wyatt saw a tall man, dressed Eastern, leaving the establishment, straightening his fancy neck rigging as he crossed the wooden sidewalk, heading for the street.

Spotting Owen walking with Wyatt, the man smiled broadly and approached. "There you are, you little scamp," he told the boy, ruffling the kid's hair.

"This is Wyatt Earp," Owen said. That explained all the chatter.

"Wyatt *Yarbro*."

"Charles Langstreet," said the dandy.

He didn't extend his hand, which was fine with Wyatt.

Wyatt glanced over Langstreet's shoulder, hoping to catch a glimpse of Sarah through the bank's front window. He didn't know much about Owen's papa—but he figured him for trouble, all right.

"You're not Wyatt Earp?" Owen asked, looking disappointed.

"No," Wyatt said. "Sorry."

"But you've got a gun and a badge and everything."

"Come along," Langstreet told the boy, though his snake-cold eyes were fixed on Wyatt's face. "Aunt Sarah has invited us to supper, and we'll need to have baths and change our clothes." His gaze sifted over Wyatt's borrowed duds, which had seen some use, clean though they were. "A good day to you—Deputy."

With that, the confab ended, and Langstreet shepherded the boy toward the town's only hotel. Owen looked back, once or twice, curiously, as if trying to put the pieces of a puzzle together.

Wyatt made for the bank. A little bell jingled over the door as he entered.

Sarah, standing behind the counter, looked alarmed, then rallied.

"Oh, it's you," she said.

Wyatt took off his round-brimmed black hat and tried for an easy smile, but the truth was, the inside of that bank felt charged, like the floor might suddenly rip wide open, or thunder might shake the ceiling over their heads. "Everything all right, Miss Tamlin?"

She blinked. "Of course everything is *fine,* Mr. Yarbro. Whyever would you ask such a question?"

"Partly because it's my job." He indicated the star on his shirt. "I'll be looking after Stone Creek while Rowdy's out of town. And partly because I just met a boy named Owen Langstreet down by the depot."

She paled. "What did he tell you?"

"Just that his father means to take the bank away from you."

Sarah tried to lasso a smile, but the rope landed short. "This bank belongs to my father, not to me. Mr. Langstreet is merely a—a shareholder. There is no need to be concerned, Mr. Yarbro, though I do appreciate it."

Wyatt nodded, went to the door, replaced his hat. "I'm a friend, Sarah," he said. "Remember that."

She swallowed visibly, nodded back.

Wyatt opened the door.

"Mr. Yarbro?"

He stopped, waited. Said nothing.

Sarah's voice trembled. "I wonder if you'd join us for supper tonight? Six o'clock?"

"I'd like that," Wyatt said.

"We'll be expecting you, then," Sarah replied brightly.

Wyatt touched his hat brim again and left.

Walking back along Main Street, toward Rowdy's office, he was intercepted repeatedly; evidently, word had gotten around town that while Marshal Yarbro was away, he'd be watching the store. Folks were friendly enough, if blatantly curious, and Wyatt offered them no more than a "howdy" and an amicable nod.

Thoughts were churning inside his head like bees trying to get out from under an overturned bucket. He meant to leave Stone Creek. He meant to stay.

He didn't know *what* the hell he was going to do.

Distractedly, he counted the horses in front of every saloon he passed—the town had more than its share, considering its size—saw no reason for concern, and went on to the jailhouse. Now that he had a supper invitation from Sarah, his spirits had lifted, though he was under no illusion that she'd asked him over out of any desire to socialize. She didn't want to be alone with Langstreet, that was all; she was terrified of him, and it was more than the threat of losing control of the bank.

Back at the jail, Wyatt collected his bedroll and saddlebags from the cell where he'd passed the night and headed for the small barn out behind Rowdy's house. He'd bunk out there in the hayloft, he'd decided, with Reb and the other horses. He'd be behind bars again soon enough, if Rowdy and Sam caught up with Billy Justice. Soon as Billy heard the name Yarbro, he'd put paid to any hope Wyatt had of living as a free man.

He could lie, of course. Say he'd never crossed paths with the gang, let alone helped them rustle cattle. His word against Billy's. Sam might even believe him—but

Rowdy wouldn't. No, Rowdy'd see right through to the truth.

Inside the barn, Wyatt tossed his few belongings up into the low-hanging loft, and the sweet smell of fresh hay stirred, along with a shower of golden dust.

Reb nickered a greeting, and Wyatt crossed to the stall to stroke the animal's long face. "You like it here, don't you, boy?" he asked. "Time you led the easy life."

Wyatt added hay to Reb's feeding trough, then to those of the other two horses. He carried water in from the well to fill their troughs.

Rowdy's spare horse was a buckskin gelding named Sugarfoot. He looked capable of covering a lot of ground—he and Sugarfoot could be a long way from Stone Creek in a short time. Maybe he'd leave a note for Rowdy, on the kitchen table, along with the badge, saying he was sorry and promising to send payment for the horse as soon as he got work.

He closed his eyes against the emotions that rose up in him then—shame, frustration, regret—and a hopeless yearning for the kind of life his younger brother had. Rowdy would understand; he'd been on the run himself. But if he found out about Wyatt's brief association with Billy's gang, he might come after him, not as a brother, but as a lawman.

And there was more.

He'd never see Sarah again, or poor old Reb.

He sighed, shoved a hand through his hair.

After a few moments, he made for the house. He'd been kidding himself, thinking he could stop running and put down some roots. Now, he was going to have to cut himself loose, and it would hurt—a lot.

Entering by the kitchen door, Wyatt noticed the envelope propped against the kerosene lamp in the center of the table right away. Took it into his hands.

Rowdy had scrawled his name on the front.

After letting out a long breath, he slid a thumb under the flap, found a single sheet of paper inside, along with three ten-dollar bills.

Thanks, Wyatt. It's good to know I can count on you. R.

Wyatt swore under his breath. He didn't doubt Rowdy's gratitude, but he suspected the marshal had an additional motive—he wanted to make it harder to leave.

He checked the clock on the shelf under the far window—it was nearly noon—and saw another slip of paper, folded tent-style. A rueful grin hitched up one side of his mouth. He hadn't gotten this much mail in a long time.

The second note was from Lark.

Wyatt—Help yourself to the food, and if you run out of anything, use our account at the mercantile to buy what you need. Make yourself at home.

He folded the note carefully and tucked it under the edge of the clock, his throat strangely tight, his eyes burning a little. He jollied himself out of the melancholies by looking around for a third note, from Gideon, or maybe even Pardner.

Neither of them had written a word, though.

He went to the larder, a wooden box with a metal handle, opened it up, and found cold meat inside. There was half a loaf of bread, too, so he made himself a sandwich and walked through to the little parlor beyond the kitchen. He hadn't passed much time in a real house since he'd left the homeplace for the last time.

His ma had cried that day. Begged him to stay and work the farm.

He'd ridden out instead. He'd had better things to do, he'd thought back then, than plowing fields and milking cows. No, he'd preferred to rob trains with Pappy.

"Fool," he said aloud, admiring but not touching the framed photographs set up on a wooden table near the windows. Lark and Rowdy, posing solemnly on either side of a Grecian pillar. Little Hank, bare-ass naked on a fur rug, in the saddle in front of a grinning Rowdy, cradled in Lark's arms in a rocking chair.

The soreness in Wyatt's throat got worse, and he had to blink a couple of times. He retreated from the row of pictures, scanned the rest of the room. There were two other doors, one open, one closed.

The open door led to the bathroom, a swanky one with a flush toilet and a copper boiler to heat water, just as Rowdy had said. Wyatt stepped inside the small room and looked into the mirror above the pedestal sink. He needed a shave, he decided, rubbing the dark stubble on his face. Rowdy had left behind a razor and a soap mug, and the tub looked mighty inviting.

Just go, he told himself. *Saddle up Sugarfoot, ask some neighbor to look after Reb and Lark's mare, and go.*

He thought about supper at Sarah's, sitting across a table from her, just for one meal. He'd make sure Langstreet didn't pose any kind of serious threat to her, and leave in the morning.

First thing in the morning, for sure.

No matter what.

In the meantime, he might as well go into the jailhouse, in case somebody came by needing a lawman.

He was amused to find, when he approached the desk, that Gideon had left a note after all. Scrawled on the back of a Wanted poster and carefully centered in the middle of the blotter.

Don't steal anything. If you do, I'll come after you for sure. Gideon Yarbro.

Wyatt chuckled. He had no doubt that

the kid was sincere. *Two lawmen in the family now, Pappy,* he thought. *And me wearing a badge, too. Guess you must be wondering where you went wrong.*

THE AFTERNOON, blessedly quiet in terms of business, passed at an excruciatingly slow pace. Sarah spent the time examining the books—column after column of figures penned in her distinctive handwriting, every cent accounted for—and wondered if Charles would believe the only lie she could come up with on such short notice.

Her father's eyesight had been very poor before Dr. Venable had arranged for a pair of spectacles to be sent up from Phoenix, and she'd fallen into the habit of managing the ledgers for him.

Flimsy, but it might work.

Carefully, she recorded the statement in her own small book, which she carried in the pocket of her skirt. Ever since lying had become a necessary art, Sarah had taken pains to record the fibs she'd told, both for the sake of continuity in conversations with others and, she supposed, as a form of penance.

God recorded both sins and virtues

in the Book of Life, according to the preachers. Maybe He'd understand, on Judgment Day, that writing down the lies she told was a form of honesty in and of itself, convoluted as the idea seemed, even to Sarah herself.

More likely, He'd order her flung into the Lake of Fire, immediately if not sooner. After all, God hated a liar, didn't He?

Sarah sighed. If the Lord was as cranky and hard to please as Brother Hickey and his ilk made Him out to be, she couldn't hope to get along with Him anyhow.

When closing time finally came—neither Thomas nor her father had returned from the visit to Dr. Venable, who was probably subjecting poor Thomas to all manner of painful cures—Sarah hung the sign in the door, locked up, and headed for home.

She'd been a fool to invite Wyatt Yarbro to take a meal under her roof—he was an outlaw, badge or no badge—but it would be better than being alone, for all practical intents and purposes, with Charles Langstreet. Owen and her father would also be present, but both of them were children, despite the vast difference in their ages.

A new worry rose up whole in her mind as she approached her front gate and stooped to pat Mehitabel, the three-legged cat, who sometimes came by to lap up a bowl of cream or sleep contentedly behind the cookstove when the weather turned cold.

What might Ephriam say when he saw Owen? Once, she could have depended on her father's discretion, but given the state of his mind, he might blurt out something the boy wasn't prepared to hear, or understand.

A chill rippled in the pit of her stomach. **Owen.**

She could adapt to almost anything, including losing control of the Stockman's Bank, if matters came to that pass, but seeing Owen hurt in any way would be beyond toleration.

Charles claimed he'd brought the boy to Stone Creek because he could not remain at school, or at home with Mrs. Langstreet; he'd simply had no other choice. Caught off guard, Sarah had accepted the explanation the way someone at the top of a burning staircase would accept a wet blanket. Now, with the storm of her thoughts abating a little, she knew there had to be another reason. Charles could have left Owen with his aging mother, prevailed upon one of his three married sisters.

Instead, Owen was there, in Stone Creek.

Why?

Certainly not because Charles felt any kindly inclination toward her. She'd begged him for photographs of Owen over the years, receiving only one, sent letter after letter to the child, revealing nothing, always signing the long missives with the spinsterly affection of an aunt. There had been no replies, but given Owen's tender age, that wasn't surprising.

Sarah blinked, realizing she was still standing at the gate, Mehitabel curling into her hem, and worked the latch. The hinges creaked as she passed through.

Are you my aunt Sarah? Owen had asked earlier, in the bank, his eyes wide and trusting.

What had Charles—or, more worrisome yet, his wife, Marjory—told the boy about his "aunt"?

The front door opened as Sarah approached, and Doc appeared in the gap. He was a stoutly built man with gentle eyes, and an old friend as well as physician to her father. The two men had met in the army, serving under General Grant, Ephriam as an infantry captain, Jacob Venable as a surgeon. Ephriam had sustained a bayonet wound to his right shoulder during a skirmish with Confederate cavalrymen, and Venable had tended him. Having a number of things in common, but primarily a shared passion for books, they'd swapped whatever rare and treasured volumes they managed to get their hands on. Both men had been at Appomattox when Lee surrendered, and taken off their hats to the living legend as he left Grant's presence, proud even in defeat. Every winter they sat smoking in front of the fire in the Tamlins' parlor, reliving that day and the events that led up to it.

Now, looking up at Doc, with his graying beard and dignified bearing, Sarah thought he resembled General Lee, for all that he, like her father, had been a Union man, born and bred.

Doc was also the only person who knew about her book of lies. She'd confided in him, one late night, while keeping a vigil by a dying neighbor's bedside.

"Is Papa ill?" she asked.

"I dosed him with laudanum and put him to bed," Doc said matter-of-factly. "He was in another one of his states—asking after your mother."

Sarah swallowed hard, blinked back tears. She felt relieved that her father wouldn't be at the supper table, unpredictable as he was. She also felt guilty for *being* relieved.

Doc took a seat in the porch swing and patted the space beside him. "Sit down, Sarah," he said gently.

"I've got to fix supper for company and—"

"Sit down, please," Doc repeated.

Sarah sat. Doc and the teller, Thomas, were the only people in Stone Creek who knew for sure that Sarah ran the bank, though there were surely others, like Sam O'Ballivan, who suspected it.

"You're not going to be able to keep up this charade much longer, Sarah," Doc told her quietly. "Ephriam's condition is deteriorating. Heartbeat's sporadic, and there are other bad signs, too. He'll need a nurse soon—if the town had a hospital, I'd have him admitted, for an indefinite length of time."

"Is he dying?" Sarah could barely force the words out. An only child, conceived late in her parents' lives—they'd both been forty when she was born—she'd never achieved true independence from them. Except when she'd attended college in Philadelphia, she'd never been away from home.

Doc patted her hand, smiled sadly. "We're *all* dying. Life is invariably fatal. But to answer your question, Ephriam could live another twenty years, or never awaken from the nap he's taking right now. The point is, he's suffering from dementia, and folks are bound to take notice, if they haven't already."

Nothing Doc said came as a surprise to Sarah, but she still needed a few choked moments to absorb it. She'd spent so much time and effort hiding and denying the problem that facing the truth was a challenge.

Doc put a fatherly arm around her

shoulders. "You've fought the good fight, Sarah," he said. "Run that bank as well as any man could, better than most. But it's time to let it go."

"You don't understand, Doc," Sarah answered miserably, wringing her hands in her lap. "Papa and I will have nothing to live on, if his salary stops coming in."

"Ephriam has always been the thrifty sort," Doc said, a frown puckering the flesh between his bristly eyebrows. "He must have saved a considerable amount, over thirty years."

Sarah's eyes burned. "There were bad loans, Doc, a couple of years back, during the worst of the drought. Papa used his own money to cover them, so the Weatherbys and the Connors and the Billinghams wouldn't lose their ranches—"

A muscle ticked in Doc's jaw. "And of course they never paid him back."

"They couldn't," Sarah insisted. "Now that the railroad's come as far as Stone Creek, things are getting better, but you know Mrs. Weatherby's a widow now, with four young children to feed, and the Connors got burned out and had to go live with their folks up in Montana. They might or might not be able to make a new start. Jim Billingham pays what he can, when he can, but it isn't much."

"Oh, Lord," Doc said. "Is the house mortgaged?"

Sarah shook her head. "The deed's in my name," she answered. She looked back over one shoulder at the big house, the only home she'd ever known. There were six bedrooms, in total, because her parents had hoped to have that many children, or more. "I suppose I could take in boarders," she said. "Give piano lessons."

Doc lowered his arm from Sarah's shoulder and took her hand, squeezed it lightly. "You're the sort who'll do whatever has to be done," he said fondly. "Ephriam's lucky to have a daughter like you."

Privately, Sarah believed her father would have been better off with a son, instead of a daughter. If she'd been born male, there'd be no question of giving up control of the Stockman's Bank—a man would be allowed, even *expected,* to take over the helm.

Sarah didn't mind hard work, but taking in boarders was one step above beggary, in small, gossipy communities like that one. There were already several women offering piano lessons, so pupils would be hard to come by. She'd be pitied and whispered about, and keeping her spine straight and her chin up in public would take some doing.

"You could always get married," Doc said. "Any one of several men in this town would put a ring on your finger, if you were agreeable."

Wyatt Yarbro ambled into Sarah's mind, grinning.

She blushed. The man was a self-confessed outlaw, despite the badge pinned to his shirt, and for all that he'd walked her home the night before, and stopped by the bank that very day to offer his assistance, should it be required, marriage wouldn't enter his mind.

Men like Mr. Yarbro didn't marry, they dallied with foolish women, and then moved on.

"I'd have to love a man before I could marry him," she told Doc forthrightly. Although she *would* have married Charles Langstreet the day she met him, and certainly after she discovered she was carrying his child—if he hadn't admitted, after

Owen's conception, that he already *had* a wife.

"Love might be a luxury you can't afford, Sarah Tamlin," Doc said. "You're a strong, capable woman, but the reality is, you need a man." His weary old eyes twinkled. "I'd offer for you, myself, if I were thirty years younger."

Sarah chuckled, though she was dangerously near tears. "And I'd probably accept," she said, rising to her feet. She had things to do—look in on her father, start supper for her guests, due to arrive in just under an hour, tidy up the parlor and lay a nice table in the dining room. She said as much, adding, "Will you stay and join us?"

Doc Venable stood, too. "I'd be honored," he said.

CHAPTER FOUR

OWEN'S FACE WAS SCRUBBED, and someone, probably Charles, had slicked down his hair. Standing on the front porch, gazing earnestly up at Sarah, he held out a bouquet of flowers and bravely announced, "Papa said to tell you he'll be along as soon as he can. He got a telegram at the hotel, and he's got to answer it."

"C-come in," Sarah said, stricken by the sight, the presence, of this boy. Accepting the flowers with murmured thanks, she stepped back to admit him.

Owen moved solemnly over the threshold, a little gentleman in a woolen suit, taking in the entryway, the long-case clock, the mahogany coat tree. Sarah wondered if he ever wore regular clothes and played in the dirt, like other children his age.

And she wondered a thousand other things, too.

"Let's put these flowers in water," she said, and started for the kitchen.

"You have gaslights and everything," Owen marveled, walking behind her. "I thought you'd live in a log cabin, and there'd be Indians around."

Sarah smiled to herself. "There are a few Indians," she said. "But you don't have to worry about them. They're friendly."

"Good," Owen said, with evident relief, as they passed the dining room table—she'd set it for five, since her father was snoring away in his room—and the plates, glasses and silverware sparkled. "I wouldn't want to get scalped or anything."

"Nobody's going to scalp you," Sarah said, with certainty.

Owen pulled back a chair at the kitchen table and sat while she found a vase for the wild orange poppies he'd apparently picked for her. "Papa says this is the frontier," he announced.

Sarah's spine tightened briefly at the mention of Charles. She hoped Doc Venable would be back from his evening rounds before he *or* Wyatt Yarbro arrived. "We're quite civilized, actually," she said, pumping water into a vase at the sink, dunking the stems of the poppies, and setting the whole shooting match in the center of the table.

"Do you live in this great big house all by yourself?" Owen wanted to know. He was small for his age, Sarah noticed, trying her best not to devour the child with her eyes. His feet swung inches above the floor, but he sat up very straight.

"No," Sarah said, taking a chair herself. "My father and I live here together. Isn't your house much bigger than this one?"

Owen allowed that it was, then added, "But I'm not there very much. If I'm not at school, I mostly stay with Grandmama. She's got all sorts of money, but she lives in a town house. That way, she doesn't need so many servants."

"Do you like staying at your Grandmama's town house?" Sarah asked carefully.

"Not much," Owen said. "You can't run

or make noise or have a dog, because dogs have fleas and they chew things up and make messes."

Sarah didn't know whether to laugh or cry. "Would you like to have a dog?"

"More than anything, except maybe a pony," Owen answered.

"Do you like school?" A thousand other questions still pounded in Sarah's mind, but it wouldn't be appropriate to ask them.

"It's lonesome," Owen said. "Especially at Christmas."

Sarah stomach clenched, but she allowed none of what she felt to show in her face. "You stay at school over Christmas?"

"My mother doesn't like me very much," Owen confided. "And Grandmama always goes to stay with friends in the south of France when the weather starts getting cold."

"Surely your mother loves you," Sarah managed.

"No," Owen insisted, shaking his head. "She says I'm a bastard."

Sarah closed her eyes briefly, struggling with a tangle of emotions—anger, frustration, sorrow, and the most poignant yearning. So Marjory Langstreet *did* blame Owen for her husband's indiscretions, as she'd always feared she might.

"My brothers aren't bastards," Owen went on, taking no apparent notice of Sarah's reaction.

"Do you get along with them?" she asked, after biting her lower lip for a few moments, lest she say straight out what she thought of Marjory and all the rest of the Langstreets. "Your brothers, I mean?"

"They're old," Owen replied. "Probably as old as you."

Sarah chuckled. "My goodness," she said. "They must be doddering."

"What's doddering?"

Just then, her father appeared on the rear stairway leading down into the kitchen, clad in a smoking jacket and the military trousers Sarah had hidden earlier. His feet were bare, and his white hair stood out all around his head. He'd forgotten his spectacles, and he peered at Owen.

"Doddering," he said, "is what I am. An old fool who can't get around without somebody to hold him up."

"Papa," Sarah said, rising, "you're supposed to be in bed."

"Balderdash," Ephriam snapped. "It's still light out. Who's the lad?"

"My name is Owen Langstreet, sir," Owen said, standing respectfully in the presence of an elder. "Who are you?"

Don't, Papa, Sarah pleaded silently. "This is my father, Ephriam Tamlin," she said aloud.

"Those pants," Owen observed, "are peculiar. How come they have yellow stripes down the side?"

"I wore these trousers in the great war," Ephriam blustered. Then he saluted briskly. "You're a mite small for a soldier. Reckon you must be a drummer boy."

"Papa," Sarah pleaded. "Please."

"I smell supper cooking," Ephriam told her. She'd fried chicken earlier; it was on a platter in the warming oven. "I'm hungry."

"I'll bring you a plate," Sarah promised. "Just go back to bed."

"I'm not a soldier," Owen said.

A rap sounded at the back door, and Doc Venable let himself in. Spotting Ephriam standing there on the stairs, he tossed Sarah a sympathetic glance, let his eyes rest briefly on Owen, then went to usher his old friend to his room.

"How come Ephriam can't eat with us?" Owen asked Sarah, when they'd gone. He looked so genuinely concerned that it was all Sarah could do not to reach out and ruffle his neatly brushed hair.

"He's sick," Sarah said.

"Why did he call me a drummer boy? I don't have a drum."

"Figure of speech," Sarah answered.

At that instant, for good or ill, someone turned the bell knob at the front door, indicating the arrival of another supper guest.

"I'll answer the door!" Owen said, and rushed off through the dining room.

Sarah gripped the back of a chair, swayed. She should have told Charles, when he invited himself to supper, that it wasn't a good time for her to entertain. Her father was indisposed, and she was frantic with worry over the situation at the bank. But she'd wanted so to pass an evening in Owen's company.

"It's the deputy!" Owen shouted from the entry hall. "Should I let him in?"

Sarah laughed, though her eyes stung with tears. She hurried out of the kitchen and through the dining room.

Wyatt Yarbro stood smiling and spruced up just over the threshold. He wore a clean white shirt, black trousers, and polished boots, and the holster on his hip was empty. He'd dusted off his black hat, which he held politely in his hands, and his dark eyes danced with a sort of somber amusement.

"Do come in, Mr. Yarbro," Sarah said. "This is my—nephew. Owen Langstreet."

"We've met," Mr. Yarbro said, stepping past the boy, who stared up at him in fascination.

"He's not Wyatt Earp," Owen said.

"I'm aware of that, Owen," Sarah replied, gesturing toward the coat tree, with its many brass hooks. "Hang up your hat, Mr. Yarbro."

Wyatt did as she'd asked.

An awkward silence fell.

"Let's have a seat in the parlor," Sarah said, flustered, leading the way.

Owen followed, and so did Wyatt.

"Nice place," Wyatt said.

"She lives here with her papa," Owen informed him, gravitating toward Sarah's piano, which was her most prized possession. "He wears blue pants with yellow stripes on them and thinks I'm a drummer boy."

"Is that so?" Wyatt asked affably, and when Sarah dared to look back over her shoulder, she saw that he was watching her, not the child.

"Sit down," Sarah said. "Please. I'll get some coffee."

"No need," Wyatt said, waiting until Sarah sank into her mother's threadbare slipper chair before taking a seat on the settee. He was leanly built, but the house seemed smaller somehow, with him in it, and warmer.

Much warmer.

Owen perched on the piano stool. "May I spin?" he asked.

Wyatt chuckled.

"Spin all you want," Sarah said, smiling a wobbly smile.

Owen moved the stool a few more inches from the piano, sat, gripped it with both hands, and used one foot to propel himself into blurry revolutions.

Sarah felt dizzy and had to look away, but her gaze went straight to Wyatt Yarbro, and that made her even dizzier. He'd shaved, and his cologne had a woodsy scent. His white shirt was open at the throat, and it was not only pressed, but starched, too.

Wyatt glanced curiously around the well-appointed, seldom-used room. "Where's Mr. Langstreet?" he asked.

"He's been delayed," Sarah said.

Owen used his foot to stop the piano stool. He looked happily flushed, more like the little boy he was than the miniature man who blithely referred to himself as a "bastard." "He got a telegram," Owen said importantly.

"Imagine that," Wyatt said, though not unkindly.

"In Philadelphia, we have a telephone," Owen added.

"Don't hold with telephones myself," Wyatt replied, mischief sparking in his dark eyes. "I figure if folks have something to say to each other, they ought to write it in a letter or meet up, face-to-face."

"Papa says someday *everybody* will have a telephone."

"Does he, now?" Wyatt asked easily.

As though to speak of the devil was to conjure him, Charles chose that moment to ring the doorbell. Sarah excused herself to answer, and Wyatt stood when she rose from her chair.

He might have been an outlaw, but someone had taught him manners.

Sarah was a little flushed when she opened the front door to Charles.

"Good evening, Sarah," he said, stepping past her when she hesitated to move out of the way. "I apologize for being late. Business. One can never escape it."

Doc Venable descended the front stairs, rolling down his shirtsleeves. His hands and forearms still glistened with moisture from the sink upstairs, where he must have washed up for supper.

Sarah made introductions all around, out of deference to the doctor. Wyatt and Charles had already met; Wyatt's expression thoughtful, Charles's elegantly aloof.

Charles looked down on Wyatt, Sarah realized, as a ruffian, and she felt a swift sting of fury. Her cheeks throbbed with it.

Supper seemed interminable. Sarah was afraid, every moment, that her father would appear, oddly dressed and confounded.

"I thought you said you couldn't cook," Wyatt teased, helping himself to another piece of fried chicken and then adding gravy to his mashed potatoes. "Tastes fine to me."

"Thank you," Sarah said, inordinately pleased and not a little embarrassed. By some miracle, she'd managed not to burn the chicken, and the mashed potatoes were thicker than the gravy, as they were supposed to be.

Charles maintained a chilly silence; he clearly resented Wyatt's presence, tossing a disdainful glance his way every now and then. Finally, he took a sip from his water goblet and condescended to remark, "Very nice."

"Is Aunt Sarah your sister, Papa?" Owen asked.

"Eat your supper," Charles told him.

"Is she?"

"No," Charles snapped.

"Then she must be Mother's sister. They don't look anything alike."

Sarah stiffened in her chair. Wyatt saw the motion, and stared diplomatically down at his plate.

"In Sarah's case," Charles said, plainly irritated and red at the jawline, "the title of 'aunt' is honorary. She's—a family friend."

"Oh," Owen said, looking dejected. He laid his fork down. He'd been sawing away at a drumstick for the last twenty minutes; Sarah had wanted to tell him it was all right to eat chicken with his fingers, but refrained. "I was thinking maybe I could visit her at Christmas, but if she's not really my aunt—"

"You may visit me whenever you want," Sarah told him, aware that she was over-stepping, and not caring. When she got Charles alone, she'd have a word with him about this "bastard" business, *and* leaving a ten-year-old boy at boarding school over the holidays.

Owen's face brightened, causing his freckles to stand out. "Really?"

"Enough," Charles said coldly. "Philadelphia is a long way from Stone Creek. Have you forgotten that we just spent a week on a train?"

Owen subsided as suddenly as if he'd been slapped.

Doc Venable cleared his throat and turned the conversation in a new direction. "I understand you're keeping the peace around town while your brother is away, Mr. Yarbro," he said.

Wyatt shifted in his chair, oddly uncomfortable with the remark. "Yes, sir," he said. "And I'd appreciate it if you called me Wyatt." His gaze moved to Sarah. "You, too, Miss Tamlin."

Sarah blushed.

"My, but we are a friendly bunch, aren't we?" Charles asked dryly. His nostrils were slightly flared, and the skin around his mouth looked tight.

"I reckon most of us are, anyhow," Wyatt said quietly.

"Can I call you Wyatt, too?" Owen wanted to know.

"Sure," Wyatt said. "Long as I don't have to call you 'Mr. Langstreet.'"

Charles reddened.

Owen giggled with delight. "Nobody calls me 'Mr. Langstreet,'" he said. "I'm only *ten.*"

Wyatt's lips twitched. "You could have fooled me," he replied. "Like I said this afternoon, I'd have said you were forty if you were a day. Just a mite short for your age."

Charles favored Sarah with a pained look. Again, she wondered why he'd brought Owen to Stone Creek, when he seemed, at least at the moment, barely able to tolerate the child's presence.

"You ever seen a man as short as Owen here, Doc?" Wyatt asked, well aware that he'd gotten under Charles's skin and clearly enjoying the fact.

"Can't say as I have," Doc said, regarding Owen thoughtfully.

Owen beamed.

"Is everyone ready for dessert?" Sarah asked brightly.

She served strawberry preserves on shortbread, and poured coffee for the adults. Earlier, she'd longed for the evening to end. Now, she realized that Charles was the only unwelcome guest. Doc, Wyatt and Owen had lifted her spirits with their banter.

Charles was the first to lay his table napkin aside, push back his chair, and stand. "I've got a meeting tomorrow in Flagstaff," he said. "It came up unexpectedly. Sarah, I wonder if I might speak to you in private."

Sarah felt a prickle of dread, but she welcomed the chance to talk to him about Owen, out of the boy's earshot. "Certainly," she said. "I'll walk you to the door."

Owen remained in his chair, his eyes fixed on his plate. He seemed to have shrunk a full size, and his head was bent at an angle that made Sarah's heart hurt.

She proceeded to the front door, Charles following.

"I can't leave the boy alone at the hotel," Charles said, before she had a chance to speak. "Will you keep him while I'm away?"

Sarah nodded, surprised. She'd expected some kind of harangue.

"I might be gone for several days," Charles warned.

"I'll look after him," she promised. "Charles, I—"

Something ominous flickered in Charles's eyes.

Sarah straightened her spine. "He refers to himself as a bastard. Owen, I mean."

"He's precocious," Charles said, taking out his pocket watch and checking it with a frown. "And he lies constantly."

"Is he lying about Christmas? Having to stay at school alone while everyone else goes home for the holiday season?"

Charles's mouth took on a grim tension. "It isn't always convenient to have a ten-year-old underfoot," he said. "Marjory's nerves are—delicate."

"*Convenient?* Charles, he's *ten.* A child."

"Marjory—"

"*Damn* Marjory!" Sarah whispered furiously. She was in no position to anger Charles, given the shares he held in the bank, but her concern for Owen—*her* son—pushed everything else aside. "What do I care for the state of your wife's nerves?"

"They'll hear you," Charles said anxiously, inclining his head toward the dining room. "Do you *want* the cowboy to know you gave birth to an illegitimate child when everyone in Stone Creek thought you were getting an education?"

"Oh, I got an education, all right," Sarah said bitterly.

Charles consulted his watch again. "I have to go," he said. "I have paperwork to do, before tomorrow's meeting."

Good riddance, Sarah thought. She'd gotten a reprieve, as far as the bank was concerned, but another part of her was alarmed. Was this "meeting" with the other shareholders? Several of them lived in

Flagstaff, a relatively short train ride from Stone Creek. Suppose Charles had asked around town, heard about some of her father's recent escapades, and made the decision to take over control? Alone, he couldn't do it. With the help of the other shareholders, though, he could be sitting behind her father's desk the morning after next.

With the first smile he'd offered all evening, Charles ran his knuckles lightly down the side of Sarah's face. "I'll be back in a few days," he said, as though he thought she was pining over his departure. "A week at the outside."

A week with Owen. A week to cover her tracks at the bank.

She tried to look sad. Might even have said, "I'll miss you," as he seemed to expect her to do, but since she would have choked on the words, she swallowed them.

He bent his head, kissed her lightly, briefly on the mouth.

She stepped back, secretly furious.

"Still the coquette," Charles remarked smoothly. "You're not fooling me, Sarah. I remember how much you liked going to bed with me."

Sarah's cheeks pulsed with heat so sudden and so intense that it was actually painful. She would surely have slapped Charles Langstreet the Third across the face if she hadn't known the crack of flesh meeting flesh would carry into the nearby dining room.

"Good *night,* Mr. Langstreet," she said.

He grinned, turned, and strolled, whistling merrily, down the porch steps, along the walk, through the gate.

Sarah watched him until he was out of sight, then turned and nearly collided with Wyatt, who was standing directly behind her.

Her heart fluttered painfully. How much had he heard? Had he seen Charles kiss her?

She could tell nothing by his expression.

"I'd best be leaving, too," he said. "I've got to count horses in front of saloons."

"What?" Sarah asked, confused.

He chuckled. "Rowdy's way of watching out for trouble," he said, taking his hat from the coat tree. "Thank you, Miss Tamlin, for a fine evening and the best meal I've had in a long time."

Something tightened in Sarah's throat. "If I'm to call you Wyatt," she heard herself say, "then you must call me Sarah."

His smile was as dazzling as the starched shirt he'd put on to come to supper. "Sarah, then," he said. The smile faded. "That Langstreet fella," he began. "Is he . . . ? Do you—?"

"He's a business associate," Sarah said. It was a partial truth, and she wondered if she ought to record it in her book of lies.

"That's good," Wyatt said. His dark eyes were almost liquid, there in the dim light of the entryway. "Because if I stay on in Stone Creek, I mean to set about courting you in earnest."

"*If* you stay?" She'd known he was a drifter, an outlaw, that he'd be moving on at some point. So why did she feel as though a deep, dark precipice had just opened at her feet?

"Reckon I'll be deciding on that further along," he said. "Good night, Sarah."

For a moment, she thought he was going to kiss her, just as Charles had—his face was so very close to hers—but he didn't. And she was stunned by the depths of her disappointment.

She watched until he passed through the front gate, turned toward the main part of town, moving in and out of the lamplight. Then she closed the door quietly and went back to the dining room.

Doc and Owen were busy clearing the table.

"Is Papa leaving me here?" Owen asked hopefully.

"Yes," Sarah said, taken aback, exchanging quick glances with Doc, who'd paused in his plate-gathering like a man listening for some sound in the distance. "But only for a few days. I thought you'd be—well—surprised—"

"Papa's always leaving me places," Owen said. His manner was nonchalant, though there was a slight stoop to his shoulders that hadn't been there before.

Doc shook his head, though the boy didn't see.

Sarah contrived to smile and moved to help with the work. "What sort of places?" she asked, in a tone meant to sound cheerful, as though abandoning a child with people who were virtual strangers to him was a common occurrence, and wholly acceptable.

"Once, I lived at a hotel all by myself for a whole week," Owen told her. "It was scary at night, but I got to have whatever I wanted to eat, and Papa gave me lots of spending money."

Sarah could not look at him. He might see what she was thinking. "Why did he do that?" she asked lightly, when she could trust herself to speak. Again, her gaze met Doc's, but this time, the look held.

"He had meetings with a lady. She wore a big hat with pink feathers on it and rode in a carriage with six white horses pulling it."

Sarah drew back a chair and sank into it, breathless.

"Are you sick, Aunt Sarah?" Owen asked, clearly frightened.

"I'm f-fine," Sarah muttered. She wouldn't have to write *that* lie in the book to remember it.

"Let's wash up these dishes," Doc told the boy, his voice a little too hearty. "Since your aunt Sarah went to all the trouble to cook it and all."

Owen nodded, but his eyes were still on Sarah. "I'll be quiet," he said. "If you have a headache—"

Sarah longed to gather the child in her arms, but she didn't dare. She'd weep if she did, and never let go of him again. "You don't have to be quiet," she told him softly.

Doc put a hand on Owen's shoulder and steered him in the direction of the kitchen. "I'll wash and you dry," he said.

CHAPTER FIVE

WHILE OWEN AND DOC WERE washing dishes, Sarah went upstairs, looked in on her father, who was sleeping soundly, then opened the door to the room across from her own. It contained a brass bed, a washstand and a bureau, and soft moonlight flowed in through the lace curtains.

The mattress was bare, since no one had used the room in months, with a faded quilt folded at its foot. Briskly, Sarah fetched sheets from the top drawer of the bureau and made up a bed for Owen.

The process was bittersweet. Tonight,

her son would sleep in this room, dreaming, she hoped, little-boy dreams. But there was a disturbing truth in Wyatt and Doc's teasing—young as he was, Owen was more man than child. He'd lived in hotel rooms by himself, and God knew what other places.

She yearned to keep him, raise him openly as her son. She wouldn't mind the scandal that would surely ensue, the extra expense, the inevitable work of bringing up a child. But she must not allow herself to think such thoughts, she knew, because Charles would come back and take him away again.

Under the law, she had no rights. On his birth certificate, Marjory Langstreet was listed as his mother.

Some of the starch went out of Sarah's knees.

She sat down on the edge of the freshly made bed, fighting back tears of hopelessness.

She'd been so young and foolish—only seventeen and far from home—when she'd given birth to Owen, in an anonymous infirmary room, a decade before. Charles, fifteen years her senior and sophisticated, a friend of her father's, had been her "protector," met her at the train when she arrived in the City of Brotherly Love, taken her by carriage to the women's college in the rolling green Pennsylvania countryside.

Homesick, regarded as a bumpkin by the other pupils in residence, most of whom had been raised in cities and not crude frontier towns, she'd quickly become besotted with Charles. She'd studied hard at school, majoring in music, but on weekends, he often came to collect her in his elegant carriage. It was all innocent at first; he escorted her to museums, to concerts, to fine restaurants.

And then he took advantage.

He said college was a waste for a woman, and suggested she leave school so they could spend more time together. He'd set her up in a fancy hotel, persuaded her not to tell her father that she'd dropped all her classes.

That was when the lying had begun. She'd written weekly letters to her parents, describing books she hadn't read, lectures she hadn't attended, field trips she hadn't taken. Someone Charles knew in the college office mailed the missives, and forwarded the replies. Sarah returned the funds her father sent for tuition and textbooks, claiming she'd won a scholarship. Her grades were forged, with the help of Charles's friend, and for a long, blissful time, the deception passed as truth.

Sitting there in Owen's moonlit room, Sarah blushed. Charles had been right earlier when he'd taunted her about enjoying his attentions in bed. Just sixteen, her body in full flower, she'd lived for his visits, reveled like some wild creature in his caresses.

Even when she realized, one eventful day, that she was carrying a child, she hadn't worried. Charles would be pleased. He would surely marry her, straight away.

She was awaiting his visit, full of her news, when a grand woman in tailored clothes presented herself at the door of Sarah's suite. She'd been tall, imperious, exuding angry confidence.

"So this is where Charles is keeping his current mistress," Marjory Langstreet had said, sweeping past a startled Sarah into the sumptuously furnished suite. "And how gracious of him to support you in such style."

Sarah had stared at the woman. "M-mistress?" she'd echoed stupidly.

"Surely you understand," Marjory had said, "that you are a kept woman? A bird in a gilded cage?"

Sarah's mouth had fallen open. This was surely some kind of cruel prank. Charles *wasn't* married. He loved her—hadn't he said so, over and over again? Hadn't he given her jewelry, bought her trinkets and clothes?

"Who are you?" she'd managed.

Marjory ran a gloved hand along the keyboard of Sarah's treasured piano. The sound was discordant, and bore no resemblance to music. From there, she proceeded to examine a painted porcelain lamp, a novel bound in Moroccan leather, a delicate Chinese fan with an ivory handle—all gifts from Charles.

"You really don't know?" she trilled, after several long moments. Then she'd turned, hands resting on her hips, and shattered Sarah's world with a single sentence. "I'm Mrs. Charles Langstreet the Third," she said, the words slicing through Sarah with the stinging force of a sharp sword.

Then, as now, Sarah had been unable to stand. She'd dropped into a chair, blind with confusion, pain and fear. Unconsciously, she'd rested a hand on her abdomen.

"Pack your things, dear," Mrs. Langstreet had said. "As of tomorrow morning, you won't be living here any longer. A back-street whore belongs, you see, on a *back-street.* If Charles wants to continue this dalliance, that's his business, but I won't be footing the bill."

With that, she'd gone, leaving the suite door standing open to the hall beyond.

Sarah had been too numb to move at first. She simply sat, waiting for Charles to come and say it was all a mistake. That *she,* Sarah, would be the only Mrs. Charles Langstreet the Third.

All day she waited.

But he didn't come.

Sarah had finally closed the door, gone to bed and lain staring up at the ceiling throughout the very long night to come.

In the morning, a tentative knock sent a surge of hope rushing through her. She rushed to the door, opened it to find, not a smiling Charles, with a credible explanation at the ready, but one of the hotel's porters. The fellow stood in the corridor, clearly uncomfortable.

He'd offered an anxious smile as two maids and another porter collected themselves behind him. "I'm sorry to hear you're leaving us," he'd said. "Mrs. Langstreet asked that we help you gather your belongings. There'll be a carriage waiting to take you to your new residence at ten o'clock."

Sarah had not protested.

She'd simply watched, stricken, as her clothes were folded into trunks and boxes, her books taken from the shelves, her jewelry stuffed into valises Marjory Langstreet had evidently provided for the purpose.

By noon, she'd been settled in a seedy rooming house, one door of her tiny room opening onto a rat-infested alley.

And still there had been no word, no visit, from Charles.

Sarah waited a week, then began pawning jewelry, a piece at a time, to buy food. Twice, she wrote long letters to her unsuspecting father, telling the shattering truth, but she'd never mailed them.

She was too ashamed.

Too heartbroken.

Several times, when hunger forced her out into the narrow, filthy streets, she'd considered standing on the tracks when the trolley came. It would be over, that way.

In the end, she couldn't do that to the baby, or to herself.

She finally sent a wire to her father, reading simply, *I am in trouble,* and listing her address at the boardinghouse.

Within ten days, he'd arrived, bent on taking her home to Stone Creek. She'd told him everything but the name of the man who'd sired her child, and patently refused to return to Arizona Territory. As much as she yearned for her own room, the sound of her mother's voice, the soothing touch of her hand, Sarah simply hadn't been able to face the inevitable gossip and speculation.

Resigned, Ephriam had enrolled her in another college, a small, private one where secrets were kept, and moved her into the dormitory.

She hadn't seen Charles again until a week before Owen's birth, in the college infirmary. They met in the library, Charles and Sarah and Charles's lawyer. Charles had stiffly informed her that he meant to raise the child as a legitimate heir, with Marjory listed as the legal mother.

Sarah had had no choice but to comply.

She'd long since sold the last of her jewelry, her rich clothes and the books. Even the Chinese fan. And she'd promised her clearly disenchanted father she would finish college, no matter what.

So when her baby boy was born, she'd handed him over to Charles's lawyer. The loss had been keen, brutal, as though she'd torn her still-beating heart from her bosom and handed that over, too.

She'd survived, somehow, doggedly arising in the morning, doing what was at hand to do, enduring more than living. She'd worked hard at her lessons, gotten her degree in music, and returned to Stone Creek just in time to attend her mother's funeral.

Nancy Anne Tamlin had never known she had a grandchild, nor had anyone else in town, except for Ephriam, of course, and possibly his best friend, Doc Venable.

Now, ten years later, miraculously, impossibly, that boy was right downstairs, in her own kitchen, helping with the dishes.

"Sarah?"

She looked up, startled, and saw Ephriam standing in the doorway. She couldn't see his face, but she knew by the way he'd spoken her name that he was enjoying one of his brief, lucid intervals.

"That boy I saw tonight. Is he—?"

Sarah felt for the book of lies, nesting, as always, in her skirt pocket, clenched it through the fabric. She swallowed, then shook her head. "No, Papa. He's just visiting."

"He looks like your mother's people," Ephriam said. "What's his name?"

"Owen," Sarah allowed, after swallowing again. "He's Charles Langstreet's son. You remember Mr. Langstreet, don't you?"

"Never liked him," her father replied. "Pompous jackass."

She saw a change in Ephriam's bearing, something too subtle to describe, but there nonetheless.

"Great Scot," Ephriam gasped. "It was *Langstreet,* wasn't it? *He* was the one who led you astray!"

"Papa—"

"And Owen is my grandson," the old man persisted, sounding thunderstruck.

Of all the times he could have recovered his faculties, it had to be now, tonight, when keeping the secret was more important than ever before.

Sarah simply could not summon up another lie. She felt drained, enervated, as though she'd relived her affair with Charles, her sad, scandalous pregnancy, the birth itself, which had been torturous, and, still worse, watched as Charles's lawyer carried her newborn son out of her room in the college infirmary. She'd been permitted to give him only one thing: his first name.

And she'd never expected to see him again.

"Yes," she said weakly. "You're right, Papa. But you mustn't let on. Owen doesn't know who I am. He calls me Aunt Sarah."

Ephriam pondered a while, silent and brooding. "I'd have killed Langstreet if I'd known," he said. "I suppose that's why you didn't tell me."

Sarah closed her eyes for a moment, summoned her will, and stood. Doc and Owen had probably finished washing the dishes by then, and they'd be wondering what was keeping her.

She stood before her father, still looming in the darkened doorway, straightening the front of his long nightshirt as though it were one of the day coats he wore to the bank.

"Our secret, Papa?" she asked.

"There are too damn *many* secrets in this house."

"Papa—"

"All right," Ephriam said. "But I don't like it. And I'm taking that boy fishing at the creek tomorrow, with or without your say-so."

Sarah's eyes stung, and she smiled. "Fair enough," she said.

She walked her father back to his room, tucked him in like a child. Kissed his forehead. Still under the effects of the laudanum Doc had given him earlier, he dozed off immediately.

When she descended to the kitchen, via the rear stairway, Doc and Owen were sitting at the pedestal table in the center of the room, playing cards. The pot was a pile of wooden matches.

Interested, Sarah stood behind Owen's chair and assessed his hand.

"Five card stud," Doc said. "Care to join us?"

"I never play poker," Sarah said. The little book in her skirt pocket seemed to pulse in protest.

Doc merely chuckled.

Sarah bent low and whispered in Owen's ear. "Bet all your matchsticks. You've got a straight with ace high."

THERE WERE ONLY THREE HORSES in front of Jolene Bell's Saloon, two in front of the Hell-bent, six lining the hitching rail at the Spit Bucket. Wyatt passed them by, making for the jailhouse.

All was quiet there, too, so he closed the place up for the night and went around back to the barn, where he planned to stretch out in the hayloft. The weather was clear, and he'd be able to see the stars between the wide cracks in the roof.

He was thinking about Sarah, and those blue eyes of hers, full of tragic mysteries and an almost formidable intelligence. There was something to her attachment to the boy Owen, though he couldn't quite figure out what it was. A sort of anxious solicitude, carefully controlled. Her gaze had constantly strayed to the child, rested on him with a certain desperate hunger.

Mulling over these things as he was, Wyatt almost fell over the dog lying in the path between the jailhouse and the barn. The critter whimpered, and Wyatt righted himself.

"What the—?"

The dog whimpered again. It was an ugly brute of a mutt, missing a chunk of one ear and so thin he could make out its ribs even in the relative darkness. Its tail had been lopped off square, close to the hind quarters, and a scab had formed over the wound.

"Run along home," Wyatt said.

The dog started to rise, dropped heavily to the ground again.

Muttering a swear word, Wyatt crouched for a closer look. "You sick, fella?"

The animal emitted a soft, keening whine, almost like a plea.

Wyatt's heart sank. He couldn't take care of his own horse, or even himself, but he couldn't walk away from this dog, either. And about the last thing he needed was a goddamned dog.

He felt the mutt's sides for obvious injuries, and found none. The legs seemed sound, too. When the brute didn't bite him, he sighed, lifted him up in both arms, and carried him into Rowdy's tidy little house.

He laid him on Pardner's rug, as gently as he could, and struck a match to light one of the kerosene lamps.

In the glow, the miserable specimen looked even uglier than he had in the dark. And there was dried blood all over his coat, some of which had transferred itself to the front of Wyatt's borrowed white going-to-supper shirt.

"If you were a woman," Wyatt told the sorry-looking critter, "you'd have to wear a flour sack over your head every time you left the house."

The dog whined again, its moist brown eyes imploring Wyatt, though for what he did not know. Mercy, perhaps. The simple privilege of living.

"No telling how bad you're hurt, looking the way you do." Resigned, Wyatt went into Rowdy and Lark's fancy bathroom and ran some warm water into the tub. He went back to the kitchen, gathered up the dog again, and lugged him in for a sudsing.

The dog endured the ordeal with the last of his dignity, and as he soaped and rinsed the critter, and soaped and rinsed him again, Wyatt's temper, subdued by two years in prison, flared inside him, a slowly spreading heat.

Someone—and God help them when Wyatt found out who—had beaten the dog with either a buggy whip or a tree branch of similar circumference, leaving deep, bloody stripes in his brindled hide.

Once he'd hoisted the dog out of the tub and dried him off with a fancy mono-grammed towel—the only thing at hand to serve the purpose—Wyatt rummaged through cabinets until he found a tin of salve. He applied it lavishly to the dog's wounds, and the poor, pitiful creature didn't even try to lick the stuff off. He just huddled there on Lark's formerly pristine bath mat, looking forlorn and waiting for another blow.

"I'm not going to hurt you, boy," Wyatt

said, his voice catching raw in his throat. "You've fallen among friends."

The dog licked his face, tentatively, and then cowered again.

Wyatt patted his head, then stood. "I reckon what you need now is something to eat and a decent night's sleep. I'll figure out what to do with you in the morning. Meanwhile, you'll require a name. 'Lonesome' ought to suit."

Lonesome looked pleased. Got painfully to his four feet to follow Wyatt out of the bathroom and toward the kitchen.

After searching the pantry shelves, Wyatt opened a can of condensed milk, emptied it into a bowl, and set it on the floor. Lonesome hesitated, then made short work of the milk.

Next, he purloined a jar of venison stew, home-preserved, and gave that to the dog, too. At this rate, he'd owe his deputy salary to Lark for the groceries he was using up.

Lonesome lapped up the stew, burped like a dry-throated cowboy swilling beer, and laved the toe of Wyatt's right boot with his tongue.

He'd planned on bedding down in the

barn, but Lonesome didn't appear to be up to walking even that far. Feeling like a squatter, Wyatt found some blankets, made himself a bed on the settee in the little parlor, with one for the dog beside it on the floor.

Lonesome settled down to sleep, after circling the blankets for a spell, and Wyatt stretched out on the settee.

Again, he thought of how the last thing he needed was something he had to look out for and feed, but he didn't have the heart to say so aloud. Might hurt Lonesome's feelings, and he'd been hurt enough already.

SOMEONE FROM THE HOTEL brought Owen's baggage over in a wagon, bright and early, along with a telegram from Charles.

Called back to Philadelphia on an urgent matter. Will return for the boy as soon as possible. Funds for his maintenance to follow.

Maintenance? Was that all Owen was to Charles—something requiring maintenance? Sarah stared at the neatly typewritten words, amazed, dangerously hopeful, and utterly confounded. Her father and Owen were seated at the kitchen table, eating oatmeal and planning their fishing expedition to the creek. Ephriam was properly dressed, though in outdoor clothes rather than his usual suit, his hair was brushed, and his eyes were as clear and placid as still water.

Indeed, in Owen's chattering presence, he seemed almost like the man he had once been. Sarah was both thrilled and terrified, knowing as she did that the change would be fleeting.

Owen, for his part, seemed delighted to be going fishing on a summer day. The creek was shallow, so Sarah didn't fret that he'd drown, and as she cleared away the remains of breakfast, she stole sidelong looks at her son.

Her son.

He *did* resemble her mother's side of the family, just as Ephriam had remarked the night before. Fortunately, Nancy Anne Owen Tamlin *hadn't* looked a thing like her fair-haired parents and siblings—she'd been stout and quite plain, with hair she herself had described as mouse-brown, ears that protruded slightly, and an exuberant laugh.

Sarah had adored her.

"I'm due at the bank," she told the man and boy at the table, as though it were a perfectly normal morning in the Tamlin household, her father bright-eyed and clear-minded, Owen gobbling up the last of his oatmeal. "Be careful down at the creek, both of you."

With that, she found her pocketbook and left the house by the front door, humming a little under her breath.

As she passed the church, Sarah opened the gate and entered the cemetery. It was something she often did, of a morning, though she never stayed long.

Intent on reaching her mother's final resting place, she didn't immediately notice Wyatt Yarbro standing nearby, gazing down at another grave. When she did, her face heated up, and she crouched in front of Nancy Anne's headstone, her skirts spilling around her, pretending she hadn't seen him.

"Mornin'," she heard him say.

Sarah looked up, shaded her eyes from the dazzling sun. Wyatt's lean frame seemed rimmed by the glare, eclipselike. "Good morning, Mr.—Wyatt."

As her vision adjusted, she noticed the speckled dog, sniffing between headstones a short distance away.

"He and I have taken up with each other," Wyatt said, grinning a little as he squatted beside Sarah in the sweet-smelling grass of that peaceful place. "You wouldn't happen to know where he calls home, would you?"

Sarah squinted. "I've seen him trying to scrounge food behind the saloons," she said, then wished she'd held her tongue, because Wyatt would, of course, wonder what business she had behind saloons. "Sometimes, people throw rocks at him."

Wyatt plucked a blade of grass, examined it thoughtfully, and then tossed it aside. "Then I guess he's my dog for the duration," he said. When his eyes met Sarah's, she had the disturbing sense of tumbling into them. The fall took her breath away.

"I've tried to get him to follow me home," Sarah said, catching herself, regaining her balance, nodding to indicate the dog. "He was just too skittish, though."

"Do you like dogs, Miss—Sarah?"

"They're God's creatures," she affirmed.

Wyatt's grin flashed, fairly knocking her back on her heels. "What I said last night about courting you—I hope you weren't offended."

Sarah didn't know how to reply, and she'd reveal too much if she tried.

"I wouldn't want to scare you off or anything," he went on, somewhat awkwardly. "But it's only right that you hear the truth about me, Sarah. I did a couple of years in prison for train robbing."

Still tongue-tied, Sarah simply stared at Wyatt Yarbro, wondering why she felt safer in the presence of an admitted criminal than she ever had with Charles.

Wyatt sighed, stood, offered a hand to help Sarah to her feet.

She took the hand, let him pull her up.

"I figured you'd be shocked," he said.

At last, Sarah found her voice. "But I'm not," she said. "Shocked, I mean." She indicated the nearby grave of his very famous outlaw father, Payton Yarbro. "Rowdy's been straightforward about his past, at least since he met Lark. It's no surprise to learn that you were caught and punished for what you did."

He studied her, his wonderful eyes slightly narrowed. "Did Rowdy tell you about me?"

Sarah shook her head. "No, and neither did Lark," she answered.

Wyatt was quiet for a long time, his gaze fixed on the far horizon, where a plume of dust rose against the sky.

"Riders coming," he finally said.

"Cowboys, probably," Sarah said, unconcerned. There were a lot of ranches around Stone Creek, and the hired hands often came to town to carouse at one of the saloons, especially when payday rolled around.

Recalling that it was the last day of August, she sighed. She'd best get to the bank and help Thomas take in the deposits. Some of the cowpokes actually had accounts, and they put a portion of their wages away, or bought drafts to send funds home to mothers, wives and children, before throwing the rest away on whiskey and women of unfortunate character.

Wyatt whistled for the dog, put his hat back on. He seemed distracted, even a little

troubled, and kept glancing toward the bil-
low of dust swelling against the south-
eastern skies.

Even though he walked at Sarah's side
as far as the churchyard gate, and held it
open for her while she passed through
ahead of him, he was far away. When they
reached the sidewalk, Wyatt touched the
brim of his hat and he and the dog
headed in one direction, while Sarah went
in the other.

The window shade was drawn at the
bank.

Frowning, she consulted the small
watch pinned to her bodice. Five minutes
past the opening time of eight o'clock. She
was late.

The door was locked.

Sarah fumbled for her key, let herself in.

Thomas stood behind the counter,
looking anxious.

Sarah rolled up the shade.

"Maybe we ought not to open for business today," Thomas said. Perspiration
glistened on either side of his nose, as well
as his forehead, and he kept wetting his
lips with his tongue.

"Nonsense," Sarah said. "It's payday on most of the ranches. Down at the feed store and the livery stable, too. People will want to make deposits."

"We shouldn't open the safe," Thomas insisted, glancing at the rolled-up shade above the front window.

"Thomas, what on earth—?"

"It's just something I overheard at the boardinghouse last night," he said. Then he walked right past her, lowered the blind again, and locked the door. "Probably nothing to be concerned about, but—"

Sarah laid a hand on his arm. *"Thomas."*

He shoved splayed fingers through his hair. "A couple of drifters stopped off at our place and asked to chop wood in return for a hot supper. Mother allowed as how she'd feed them, all right, but they had to eat outside because they were strangers and she didn't like the looks of them."

"And?" Sarah prompted.

"It was hot, so Mother had a window open in the kitchen, and I went in there to shut it. That's when I heard them talking outside. The drifters, I mean."

Sarah pressed her lips together, waited.

"They said there was money to be gotten, in a place like Stone Creek, and they wouldn't have to ride for the likes of Sam O'Ballivan to get their hands on it."

Sarah remembered the dust on the horizon, and the way it had caught Wyatt's attention. She felt a little prickle of alarm, not so much because the bank might be robbed—that was preposterous—but because Owen and her father were down by the creek, fishing, and the trail into town ran right past it. And because, if there was trouble coming, Wyatt would most likely face it alone, with Sam and Rowdy away.

Thomas prattled on, apparently unable to stop talking now that he'd gotten started. "I wanted to come right over to your house and tell you," he said, "but Mother said you had company and I'd be intruding." He reddened. "Sarah, what if they mean to hold us up?"

"Don't be silly, Thomas. No one has *ever* held up the Stockman's Bank."

"Folks know Rowdy Yarbro's out of town, and Mr. O'Ballivan, too," Thomas argued, albeit respectfully, "and this is the only place in Stone Creek where there's any amount of cash money—"

Sarah shook her head. "You've been reading too many dime novels," she insisted. "This is 1907. The *twentieth century,* not the old West. Anyway, if we lock up on a Tuesday morning, it might start a panic."

"I feel sick," Thomas said. "Can I go home?"

Sarah sighed. Thomas was a faithful worker; he was *never* sick. His salary was small, but he never complained, or refused to run errands or other tasks outside his job as a teller.

"Very well, then," she said, somewhat snappishly. "Go home."

"I don't like leaving you here alone," Thomas fretted, but he was already making for the door, fumbling with the lock.

"Give my kindest regards to your mother," Sarah said.

Thomas nodded, and fled.

Sarah rolled the window shade back up, smoothed her hair and her skirts, and walked behind the counter, resigned to doing Thomas's work, as well as her father's and her own.

She checked her bodice watch again. At three o'clock, she would close the bank, walk down the street toward home as usual, and duck around behind the Spit Bucket Saloon when she was sure no one was looking.

CHAPTER SIX

HOW MANY RIDERS would it take to raise a
dust cloud like that one? Wyatt wondered,
as he moved briskly toward the jailhouse,
hoping poor old Lonesome could make it
that far without collapsing. Much restored
by a little kindness and a lot of breakfast,
the dog was puny, just the same. He'd
need some time to heal up proper.

Reaching Rowdy's office, he had to
pick Lonesome up in both arms to get him
over the threshold. The critter's tongue
hung to one side of his snout, and he was
panting hard.

He settled Lonesome in front of the

cold stove, took the washbasin outside, and pumped cold water into it. Then, having set the basin within Lonesome's reach, he drew his Colt, spun the cylinder to make sure it was fully loaded.

It was, since he'd had no cause to shoot, except to pick off the occasional rabbit for his supper out on the trail. Pappy had been a great advocate of regular target practice, but Wyatt hadn't been flush enough to waste good bullets plunking at tin cans for a long time.

Fortunately, Rowdy kept enough ammunition in the bottom drawer of his desk to supply an artillery regiment.

Leaving the dog in peace, Wyatt stepped back out into the street.

He guessed at least a dozen riders were bearing down on Stone Creek, and even though they were most likely harmless cowpokes, looking to wet their whistles with a little whiskey and maybe visit a loose woman, a familiar uneasiness prickled in the pit of his stomach. He'd felt it last just before the stampede, down by the border.

There was no fear—just a sense of standing a rung or two above it on an invisible ladder. That was another thing he'd learned from Pappy—fear was a luxury an outlaw couldn't afford. When trouble came, a man had to stand up on the inside, ready to play whatever cards he might be dealt.

Wyatt looked up and down the street, found it deserted, where a quarter of an hour before, the place had been bustling with morning business. He spared a moment to wish that Sam and Rowdy were around, but no more than that. Clearly, if trouble was on its way, he'd be the one facing it down.

The riders were getting close—he could hear the hoofbeats of their horses now—probably within minutes of town, and Wyatt's thoughts strayed to the bank. Or, more properly, to Sarah.

He headed in that direction, not at a lope, as instinct urged, but with long, sure strides. In his head, he heard Pappy's voice, as he often did. *You've got to look tough, boy, even if you're down to your last pint of blood and plumb out of ideas. Show any weakness, and they'll be on you like wolves.*

At the moment, Wyatt had only one

idea, but his blood was pumping just fine. It wasn't a matter of looking tough, either. He knew he was. Two years breaking rocks in the hot Texas sun had given him that, if nothing else.

He reached the bank, tried the door, found it open.

Sarah stood alone behind the counter, pale and straight-shouldered. Relief flickered in those astounding blue eyes of hers, though, and a little color came into her cheeks.

"Everything all right here?" Wyatt asked.

"So far," Sarah said, but a note of worry echoed in the air after she spoke.

"You're alone?" He knew she was, but it seemed odd, so he had to verify the suspicion.

"I was," she replied. "Until you came. Is something wrong?"

"Probably not," Wyatt said, though his senses told another story entirely.

"Thomas has some silly notion that the bank is about to be robbed," she said, in the same voice she'd used the night before, at supper, to offer him a second helping of fried chicken.

"Where is he?" Wyatt asked, watching

the street through the glass window in the front door. He saw three riders in the lead, but there were a lot more coming up behind, raising as much dust as they had on the trail outside of town. He upped his estimate of their numbers to twenty.

"He was frightened, so I sent him home."

Wyatt gave a huff of disgust at that.

"There's no cause for concern, I'm sure," Sarah said brightly. "It's payday on the ranches, being the last day of the month, and cowboys come from all over to spend their wages and—"

Wyatt glanced back at her. "Just the same," he said evenly, "you ought to slip out the back door, if there is one, and go on home."

She hoisted a shotgun in one hand. Evidently, she kept it stashed behind the counter. "I'm not afraid," she said, straightening her spine to confirm the assertion. "And besides, those men are harmless. You'll see."

He had to admire Sarah's grit, though he still wished she'd do as he said and go out the back way.

Out front, men began to dismount, leaving their horses untethered, and tromping, spurs jingling, up onto the wooden side-walk.

Three of them, the same men he'd seen riding in the lead, headed for the bank's door.

Wyatt stepped back to admit them. The .45 seemed to vibrate against his hip, the way the ground trembled when a herd was passing at a high run, but he didn't draw. No cause for that—yet.

The first galoot through the door was big as a mountain. Despite the heat, he wore a long coat, and every part of him, from the top of his hat to the worn boots on his feet, was covered in a fine layer of yellowish-red dust. Wyatt noticed immediately that he'd pushed the side of his coat back, so it caught behind his gun and holster.

Wyatt's nape tingled, but he stood with his arms folded, a slight but deliberately cordial smile curving at one side of his mouth. An experienced desperado himself, he figured the men would have worn ban-dannas over their faces if they intended mischief. On the other hand, though, word of Rowdy's absence had probably gotten around that part of the territory. With the cat away, the mice were inclined to play . . . .

The big man's attention went straight to the star pinned to Wyatt's vest, and his eyes, small and set deep in their grimy sockets, sparse lashes coated in dirt, widened a little. He glanced toward Sarah, his countenance seeming to droop a little.

"Thought you was gone to Haven," the giant told Wyatt, his tone moderately resentful.

Two facts registered in Wyatt's mind: the big man didn't know Rowdy by sight, only reputation, and finding a lawman in the Stockman's Bank put some kind of hitch in his get-along.

"Would you like to make a deposit?" Sarah chimed sunnily.

A muscle contracted, hard, in Wyatt's jaw. It was no time for feminine chatter. While the situation looked ordinary on the outside, he knew in his gut it wasn't.

Two more of them crowded in behind the yahoo. Their eyeballs stood out starkly in their dirt-caked faces—they reminded Wyatt of coal miners, just coming up from underground, startled by daylight.

"Where can a man get a drink around here?" the big man boomed, suddenly jovial.

"You don't want to make a deposit?" Sarah asked, sounding disappointed.

Wyatt didn't take his eyes off the trail bum. These men weren't riding for a brand—they were on their own, and traveling in a bunch because, at the core of things, they were cowards. "Oh," he answered dryly, his arms still folded, "maybe in one of the three or four saloons you passed getting to the bank."

More men crammed themselves into the doorway, clogging it like hair in a drain. The big man put up a hand to stop the flow from the street.

Wyatt was Yarbro-fast with a gun, but he was only one man, Sarah only one woman, shotgun at the ready or not. With a score of men in the street and stuffed into the doorway, they wouldn't have a chance. But Wyatt could take out the first half-dozen comers with no problem, and the big fellow seemed to know that, if the others didn't.

"You have a name?" Wyatt asked easily,

never taking his eyes off the stranger. Cowards, he knew, were especially dangerous.

"Not one you need to know," the other man blustered, offended.

"I can always check the Wanted posters back at the office," Wyatt said. *If I chance to live that long.* "If you gentlemen don't have honest business in this establishment, I'd suggest you go elsewhere. I hear they don't water down the whiskey— much—over at Jolene Bell's place."

"What's *your* name?" the big man demanded.

"It's one you do need to know—and remember. Wyatt Yarbro."

"Oh, I'll remember, all right."

"If any of you have wages to draw on one of the big ranches," Sarah put in, "we'll be happy to cash the vouchers for you."

Wyatt willed her to shut up. It proved futile, however, as it usually did with women.

"We offer one-percent interest on our savings accounts," she prattled on.

The big man looked flustered. Clearly,

he'd come to make a withdrawal, not a deposit, and he didn't give a rat's behind about interest rates.

"Stone Creek's a friendly town," Wyatt said affably, still sensing that he had an advantage in this situation, though he'd be damned if he knew what it was, since he was outnumbered and the menfolks hereabouts didn't seem inclined to stick their heads out of their homes and businesses, let alone stand with him. "We do have an ordinance, though, in regard to firearms. Drop your pistols and rifles off right there on the counter and collect them at the jailhouse when you're ready to ride out."

The big man blinked. "I never heard about no *ordinance*," he protested.

His cohorts were clustered in front of the window, peering in, and Wyatt thought he recognized one of them as Billy Justice's younger brother, Carl, but he couldn't be sure. Like the others, Carl resembled a dust statue, come to life.

"I reckon there are a lot of things you haven't heard about," Wyatt responded. "The law is the law—" now, where had *that* come from? "—and if you won't comply, I'll have to arrest you."

"Look, we don't want no trouble," the big man said.

"Hand over those firearms and you won't have any," Wyatt promised. What had turned these yahoos from their obvious intention to rob the Stockman's Bank while Rowdy was away? Surely the Yarbro name, widely known in the West and even parts of the East as it was, hadn't been enough to stop twenty armed men in their boot prints. Most likely, they'd counted on an easy morning's work, with no one but an elderly banker, his daughter, and a clerk to impede them, and now that they'd encountered a single deputy marshal, they'd lost their gumption. If Pappy had decided to clean out the vault, he'd have taken care of business and ridden for the hills in half the time these would-be bandits had spent jawing and jamming up the doorway.

Reluctantly, the big man drew his hog-shooter and stepped up to lay it on the counter. "All right then," he said, signaling the others to do the same. "But I don't like it."

"No ordinance says you have to like it," Wyatt offered, letting out an inward breath in relief. He'd never been worried for his own safety, but he'd been *plenty* concerned about Sarah's.

She watched, clearly amazed, as man after man trooped in and surrendered his firearm. Within a minute or two, the counter top was piled high with six-guns, rifles, and even a Bowie knife or two.

"Much obliged, fellas," Wyatt said. Carl Justice was at the tag end of the line, and when he'd laid his ancient pistol on the counter, his gaze connected with Wyatt's, then skittered away.

As he turned to go, Wyatt caught him by the back of his canvas duster and held him fast.

"We'll have a word or two," Wyatt told Carl.

Carl's Adam's apple moved the length of his throat when he swallowed, but he didn't try to walk away.

"Phew!" Sarah said, when all the men but Carl had gone.

Wyatt sliced a glance in her direction. He wondered if she still thought the big man and his gang had come in to put part of their wages by for their old age. "I'll need something to carry those guns in," he told her mildly.

She nodded. "There's a wheelbarrow over at the livery stable. I'll borrow it."

A moment later, she was gone.

Fine time to clear out. For such a smart woman, she sure was naive when it came to the intentions of others.

"What are you doing here?" Wyatt demanded of Carl, getting him by the lapels of his coat as soon as Sarah passed the front window.

Carl smirked, though his eyes said he was scared. "I could ask the same thing of you," he countered. "Billy's bound to kill you dead. He knows you were in with them vigilantes that jumped us down at Haven right after you run off. Me and Billy and Clyde and Jack, we got away, but Billy's best friend Pete got lynched, right along with poor old Hannibal. Billy said their tongues hung out and turned black while they was chokin'."

"Where's Billy now?" Wyatt asked coolly. He'd taken a careful look at the outlaws as they turned in their weapons, one by one, but there had been no familiar faces among them, save Carl's.

"You think I'm fixin' to tell you that?" Carl scoffed. "After what you done to us?"

He glanced at Wyatt's star, and if he'd been a braver man, Carl probably would have spit in his face. He was yellow-bellied, though, which in this case was a prudent approach.

Wyatt felt no need to defend leaving the Justice gang to look out for themselves. He took a tighter grip on the front of Carl's filthy coat, which was stained with tobacco juice and spilled whiskey, among other things. "That big fella, the one who did all the talking. Who is he?"

Carl tried to shrug off Wyatt's hold on his duster, to no avail. "Hails to Paddy Paudeen. He was a strike-breaker, up in Wallace, Idaho, and other places, too, so you'd best not push him overmuch."

Wyatt made a mental note of the name. It wasn't familiar, but it wouldn't be hard to remember. "You were planning on holding up this bank." It was a statement, not a question.

Carl's attempt at bravado was pitiable. "Nah. We was just lookin' for a saloon, like Paddy said."

"You don't know a bank from a whiskey joint? Damn, Carl, even *you* can't be that stupid."

Carl gulped loudly. "No harm done. Can I go now?"

Wyatt let him go with a flinging motion that made him stumble backwards a few steps. "If you happen to have any contact with your big brother Billy, tell him I'd like to see him."

"Ain't seen him since we scattered to get away from them vigilantes," Carl lied, edging toward the door.

"If you send him a wire, say, I'll know it, Carl."

"I cain't send no telegram. Only got so much money in my pocket, and it's goin' for whiskey and a woman. And, anyways, I don't know where he is."

Just then, Sarah appeared in the open doorway, pushing an empty wheelbarrow. Her cheeks were pink from the effort, her hair all flyaway and stuck to her cheeks and the sides of her neck from the heat.

Wyatt's gut clenched at the sight of her, like it had the very first time, when he'd walked into that revival tent down by the creek.

Carl all but scrambled over the top of the wheelbarrow to get past her.

"I thought at least one of them would be fiscally responsible," she said.

Wyatt laughed outright. He could have used a drink himself, right about then, but with Paddy Paudeen and his outfit in town, he didn't have the option.

"What," she demanded, flushed again, "is so funny?"

"You," Wyatt said. He took the handles of the wheelbarrow from her, rolled it over to the counter, and started loading up guns, emptying each one of bullets and dropping these into the bottom of the barrow in a jumble.

Vexed, Sarah stepped inside and shut the door, whispered as though there were folks outside with their ears against the walls. "There *is* no ordinance against the possession of firearms in Stone Creek," she said.

"There is now," Wyatt replied, unconcerned.

Out of the corner of his eye, he saw her put her hands to her hips. Yes, sir, she was vexed. Not the least bit grateful that he'd just saved the cash holdings of the Stockman's Bank, whatever they amounted to, and possibly her life and virtue in the bargain.

"You can't just make up laws," Sarah challenged, "like some—some *potentate!*"

"Can't I?" Wyatt countered.

"No!" she sputtered.

"Well, darn," Wyatt said, grinning. "Somebody should have told me that before I went ahead and did it." He'd filled the wheelbarrow; now, he'd trundle it down the street to the jailhouse. Look in on Lonesome and see how the old dog was faring. If he was still feeling poorly, Wyatt planned to take him to see Doc Venable. Maybe there was a way to perk the mutt up a little.

"Suppose those men intended to trade honestly with this bank?" Sarah persisted. "Now, they'll never set foot in here again, thanks to you!"

Wyatt shook his head as he wheeled the load of guns past her, leaned to open the door. So *that* was what was getting under her hide. She thought she'd lost a valuable business opportunity. "It would be a good thing if they didn't," he said, over one shoulder. "Since they meant to empty your safe." Sarah was mad, all right, and he hoped she wouldn't get over it too quickly. Anger was becoming on her, making her eyes flash like blue fire and her cheeks blossom pink as the tea roses growing behind his ma's springhouse back on the farm.

He set the wheelbarrow down on its three wheels and turned, standing on the sidewalk, to look at her.

He never knew what came over him. Maybe he was just glad Paudeen and the others hadn't called his bluff. He could still feel the hot August sun on his face, the breath in his lungs, the steady, strong beat of his heart.

Maybe it was the way she looked, standing there.

In any case, Wyatt stepped over the threshold, took her by the shoulders, and backed her across the room until she was pressed against the counter. Then he caught her chin in one hand, lifted, and kissed her square on the mouth.

She stiffened, then opened to him. Her hands came up slowly, tentatively, and linked at the back of his neck.

A thousand thoughts flashed through Wyatt's mind as the kiss lengthened—he imagined bedding Sarah, right and proper, and all the pleasures that would entail. Her response was neither innocent nor awkward, but seasoned.

This was no virgin spinster, an insight that both troubled Wyatt and intrigued him.

When they finally broke apart, Sarah stared up at him, baffled and flushed, her hair even more askew than before. He accepted the truth then—he wasn't leaving Stone Creek anytime soon. If Billy Justice came, looking to gun him down, all the better—he'd like to get that particular confrontation out of the way anyhow.

If Rowdy and Sam came back, knowing he'd been part of the rustling operation down near Haven and bent on arresting him, he'd take his medicine, even if it meant going back to prison. Whatever happened, he wanted as much time with Sarah as he could get. Every minute spent away from her was a wasted one.

She seemed breathless and a little frazzled. Instead of moving away, out of his embrace, as another woman might have done, she was in no hurry to lower her hands to her sides. They were still resting against the back of Wyatt's neck.

"Of all the nerve," she marveled, in a strangled whisper.

Wyatt kissed her again, lightly this time, and all too briefly. God, what he wouldn't have given to lay her out on a soft bed, or in deep, fragrant grass, and pleasure her into feverish distraction. His whole body hardened at the prospect, and she must have noticed, because they were still pressed close together; her breath caught and her cheeks got pinker.

She slid her hands down over his shoulders and chest before sidestepping him, and he knew by the way she moved that she'd wanted him as much as he wanted her. He'd taken willing women in broad daylight before, and in some unorthodox places, too. But Sarah Tamlin was, for all her tantalizing secrets, a lady. When he had her, it would be a proper seduction, slow and easy, in a real bed.

"You might want to close up early," he said, sounding hoarse. He went back to the wheelbarrow, took hold of the handles.

She wouldn't look at him, nor did she speak, but he saw her give a brisk nod.

As soon as he'd stepped away from the door, he heard the lock turn behind him.

Wyatt wondered if she wanted to keep Paddy and his gang out, or the new deputy marshal who'd just kissed her, and soundly.

KITTY STEEL OPENED the back door of the Spit Bucket Saloon when Sarah knocked lightly, two full hours after she'd closed down the bank. Skirting Main Street, Sarah had rushed to Stone Creek, and found her father and Owen safe beside the sparkling stream, fishing. They'd caught a mess of trout.

"Is something the matter?" Ephriam had asked, squinting at her. He'd left his spectacles at home, evidently, or tucked them into his shirt pocket. To look at him, one would never guess he had episodes when he truly believed an invasion of the Confederate army was imminent.

They were safe. That was all that mattered to Sarah.

"No," she'd said cheerfully. "I just decided to close the bank early today. Let's go home and fry up those fish for lunch."

"Ephriam showed me how to clean them," Owen had told her proudly, on the walk back to the Tamlin house.

"I believe I could use a nap, after we

eat," Ephriam had observed, once they were inside.

"A *nap?*" Owen had looked positively crestfallen. "I thought only *babies* took naps."

"Old coots do, too," Ephriam had replied fondly. His eyes seemed to caress the boy.

Sarah fried up the fish, managing not to cremate them in the skillet, and even though she was still shaken—not by what *might* have been a near robbery, but by Wyatt Yarbro's kisses. When the meal was over and she'd cleared the table, Ephriam retired to his room, and Owen, despite his position on naps, began to yawn.

"Just lie on your bed and close your eyes," Sarah had told him gently. "You needn't actually sleep." Her mother had used that trick with her, when she was small. *Just rest,* she'd said, knowing Sarah would drift off.

Full of fresh air and fish he'd helped to catch, Owen considered the suggestion, finally nodded, and went up to his room. When Sarah peeked in, he was sound asleep.

She'd waited half an hour, then set out,

via backstreets and alleys, for the Spit
Bucket Saloon.

"It won't be the same without Maddie
and Lark," Kitty said now, as Sarah entered
the shadowy little room where the Tuesday
Afternoon Ladies Only Secret Poker Society met.

The Society, as the members referred
to it, had been founded three years before,
when an epidemic of grippe struck the
brothel above the Spit Bucket. Kitty, as well
as several of the other soiled doves, had
been desperately ill.

Doc Venable had run himself down to a
nub, trying to look after them, and finally
issued a plea for help during the weekly
church services. Of all the ladies in attendance, only Sarah had been willing to set
foot in any part of the saloon, let alone the
infamous chambers upstairs.

During Kitty's long recovery—two of her
friends had perished—she and Sarah
had become friends. In an effort to repay
Sarah's kindness, Kitty had taught her to
play poker.

Sarah, with her head for numbers,
found the game fascinating. At first, she'd
played with Kitty and some of the other

girls, but eventually, word had leaked out
and traveled along the female grapevine.
Soon, Fiona had joined in, then Mabel
Hemmings, who worked at the mercantile. When Maddie married Sam O'Ballivan and moved to Stone Creek, she joined,
too. Lark Yarbro had started attending
over the winter, sometimes bringing her
baby boy, sometimes leaving him in
Gideon's or Rowdy's care.

Today, Fiona had arrived early. She
greeted Sarah with a slightly brittle smile.

Sarah deliberately sat down next to her.
From the looks of things, there would only
be three of them in attendance that day,
although Mabel was often late, and usually came tearing in after the first hand
was dealt, struggling out of her apron as
she burst into the room.

"I hear there were *two* handsome men
dining at your house last night," Fiona
said tightly, losing her grip on the smile
but trying valiantly to sustain it. "Deputy
Yarbro *and* that Eastern fellow, with the
little boy."

The mention of Owen jabbed at Sarah.
If Fiona suspected any blood connection
between her and the child, the news would

be all over Stone Creek within an hour after the poker game ended. And speculation would be rife.

"Charles Langstreet was there," Sarah said moderately. "He's a business associate of my father's."

"But handsome," Fiona reiterated.

"I suppose," Sarah replied, careful not to look at her friend. And simultaneously realizing that Kitty was staring at her from across the table. Like many women in her scandalous sisterhood, Kitty had been widowed at a young age, left with two children and no means of supporting them. She'd scoured Denver for work, after her miner husband's death during a riot—the union members had called him a "scab"—but there was none to be had. Every door had been slammed in her face.

In the end, she'd had no choice but to leave her small daughters in an orphan's home and search elsewhere for a way to earn a living. Finally, she'd found work on a cattle ranch outside Durango, cooking for the crew, since the lady of the house was ailing. With her first month's salary and permission to bring her children back with her, as long as they didn't get underfoot, she'd hurried back to Denver to reclaim her children.

When she reached the home, breathless with anticipation, clutching stagecoach tickets for all three of them to make the return journey to Durango, she was informed that the little ones had been adopted by a wealthy physician and his wife, and taken back East somewhere. Stricken to the soul, having stressed that the arrangement was temporary when she left her girls, Kitty had begged for more information, desperate to track her babies down, but the officials at the orphanage refused. The adoptive parents' last name was "confidential," she was told, and besides, the children would have a better life with their new family.

Kitty had never gone back to the ranch outside Durango.

She'd asked questions of everyone she could find, but if anyone knew where her babies had gone, they weren't telling. Frantic, half-wild with grief, Kitty hadn't eaten or slept for days. She'd taken shelter in churches and alley doorways at night, and finally, when a man offered to buy her a drink, her destruction was complete.

She'd accepted, found a dark and instant solace in the strong liquor, and asked for another. After that, she'd gone to the man's room with him, and given over the terrain of her body, and been surprised to feel nothing at all when he degraded her. Offering herself to men was an easy way to get more whiskey and sustain the numbness that allowed her to live.

Kitty had told Sarah all this while she was recuperating from her nearly fatal illness. Sarah had been heartbroken by the story, and outraged that, as a woman and a mother, Kitty had no legal rights at all. Eventually, with Maddie's help and then Lark's, she'd begun writing letters to far-away churches and charities, hoping to find Kitty's daughters. When Kitty found out, she'd asked them to stop. Little Leona and Davina had forgotten her by now, she said, and that was for the best, given what she'd become since losing them.

Of all the women she knew, Sarah figured Kitty was the most likely to understand what she'd suffered, giving Owen away. She felt an overwhelming need to confide in someone—Kitty, or even Wyatt

Yarbro—though she had no intention of doing so.

Wyatt might think ill of her, and Kitty, who still had occasional bouts with the bottle, might let something slip when liquor loosened her tongue. When she succumbed, albeit rarely, she babbled to anyone who would listen about her little girls. Sarah could not afford to have her spilling the story of Owen's birth, too.

The game began, and at first, Sarah's cards were good ones. The ladies of the Society did not bet with matchsticks or buttons, like the more sedate Canasta club meeting in various parlors around town, but with real money. Sarah kept a stash of coins and small bills at home, in a coffee can tucked away on a pantry shelf, expressly for the purpose.

Soon, though, luck began flowing in Fiona's direction.

And Kitty was still watching Sarah at intervals, stealing surreptitious glances over the top of her fan of playing cards.

When the "meeting" was over, Fiona flounced off with copious winnings weighing down her handbag, and Mabel left, too, muttering that gamblers always died broke.

"Guess there was quite a scene over at the bank this morning," Kitty said when the others were gone, making no move to rise from her chair. She gathered the scattered cards expertly, though, her gaze fastened on Sarah. "A lot of our customers are grumbling that the deputy took their guns away."

Sarah didn't comment.

"Sarah?" Kitty pressed.

Sarah met her friend's eyes. "What?"

"You want to look out for that lawman," Kitty said.

"Wyatt? Why?" A little thrill of apprehension went through Sarah. She couldn't help recalling the kisses, and how they'd made her feel. "Do you know him?"

"Met up with him five years ago, out in Kansas City," Kitty answered. "He's Rowdy's brother, folks say."

Sarah waited, singularly alarmed, even though she thought she knew what Kitty was about to tell her—that Wyatt was a train robber, and he'd done time in prison for his crimes.

"Whatever he's telling you," Kitty said implacably, "it probably isn't true."

CHAPTER SEVEN

THE DOG HADN'T MADE a turn for the better.

After stowing all the guns he'd taken off Paddy Paudeen and his crew in the lone jail cell, locking the door, and dropping the key into his vest pocket, Wyatt loaded Lonesome into the wheelbarrow, being as careful as he could, and rolled him outside and down the sidewalk.

Having met and liked Doc Venable the night before, at Sarah's supper, Wyatt had confidence in the man. Venable mainly leaned toward people-doctoring, most probably, but surely he knew a thing or two about four-legged critters, as well.

There were too many horses tied up outside the saloons, Wyatt acknowledged to himself, as he and Lonesome made their procession through the center of town, but he'd averted the immediate crisis, and right now, the mutt was a priority. As they passed the Stockman's Bank, he noted with relief that Sarah had taken his advice and shut it down.

He could get Lonesome looked after without shirking his duties.

They drew some looks, Wyatt and the dog, and a few sheepish smiles, along the way. Wyatt asked the storekeeper, a balding man about as wide as he was high, the way to Doc Venable's place, and was told he'd find the house directly behind the Spit Bucket Saloon, on the next street over.

Since Lonesome seemed a mite embarrassed by all the attention, Wyatt decided to take a short cut between the Spit Bucket and the telegraph office. Careful not to jostle the dog too much while traversing the narrow and bumpy passage, the ground being littered with old whiskey bottles, a lone boot and other debris, Wyatt was taken by surprise when

they emerged into the alley and practically ran right over Sarah. She'd plainly
just left the saloon; the door was still half-
open behind her.

On taking a second look, Wyatt saw
another familiar face peering out at him
through the crack—a painted-up female
with sorrow-worn features, a skimpy dress
made of some shiny green fabric, and
piles of dyed red hair.

Now, where had he seen that woman?

She pulled the door to before he could
ask.

Sarah, blushing a little, approached.
She'd started when she saw him, but now
she'd recovered her composure. Mostly,
anyhow.

Upon taking a closer look at Lonesome,
her face changed. She drew a half step
nearer. "Is—what's the matter with him?"

"He's under the weather," Wyatt said,
watching her with amusement and the
usual appreciation of all her physical
virtues. She was clearly abashed at being
caught sneaking out the back door of the
Spit Bucket, but compassion for a dog
fallen on hard times had distracted her.
"I'm taking him to Doc Venable in the

hope that he can dose him up with something, so maybe he won't hurt so much."

Sarah came nearer. He smelled cigar
smoke on her, and pondered the possibility that Rowdy had been right in maintain-
ing that she had a tobacco habit. Wyatt
didn't approve, but it added to her appeal
in a strange way, too. She was a complicated woman, and there was a lot to find
out about her.

Reaching down, she stroked Lonesome's head. "Poor thing," she murmured.

Wyatt was surprised to learn that he
couldn't hold back the question hammer-
ing in the back of his mind. "What were
you doing in the Spit Bucket Saloon?" he
asked.

She touched the pocket of her skirt in a
subtle, fretful gesture, and then looked
him directly in the forehead, neatly avoiding his eyes. "Kitty Steel is a friend of mine,"
she said. "I like to visit her sometimes." A
pause, a deep, indrawn breath that made
her fine breasts rise for a moment. "Is
there an *ordinance* against that, deputy?"
she asked.

Wyatt chuckled, but when Lonesome
gave a pathetic whimper, he sobered

again. "No ordinance," he assured her, inclining his head toward an unpainted house on the other side of the dirt alley. "Is that Doc's place?"

"Yes," she said. Wyatt had expected her to veer off toward home, but instead, she walked beside him.

Doc appeared in the back door of his house, probably having seen them coming through a window, and descended the steps to open a second door at ground level. "Bring that animal in this way," he said.

Wyatt wheeled the dog across Doc's overgrown yard and inside. Sarah came right along, murmuring soft words to Lonesome. It almost made Wyatt wish *he* were the one being hauled in a wheelbarrow and in need of copious female sympathy.

Venable's office was cluttered, but there was an odd order to the chaos. He patted the examination table, with its worn leather top. Light streamed in through a side window in a wide, convenient shaft. "Set him here where I can get a good look," he said.

As careful as Wyatt tried to be, Lonesome gave a whine of pain when he was lifted out of the wheelbarrow.

Doc Venable waved Wyatt and Sarah aside. "Give us some room," he said brusquely, fitting his stethoscope into his ears as he spoke.

Wyatt stood nervously by while the doctor listened to Lonesome's insides, poked and prodded here and there with gentle fingers. Sarah remained beside him, so close their arms were touching.

"I'd say he's sound on the inside," Doc finally said, and Wyatt let out a long breath. "He'll be sore for a while, though." The old man frowned at the lash marks on the dog's back, glistening with the salve Wyatt had applied the night before, and stroked him lightly. Crossing to a cabinet, Doc took out a small brown bottle and brought it to Wyatt. "Laudanum," he said. "Put a drop or so on his tongue, three times a day. It'll make him sleep, and that's what he needs to heal up. If he bleeds or goes into convulsions, send for me right away."

Wyatt gulped. He'd squared off with a score of ill-intentioned men just that morning, but the possibility of a medical emergency involving a dog almost undid him.

God only knew how he'd react if his *horse* ever took sick. "Convulsions?" he asked.

Doc smiled. "Not very likely that'll happen," he assured Wyatt. "But he'll be in no fit state to ride in a wheelbarrow if it does."

Wyatt dropped the vial of laudanum into his pocket, where the cell key rested. "What do I owe you, Doc?"

"On the house," Doc said, with a dismissive wave. "Way I heard it, my life savings, such as they are, might have gone down the road with that bunch whooping it up in the saloons if it hadn't been for you."

Sarah stiffened. "They weren't going to rob the bank," she said.

Wyatt and Doc exchanged glances.

"Sarah always believes the best of folks," Doc said.

"If Deputy Yarbro runs off every bunch of cowboys that come into my—the bank, we'll soon be closing our doors for good!"

Doc chuckled, but the expression in his eyes was serious when he turned to Wyatt. "You be careful," he said. "Might be in your best interests, in fact, to wire Rowdy and Sam and tell them to hightail it back here and tend to home business instead of gallivanting after a pack of vigilantes."

Wyatt missed Rowdy, since their reunion had been so brief, and he was looking forward to handing in his badge and going to work for Sam out at Stone Creek Ranch, provided he didn't wind up in jail for rustling first, but he wasn't ready to run a white flag up the pole just yet.

"I'll send for Rowdy if I see the need," Wyatt said.

Doc took back the laudanum, opened the bottle, wet the tip of his finger with the stuff, and put the droplet on Lonesome's tongue. "Like that," he said. "Better give you a tin of salve, too, for these welts of his."

Since Wyatt had been using Lark's salve, as well as her canned milk and preserves, he accepted Doc's generous offer.

"I'll fetch us some coffee while we wait for that laudanum to take effect," Doc went on, heading for an inside staircase. "You wait here and see that he doesn't fall off the exam table."

Wyatt nodded, conscious of Sarah and the tender way she comforted the dog. If he hadn't left his hat behind at the jail, he'd have been able to turn the brim in his hands, give himself something to do. Because all of a sudden, despite taking supper at her table and kissing her in the broad light of day, he felt shy as a smitten schoolboy in the presence of this woman.

She wasn't looking at him, but he could see that she felt almost as uncomfortable as he did. "Kitty says she knew you in Kansas City," she ventured quietly, "and whatever you tell me is probably a lie."

Wyatt felt as if somebody had struck him behind the knees.

Kitty Steel.

She'd niggled at his recollection, watching him from the back door of the Spit Bucket the way she had. Now that the image had had time to percolate a while, he remembered her.

"I guess you must have been one of her—customers," Sarah said, when Wyatt didn't answer right away.

Wyatt shook his head. "I've been with women like Kitty," he said. He wasn't a talker, but words were spilling out of him now, like beans through a hole in a burlap sack. "I don't deny that. But all Kitty and I did was play poker. She was working at a saloon called the Last Dollar, dealing cards when she wasn't upstairs, and I was living high off the proceeds from a train robbery."

Sarah turned slightly, and he saw hope in her eyes, mingled with the fear of believing too readily. "That doesn't explain why she called you a liar."

Wyatt sighed. "She kept talking about her daughters. She'd lost them, some way, and then found them again, she said, and she could get them back if she had a husband. She wanted me to marry her—said I wouldn't have to do anything but say the words in front of a preacher and sign the papers. I told her I already had a wife—hell, I was on the run. I guess Levi or Ethan—my brothers—must have told her the truth."

Sarah absorbed his answer, seemed to resolve something in her own mind. She gave a little nod.

Doc returned before they could pursue the matter further, carrying a tray in both hands, with three cups of coffee steaming on top. Lonesome began to snore.

Doc, Wyatt and Sarah sat down in hard wooden chairs.

The coffee was downright awful, stout and bitter as axle grease, but Wyatt figured the least he could do, after Doc had been so kind to Lonesome, was act as if he liked the stuff. The old man seemed a little down-hearted, there in his cramped office. Eager for company.

Wyatt, for his part, felt restless. He had a town full of potential trouble, and a sick dog to take care of. He needed to be on the street, making sure things stayed peaceful.

As long as those guns were locked up, though, he had no reason to expect a disturbance.

So he drank his coffee and chatted with the doc, and didn't notice for a long time that the old man's questions weren't idle ones. He was sizing Wyatt up, deciding whether he was friend or foe. Most of all, Venable wanted to know what his intentions were toward Sarah, his best friend's daughter.

Already high in Wyatt's private estimation, Doc went up a notch or so. He was looking out for Sarah, pure and simple.

As things turned out, it was Sarah who ended the festivities. "I'd better get home and see to Papa and Owen," she said, rising from her chair and causing both Doc and Wyatt to leap immediately from their own. "They'll be wanting supper soon enough. Will you join us, Doc?" She paused and colored up, probably thinking she'd just roped herself into extending an invitation to Wyatt, too.

"Not tonight," Doc said. "There's a baby due out at the Starcross Ranch and I'm betting on twins. The mother's a little gal, and she'll need some help, I reckon. I was all set to hitch up my buggy and drive out there when you and the deputy here showed up with the dog."

Sarah nodded, embarrassed, and turned to Wyatt. "You're welcome to eat with us," she said quietly. "It's just leftover trout, but there's plenty."

Wyatt wanted to accept, but he wouldn't, because he knew Sarah hadn't planned on including him in the invitation to Doc. He shook his head, muttered, "No thanks." He had work to do, and he needed to get Lonesome settled down back at the jail so he could tend to his job.

With Doc's help, he put a still-snoring Lonesome back in the wheelbarrow and made for the door.

Sarah followed him, but instead of turning in the direction of her house when they reached Main Street, she stayed right on his heels.

"Wait," she said.

He stopped, turned around, pretending he was surprised to see her there. Actually, though, he'd been aware of her in every part of his mind and body, and maybe the outskirts of his soul, too.

"I think Lonesome ought to stay with us for a few days," Sarah told him. "Papa and Owen could mind him, while I'm at the bank."

Sorrow balled itself up and rolled over inside Wyatt, to think of giving up that mutt, even considering the critter's sorry state of health. Still, he couldn't hang around the jailhouse all the time, playing dog-nurse. Stone Creek wasn't quite the quiet, peaceful place Rowdy had made it out to be.

"I don't like parting with him," Wyatt admitted, his voice hoarse.

Sarah's face softened. "It's only temporary, Wyatt," she said. "And you can visit him whenever you want."

An excuse to call on Sarah made the idea a sight more palatable.

"All right," he said. "But don't you reckon the boy might get attached to Lonesome and find it hard to turn him loose when the time comes?"

Sadness moved in Sarah's eyes, like a shadow under sky-blue water. "Owen's only visiting," she said. "His father will be back for him."

Something ached inside Wyatt, and it had nothing whatsoever to do with the dog. "Oh," he said, because nothing else came to mind.

Together, Wyatt and Sarah headed for the Tamlin house, Wyatt swerving to avoid ruts in the street, so Lonesome could snooze on. While they walked, Wyatt wondered what he was going to have for supper.

He had thirty dollars in his pocket, thanks to Rowdy. He decided he'd visit the mercantile, stock up on sardines and crackers and maybe some canned peaches. While he was in prison, he'd so craved sweet fruit that he hadn't been able to get enough of it since.

Soon as they reached the front gate, Owen burst out of the house and came running down the walk.

"A dog!" he shouted, overjoyed. Then a

frown crossed his face as he took in Lonesome's mode of conveyance, and the well-greased welts striping his hide. "Is he hurt?"

"He'll be all right," Wyatt said. The boy's pleasure, like Sarah's presence, lifted his spirits. "Just needs to rest up a bit."

"He can't chase sticks or anything?" Owen asked, disappointed.

"Not for the time being," Sarah told the boy, moving to ruffle his hair, then drawing her hand back just short of it. "But you can feed him, and make sure he has fresh water to drink, and help him go outside when he needs to."

Owen squared his small shoulders manfully. "I can do that stuff," he said. "What does he eat?"

"Table scraps ought to do," Wyatt said. "And he likes some canned milk, now and then, if you have it."

"Do we have canned milk?" Owen demanded of Sarah, his voice urgent.

She smiled. "Yes," she said. "His name is Lonesome."

Wyatt stood pondering on why she'd held herself back from touching the boy, when it was plain that she wanted to so badly.

With Owen getting in the way a lot,

Wyatt left the wheelbarrow on the sidewalk and carried Lonesome into the house. Sarah hurried to fetch a quilt from upstairs, and made a bed for him, right in the kitchen, precisely where Wyatt would have put him—next to the stove.

"Well, now," Ephriam Tamlin said, coming through the doorway to the dining room, "what do we have here?"

"A dog!" Owen crowed. He was on his knees next to Lonesome, pouring milk from a can into a dish that was probably too pretty for the purpose.

Ephriam laughed heartily.

Deftly, Sarah replaced the china bowl with an old pie tin. She looked happy, with the boy and the dog and her father there. In fact, she might have been a different person from the matter-of-fact, briskly efficient woman she was at the bank.

Wyatt was confounded by the things he felt, watching her bustle around that kitchen, making coffee, putting the laudanum and salve he gave her on a handy shelf, planning supper.

He missed his ma and the homeplace. They'd kept a dog when he was a youngster, and Ma had let it live in the house, sleep on an old blanket near the stove. Back then, he'd been part of a real family.

"I reckon I'd better go," he said, thinking nobody would hear him in all the hubbub.

But Sarah did hear, though he'd spoken softly. She paused and looked at him with wide, knowing eyes. "Won't you stay for supper?" she asked.

"Another time," Wyatt said. And then, finding himself unable to bid the dog farewell, he turned and headed for the back door. Let himself out.

He knew looking back wasn't smart, but he did it anyway.

Sarah was standing on the small porch off the kitchen, watching him go.

Supper was over, and Sarah had assigned her father the task of heating water so Owen could take a bath. Owen had protested that he was "clean enough," and anyhow he wanted to sleep on the quilt with Lonesome that night, so he'd just get dirty again.

Sarah replied that he wasn't sleeping with Lonesome, but if he agreed to the bath, she'd let him spend the night in the spare room in back of the kitchen. That way, he'd be close by if the dog needed him.

Owen had agreed, none too graciously, and Sarah had gone out for a walk, so the bath could be endured in private.

Sarah often walked at night, and she had an accustomed route—down to the schoolhouse, around past Doc Venable's, then home.

Tonight, she took Main Street. The saloons were swelling with gaslight, bawdy music and noise, as if their very walls might burst. Horses lined every hitching rail, and there were lights burning in the jailhouse, too.

Sarah headed straight for it, lifting her skirts to keep them out of the horse manure littering the street. She'd been purposeful enough—until she reached the open doorway of Rowdy's office. Then she hesitated on the sidewalk.

Would Wyatt think her forward for paying an unexpected call on him, after dark?

He'd *kissed* her twice that day.

What if he got the impression that she wanted him to do it again?

Her face burned in the warm darkness. She was about to turn and hurry away when he came to the door and caught her standing there, like a fool.

He grinned, and all of Stone Creek went on the tilt for just a moment.

"Evening, Sarah," he said.

"Owen is taking a bath," she explained, and then felt all the more idiotic for making such an inane remark. It wasn't as if the town deputy had to be informed of people's personal hygiene habits, after all.

"Come in, if you think it's proper," Wyatt drawled. He'd rolled up his shirtsleeves, and his forearms were sun-browned and muscular.

Sarah had never actually been inside the jailhouse. She told herself it was mere curiosity that sent her over that threshold.

Wyatt stepped back so she could pass, but not far enough that they could avoid brushing against each other.

"How's Lonesome?" he asked.

"He's fine," Sarah said, looking around. She saw a desk, chairs, an old potbellied stove, and a single cell with rusted bars and two cots inside, but, thankfully, no prisoner. "I gave him milk toast for supper, and more laudanum, like Doc said, and he was sleeping when I left."

"Good," Wyatt said, watching her.

Sarah approached the cell, saw the stockpile of guns and rifles inside. Turned to face Wyatt and found him standing directly behind her, but at a decent distance.

"Kitty told you she'd found her children?" she asked, realizing only as she spoke the words that she'd come here to say them. She and Maddie and Lark had written letters into the wee-small hours, searching for Kitty's daughters. Had Kitty known where they were the whole time?

Wyatt looked blank for a moment, then remembered their exchange in Doc's office, while he was upstairs getting the coffee. "Yes," he said. "She had a letter from some lawyer. They were living someplace in Illinois, I think. Why?"

Sarah sighed, looked away from his face, looked back. "I'd have to speak with Kitty before I answered that," she said. Five years ago, in Kansas City, Kitty had been willing to marry a stranger to recover her children. She'd apparently known exactly where to find them. Yet when she'd roused Sarah and the others to such a state of righteous indignation that they'd begun to search for little Leona and Davina, through the mails and every other means they could think of, she'd called a halt to it. Had something happened to change her mind, in the years and places between Kansas City and Stone Creek? Or did Kitty's daughters actually exist at all? Perhaps it had just been a story, a ploy for sympathy, and nothing more.

It was all too confusing. And Sarah felt stung, even betrayed. She lived in the figurative glass house and certainly couldn't afford to throw stones at Kitty for lying, but the discovery hurt, just the same.

Wyatt pulled a chair into the center of the room and gently lowered Sarah into it. "Don't they get heavy? All those secrets you're carrying around, I mean?" he asked quietly, his face close to hers.

"I don't have any secrets," Sarah said.

Wyatt straightened, took a seat behind the desk. "Langstreet sure took off in a hurry," he said, after a few moments had passed. "It's almost as if he came here meaning to leave the boy with you."

Sarah's throat hurt. She swallowed, but it didn't help, and her eyes suddenly burned. Wyatt, she knew, was a hairsbreadth from guessing that Owen was her child, and she wished she could tell him he was right. It would be like laying down a heavy burden, one she'd been carrying for too long.

"I'm sure he didn't expect to be called away so suddenly," she said lamely.

"Or so he claimed," Wyatt replied, kicking his boots up onto the desk top and crossing them at the ankles.

Sarah didn't answer.

"I've watched you with Owen, Sarah," Wyatt went on. "Sometimes, you reach out to touch him, then draw your hand back instead. He's more to you than the child of a family friend."

Sarah thrust herself to her feet. "I shouldn't have come here," she said, more to herself than Wyatt. "It's getting late, and I have to open the bank in the morning—"

Wyatt rose, too. "I'll walk you home," he said.

She shook her head, rattled. "I've lived in Stone Creek for most of my life," she told him. "I can get home just fine on my own."

He took her arm, at the elbow. "There are some pretty rowdy strangers in town right now," he said. "They've been swilling whiskey all day and, with or without guns, they're not fit company for a lady. And do you really think it's a good idea to open the bank while they're still around?"

Sarah knew Wyatt was going to walk her home, whether she wanted him to or not. So she resigned herself to that much, though she did jerk her elbow out of his hand. "The Stockman's Bank is our family business," she said. "Of *course* I have to open it tomorrow morning, right on time."

They'd gained the sidewalk, and Wyatt walked on the outside, shortening his stride a little so she could keep up, his eyes roving up and down the street, one side and then the other, as they went.

"Will your father be there?"

"I don't know," Sarah said. "He hasn't been well lately."

"He seems fine to me," Wyatt observed. "At first, I thought he might be a little touched in the head, but he looked well enough when we brought Lonesome to your place after we left Doc's."

"My father," Sarah said sharply, "is not 'touched in the head!'"

Two cowboys burst suddenly through the

swinging doors of Jolene Bell's Saloon, just ahead, and Wyatt shoved Sarah behind him so quickly that she stumbled and had to catch her balance.

She watched, her heart seizing in her chest, as he laid a hand on the butt of his pistol.

One of the cowboys shoved the other into a horse trough, and there was a lot of shouting and swearing, plus some splashing.

Wyatt let go of the pistol butt. Walked on past the cowboys, with a chuckle, pulling Sarah along behind him, double-time.

"Surely," Sarah huffed, in a whisper, still trying to breathe properly, "you don't think I've never encountered drunken cowboys before!"

"I think," Wyatt answered calmly, "that you don't have the good sense to know when you ought to be careful."

"I beg your pardon?" Sarah tried to pull free, but he held fast to her arm and kept walking. "I happen to have a *lot* of sense!"

"Do you?" Wyatt retorted.

Sarah knew he was thinking of the way she'd welcomed those men into the bank

that morning. Well, it was just good business. "I have a college *education,* Wyatt
Yarbro. I run a *bank,* single-handedly—"

He stopped so suddenly that she collided with him.

"Single-handedly?" he asked.

"Well, I mean, I help my father, of
course—"

"Sarah."

She looked around frantically, was
relieved to see that there was no one
nearby to overhear their conversation.

Wyatt gripped her shoulders, firmly but
gently, too. "Owen told me his father came
to Stone Creek to take the bank away
from you. Not from your father. From you."

"Owen is a child, he—"

"Sarah, stop. Tell me the truth, or don't
talk to me at all!"

Sarah pressed her lips together. She
knew by the look in Wyatt's eyes that he
wanted to shake her, but he didn't. She felt
delicate in his hands, like something precious and breakable.

"Sarah," Wyatt said again.

"You mustn't tell anyone," Sarah whispered, her eyes filling with tears. "Not
Rowdy, and certainly not Sam O'Ballivan."

She paused, drew a shaky breath, let it out again. "Do you promise?"

"Depends," Wyatt said, "on just what sort of secret this turns out to be."

"M-my father suffers from spells. Times when he gets mixed up, can't remember things. So I do his work for him, whenever I can. If Charles and the other stockholders find out—well . . . we could lose everything—"

Wyatt sighed again. "Sarah, Langstreet suspects something. That's why he came to Stone Creek, though the boy plays some part in it, too. You're on borrowed time until he gets back."

Sarah let her forehead rest against Wyatt's strong chest.

He held her, brushed a light kiss onto her temple.

"Will you help me?" she asked softly.

His arms tightened around her. "Yes," he said. "Yes."

CHAPTER EIGHT

WILL YOU HELP ME?

Wyatt wondered how long it had been since Sarah Tamlin had uttered those words—to anybody. That she'd said them to him was a peculiar honor, considering the extent of her pride.

He'd said yes.

Now, he thought, as he held her front gate open so she could pass ahead of him, all he had to do was figure out *how* he'd go about keeping his word.

As they'd walked to her house she'd confessed that she'd made some bad loans and replaced the funds with her own and her father's money. While that wasn't illegal, at least as far as Wyatt knew, she and Ephriam could end up as paupers if Langstreet and the other stock-holders caught on. The first thing they'd do, once they learned about Ephriam's "spells," would be to show him the road. With no salary coming in things would get tight around the Tamlin place, money-wise, and fast.

On the front porch, Sarah looked up at Wyatt with bleak vulnerability in her eyes—blue as bruises, they were—and he thought he saw the glimmer of tears. "You won't tell anyone?" she asked very softly. "About Papa, I mean? And me run-ning the bank? And the loans?"

Wyatt sighed, holding his hat in one hand. "I can't promise you that, Sarah," he said. She hadn't done anything wrong, to his way of thinking, but a lot of folks had entrusted her with what savings they could scrape together and lay by against hard times. "I need to think it over."

She started to speak, stopped herself, nodded once.

He touched the smooth skin of her cheek with the backs of his fingers. She felt as soft as condensed moonlight. "I meant it when I said I'd stand by you," he told her. "For now, for tonight, that has to be good enough."

She sniffled, nodded again. "Good night, Wyatt."

He leaned down, brushed his mouth against hers. "Good night," he replied.

Behind them, toward the center of town, shots erupted. Six of them, rapid-fire.

"Damn!" Wyatt cursed, turning from Sarah, starting for the steps.

She caught hold of his arm, and he was surprised by the strength of her grip. She was a small woman, delicately made, but her fingers felt steely against his flesh.

Don't go, her eyes said.

Gently, Wyatt patted her hand and then removed it from his arm. He turned, sprinted down the walk, and vaulted over the gate, not wanting to spare the time to open it.

More shots splintered the night.

As he ran for Main Street, Wyatt told himself it was just a few of the boys, whooping it up on payday, and he wouldn't have to shoot anybody, or get shot himself, but all the while he knew he was joshing himself.

There'd been a gunfight, directly in front of Jolene Bell's, and three men lay in the street, sprawled on their backs and bleeding, their arms flung out wide from their sides. The smell of gun smoke still tainted the air, though he figured the battle must have been over, because a dozen other men were riding out at top speed, and ordinary folks had begun to gather on the sidewalks.

Keeping the .45 at the ready in his right hand, Wyatt scanned the crowd, reached the first victim, crouched to put a hand to the pulse at the base of his throat, though he could see the man had been hit square in the center of the forehead. His eyes were wide-open, staring in affronted surprise at the starry sky.

There was no heartbeat.

Using two fingers on his left hand, Wyatt closed the man's eyes.

Doc Venable elbowed his way through from the sidewalk as Wyatt squatted beside the second man. Carl Justice gazed up at him, blood gurgling, a crimson fountain, through a wound in his throat. He was going to drown in the stuff.

"Doc!" Wyatt growled, knowing full well that there was no saving Carl.

Venable knelt opposite Wyatt, fumbling with his medical bag. "Turn him onto his side," he said.

Wyatt did as he was told. How old was Carl, anyway? Seventeen? Twenty? Whatever age he was, he wasn't going to get any older, and sorrow ambushed Wyatt, surging up from somewhere in his middle. Carl was a rustler for sure, and he was probably guilty of other crimes, too, but he was hardly more than a kid. He might have turned around, if he'd gotten the choice.

"That third fella is a goner," Doc said, when Wyatt moved to rise, pumping something into a syringe and looking for a place on Carl's blood-drenched body to stick the needle. "No need to bother with him."

"What is that?" Wyatt asked, momentarily light-headed. Blood didn't bother him, but even the sight of a hypodermic needle made him woozy.

"Pure morphine," Doc answered, in a

gruff whisper. "There's no bringing this boy back, but it'll take him three or four minutes to die, and it doesn't have to be that way."

Carl gave a strangled cry, and his blood wet the thighs of Doc Venable's pants. When the kid gave a violent shudder and went still, Wyatt got to his feet, surveyed the gathering on the sidewalk.

Folks were keeping to the shadows.

"Who shot these men?" he asked.

Nobody spoke, and nobody moved.

Wyatt waited, staring into every pair of eyes he could catch.

Finally, Kitty Steel stepped down off the sidewalk and approached.

"They shot each other," she said.

"I took their guns," Wyatt said. "How did they happen to be armed?"

"A man can always get a gun," Kitty sighed, looking glumly down at the dead men at her feet. "They were arguing over a hand of cards. It got out of hand. They borrowed what pistols they could from the regulars in the saloon and came out here to settle up."

Wyatt shoved a hand through his hair. He'd lost his hat, somewhere between

Sarah's place and here. In the morning, he'd saddle Sugarfoot and ride out after the others. Chasing after a dozen men in the dark would be futile—best he could hope for was a bullet fired from behind a rock or a Joshua tree.

"Help me with these bodies," Doc Venable ordered, addressing the gaping spectators on the sidewalk. "We'll lay them out in my office, bury 'em proper tomorrow."

A few men shuffled forward, hesitant and shame-faced.

Wyatt crouched beside Carl again. "Is he dead?"

Doc nodded. "Facing his maker," he said.

Bile scalded the back of Wyatt's throat. Because he'd ridden with Carl, though they certainly hadn't been friends, he hoisted the slight, inert form off the ground, draped it over one shoulder, and started for Doc's.

Sarah was already there. She tied on one of Doc's aprons and cleared space for the corpses and even filled some basins with hot water.

"You oughtn't to be here," Wyatt said, when he saw her.

"Are any of them alive?" she asked.

Wyatt laid poor Carl on the examination table where Lonesome had rested, just that morning. "You shouldn't be here," he said again.

"I always help Doc when things like this happen," she told him, unruffled. She got a basin and a cloth and began to wash Carl's face as gently as if she thought he could feel the touch of her hands, and might feel more pain if she was rough.

"When Till Crosly damn near cut his foot off chopping wood," Doc contributed, "Sarah helped me sew it back on."

Wyatt felt queasy.

"Better look and see if they've got any kind of papers with their names on them," Doc said. "Like as not, they have folks someplace."

The second body was placed on the leather settee, the third on wooden chairs hastily scraped into a row.

Wyatt dug through blood-soaked pockets, but he found nothing but a bag of tobacco and an old watch with a picture of a pretty woman painted on the inside of the case. Searching Carl, Doc came up with a worn letter and handed it off to Wyatt.

"Probably from his mama," Doc said.

Wyatt glanced at the return address, penned in a woman's fine and flowing hand. *Home,* was all it said. She'd sent the letter to Carl in care of general delivery, Denver. He tucked the envelope, smudged and much-handled, into the inside pocket of his vest. Said nothing.

"I'll get Willie to take pictures of them," Doc said, as calmly as if things like this happened in Stone Creek every day of the week and twice on Sundays. "That way, if their kin should come looking for them, we'll know who's who."

Wyatt gulped back more bile as Sarah dunked a bloody rag in the basin and wrung it out before wiping at Carl's face again. When the dead man's eyes popped open, she closed them matter-of-factly, and weighted them down with pennies from a little bowl on a nearby table.

Doc dismissed the bystanders, leaving himself and Sarah and Wyatt alone with the bodies.

Now that Sarah almost had his face wiped clean of blood, Carl looked more like his usual self—except, of course, for the pennies on his eyes.

"You going to wash all three of them

down?" Wyatt asked, and then gulped again, and colored up. Decomposition hadn't begun, but the bodies stunk to high heaven, because bodies, when they die, discharge worse things than blood.

"Of course," Sarah said. "We can't bury them like this."

Wyatt's stomach did a slow, backward roll. "Why not? Who's going to see them, once the coffin lid is nailed on?"

"It's the decent thing to do," Sarah replied, trying to pull off Carl's blood-sodden coat. Next, she'd be stripping him naked.

"I'm not sure I agree on the decency aspect," Wyatt said.

Sarah surprised—and comforted—him with a sudden smile. "They're *dead,* Wyatt."

"Yeah," he said. "A person can't help but notice."

Doc took blankets from the cabinet he'd fetched Lonesome's medicine out of, a lifetime ago, when Wyatt had believed Stone Creek to be a relatively serene community, the incident at the bank notwithstanding. He covered the other two bodies—decency, again, Wyatt supposed—then began pulling off Carl's boots.

They were worn at the soles, and lined with old newspaper, evidently contrived to double as socks.

Wyatt felt the sadness again. Wondered about the letter in his vest pocket, and if Carl and Billy had a ma, like Doc thought, and maybe other kin, too, watching some country road for their horses.

On a less sentimental note, he reckoned if Billy wasn't someplace around Stone Creek now, he soon would be. Word of Carl's shooting would bring him on the run, with blood in his eye. Soon as Billy Justice knew Wyatt had been in town when the shoot-out took place, Billy would lay the blame at his feet and come gunning for him.

It was the only bright spot in this whole dismal mess.

"If you're not going to help," Sarah told him, "please get out of the way."

Wyatt blinked, stepped back. Stepped forward again. "*I'll* help Doc bathe these yahoos," he said. "You go home and look after Owen and Lonesome and your father."

Sarah bristled.

"Go," Doc told her. "Wyatt's right. This is no fit work for a woman."

"What work *is* 'fit for a woman,' Doc?" Sarah demanded.

"This is no time to talk women's suffrage," Doc said. "Go."

"I'm sure the deputy wouldn't allow me to walk home alone," Sarah said tartly, hands resting on her hips. "After all, I could be accosted on the street!"

Three dead men, all that blood and a stench that made him want to gag, and she'd almost made Wyatt laugh.

Almost.

Doc took the basin and the rag out of her hands and set them aside. "I delivered twins a few hours ago, Sarah. It was a five-mile ride, there and back, on that cussed old mule of mine. Now I've got bodies to wash down and embalm. I simply do not possess the inclination to argue with you."

"It's true that she oughtn't to walk home alone," Wyatt said.

"Ha!" Sarah spouted, with a triumphant motion of one hand.

"At least go upstairs, then, and make us a pot of coffee," Doc replied coolly. He'd had more experience handling Sarah than Wyatt had, and Wyatt was bent on watching and learning.

"Women's work!" Sarah said, flinging up both hands this time.

But she gathered her skirts and tromped up the staircase to the second floor. The kitchen must have been directly overhead, because things took to clattering and clanking straightaway.

Wyatt smiled again. Then helped Doc strip down the bodies, one by one, and bathe them. This involved going upstairs, from time to time, to dip more hot water from the reservoir on Doc's wood-burning cookstove. Wyatt undertook the task, each time hoping Sarah might spare him an amiable word, or even a glance, but she'd put a pot of coffee on to brew, sat herself down in a rocking chair turned to face a window, and paid him no attention whatsoever.

When the awful work was done, the bodies blanket-draped, Wyatt wanted nothing so much as to get naked himself and slide chin-deep into Rowdy's big-city bathtub. Well, there was one thing he wanted more than a bath hot enough to scald his flesh and some good old-fashioned lye soap, but he wasn't going to get it.

Not that night, at least.

So he and Doc scrubbed up, as best they could, and sank into chairs to drink Sarah's coffee. For all her bad reputation as a cook, the brew was a lot better than the acid slop Doc had served them after seeing to Lonesome.

Sarah didn't join them, but she made a point of pouring the hot liquid into their cups, her skirt sweeping past the backs of their chairs as she moved.

"I reckon I need some shut-eye," Doc finally said, to break the silence. He'd had three cups of coffee by that time, but apparently, he didn't expect it to disturb his rest. "That was fine coffee, Sarah," he told her. "Could have done with a dash of whiskey, though."

Sarah, still miffed, evidently because Doc didn't let her wash down naked dead men in his cellar, flounced toward the door. "You're *welcome*," she snapped, wrenching at the knob.

Wyatt rose wearily from his chair, aching in every bone and muscle. He needed to find himself an easier job—like breaking rock with a sledgehammer in the belly of some mine, or breaking devil-horses to ride.

"Thanks for the help, Wyatt," Doc said, and his half smile was tinged with good-natured sympathy.

He'd been about to offer a word of thanks to Doc, for taking charge of the situation out in front of Jolene Bell's Saloon the way he had; now, he just nodded.

Wyatt followed Sarah outside and down the porch steps. She was moving fast, so he had to hurry.

"Sarah," he finally protested, catching her by the arm. "Slow down."

She stopped, but only because she didn't have much choice, given the grip he'd taken. He loosened his fingers, worried that he'd bruised her.

"I was only trying to spare you," he said.

"I don't *require* sparing," she shot back. "I've helped Doc prepare folks for burying *plenty* of times."

"Doesn't this town have an undertaker?" Wyatt asked, exasperated. Why was a task that would have most people either running in the other direction or heaving up their socks so damn important to her?

"Yes," Sarah said acidly, "Stone Creek has an undertaker. Doc."

She'd managed to pull away, and now she was walking fast again. She'd cleaned up a little at Doc's place, but her skirts and the bodice of her dress were stained red, and she smelled.

Or was that him?

Wyatt stopped to look down at his ruined shirt—more properly, *Rowdy's* ruined shirt—and when he did, she got farther ahead of him, and he had to scramble to catch up. He wasn't just hell on the grocery bill, he concluded grimly. He was hell on his brother's wardrobe, too.

"Doesn't it bother you?" he asked, beside her now. "Bathing dead people, I mean?"

She halted again, put her hands on her hips, and glared up into his face. "I love bathing dead people!" she shouted. "It's one of my *favorite* things to do!"

Wyatt started to laugh.

Sarah started to cry.

He took a gentle grip on her shoulders. "I'm sorry," he said.

"S-Somebody has to tend to them—" Sarah blubbered.

Wyatt pulled her close. "Hush, now," he said. "Hush."

"It was awful," Sarah said, her voice muffled by his shirtfront, vibrating through his heart. The crying intensified to outright sobs. "And you stink!"

Wyatt chuckled. "So do you."

They stood like that for a while, and Sarah's close proximity caused a shift inside Wyatt. He stopped thinking about death; life was on his mind, and all the good things that it had to offer.

"I'd give *anything* for a hot bath," Sarah wailed.

"I might be able to help you out with that," Wyatt said, and waited for the explosion.

She looked up at him, sniffling and teary-eyed and covered in gore, and still as beautiful as an Arizona sunset blazing across the sky. He'd expected her to give him what for, even slap him, but instead she said, *"Lark and Rowdy have a real bathtub!"*

"They do," Wyatt said, amused. "And you're welcome to use it if you want to." Generous of him, he thought. Wyatt respected other people's belongings, but just about then, he'd have helped himself to Rowdy and Lark's bed, too, if he could lie down with Sarah Tamlin.

It was too early for that, though.

"What would I do for clean clothes?" Sarah asked.

"Reckon you could borrow one of Lark's dresses. She's about the same size as you are."

Sarah blinked. "It would be *scandalous,*" she breathed.

"Absolutely," Wyatt agreed solemnly.

"You'd have to promise not to look until I'm dressed again."

Wyatt raised a hand, a man swearing an oath he'd love to break. "I promise," he vowed.

Sarah's eyes widened. "I *couldn't.*"

"Sure you could," Wyatt said. "Just think of it. Peeling off that getup you're in now. All that hot water. Scented soap—"

"Stop," Sarah pleaded.

Wyatt grinned. "Up to you," he said. And he turned, betting that she'd follow.

She did.

Five minutes later, having taken a roundabout way, in the hope no one would see them, Wyatt and Sarah stepped into the little house behind the jail.

"That way," Wyatt said, pointing from the kitchen doorway.

Everything ground inside him, he wanted so badly to follow her, strip off his own clothes, get right into the tub with her.

Easy, cowboy, he told himself. Sarah was as skittish as a wild mare scenting wolves on the breeze, and if he made any sudden moves, he might scare her off for good.

"I know where the bathroom is," Sarah said, lofty now. Even a little imperious, for all her tumbledown hair and her stained dress. "Lark showed it to me when it was her turn to host the Canasta club."

Wyatt grinned. "I'll see to the horses," he said, though the horses didn't need seeing to, since he'd given them hay and filled their water troughs earlier in the evening.

She didn't move until he'd gone out the back door and closed it behind him.

SARAH FELT WANTON, bathing in someone else's bathtub, even if that someone was a close friend. She knew Lark wouldn't mind, but it was still a very improper thing to do. She was, alas, alone in a house with an unmarried man, and naked to the skin in the bargain.

Oh, but the hot water was glorious.

There was real shampoo, in an actual bottle.

At home, Sarah lathered her hair with a bar of soap and rinsed it with rainwater.

She alternately scrubbed and soaked, but when she heard a door open and close in the near distance, she bolted upright. Scrambled for a towel. Her hair down and dripping, she stood in the water, listening.

"Wyatt?"

"Yup," he replied. "Are you decent?"

Sarah flushed from the roots of her hair to the soles of her feet. "No!"

She heard him laugh. Then the door opened a little way and his hand came through, holding out a calico dress.

Sarah rushed over, snatched it from him, and almost shut the door on his arm.

"Go away," she said.

"You're welcome," Wyatt replied.

She pulled the plug in the bathtub, dried herself off, wrapped her hair in the towel, turban-fashion, slipped on her dress, and crept out into the main part of the house.

Wyatt was sitting at the table, his head bent over an open book. His clothes looked as though he'd passed the day in a

slaughterhouse and his hair, shiny as a
blackbird's wing, was mussed. She imagined he'd have to bathe, and thinking of
that made her turn red all over again.

"I should go home," she said.

"Yes," Wyatt agreed, closing the book
slowly, almost reverently, and getting to
his feet. "Feel better?"

She nodded, oddly spellbound. Something about seeing Wyatt that way, intent
on a book, made her heart flutter. She put
a hand to it. "I th-thought you were going
to try to seduce me," she said, and could
have bitten off her tongue.

"I'd like nothing better," Wyatt said, his
gaze sweeping over her, "but when I have
you, it won't be in somebody else's bed.
Since I don't have one of my own as of
yet, I reckon it will have to be yours."

Sarah's breath flowed shallow, and she
felt her nipples harden beneath the bodice
of Lark Yarbro's calico dress. She knew
she should have waxed indignant; instead,
she wished he didn't have so many scru-
ples. "Where do you sleep, if you don't
have a bed?" she asked.

One corner of his mouth tilted slightly
upward. "Out in the hayloft," he said. "I

passed one night on a cot in the jail, but it brought back too many memories, so I moved to the barn."

"Oh," Sarah said.

He extended a hand to her. "Let's get you back to your place while the getting's good," he said. She came to him, and he took the towel from around her head and watched her hair fall, spiraling with the damp, around her shoulders and breasts.

There was something so sensual about the act that Sarah's breath stopped in her throat, broke free with a little gasp.

If Wyatt had kissed her then, she couldn't have resisted him.

But he didn't.

He took her home, the two of them moving through the shadows and alleys like a pair of illicit lovers returning from a tryst. He waited until she'd let herself in through the kitchen door.

And then he left.

"Sarah?" It was her father's voice. He came down the back stairs, a lantern glowing in one hand. "Where have you been? What happened to your hair?"

She went to meet him, midway up the stairs, and gently took the lantern from him.

"Papa," she said, gently stern, "I've asked you not to carry these around when they're lit. You could start a fire."

"Oh, for heaven's sake, Sarah, I'm not a blithering idiot!"

"Hush," Sarah said. "Owen will hear you."

"That boy's sound asleep," her father replied. "He and the dog are sharing the spare room." His spectacles glinted in the light of the lantern. "What have you been doing? Your hair is down, and it's wet—"

Sarah retreated to the kitchen, set the lantern in the middle of the table, and went about making tea. She needed something to settle her nerves—and since she wasn't a drinker, orange pekoe would have to do.

She'd half hoped Ephriam would retire to his room again—she wasn't used to all this lucidity on his part and found, to her quiet astonishment, and no little shame, that she missed her father's normal befuddlement.

Of course he did *not* retire, nor did he cease asking questions.

"You haven't been with a man, have you?" he asked, causing her cheeks to flame.

"No!" Sarah cried, and in that instant,

she froze. She'd left her soiled dress at Rowdy's place—and the book of lies was in the pocket. Slapping a hand to her mouth, Sarah sank into a chair at the table.

Just then, Owen appeared, yawning and blinking, in the doorway of the spare room. "Why's everybody fussing?" he asked sleepily. "You woke Lonesome up, and now he's crying."

"Crying?" Sarah echoed, confused. Then she realized that Lonesome's last dose of laudanum had probably worn off, and he needed another. She fetched the bottle from its shelf and followed Owen into the small bedroom just off the kitchen.

Lonesome whimpered.

"Poor thing," she said, and knelt to put a drop of medicine on the dog's tongue.

But Lonesome didn't stop the pitiful noise he was making.

"I think he wants Wyatt," Owen said wisely. "He's homesick."

"He can't be," Sarah said, stroking the dog, trying to calm him. What should she do? She couldn't wake Doc—he was exhausted. He'd delivered twins today, and then attended to the gruesome business of preparing three bodies for burial.

Tears shimmered in Owen's eyes. "*Do something,*" he pleaded.

Sarah turned her head, expecting to see Ephriam in the doorway. "Papa—"

But he wasn't there.

"Papa?"

"Bet he went to get Wyatt," Owen said, with such hope that Sarah prayed it was true, for the boy's sake as much as Lonesome's. In the next instant, though, she remembered that her father had been wearing a nightshirt and nothing else.

"Stay with Lonesome," she said, rushing for the kitchen.

Ephriam was gone, and the back door stood open. Outside, in the grass, crickets chorused.

Not wanting to rouse the neighbors and have them looking out their windows to see Ephriam Tamlin, president and chief stockholder of the Stockman's Bank, marching down the street in his nightshirt, Sarah called out softly. "Papa! Papa, please come back."

He was nowhere in sight.

Suppose he'd gotten befuddled again? What if he ended up wandering around out there in the dark countryside, where all manner of terrible things could happen to him, a defenseless old man, alone?

Panic clutched at the inside of Sarah's throat. She couldn't leave Owen by himself to go chasing off after her father, especially when he was so worried about Lonesome.

Offering a prayer that Ephriam would be kept safe and, if possible, unseen crossing town in his bedclothes, Sarah closed the door and went back to the spare room.

Lonesome had settled down a little, but his grief was heartrending. Great, shuddering tremors went through him. Was he dying? Had she given him too much medicine?

Tears slipped down Owen's cheeks. "Help him, Aunt Sarah. Please, help him."

Both of them were kneeling now, beside the dog. Sarah put one arm around her son's shoulders and used the opposite hand to stroke Lonesome's quivering back, hoping to soothe him.

She couldn't have said how much time passed—ten minutes? A half hour? Longer?

Her heart leapt when the back door

opened and she heard her father say, "In there."

And then Wyatt was in the room.

Lonesome tried to get up and go to him, but he was too weak.

"Lie still, now," Wyatt told the dog, with gruff tenderness. He crossed and crouched, opposite Sarah, and stroked Lonesome's head. Lonesome licked Wyatt's hand and fell silent.

"I told you he wanted Wyatt," Owen said, sinking against Sarah's side. "Will you stay with him, Wyatt? So he doesn't cry? You can sleep here in the spare room, and I'll go upstairs—"

Wyatt started to speak, stopped himself. Looked directly into Sarah's eyes. He'd had a bath, and he was wearing clean clothes. His hair was still damp, and smelled of hard soap.

"I think that's a fine idea," Ephriam said. Bless him, he'd gone all the way to the other end of town, found Wyatt, and brought him back.

Sarah offered a silent prayer of gratitude.

"So do I," Sarah said, gazing at Wyatt.

"Then let's all get ourselves bedded

down for the night," Ephriam suggested. "Do you people have any idea what *time* it is?"

Sarah stood, ushered Owen out of the spare room with as much dignity as she could manage. Ephriam and Owen went upstairs together.

And Sarah stopped cold. A small volume lay in plain sight on the kitchen table, next to the lantern.

It was the book of lies.

CHAPTER NINE

WYATT SAT ON THE EDGE of the narrow cot in Sarah's spare room, looking down at Lonesome, who lay contentedly at his feet, staring up at him with a kind of adoring devotion he'd never experienced before.

"I can't stay here," Wyatt told the dog, keeping his voice low. "Folks will see me leave the house in the morning, and think the worse of Sarah because I spent the night."

Lonesome gave a companionable sigh and laid his ugly muzzle on his forelegs, perfectly contented now that he had things just the way he wanted them.

"And I've got things I ought to be doing," Wyatt went on. Out on the trail, he'd sometimes carried on long conversations with his horse. Old Reb was a compassionate listener. "Guarding those guns locked up at the jail, for one thing. For another, tracking those men who tore out of town tonight, after the shooting. But here I sit, playing nursemaid to a damn dog."

A light rap sounded at the spare room door.

Wyatt got up, crossed to open it. Sarah stood on the other side, still clad in Lark's dress, though she'd plaited her damp hair so it rested in a thick ebony rope over her right shoulder. The little horse-tail rigging at the bottom, tied off with a pink ribbon, touched her waist.

"You brought back my book of—my diary," she said, watching his face closely. "I found it on the kitchen table."

Wyatt nodded, a little confused. "I burned your other dress in the kitchen stove at Rowdy's place, along with my own gear. No amount of laundering was going to save *those* duds. When I felt something in the pocket, I took it out."

She drew a deep, slow breath, and let

it out again just as slowly. "You didn't read it?"

"Sarah, of *course* I didn't."

She sighed, relaxed a little. "Well, then," she said. "Thank you."

"For bringing the book back, or not reading it?"

She managed a sparse little smile. "Both."

"You're welcome," Wyatt said. "Sarah, I can't stay here overnight. Is that wheelbarrow around here someplace? I'll load Lonesome up and haul him on back to Rowdy's."

"It's in the shed out back," Sarah said, but now she was looking troubled again. "Why can't you stay?"

"If I do, the whole town will say we— well—" he paused, felt his neck heat up. "It just wouldn't be good, that's all."

"Nonsense," Sarah said. "Unmarried men rent rooms in private houses all the time. You said yourself that you don't want to sleep in the jail cell, or Rowdy and Lark's bed, so you bunk in the hayloft. Room and board is two dollars a week, twice that if you eat second helpings at supper."

Wyatt considered the idea. It *was* common for single men—and women, too—to take rooms in other people's homes. He'd be under the same roof with Sarah, at least part of the time, and so far, he'd deemed her cooking passable, if not something to write home about.

Not that he actually had a home, with his ma gone all these years.

"When Sam O'Ballivan gets back, I'll be going to work for him on Stone Creek Ranch," he said, fumbling in his pocket for his money. He'd spent some at the mercantile, buying the sardines, crackers and canned peaches, but he had plenty left, since he didn't use tobacco and rarely took a drink. "The job comes with living quarters."

Sarah simply held out her hand, palm up, smiling a little.

Wyatt counted out eight dollars. "Two weeks," he said. "With second helpings."

She laughed.

"Are you going to wash and iron my shirts?"

"No," she told him. "I am not. And since you're a boarder in this house now, I'd better go back to calling you 'Mr. Yarbro.'"

"Fair enough," Wyatt said. He kind of liked the sound of that. Paradoxically, the very formality of it lent a certain intimate spark to their exchanges.

"I'll say good-night, then," Sarah replied, turning to go.

Wyatt watched her cross the kitchen and start up the back stairs, wanting to follow her, knowing he couldn't. Like her calling him Mr. Yarbro, being in such close quarters gave a sort of festive little quiver to the whole situation.

Wyatt closed the door quietly, went back to the cot, sat down on its edge, and pulled off his boots. Lonesome was already dead to the world, snoring away on his folded-quilt bed.

"Don't get used to all this luxury," Wyatt warned the sleeping dog. "Once you're fit for it, you'll be herding cattle right along-side me."

With that, he turned down the wick in the kerosene lamp on the bedside table, stretched out on top of the covers in his clothes, and went to sleep.

THE EXPLOSION RATTLED the windows and sent Sarah shooting bolt upright in bed.

Somewhere, though whether from inside the house or the street, she couldn't say, someone shouted, "Fire!"

Dear God, she thought, scrambling into a wrapper. Papa had finally tipped over a lantern and set the place ablaze. She had to get Owen out, and her father, and Wyatt and his dog were sleeping in the spare room.

Frantically, she sniffed the air for smoke. Wrenching open the bedroom door, she stepped into the corridor and found Owen and Ephriam already there, sleepy-eyed and blinking.

She heard the back door slam, and knew Wyatt had gone. For a moment, she was stung, thinking he'd left them behind in a burning house, bent on saving himself.

She stared at her son and her father, momentarily paralyzed, incapable even of speech.

"Something blew up," Owen said cheerfully, breaking the silence.

Ephriam nodded, and they all scuttled down the stairs.

No smoke.

No flames.

Sarah calmed down a little.

"I'm going after Wyatt," Ephriam announced, and headed for the door.

"Me, too," Owen agreed.

And they both dashed out, in their night-shirts, ignoring Sarah's startled, "Come back!"

Muttering, she paused only long enough to look in on Lonesome, who, remarkably, was still sound asleep. "You're on your own," she told him, and hurried after her son and father.

People seemed to fill the streets, all rushing toward the center of town. Since everyone else was wearing their night-clothes, too, Sarah stopped fretting about her own state of dress. For once, Ephriam wouldn't look out of place, with the hem of his long flannel nightshirt flapping in the breeze.

Smoke and flames billowed from the windows and eaves of the jailhouse, and a series of deadly pops filled the night air.

"Everybody stay back!" Sarah heard Doc yell, from somewhere in the surging crowd.

Sarah recalled the guns Wyatt had locked up in the jail cell. *Oh, Lord,* she thought. They must have been the cause of the explosion. Had someone set the jail afire on purpose? Or was it simply an accident?

Wyatt.

Where was Wyatt?

Sarah began fighting and flailing her way through throngs of neighbors and friends, standing on tiptoe trying to catch some glimpse of him, however brief.

But he was nowhere to be seen.

Sarah saw Owen and Ephriam up ahead, and pushed through to reach them. Doc was there with them, as comical a figure as Ephriam in his night garments, with his graying brown hair all a-tousle.

"Have you seen Wyatt?" Sarah asked, grasping his arm.

"He and some other men went around back to get the horses out of Rowdy's barn, in case it catches."

The fire-wagon arrived, with its great tank always kept full of water, and a hose was unfurled. Buckets were taken from the livery stable and even the mercantile, and everyone, man, woman and child, fought the fire.

It was a threat to all of them.

If the blaze spread, it could devour the town, with all its wood-frame buildings, in a matter of minutes. Even Kitty and the other saloon women came, and a long bucket-brigade line was established, stretching all the way from the creek to the jailhouse.

The fight was long, hot and hard, but there were no more exploding bullets from inside, and the townspeople managed, though barely, to keep the blaze confined to the jailhouse.

It was almost dawn when the battle was won.

Exhausted, Sarah looked around her at all the sodden, soot-covered faces. Ephriam had long since taken Owen home, to her profound relief, but she doubted that either of them had slept.

When Wyatt found Sarah, his clothes were singed and blackened, and there were blisters on his hands. He looked all done in, yet ready to fight fire, or any other threat, for *another* six to eight hours, if it proved necessary.

It was in that moment, both of them standing there, blackened by greasy smoke, that Sarah came to an equally heartbreaking and joyous realization.

She loved Wyatt Yarbro. Deeply, truly and forever.

Tears stung her already burning eyes.

Oh, no, she thought. *Oh, no.*

"Your hands—" she whispered.

"I'm all right," Wyatt said. "You?"

"Fine," she replied. Except that a whole new landscape, filled with darkness and light, deep valleys and high mountains, had just opened up within her, forcing out so many of the things she'd always believed about herself.

That she'd never love again, after Charles.

That if she married, it would be for companionship and convenience, not because her very soul seemed to crave the passion of one man in particular.

Well, that man was standing before her, soot-stained and blistered and bleakly resigned to a fresh disaster.

"How did the fire start?" she heard herself ask. "Do you know?"

Wyatt's jawline tightened, and he nodded once, sharply. "Dynamite," he said. "Somebody figured on getting at those guns I locked up in there." He let out a grim chuckle, entirely void of amusement.

"Stupid bastards. Now the guns are gone, and so is my brother's jail."

Sarah touched Wyatt's arm, but tentatively, because all that she was feeling was so new, a fierce and fragile flame, burning inside her. "There's nothing more you can do right now," she told him. "Let's go home."

Home.

The word seemed to tremble between them.

He nodded.

Folks were already dispersing, heading wearily for their houses, talking in relieved whispers.

Stone Creek was still standing.

For the moment, it was enough reason to keep going.

At home, Owen and Ephriam were both up and dressed. They'd moved Lonesome's bed out into the kitchen, and he was lying on it, lapping from a pie tin of canned milk.

There was coffee, too.

"Sit down," Ephriam told Sarah and Wyatt. He gave them coffee and served up a platter of biscuits and a bowl of gravy lumpy with sausage, heretofore stashed in the warming oven over the stove.

Sarah was ravenous, but she fetched Lonesome's salve first, and asked Owen for a basin, water and a clean washcloth.

Wide-eyed, the child rushed to do her bidding. He kept stealing glances at Wyatt, his eyes full of hero worship.

Wyatt winced a few times while Sarah washed his hands and treated the blisters with salve, and his eyes never left her face. For Sarah, the experience was deeply sensual—just touching Wyatt in this innocent, practical way aroused yearnings within her that she'd never experienced before, even at the height of her romantic, whirlwind affair with Charles Langstreet.

Now, she wished she'd saved herself, in true Victorian fashion. She'd wished that often, over the years, but not in the same way. Before, she'd only regretted her foolishness, her gullibility, and the terrible emotional price she'd had to pay: giving up her baby. This new and poignant regret ran much deeper. When she lay with Wyatt Yarbro—and she knew she would, once or a thousand times—he would know she'd given her most precious gift to some other man, long before.

Desolation clenched at her heart, forced fresh tears to her eyes.

"Sarah?" Wyatt said quietly. He missed no nuance, this man. He would be hard to lie to, if not impossible. And Sarah, having lied so long, had forgotten how to tell the truth.

"I'm just tired," she said. *I love you,* said her heart.

"Eat," Ephriam ordered. "Both of you."

"Where are you going to put outlaws?" Owen asked Wyatt, almost breathless with interest. "Now that there isn't any jail?"

Wyatt winced again, the way he had when Sarah was doctoring his hands, but this time, the motion was accompanied by a dry grin. "Got to catch some, before I worry about where to put them," he answered. "This is good food, Mr. Tamlin," he added, turning to look at Ephriam, now seated directly opposite of him. "Maybe you ought to work as a cook, rather than a banker."

Sarah stiffened at the reminder that she had more problems than just being hopelessly in love with an outlaw deputy who'd served two years in prison. There was the bank to think about, and she constantly dreaded Charles's return to Stone Creek, because of that and even more because of Owen. When Charles came back, he would take the boy away from her as easily as he'd handed him over.

She could feasibly survive, if Wyatt left town for good. Oh, she'd grieve and pine, and become more spinsterish with every passing day, but she'd live on.

When it came to parting with Owen, though, she wasn't so confident. Losing him the first time had been hard enough; losing him again might be more than she could bear.

The pain of these prospects—Owen's going, and Wyatt's—all but doubled her over. She sat rigidly in her chair, unable to force down another bite of the delicious breakfast her father had served.

Wyatt saw it all, though of course he had no way of knowing what was tormenting her so. "Get some rest today, Sarah," he said. "You've got dark circles under your eyes."

"Probably soot," she said, trying to make a joke and failing miserably.

"Just the same," Wyatt said.

"I'll attend to the bank," Ephriam added.

"And Lonesome and I will be really, *really* quiet," Owen promised.

"You're all ganging up on me," Sarah protested, touched.

She wasn't even allowed to clear the table and wash the dishes.

Finally, Sarah gave up. She went upstairs, fell face-first onto her bed, and was asleep within moments.

LONESOME TOOK HIS MEDICINE and seemed affably resigned to staying at the house with Owen, so Wyatt cleaned up and headed into a day that was bound to be difficult.

There were the three dead men to bury.

The jailhouse was in smoking ruins.

He had some outlaw-chasing to do, and no posse.

First off, he stopped at the telegraph office. From there, he sent a wire to Rowdy in Haven, in the hope that somebody would track him down to deliver it. It was simple and to the point, that telegram:

Jailhouse blew up. Nothing left of it. Wyatt.

If Rowdy and Sam chose to come back to Stone Creek upon receipt of the message, so be it. He'd have to help them round up the galoots who'd dynamited the jail, that was only right, but beyond that, the responsibility for the safety of the people and property hereabouts would be theirs, Rowdy's and Sam's, not his.

After sending the telegram, Wyatt looked up Kitty Steel. He found her drinking coffee in the still-closed Spit Bucket Saloon, with a flock of other faded whores, all of whom fled when he came through the swinging doors.

All except for Kitty, that is. She watched him approach with dull, stoic eyes. She was used to enduring things, Kitty was.

"No whiskey before we open at ten," she told him. "But I can serve you some coffee."

A battered metal pot stood cooling on the bar. Wyatt took a mug that looked reasonably clean and filled it with coffee. Joined her at the table.

"If you know who blew up the jailhouse," he said companionably, "you'd better tell me."

Kitty let out a scoffing huff of a laugh. "It

was Paddy Paudeen," she said. "And you know it."

Wyatt *had* known, but he'd played no-holds-barred, cutthroat poker with Kitty Steel, out in Kansas City, and he was sure she hadn't laid down all her cards. "They were in here? Paudeen and his bunch?"

She gave a slight nod, leaned back comfortably in her chair. Let one side of her faded silk wrapper slide down to reveal a bare shoulder. "Yes," she said. "They made the rounds of all the saloons, but Paddy was here, all right. He likes Nola—" She cocked a thumb toward the stairs. Upon Wyatt's arrival, most of the fleeing whores had headed that way. "Pays her well and never actually gets around to the actual deed, if you know what I mean. He's always too drunk by that time, and just passes out in her bed."

"I'd like to talk to her," Wyatt said. "Ask her some questions."

"Second door on the right," Kitty replied, with a shrug and a sly little smile. "Though I must admit, I was hoping you'd take a fancy to me instead."

Wyatt had taken a fancy, all right—to Sarah Tamlin. He flat-out wasn't interested in anybody else, be they saint or sinner. "Get her down here for me," he said.

Kitty sighed, threw her head back, and bellowed, *"Nola!"*

Wyatt jumped.

Kitty chuckled.

And a small blond woman appeared on the upper landing and crept down the stairs, clutching the rail in both hands like a sailor about to blow off the deck of a ship in a typhoon.

"I'm twenty-one," Nola said, her eyes fixed, fearful and huge, on Wyatt's face. Or was it his badge she was looking at? "It ain't against the law for me to work here."

Wyatt pushed back his chair and stood. Nola surely wasn't a lady, but she was female, and therefore entitled to the normal courtesies. "I'm not here to give you trouble," he told the girl, who probably wasn't a day over sixteen. "I just want to talk to you about Paddy Paudeen."

The girl's eyes grew even wider. She'd reached the bottom of the stairs, but she didn't come a step closer. "What about him?"

"I figure he was the one who blew up the jailhouse last night," Wyatt said. He felt

Kitty's gaze on him, assessing, measuring, but he ignored her. "Did he say anything when he was with you, Nola? About where he and the others are holed up?"

Nola bit her plump lower lip. She was a pretty little thing, for all the war paint and the come-hither clothes. Wyatt wondered how she'd wound up in the business of laying down for men. It was one of the things he couldn't afford to dwell on, and usually pushed to a back burner.

"He'd kill me if he ever knew I told," she said, plenty fearful.

"I won't let that happen," Wyatt said.

"Don't trust him," Kitty warned the girl.

Wyatt looked down at her, sidelong. "Shut up," he told her.

Kitty smirked. "They usually set up camp out on the old Henson place. It's been abandoned for years. If Paddy asks who told you where to find him, you tell him it was Kitty Steel."

"They come to town often? Paudeen and his outfit, I mean?"

Nola slunk back up the stairs and disappeared.

"Every couple of years," Kitty said. "The

bunch changes, but Paudeen is always heading it up. He's steered clear, of late, because of Rowdy and Sam. I'm not so sure he's scairt of you, though."

"If he isn't," Wyatt said, "he will be."

"You talk tough, Deputy Yarbro, but you're only one man. And the way I heard it, you're an outlaw yourself, with a prison term behind you."

Wyatt nodded. "It gives me a certain advantage," he said, "over the law-abiding types like Sam O'Ballivan. I know how outlaws think."

"Sarah's taken with you," Kitty said, surprising him. "For her sake, I'd like to see you stay alive. Don't go after Paudeen. Wait till Sam and Rowdy get back, and raise a posse. Stone Creek needed a new jailhouse, anyhow. They'll pony up the money to rebuild."

Wyatt's pride stung a little. First Doc, now Kitty. Why did everybody think he needed Rowdy and Sam's help to get anything done—including bringing in Paddy Paudeen and his band? "You think I'm scared of those yahoos?"

Kitty chuckled, shaking her head. "That

would be giving you too much credit. You don't have the good sense to be scared, I'm guessing."

"Sarah knows you found your daughters," Wyatt heard himself say. He hadn't planned on bringing the subject up, since it was none of his business. "I told her about Kansas City. How you wanted me to marry you, so you could get the little girls back."

Kitty paled, but quickly recovered. Said nothing.

"Why did you lie about it, Kitty? To Sarah, I mean."

"Sarah's a lot more comfortable with lies than the truth," Kitty said. The remark was calculated to get under Wyatt's hide, and it did. In fact, it burrowed in and commenced to festering.

"Don't you want to see them? You were so all-fired determined to get them back, out in Kansas City—"

"My girls are young women now," Kitty answered. "Leona was married last year, to a man who built her a house and wears a suit to work every day. Davina is about to graduate from normal school. I'd like to see them, sure, but I don't kid myself that the feeling is mutual. What would two fine ladies want with a whoring mother?"

Wyatt set his hands on the back of the chair he'd been sitting in. "If you're so friendly with Sarah," he began, "then why did you say what you did a few minutes ago, about hoping I'd choose you over Nola?"

Kitty smiled, sat back, and lit a long brown cigar. Drew on it and blew a smoke ring that floated up over Wyatt's head, like a passing halo. "When it comes to plying my trade," she said, in a crooning drawl, "friendship has its limits."

Wyatt turned to leave. He was still hoping to find his hat, lost when he'd gone to investigate the gunshots that left Carl Justice and two other men dead, and then he'd saddle up Sugarfoot and go find the Henson place. They'd tied one on for sure, the night before, Paudeen and his crew. The chances were good they'd still be passed out from celebrating the destruction they'd wrought in Stone Creek. Even if they were up and around, they'd be hung over, and that might make it one hell of a lot easier to get the drop on them.

"Wyatt?" Kitty called after him, when he was almost to the swinging doors.

He stopped, turned his head, waited.

"The Henson place is three miles east of town, in a little valley. If you stick to the trail, they'll see you. Go overland, and leave your horse in the stand of cotton-woods on the ridge."

He nodded, and then left.

He found his hat at the base of a street-lamp, near Doc's place. It was some the worse for wear, but the sun was blazing hot in a clear blue sky, and he'd need to cover his noggin if he didn't want a temple-pounder of a headache.

When he got to the livery stable, a few of the cowboys from local ranches were hanging around, like they had nothing better to do, chewing the fat.

One of them, a young fella with curly brown hair and greenish eyes full of affa-ble goodwill, came forward as Wyatt approached.

"You goin' out to look for the men who blew up the jail and shot those poor bas-tards laid out over at Doc's, Deputy?"

Wyatt nodded. Went inside to saddle Sugarfoot. Reb and Lark's mare were in stalls on either side of Rowdy's gelding, munching grass-hay.

The kid followed him. "Me and the boys, we thought we'd go along to help, if you don't mind." He grinned, cocky and confident, probably a great favorite with the girls. "Name's Jody Wexler," he said, putting out a hand. "My pa owns the Star-cross Ranch."

The ranch name was familiar—Doc had mentioned it the day before. "Your ma just give birth to twins?" Wyatt asked, leading Sugarfoot out of his stall.

"My stepmother," Jody said. "Pa wears out his women—put three in the ground so far, from having babies. There are seven of us, counting the new ones. The last wife died having my three-year-old brother, Harry."

"You don't look old enough to track outlaws," Wyatt said, throwing a blanket and then a saddle, also Rowdy's, onto Sugarfoot's back. Buckling and tightening the cinch.

"I'm twenty-two," Jody replied, unruffled. "Do you want company, or not?"

Wyatt paused, patted Sugarfoot's golden neck before putting the bridle on. Jody

Wexler was wearing a six-gun, low on his left hip, and he was probably just a shade too fast for his own good. Not entirely sure Wexler and his pals weren't up to something, maybe planning to jump him outside of town, Wyatt figured he had to take the chance, nonetheless. Kitty had been right—he didn't have the common sense to be scared—but the odds of rounding up Paudeen and the rest would be better if he had a posse.

"All right," he said. "Long as you and your friends understand that this is serious business. You could get shot, among other things."

"I could get shot any day of the week," Jody answered, unfazed. "Look what happened when that gunfight broke out in front of Jolene's yesterday." With that, the boy sprinted out of the barn, calling to his friends to mount up, they were going after some outlaws.

Wyatt shook his head, led Sugarfoot out into the dazzling sun, and swung up into the saddle. Jody introduced his four companions as they all rode east, out of town. Wyatt didn't even try to remember their names; his head was full of things that could go wrong, and what he'd do if they did.

Turning at the top of the little hill on the sunrise side of Stone Creek, Wyatt looked down at what was left of Rowdy's jailhouse. It was pure luck and hard work on the part of the whole town that the house and barn hadn't gone up, too.

A pang of guilt struck Wyatt, square in his middle, strong as the blow of a fist.

Rowdy had entrusted the town to him.

And there, still smoldering a little, was the proof that his brother's trust had been sorely misplaced.

CHAPTER TEN

ALL DURING THE LAST mile of the ride to the old Henson place, Wyatt knew he wouldn't find Paudeen there. It was something about the silence, undisturbed and long-standing. Contrary to the dime novels, the average outlaw was neither brave nor honorable, let alone heroic, but flat-out stupid and usually vicious. Still, even the idiots among them occasionally got things right.

Wexler and the other members of the posse, all of them still wet behind the ears, for all their bold confidence, were plainly disappointed when they drew up on the ridge Kitty had mentioned to look down on the homestead.

The roof of the house was caving in, and the barn had fallen long ago. Old wagon wheels, rotted harnesses and broken barrels littered the ground. Wyatt had a strange feeling, looking at it. He wanted to dismount, push up his sleeves, and set the place to rights.

He even imagined Sarah inside that tumbledown hut, walls and roof restored, and real glass in the windows, and himself chopping wood in the dooryard, Lonesome near at hand, too, playing tag with Owen.

He shook his head, but the pictures stuck in his mind.

"Damn," Jody Wexler said. "They're gone."

"They were never here," Wyatt said, wondering if Kitty had sent him on a wild-goose chase, as a favor to Paudeen, or if she'd really been trying to help. With a woman like Kitty, practiced at playing situations to her best advantage, it was hard to know.

Wyatt reined his horse around to head back to Stone Creek. The town was unguarded, and there were three men to bury. Paudeen might be long gone, but then again, he could just be lying low up in the hills somewhere.

"You just going to give up?" Wexler asked, catching up with Wyatt and Sugarfoot on his own sure-footed pinto pony. The kid wore a blue corduroy jacket, and his hat was set at a jaunty angle. He'd been looking forward to wrangling outlaws, that was clear.

"We'll find them," Wyatt said. "Maybe not today, though."

"Me and the boys could go looking on our own," the boy said.

"No," Wyatt answered, a little sharply. "The last thing I want is to ride out and tell all your mamas that you're laid out on a slab at Doc's place because you ran into something you couldn't handle." Paudeen and his men were no geniuses, having destroyed their own guns, as well as the jailhouse, in an effort to reclaim them. But they were hardened and bitter and probably drunked-up good, and they wouldn't hesitate to pick off five kids on cow ponies and field horses, likely to ride right into their midst.

Wexler sat up straighter in the saddle,

clearly affronted. "I'm a fair hand with a gun," he said. "And so are my friends."

"If you're smart," Wyatt said, feeling weary and a lot older than his thirty-five years, "you'll hang those guns up for good and live by your wits instead."

Wexler's gaze dropped to the Colt on Wyatt's hip. "Like you did?"

"If I had my life to live over again, I'd do things differently," Wyatt replied, and grinned a little, though it felt more like a grimace from the inside. Now *there* was an understatement, if he'd ever uttered one.

If. What a useless, empty word that was.

"A man needs a gun out here," Wexler insisted.

Wyatt wondered how long the kid had been shaving. A few years at most, if not a few months. Wexler and the others thought they were men, because they could shoot, swill whiskey and perform well upstairs in a whorehouse. In Wyatt's mind, being a man meant hard work, facing down trouble when it came, no matter how bad the odds were, loving one woman, protecting and providing for a family.

Once, though, his definition would have been about the same as young Jody's.

Raise hell, chase women, and delude himself that he was safe in a dangerous world because he had a pistol on his hip and knew how to use it.

"I reckon hard experience will bring you around to my way of thinking, eventually," Wyatt said. "I just hope you live long enough to figure out what really matters."

"Rowdy wouldn't just let those outlaws ride free," Jody protested, reddening up a little. It was meant as a jibe, and it found its mark, just as Kitty's remark about Sarah being more comfortable with lies than the truth had done. The thing about jibes was, they hurt, but they didn't do any lasting damage.

"Maybe not," Wyatt agreed. "But he sure as hell wouldn't let you and your friends go off beating the brush for Paudeen on your own, either. If you want to be of some real help, Doc and I could use grave diggers right at the moment."

Jody sighed. "We'll help," he said, and Wyatt silently put a mark in a mental column, under *character.*

"While you're digging," Wyatt advised, "keep in mind that it was packing a gun that brought those men low."

Grudgingly, Jody nodded. He didn't think death could happen to him—though if challenged, he would have claimed that any fool knew it could. He was too young, too full of sap and piss and vinegar to truly understand that all that could stop with one bullet.

When they got back to Stone Creek, Wyatt led the way straight to Doc's house. He tried not to look at the ruins of the jail as he passed them, but the smell of burned wood was acrid in his nostrils and the place itself seemed to tug at him, demanding his attention.

The bodies were laid out in coffins, in Doc's office, all wearing donated clothes. Doc had stitched their eyelids down, and they all had a blue-gray pallor. Wyatt would have sworn they were breathing.

"Fast work building those caskets," Wyatt remarked to Doc, who was signing papers at his cluttered desk, taking off his hat because he was in the presence of the dead. Wexler and the others, crowding in behind him, followed suit.

"I keep a few on hand out in the shed," Doc answered, turning around, his smudged spectacles barely clinging to the tip of his long nose. He took in Jody Wexler and the boys. "Somebody sick?"

Jody and his chums gathered round the coffins, swallowing and silent, fidgeting with their hats.

"Nobody's sick, Doc," Wyatt said. "I recruited them to dig graves."

Doc nodded, huffed out a sigh. "Good," he said. "I'm not up to the job myself, and most of the townsfolk are probably tucked up in their beds, spent from fighting the fire." He turned to the boys. "Grave digging will pay a dollar apiece. You'll find shovels in my shed, and I'll show you where the holes ought to be."

None of the boys spoke. They were staring at the stitched-up eyes and the hard, waxen skin of the dead men.

"Look your fill," Wyatt told them quietly, after exchanging a glance with Doc. "That's what comes of living by the gun."

Doc's glance slipped to Wyatt's .45, just as Jody's had earlier.

"Isn't there going to be a funeral?" one of Jody's friends asked. He was a redheaded kid, skinny and freckled, probably no older than Carl Justice. His name, if Wyatt recalled it correctly, was Clarence.

Doc shook his head. "If they've got folks, it'll take time to find them. We have to get them in the ground—fast." He paused, looked the boys over with a benign expression of weary resignation in his eyes. He was probably thinking the same thing Wyatt was, that it would be a shame if these young fellas ended up in pine boxes before their time. "You get shovels and go on over to the churchyard and wait for me. I'll make arrangements at the livery stable for a wagon to haul these coffins, and then meet you."

The boys nodded and trooped outside.

"They think they're a posse," Wyatt said to Doc. The conversation had reminded him of the letter they'd found in Carl's pocket; he had yet to read it, what with all that had been going on of late. Now, he handed it over, unopened.

Doc accepted the missive, glanced at it, then set it aside before hoisting himself out his chair; Wyatt almost expected to hear his bones creak. "They're the future of this town, those young men. Good boys, all of them. I hope they'll pay some mind to what you said, but I don't reckon they will."

"Seemed to bring them up short a little, seeing these bodies."

"They've all seen death before, and plenty of it—mothers, fathers, sisters and brothers—but as far as I know, nobody who got himself shot for nothing but too much whiskey and a hand of cards."

Wyatt helped Doc center the lids over the coffins, nail them down. It was solemn work, but it had to be done. Doc chalked a number on two of the boxes, probably corresponding to the ones he'd inscribe on the back of the men's pictures, once the photographer had them developed. He wrote *Justice* on Carl's.

While the graves were being dug, under a high, hot and merciless Arizona sun, Doc sat in the shade of an oak tree, carved those same numbers into slabs of rough wood, using his pocket knife. He was determined to keep the bodies straight, in case kinfolks came to mourn.

Wyatt helped with the digging, rode back to Doc's place when it was finished, along with Jody and the boys. They loaded the coffins, one by one, and brought them to their final resting places. Carl's marker at least had a name on it; the other two men had only numbers.

It was, Wyatt thought, a sad way to wind up.

Once the coffins had been lowered, on slings of rope, into the ground, there was more shoveling to do. Doc stood by the whole time, retreating to the oak tree again, as soon as he'd made sure the markers were right, puffing on a pipe.

A few townspeople gathered, keeping their distance, but no words were said, so it wasn't a funeral.

The blisters on Wyatt's hands had broken open, with all the shoveling, and Doc said, "Come on back to the office. I'll put something on those sores. Hell of a thing if you got infected."

Wyatt nodded. The skin on his hands burned like fire, but the heaviness in his heart was worse. Doc gave Jody and the boys a dollar each, as promised, and they headed straight for the Spit Bucket Saloon.

Doc shook his head, smiling a little.

"Things all right over at the Tamlins'?" the old man asked, as they walked back toward his place, Wyatt leading Sugarfoot behind him. "I noticed Ephriam opened the bank all by himself this morning."

"Far as I know," Wyatt said, offering no comment on Ephriam or the bank. "I'm rooming with them now," he added, in case Doc thought there was anything amiss. He was a sharp-eyed old coot, and he'd surely noticed the tension—or whatever it was—between Wyatt and Sarah.

"I'd have said Sarah was too proud to take in a boarder," Doc said. "I reckon you must be special."

Wyatt felt a slight rush of blood up his neck and hoped it didn't show under all the dirt and sweat from the day's exertions. He didn't answer, since he couldn't seem to find the right words.

If he was special to Sarah, for any reason, it would be a damn fine thing. So fine, in fact, that it was too much to hope for.

"She's a good woman," Doc went on. "Decent and upstanding."

"I've heard she's prone to stretch the truth a mite," Wyatt offered, feeling awk-

ward. It made his voice come out sounding gruff, but that might have been a
residual effect of last night's fire.

"That little book she carries around?"
Doc confided. "She records the lies she
tells in it, so she'll remember and keep
her stories straight."

Wyatt frowned. He'd found that book in
her pocket, before he burned her dress in
Rowdy's cookstove the night before, and
the temptation to open it had been nearly
overwhelming, though he hadn't given in.
He was about to ask Doc why he'd said
what he did, but they were interrupted by
the telegraph operator, chasing them down
Main Street.

"Deputy! Mr. Yarbro!" the fella yelled.
"I've got a wire here for you!"

Wyatt stopped. The pit of his stomach
seemed to open like a trapdoor to hell.
Rowdy had received his message about
the jailhouse, and this was his answer.

He dreaded reading it.

The operator handed him a sheet of
yellow paper. Wyatt thanked him, gave
him a nickel for his services, and steeled
himself to catch hell.

On our way, Rowdy had written.

And that was all.

Wyatt was both relieved and unsettled. It was like Rowdy, like Wyatt himself, for that matter, to send a three-word telegram and let the recipient guess at everything else that might have been said.

Did Rowdy know about his brief involvement with the Justice gang? Might be, that was where Billy was right now—in jail down in Haven and chattering like an old woman at a pie social.

"How long do you reckon it will take them to get here?" he asked, after handing the yellow sheet of paper to Doc.

"A week if they bring the women and babies," Doc answered, watching Wyatt's face closely. "Three days if they come on horseback, and the day after tomorrow if they take the train. If you'll pardon my saying so, you don't look too glad they're coming."

Wyatt sighed. He'd been given a job as a deputy marshal, and he not only hadn't accomplished anything, he'd gotten the jailhouse blown to smithereens by locking up those guns. "Rowdy trusted me," he said, as much to himself as to Doc.

Doc slapped him on the shoulder. "I'd say he was right to do it. Now, let's get those hands of yours treated."

WYATT HAD BANDAGES on both hands, and he looked disconsolate, as well as dirty from head to foot.

Sarah, who had slept away the morning, was up and dressed now, about to put the midday meal on the table. Her father would be home from the bank soon, to have his lunch, and Owen was playing in the back-yard, with Lonesome, who was slow but managing to move about a little.

She would have been pleased to see Wyatt standing there, if it hadn't been for the bandages.

Seeing her concern, Wyatt managed a slight smile. "I'm all right, Sarah," he said. "Doc just wanted to fuss a little, so I let him."

Relief swept through her. "Sit down," she said. "You must be starved."

He nodded, almost shyly, drew back a chair, and sat.

"You've been with Doc all morning?" Sarah prattled, unable to help herself.

"Most of it," Wyatt said. "We had to bury those bodies."

Sarah sobered, nodded. Set a cup of fresh coffee and a plate of sandwiches before him, loving the feeling it gave her. For the briefest fraction of a moment, before her practical side took over again, she allowed herself to pretend they were husband and wife.

The bandages made eating his sandwich an awkward proposition, but Wyatt bravely undertook it. He was clearly starved—the breakfast Ephriam had prepared had probably worn off a long time ago.

"You're entitled to a second helping," Sarah said, when he'd finished.

He grinned. "Thanks," he said, "but the first will hold me, I think. Aren't you going to eat?"

Sarah merely shook her head. Then she went to the back door and called for Owen. The dog followed him inside, laboriously, but with an eagerness that touched Sarah's heart in a very tender place. She gave Lonesome a plate of cold sausage gravy, and he lapped it up gratefully while Owen washed his hands at the sink.

Sarah knew perfect happiness in those few minutes; the world, always fractured before, seemed, well, *complete.* Made whole by the mere presence of a man, a boy and a dog.

When the back door sprang open, though, and Ephriam stomped in, the fleeting joy was gone. Clearly, from his red face, quivering whispers, and one waving hand, something was wrong.

"Telegram from Charles Langstreet," he announced.

Sarah felt the floor go soft beneath her, like a thin blanket suspended by its four corners and ready to rip. *Don't be alarmed,* she told herself. *It probably concerns the money he promised to send for keeping Owen.*

Owen, who had just taken his seat at the table, face and hands still wet from washing up, stared at Ephriam with an expression just shy of terror.

Her hands trembling a little, Sarah took the wire, which was inside an envelope, and broke the seal. Inside, she found a Western Union voucher for a sizable amount of money and a terse message.

Marjory ill. I will be detained in Philadelphia, once I arrive there, for

several weeks, if not longer. Please see that Owen enrolls in school. C.L.

Sarah felt relief—and fury. Charles had sent money and instructions. But *not one affectionate word* for his son.

"Is he coming for me?" Owen asked, pale. "Do I have to leave Stone Creek?"

Sarah went to her child, laid a hand on his shoulder, though she would have preferred to gather him into her arms and hold him very close. "No, Owen," she said quietly. "Your mother is unwell, and he may be detained for a few weeks. He's asked me to put you in school."

It was the first day of September—classes would be starting up at the schoolhouse soon, with Fiona officiating.

"I hope he never comes back," Owen said.

Wyatt, Sarah and Ephriam all looked at him.

"Owen," Sarah scolded, "what a terrible thing to say!"

"He'll just leave me somewhere else," Owen insisted, sticking out his chin and folding his arms across his narrow chest. "If I'm going to be left, why can't I stay here with you and Ephriam and Wyatt and Lonesome?"

Out of the corner of her eye, she saw Wyatt react to the child's words. "Lonesome and I won't be around long," he said. "Rowdy and Sam are on their way home, on account of the jailhouse blowing up, and we'll be living out on Sam's ranch."

"Can I visit you?" Owen wanted to know.

Sarah put her hand to her throat. She'd known Wyatt's plans, but she'd hoped for a little more time before he moved out.

"I reckon you'll be in school," Wyatt said.

"I'm already smart," Owen said. "I don't need school."

"You definitely need school," Sarah said.

"All I've got are stupid back-East clothes," Owen argued. His trunks had been brought over from the hotel upon Charles's hasty departure, and they were filled with velvets and wool. "The other kids will call me a sissy."

Sarah waved the Western Union voucher. "We'll go over to the mercantile and get you some new ones," she said.

Owen brightened a little. "Long pants? Boots, like Wyatt's?"

"Long pants and boots like Wyatt's," Sarah confirmed, smiling, even though her throat felt thick and her eyes stung.

"And a six-gun?" Owen pressed.

"No six-gun," Sarah said.

Ephriam, who had watched the whole exchange in silence, hung his hat on the peg with a harrumph, washed his hands at the sink, and sat down next to Owen.

Sarah served them both lunch, and refilled Wyatt's coffee cup.

"Best put the Henson place up for sale," Ephriam said, causing Wyatt to sit up straighter in his chair, for a reason Sarah did not understand. "We've got too many abandoned farms and ranches on the books."

"How much?" Wyatt asked.

"How much what?" Ephriam boomed, grabbing up a sandwich with both hands.

"How much are you planning to ask for the Henson place?"

"Three hundred and fifty dollars," Ephriam said decisively. "It would have been worth five, if it wasn't so run-down. Sarah, we can't be lending money to every footloose yahoo with a yen to start up in the cattle business. What possessed you to let Hiram Henson have that place on a five-dollar down payment?"

Sarah stood perfectly still, watching Wyatt. Her heart rose into her throat and fluttered there, though she could not think of a single reason why she ought to be excited. She was, though. She surely was.

Then she remembered the question her father had put to her. "Hiram seemed like a hard worker," she said, "and he had a family, so he needed what he had to buy food for the winter."

Her father harrumphed again. "We're running a bank, Sarah, not a charity."

Wyatt, interested only a moment before, was now staring down into his coffee cup. There was a slight stoop to his broad shoulders.

Had he been thinking of buying the Henson place? Sarah wondered. Settling down, right outside of Stone Creek? Her heart fluttered even more.

"Of course," Ephriam went on, intent on his sandwich, and talking between bites, "if I could find somebody handy enough to fix it up, we could write the mortgage for the full three hundred and fifty and count the work as a down payment."

Wyatt lifted his head, and his shoulders straightened. "How much land comes with it?" he asked quietly.

"Fifty acres or so, if I recall correctly, and there's a spring, too." If Ephriam had guessed that Wyatt wanted that old place, he gave no sign of it. On the other hand, he was a crafty old cuss when he was in his right mind, and the chances were good that he knew exactly what he was doing. "You ever done any carpentry work? Rowdy's pretty handy with a hammer and saw. Does it run in the family?"

Wyatt's grin dazzled Sarah, bright as a winter sun gleaming on snow. "Yes, sir," he said. "It sure does."

Sarah wanted to hug her father.

"Reckon you ought to ride out and take a look at the place, then. If you're of a mind to take up ranching, I can have the mortgage papers ready by closing time. First payment is due one year from today, and if you fail to meet it, don't think I won't foreclose."

Wyatt stood up, put out a bandaged hand to Ephriam, who looked at it with raised eyebrows, then turned a satisfied little smile on Sarah.

"I'll have another sandwich, if you please," he said.

Wyatt thanked Sarah for the meal, set his plate and coffee cup in the sink, and went out.

"Time to give Lonesome some more medicine," Owen said.

Sarah did the honors, and the dog lapsed into sleep again.

"Can we go buy my school clothes now?" Owen asked. "Can we go see the school?"

"Yes," Sarah said, giving in, for the first time, to the urge to ruffle his hair. It felt like silk between her fingers.

Sarah crossed the room, put out a hand to her father. "Thank you, Papa," she said, as he squeezed her fingers affectionately.

"It feels good to be running the bank again," Ephriam said. "No telling how long it will last, though. You've done a good job, Sarah, but you're too softhearted to be a banker."

She smiled, bent, and kissed the top of Ephriam's head.

Soon after that, she and Owen went out, heading for the mercantile. Ephriam remained behind to eat his second sandwich.

While Owen was trying on long pants, cotton and flannel shirts, and boots, selecting tablets and pencil boxes, Sarah stood at the mercantile window, watching as her father reopened the bank, having closed it for the lunch hour, as he always had.

He had come back, the strong, confident father she had always known. With luck, the interval would last until Charles had returned, gone through the ledgers at the bank, and found everything in good order.

But when Charles left the second time, he would take Owen with him.

Sarah blinked back tears at the thought.

"Sarah?"

She turned, saw Kitty standing behind her. She hadn't realized the other woman was in the store.

Kitty's face was waxen; she hadn't applied the usual paint and powder and kohl to darken her eyelashes. "I had a letter," she said, in a strangled whisper.

All thoughts of asking Kitty why she'd lied about finding her children fled Sarah's mind. The woman looked shattered, even shrunken, standing there in her ordinary calico dress. If not for the improbably red hair, she might have been a ranch wife, come to town for supplies.

"A letter?" Sarah asked, concerned. She took Kitty's arm and led her over to the bench where people sat to try on shoes, sat her down firmly.

"It's from—it's from Davina," Kitty said. Tears rose in her eyes, and she sniffled.

"Is she all right?" Sarah asked.

"She's coming here," Kitty replied, fitful, almost moaning the words. "She's been hired to teach school right here in Stone Creek!"

Sarah took Kitty's hand in her own. "But we already have a teacher—"

"I don't know about that," Kitty said. "All I know is, my baby is coming to Stone Creek, and she's going to find out—"

"You've been corresponding with her?"

Kitty bit her lower lip, nodded. When she met Sarah's gaze, her eyes were full of sorrow. "I'm sorry I lied to you, Sarah. I don't know why I did it—I guess I liked having you and Maddie and Lark act like friends—"

"Kitty, we *are* your friends." Sarah watched as Owen gathered school things, laid them on the counter in a pile to be paid for. She understood only too well how Kitty felt, and all the reasons there were to lie. All the countless reasons, every one of them a trap bound to spring at the least opportune time.

"I've got to move on," Kitty said frantically. "Pack up and go. I told Davina I was a rancher's wife. The minute she steps off that train, she's going to know what I really am."

"Kitty, you're her mother. You must want to see how she's turned out—"

"I want that more than I ever wanted anything," she said. "But it's too late, Sarah. I've told so many lies. And Davina grew up with a doctor and his wife. She's educated, and cultured. I can't meet her train like—like I am."

Sarah was subdued. She'd chosen a different path in life than Kitty had, it was true, but if it hadn't been for her father's understanding and support, she might well have ended up in a brothel herself.

Her degree in music wasn't worth much
when it came to earning a living—her parents had insisted on it, primarily because
they wanted her to attract a husband with
a taste for the finer things—and she knew
only too well how despair could drag people down into circumstances that would
normally be far beneath them.

Sarah could not judge, lest she be
judged herself.

"What am I going to do?" Kitty begged,
in a broken rasp.

"We'll think of something," Sarah said.

More lies? Some kind of elaborate
ruse? Kitty, boarding at Sarah's house
and pretending to mourn a rancher husband who had never existed?

It wouldn't work, of course. Just as Kitty
said, as soon as Davina alighted from the
train, folks would be eager to tell her that
her mother served liquor and sold her
body in the Spit Bucket Saloon.

None of Kitty's finer points would matter. And Kitty *did* have finer points. She
was a good poker player, for one thing,
and she sewed beautifully and painted
delicate florals in watercolor, too. Last
night, after the fire broke out, she'd fought

the blaze toe-to-toe, just like everybody else in town.

"It's no use," Kitty said. "I'm going to get my savings out of the bank and catch the first train out of here."

Kitty, unlike many of the respectable women in town, had a bank account of her own. She hadn't saved a fortune, but she'd have enough to start fresh somewhere else.

"Don't go yet, Kitty," Sarah said. "Give me a chance to think."

Kitty didn't answer. She just rose off the bench and hurried out of the store.

And Sarah watched her son, eagerly preparing to enter school.

She wasn't free to tell him the truth— Charles had a say in the matter, too, whether she liked it or not. But one day, far in the future, he might come back to Stone Creek, full-grown, like Davina, and want to know why everything she'd told him had been a bold-faced lie.

CHAPTER ELEVEN

WHERE THE HELL, Wyatt asked himself, as he rode alone down the ridge to take a closer look at the Henson place, was he going to get three hundred and fifty dollars? Or even the money to buy nails, lumber and tools to put the homestead back in working condition?

And those questions were only the first of many.

Rowdy and Sam were on their way back from Haven, where they'd been tracking not only murderous vigilantes, but Billy Justice and the rest of his gang. Rowdy was Wyatt's favorite brother, and there had always been a deep bond between them, but if Rowdy had stumbled across the truth about that failed attempt at rustling, he wouldn't hesitate to arrest him. Rowdy was that sort of man—he did everything to the fullest extent of his knowledge and ability, whether it was outlawing or keeping the peace. The badge he wore might have been a mere convenience to some folks, but it *meant* something to Rowdy, and he would stand behind it, in conscience and in action.

Wyatt grinned soberly at the thought, leaning back in the saddle a little as Sugarfoot navigated the steep descent. Rowdy had grit, and he had gumption, both of which were qualities Wyatt knew he too possessed, but he hadn't used them in the same way.

He'd been a train robber, an intermittent cowpoke on various ranches all over the West, but he'd never built anything, never owned anything. Never chosen a way of life, planted his feet on a piece of ground, dug in his heels and held on. Much as he'd wanted a wife and family, it had always been a pipe dream, something he consoled himself with when he got lonesome, which was often. The woman in his flights of fancy had never had a face—she was a figure in a calico dress, albeit a shapely one, calling him in to supper after a day of hard work.

Now, she was Sarah Tamlin.

Reaching the dooryard of the old house, Wyatt felt fresh despair, a bittersweet desolation that ached in his very soul. How could he bring Sarah, a genuine lady used to all the better graces—pianos and china dishes and spare rooms—to live in a place like this?

With a sigh, he swung down out of the saddle and left Sugarfoot to graze untethered on a patch of overgrown grass by the well. The threshold of the house—more of a cabin, really—was low. Wyatt ducked his head to keep from bashing it against the door frame and stepped over.

He could see the sky through the gaps left by the fallen roof, most of which lay in the center of the cabin. Vermin scuttled through the wreck. One room, with a potbellied stove and a stone fireplace. The stove was rusted, the fireplace was crumbling. Like as not, there were birds and mice nesting in the chimney.

Wyatt added mortar to the list of things he couldn't afford to buy.

He shoved a hand through his hair, trying to imagine Sarah there.

The effort was a bust. Her bedroom in town was probably bigger than this whole place.

He picked his way over to the potbellied stove, opened the door and looked inside. A snake hissed, raising its head to strike.

He slammed the stove door shut again and straightened.

Went back to the threshold and stood looking out over the property, gripping the door frame with his hands—a well falling in on itself, a shell of a barn that would have to be razed and cut up for firewood. And fifty acres of decent grass—not enough to call a ranch, really, but he could run a few cattle. But it would probably be a couple of years before he made a profit, and in the interim he'd have to make at least two mortgage payments.

Where was he going to get the cattle in the first place?

He gave a raspy chuckle. He could always rustle a few, he supposed. Tricky, though, when the curious decided to inspect the brands.

Again, Wyatt took off his hat and raked his fingers through his sweat-dampened hair. He had less than thirty dollars to his name, and he'd inherited his ma's fear of debt. There had been a lot of lean years when he was a kid, years when Pappy didn't send home enough to buy a twenty-pound sack of flour. Time and again, Miranda Yarbro had put on her Sunday best, donned a bonnet, driven herself to the bank in town, and borrowed against the farm, and on three different occasions, they'd faced foreclosure. Once, they'd gone so far as to load the household goods in the back of a wagon, headed out to who-knew-where with only a worn-out pair of plow horses to pull them, and at the last possible moment, Pappy had ridden up with a pocket full of money.

It was one of the few times Pappy had saved the day. Why had he chosen to follow Pappy's lead, instead of his ma's?

Wyatt gave another sigh. He wasn't even riding his own *horse,* for God's sake. And he'd have to work for Sam O'Ballivan—if the job offer was still open, given his poor

showing as deputy marshal of Stone
Creek—just to survive. Hammer and saw
on the Henson place in his spare time,
which, given the nature of ranch work,
would be nigh onto impossible.

He imagined what Pappy would say, if
he'd been standing there. *Take Rowdy's
horse and go hold up a train—better yet,
a stagecoach. Easy pickings, a stagecoach. Then keep on riding. Forget Sarah.
Forget Stone Creek. And for sure forget
that worthless hound you call Lonesome—
all he'll do is slow you down.*

Pappy's image faded, replaced by the
small but fierce figure of his mother,
Miranda. He could almost hear her voice,
see her shaking an index finger under his
nose. *Stop running, Wyatt Yarbro. Buckle
down and work. That's how you get what
you want in this life.*

"It's impossible, Ma," Wyatt muttered.

*Things are only impossible before you
do them,* she would surely have replied.
*Do you think I had an easy time, keeping
a family of hungry boys together while
your pa was off gallivanting? No. I just did
what was there before me to do, whether
it was impossible or not. I clawed a living*

out of that Iowa dirt. I milked cows and kept chickens and sold eggs and butter at the store in town. I mended shirts until my fingers bled. But I kept you all under my roof and fed, long as you needed a home.

He'd have to choose, Wyatt realized, once and for all. Choose between Pappy's way, and his ma's. He couldn't go on doing one thing, wanting all the while to do another.

He'd tried Pappy's method. Wound up in prison, first off, then as a drifter and erstwhile rustler.

His ma's way was harder, there was no denying that. Claim a patch of ground and earn the deed to it. Stand up on the inside, so he could count himself a man.

Wyatt strode through the space where the images had stood, went to peer down into the well. It was crumbling, like the rest of the place, but there was water down there. He could see the faint, muddy glimmer of it, catch the scent of it.

Water. For an Arizona rancher, it was as good as oil to a Texan.

Sugarfoot nickered companionably as Wyatt passed him, set on examining what remained of the barn. His first impression had been right—there was nothing to do but rebuild it, from scratch.

He paced off some of the land, close in to the house, and found the spring Ephriam had mentioned, a grassy oasis of pure water, feeding into the well from underground. Until he got the latter mucked out, he could hike back and forth with buckets.

He began to feel cautiously hopeful. Sure, the house was small—but so was the one Rowdy and Lark lived in, and they certainly seemed happy enough, and he could always build on more rooms when he'd had time to acquire a bank account.

He smiled. Not that he'd put a cent of his money into the Stockman's Bank. The establishment was the proverbial sitting duck, and it was only a matter of time before some band of yahoos rode in and robbed it bare.

Yahoos, he had to allow, who had not reckoned on Rowdy Yarbro, Sam O'Ballivan, or himself.

All he asked of a benevolent fate, if there was such a thing, was that Sarah wouldn't be in the bank when it happened.

Memories of the stampede down south,

when both he and Reb should have been killed, flashed in his mind. He wasn't prepared to call whatever had saved their hides "God," but *something* had kept them out of harm's way that night.

Maybe there was a reason.

Thoughtful, Wyatt mounted up and rode back to town. Headed straight for the bank.

Ephriam was there, with the teller, introduced as Thomas, though whether it was his first name or his last, Wyatt didn't know. Or care.

There was no sign of Sarah. Most likely, she and Owen were still out buying the boy's school gear. Wyatt felt a pang, picturing that. He was gone on Sarah, had been from the first sight of her, but now he was starting to get attached to the kid, too. Owen was another man's son, he reminded himself, and the kid was only visiting in Stone Creek.

"I reckon if you have those mortgage papers drawn up," Wyatt said to Ephriam, belatedly remembering to remove his hat, "I'm ready to sign them."

Ephriam smiled, and it seemed to Wyatt

that there was a lot behind the expression. Cordiality, surely, but a certain sad resignation, too. Nobody knew better than he did, after all, that the clear-minded state he was enjoying now was most likely temporary. "Come into my office," Tamlin said. "Thomas, you'll be all right out here alone?"

Thomas reddened, affronted by the question. Wyatt felt little sympathy for the youth, given that he'd warned Sarah of plans to hold up the bank, then left her to face twenty men alone. "I'll be *fine,*" the teller said.

Wyatt spared Thomas a glance as he passed him.

The young man bristled.

Ephriam's office was small and cluttered, like Doc's, but here, as at Venable's place, there was a sense of underlying order.

"Sit down, please," Ephriam said, taking the chair behind his desk, sort of sinking into it, as though he suddenly found his own weight too great to carry.

Wyatt drew up a chair. Set his hat aside on the floor.

"You've been out to the Henson place?" Ephriam asked, tenting plump fingers beneath a series of chins.

"Yes, sir," Wyatt said. "I believe I can make something out of it."

It was only by giving voice to the statement that it became true for Wyatt.

The spread would never be fancy, but it would pay a modest living—someday, that was, and with a hell of a lot of elbow grease.

Ephriam regarded him in somber, measuring silence for a long time. Then he asked, "What are your intentions toward my daughter, Mr. Yarbro?"

Wyatt was caught off guard by the question, though he supposed he should have anticipated it. "I want to marry her," he heard himself say. "But right now, I don't have much to offer in the way of support, so it'll be a while." He paused, cleared his throat, sat up a little straighter in the chair. "I do mean to court her, though, and I know I ought to ask your permission, but the plain truth is, I'll be making a case for myself with her, whether you approve or not."

The banker chuckled at that. "I'm willing to overlook that formality," he said. "You have my permission, for what it's worth. The one thing I would ask is that you take good care of Sarah." He spread his hands, apparently drawing Wyatt's attention to their surroundings. "I started with a few hundred dollars in a cash box. Got it mining, in various places. I lived over at Mrs. Porter's, in a room under the stairs, and lent money at interest, five, ten, twenty dollars at a time. Mrs. Porter's husband ran Stone Creek Bank—he was my only competitor. It's closed now, of course."

Wyatt had seen the other bank, its windows boarded up and an Out Of Business sign tacked to the door. Rowdy had mentioned some bad business concerning the Porters, sometime back, in a letter Wyatt had received in prison, but it had just been a story to him, and since he'd arrived in town, he'd been too busy falling in love with Sarah Tamlin and getting the jailhouse blown sky-high to give the tale much thought.

Now, Wyatt nodded, as if he knew more about Stone Creek's past than he did.

"I hear you turned to and helped Doc get those three men buried, too," Ephriam said, still studying Wyatt as though there were words written on his face in an illegible hand.

Thinking back on things, Wyatt couldn't recall Rowdy ever saying anything about Doc, but then, he hadn't described anybody else, either, except for Lark. The pages of his few recent letters had been filled with her—how pretty she was, and how smart. How he'd never known another woman like her.

Wyatt's throat constricted. "I thought the only doctor in Stone Creek was Chinese," he said, recalling something Lark had said, that first night, at the supper table.

"Doc went through a bad patch," Ephriam said. "Took to the drink, after his wife and daughter died of a fever. Got so bad, hardly anybody even thought of him as a doctor anymore. Made his living as an undertaker. Then, just last spring, he answered the altar call in church one Wednesday night and got himself saved. It took, I guess. He's been stone sober ever since."

Wyatt had heard of stranger things— like living through a stampede. He didn't speak, because he knew Ephriam had more to say, and he wanted to hear it, especially if it concerned Sarah.

"Doc managed to keep his hand in, though. Tended broken bones for folks who didn't want a Chinaman looking after them. He and Sarah spent twenty-four hours of the day upstairs at the Spit Bucket, when the women came down with some kind of grippe. Lost a few of them. Doc gave them medicine Hon Sing brewed up for him, and most pulled through."

Wyatt thought of Sarah, risking her own health to soothe and minister to the sick. If it came down to a choice between smoking cigars and courting maladies that could easily be fatal, he'd rather she indulged in tobacco.

Not, he reflected with a smile, that Sarah would be swayed by his opinions if she had that mind of hers hitched up to go in a different direction from his.

"I won't ask if you love my daughter," Ephriam said, making Wyatt sit up straighter again. "I reckon that's your personal business, and hers. She's taken with you, though, I can see that. A lot of men might think we have money of our own put by, Sarah and me. If that's what's on your mind, Mr. Yarbro, you're sorely mistaken. We own the house, and not much else.

Sarah made some shaky loans, and then covered them."

"I know about the loans, sir," Wyatt said, feeling his neck redden up a little. "And if I'm lucky enough to marry Sarah, it won't be for money."

Ephriam was a shrewd man, when his head wasn't in a fog. It must have been a living hell for him, Wyatt thought, forgetting everything the way he seemed to do. "There's another possibility, of course," the old man went on. "You're Payton Yarbro's flesh and blood. While he was famous for robbing trains—right now, this very day, you could go over to the mercantile and buy any one of a dozen dime novels, full of his exploits—I don't imagine he raised his sons to turn their nose up at the loot from a small-town bank, guarded only by a woman, an old man who can't recall his own name some days, and a single teller who's scared of his own shadow."

"If I'd meant to hold up the Stockman's Bank, Mr. Tamlin," Wyatt said, his neck feeling hotter still, "I'd have done it as soon that train pulled out of town with Rowdy and Sam on it."

Ephriam smiled again. "Well, I guess

Payton raised Rowdy, too, and he turned out all right."

"Pappy didn't raise any of us," Wyatt said. "Our ma did that. Then, when we got old enough, we went off with our pa to learn thieving. I make no secret of that, Mr. Tamlin. I did two years in prison, and while I didn't come forward at a revival meeting like Doc, something did happen that made me want to be a better man."

"I don't suppose you'd care to tell me what that was?" Ephriam gave a gruff, rueful chuckle. "Hell, I'll probably forget, anyway."

"I'd as soon not share it, sir, at least until I've told Sarah."

A look of respect came into Ephriam's weary old eyes. He pulled off his spectacles, wiped the lenses with part of his banker's coat. "She knows you've been in prison?"

"I let her know that right off," Wyatt said. There wasn't much about his life he could boast about, but living under his right name and claiming his past with no excuses was a point of pride with him. It was what his ma would have wanted, what she'd prayed for, all those nights, when she'd knelt by her sons' beds and offered them up to the care of the God she so completely, thoroughly trusted, no matter how hard things got.

Ephriam slid a stack of papers toward Wyatt. "Read these over, and sign them if you agree with the terms. I made the loan for four hundred and fifty dollars, instead of three hundred and fifty, figuring you'd need lumber and the like to fix up the Henson place." He chuckled again as Wyatt picked up the papers. "Guess we ought to call it the *Yarbro* place, once the ink dries."

For the first time since he'd set foot in Ephriam's office, Wyatt smiled. "The Yarbro place. I like the sound of that," he said. "And I'm obliged for the extra money." Then, because he was his mother's son, as well as his father's, he read every single word in those papers, made sure of his understanding, and then put his signature to the whole works.

That one hundred dollars, given to him in cash by Mr. Tamlin, meant an extra annual payment, and that was serious business to Wyatt. Still, if he wanted a roof and a floor and clean well water, he had to accept it.

He and Tamlin shook hands on the deal, and Wyatt left the Stockman's Bank.

He didn't kid himself that he owned that fifty acres and broken house. The bank did; all he owned was the mortgage. But there was a spring in his step, just the same, as he stepped out into the sunshine, looking up and down the street as he crossed, automatically counting horses in front of saloons. Since lumber and tools were sold out of the mercantile, he made his way there.

SARAH PUT Owen's new clothes, tablets, pencils and other school equipment on her account, since she hadn't taken time to cash Charles's voucher at the bank. They were just leaving when Wyatt stepped up onto the sidewalk from the street.

Seeing her, he stopped and tugged at the brim of his hat.

Since Owen's purchases were to be delivered at the house later in the day, there having been too much for the two of them to carry, Sarah's hands were empty. Owen clutched a parcel wrapped in brown paper and tied with string, unwilling to let it out of his sight.

Knowing Wyatt would have offered to carry things home for her, if she'd had any, Sarah almost regretted asking that the order be delivered.

Owen shoved the package out to show Wyatt. "I've got long pants in here," he said. "Just like yours. And a shirt, too. Aunt Sarah says it looks like it was cut from a flour sack, but *I* like it!"

Sarah laughed, rising, once again, on a swell of fragile and very temporary joy. "Lunch is included in your room and board," she told Wyatt. "If you're hungry."

Wyatt's white teeth flashed as he grinned. If they had a baby together, would it have Wyatt's fine, strong teeth, his rugged yet pleasing features?

She blushed, just to catch herself thinking such a thought, and on Main Street, too. In broad daylight.

"I'll be along directly," he said. "I have some business in the mercantile, but it shouldn't take long."

Hope quickened Sarah's heart. All morning long, despite helping Owen select his new clothes and grappling with what Kitty had told her, about her daughter's imminent arrival in Stone Creek to teach school, she'd been recalling breakfast, and the conversation her father and Wyatt had had about the Henson place.

She wanted to ask if Wyatt had bought the property, but couldn't quite bring herself to be that forward.

He must have seen it in her face, the longing to know if he'd be staying or moving on, because he said, "I've got a mortgage now. If there's one thing worse than a former train robber, it's a former train robber up to his gullet in debt."

Sarah wanted to shout, to whirl, right there on the sidewalk, the way she used to do as a child in her mother's parlor, when Nancy Anne Tamlin sat down at her piano and filled the house with sweet, soaring music, coaxing whole concertos from the time-yellowed keys. Suddenly, she didn't trust herself to speak.

Wyatt didn't say anything, either.

They just stood there, the two of them, looking into each other's eyes.

It was Owen who broke the impasse. "Can I put these pants on when we get home, Aunt Sarah? I look *sissified* in this getup!"

Wyatt chuckled. "I wouldn't go so far as

to say 'sissified,'" he told the boy. "Just—well—*Eastern.*"

Owen made a face. "I wanted to put them on inside the store, but Aunt Sarah wouldn't let me. She said I'd get them dirty."

"A boy's meant to get dirty," Wyatt said.

Sarah laughed and steered her son in the direction of home. She cast a look back over one shoulder and saw that Wyatt was still standing outside the mercantile, watching her go.

A HUNDRED DOLLARS WOULDN'T buy all the lumber Wyatt needed, but it was enough get him started. If things stayed calm in Stone Creek until Rowdy and Sam showed up, he could start replacing the roof out home.

Home. He hadn't had one, since his ma had died giving birth to young Gideon. When he'd gone back to pay his respects at Miranda Yarbro's final resting place, the farm had already been sold to the son of their late neighbor, John T. Rhodes.

Rhodes had been a friend to Miranda, and to Rowdy, although Wyatt hadn't approved of his ma associating with an unmarried man, while she had Pappy's wedding band on her finger. She'd mended John T.'s shirts, darned his socks, and let him drive her to church of a Sunday, too.

Looking back, Wyatt reckoned he'd taken too harsh a view of John T. Rhodes. The man had surely loved Miranda, but as far as Wyatt knew, he'd never over-stepped the bounds of propriety. Unlike Pappy, John T. had been *there,* and if Miranda had been fond of him, and no doubt grateful, too, who was Wyatt to judge?

He went inside the mercantile, took off his hat, and ordered a wagon load of lum-ber, a hammer and saw, and a keg of nails. He could hardly wait to get out of the lawman racket, and get started, though he knew he wouldn't have much free time once he started riding for Sam O'Ballivan.

"You'll be staying on in Stone Creek, then?" asked the storekeeper's wife, evi-dently pleased. The question came after she'd introduced herself as Mabel. "Word's all over town that you're sweet on Sarah Tamlin, but a body can't take common gossip as gospel, now can they?"

"No, ma'am," Wyatt said, amused and,

at the same time, feeling shy. "You can't trust gossip, I mean. I do mean to stay on, long as I'm welcome, and I'm right fond of Sarah Tamlin."

Mabel blinked, probably surprised by his straightforward answer. She was plain, but good-natured, with crooked teeth and eyes that didn't seem to focus right. She most likely needed spectacles, but a lot of women were too vain to wear them. It was one of the many things Wyatt did not understand about the female gender. They cinched themselves into corsets and pulled the strings so tight, they swooned. They wore shoes in the size they *wanted* their feet to be, not the size they actually were.

Strange creatures, but intriguing.

"We'll be selling a pile of lumber for the new jailhouse," Mabel said, once she'd recovered from a good dose of plain talk. "Lucky thing you placed your order right away."

"Lucky thing," Wyatt agreed.

"Rowdy's been wanting a new jail for a long time," the woman ran on. "He always said a town this size needed more than one cell."

"Is that right?" Wyatt said idly, counting out payment for his purchases. Maybe he'd been worrying about Rowdy's reaction to the fate of the old jailhouse for nothing. Could be, if the storekeeper's wife had it right, he was *happy* it was gone.

"He and Lark are planning to build a new house, too. A big one." Mabel leaned forward, halfway across the counter, to confide in a loud, carrying whisper, "She has money, you know. Lark, I mean."

"So I hear," Wyatt said, uncomfortable discussing his sister-in-law's financial situation, anxious to make his departure and see what Sarah was going to serve up for lunch.

"*Lots* of money," the store-mistress prattled on. "When she came to Stone Creek, she *pretended* to be a schoolteacher. We all thought there was something very peculiar, since her clothes were all so expensive—"

Wyatt pulled out his pocket watch; it had belonged to his maternal grandfather, T. M. Wyatt, and his ma had given it to him because he was her eldest son and bore her family name. "I'm in sort of a hurry," he said.

The woman had the good grace to blush. "Well, of course you are," she said. "My husband will deliver the lumber tomorrow, or tonight after supper. Where should he take it?"

"The old Henson place," Wyatt said, with a rush of pride.

The woman's eyes widened. "I've heard it's a hideout for outlaws," she told him anxiously.

"Not anymore, it isn't," Wyatt replied. Then, after collecting his change, he turned and hurried out of the mercantile. Walked with long strides toward Sarah's place. The store-mistress hadn't really said anything untoward about Lark, but he felt a little guilty just for listening to her.

Idle hands might be the devil's workshop, his ma used to say, but idle *words* were even worse. And he'd probably started a large-scale tongue-wagging session by saying straight out that he cared for Sarah Tamlin.

He was passing the telegraph office when the woman who'd given him a plate of food that first day, outside the revival tent, stepped out onto the sidewalk. She pressed a lace-trimmed hanky to her eyes and sniffled, and seeing Wyatt, made a subtle move to block his way.

He struggled to recall her name, but came up dry. Stopped and tugged at the brim of his hat.

"Fiona," she said, putting out a gloved hand to him.

"Fiona," he repeated, to lodge the name in his mind, in case he ever needed it. He glanced at the hanky clasped desperately in her left hand while he shook the right one, being careful not to tighten his grip. "Is something the matter?"

"My poor aunt Lavinia," she said. "She's been ailing for months, and now she's taken a turn for the worse."

"I'm sorry to hear that," Wyatt said.

"It's not widely known," Fiona confided, leaning in close to Wyatt, "but I've tendered my resignation and I won't be teaching at Stone Creek School when the new term starts next week. I've been sure right along that I'd need to go back to Chicago and take care of dear Aunt Lavinia, but it's still a *terrible* wrench to leave."

"Yes, ma'am," Wyatt said, at a loss.

"I have so many friends here," Fiona said.

"I reckon you probably do." Did Sarah have lunch on the table? Was she wondering what was keeping him?

"And it's only out of pure friendship that I'd say this—"

Wyatt braced himself, knowing there would be no escape. Waited.

"I'm convinced," Fiona told him, "that Sarah Tamlin hasn't *saved herself.*"

For a moment, Wyatt was adrift. Sarah played the organ at revivals and in church. It seemed probable that she would have gotten around to getting saved at some point, not that Wyatt required salvation of a wife. Just fidelity, the truth, and a willingness to bear his children.

Then he realized what Fiona was really saying. "Those," he said, "are not the words of a friend." He started around Fiona, not bothering to tip his hat a second time.

She chased after him, caught at his arm. "She got into some kind of trouble when she was in college," she sputtered, "and some folks are even saying that boy she's keeping for Mr. Langstreet is *her son.*"

Wyatt felt as though he'd been kicked by a mule, square in the center of his stomach. The breath went out of him. So *that* was why she looked at Owen the way she did, why she reached out to muss his hair and then quickly withdrew her hand.

"And," Fiona went mercilessly on, "Sarah's mother's maiden name was *Owen.*"

Wyatt was annoyed—with himself, for not guessing at something so obvious, with Fiona for talking behind Sarah's back. Once he'd gotten over the initial shock, though, he felt the same nervous jubilation he had signing the papers to buy fifty acres and a shack.

Sarah's secrets were unraveling, one after the other.

Before long, he'd know all about her.

CHAPTER TWELVE

SARAH HAD BEEN ENJOYING a run of good luck with her cooking, but that day, the tide turned. She'd put a pot of potato soup on the stove to simmer, before going with Owen to the mercantile, and when she and the boy came through the kitchen door, the room was full of scorched-smelling smoke. Lonesome, confined to the spare room during their absence lest he chew a table leg or gnaw on the piano stool cushion, barked frantically.

Sarah rushed to take the pan off the stove, dumping it into the sink. She flung up the kitchen window and surveyed the room, looking for flames.

Fortunately, there were none.

Owen hurried to set Lonesome free.

The dog hobbled out of confinement and gazed at a coughing Sarah in baleful curiosity.

Now what was she going to do for food? Wyatt and her father would be along at any minute, probably ravenous, and she would have nothing to give them.

Owen ducked back into his room, followed by Lonesome, and when he came back, he was wearing his stiff new dungarees and the flour-sack shirt, blue with tiny white dots in the pattern. "Me and Lonesome," he said solemnly, "could go back to the mercantile and get some bologna."

"Good idea," Sarah said, fanning the room with a dish towel in a fruitless effort to disperse the smoke. She paused in her efforts long enough to take a coin from her handbag. "Buy a loaf of bread, too. If Mabel asks why I haven't done my baking, tell her I've been too busy."

Owen accepted the coin.

"Maybe Lonesome ought to stay here

with me," Sarah suggested, eyeing the dog worriedly.

"He'll pine," Owen objected. "Anyhow, Wyatt told me Lonesome should move around as much as he can."

"Very well," Sarah allowed, distracted, "but if he gets too tired, bring him back home immediately."

Owen nodded and left the house, Lonesome padding stoically along behind him.

Sarah went back to fluttering her dish towel.

Several minutes had passed, she supposed, when she heard Wyatt's chuckle and turned to see him standing, hat in hand, in the open doorway leading into the side yard.

She flushed, oddly mortified. "I've burned the soup," she said.

He set his hat aside on the old chest beside the door, and entered the room. Crossed to the sink and peered into the kettle still smoldering there.

"I think that pan's seen its last," he said. "What kind of soup was it?"

It was unlike Sarah to fuss, especially over food. To her, it was just something one had to consume to keep going, like

coal shoveled into a boiler in a locomotive. *"Potato!"* she wailed, and then burst
into tears.

Wyatt turned from the sink, came to
her, pulled her into his arms. "There, now,"
he said, holding her close, resting his chin
on the top of her head. "It was only soup."

Sarah sniffled, making a mighty effort
to pull herself together. What was it about
this man that turned her into a person
who cried over *soup?*

They were still standing like that when
Lonesome joined them.

"I met up with Owen and the dog at
the corner," Wyatt explained. "Lonesome
was getting tuckered, so I brought him
home."

Glad of something to do, besides stand
there in Wyatt's embrace weeping like the
heroine of some silly road-show melo-
drama, Sarah went to fill the dog's bowl
with fresh water and shut the door. Most
of the smoke was gone, but the flies were
getting in.

That was life for you, she reflected. You
dealt with one problem, only to find that,
by doing so, you'd opened the way for
another.

When she glanced over one shoulder at Wyatt's face, alerted by some new tension in the air, she saw that he was watching her, his eyes somber, and a shade or two darker than usual.

"I met Fiona, coming out of the telegraph office," he said, as though this were a thing of portent, and not an ordinary occurrence.

Sarah wondered at his sudden solemnity; he'd seemed amused over the potato-soup debacle. "She'll be leaving us soon," she said mildly, taking butter from the icebox. Due to flies, she didn't take the lid off the dish, as she normally would have, but set it on the table. Doc said flies carried disease, and she believed him.

Wyatt started to speak, stopped himself. Clearly, he was in the grip of some dilemma.

Sarah stopped fidgeting with kitchen things, alarmed now. "Wyatt," she said quietly, "what's the matter?"

"I can't work out whether it's right to say what's on my mind or keep it to myself," he answered, looking pained.

Sarah donned an apron, tied it briskly at the small of her back, smoothed it with anxious, damp-palmed hands. "Tell me," she said.

"There's talk, Sarah," Wyatt said, and he looked miserable.

"This is a small town," she said, though her nerves were jittery now. "There's *always* talk. Did Fiona find out I took a bath at Rowdy's place the other night, after we washed down those poor men for burying?"

Wyatt shook his head. Swallowed. Glanced toward the still-closed door before looking Sarah in the eye again. "According to Fiona, folks are saying that Owen is your boy."

The silverware in Sarah's hands clattered to the floor, and she felt the blood drain out of her face. *"What?"*

"Is it true, Sarah?" She could tell nothing of his feelings by his expression, nor did she try. She hauled back a chair at the table and fell into it, windless.

Wyatt simply waited.

Sarah's eyes filled with a fresh wash of tears. She didn't mind the scandal for herself so much, but she minded for Owen. For her father. And even for Wyatt Yarbro, who would know if she lied, and walk away if she told the truth.

"Yes," she said brokenly. "Yes, it's true."

Wyatt did not walk away. He came over, pulled back the chair next to hers, and sat down, turning himself and the chair with him to look into her face. "And the boy doesn't know?"

Sarah shook her head.

Wyatt handed her a table napkin, and she swabbed at her eyes. Owen would be back at any moment with the bread and bologna for their lunch, and he mustn't see her like this.

"Langstreet?" Wyatt asked.

Sarah nodded. "I was such a fool," she said. "Young and far from home—"

Wyatt took her hand. Squeezed it lightly. "By my reckoning," he answered, "*Langstreet's* the fool. Why didn't he marry you?"

Sarah heard the side gate open, creaking on its hinges. Either Ephriam or Owen would come inside in a moment or so. She hastened to the sink, pumped cold water onto the table napkin, and pressed it to her burning eyes.

"Sarah?"

She turned. Footsteps sounded on the porch.

"Not now," she said.

Wyatt nodded, and Owen burst in, carrying a package, Ephriam directly behind him. For a while, Sarah was blessedly busy slicing bread and bologna for sandwiches, though at one point Ephriam asked if she'd been crying.

Owen had spared her from answering by announcing, his little face radiant with delight over the adventure, "She made soup and it caught fire!"

"It did not catch fire," Sarah protested.

"Almost," Owen avowed.

"There'll be no saving the kettle," Wyatt added.

Ephriam laughed, but the look of sadness in his eyes troubled Sarah. Silently, she scolded herself for not noticing earlier.

"Is everything all right at the bank, Papa?" she asked.

"Things are fine at the bank," Ephriam replied.

She had been bustling around the kitchen, too unnerved over her earlier conversation with Wyatt to eat. Now, she went to stand beside her father's chair, laid a hand on his shoulder, then checked his forehead for fever. His skin felt cool, taking the very warm weather into consideration.

"You don't look well," she murmured. "Perhaps you should lie down."

"Sarah, don't fuss," Ephriam said, pushing away his plate. He usually had a good appetite, but today he'd eaten less than half of his sandwich. Lonesome waited politely for the leftovers, sitting on the quilt over by the stove.

"I'll go over to the bank and finish out the day for you," Sarah said. "Maybe have Doc stop by and look you over."

"I'm *fine,* Sarah!" her father barked.

It was so unusual for him to raise his voice that Sarah started a little.

Owen looked on with wide eyes, and Wyatt was clearly wishing he'd gone somewhere else to have his lunch.

Ephriam gave a great sigh. "I'm sorry," he said. "Maybe I am a little tired. There was a lot of excitement last night, what with the fire—"

"If Ephriam takes a nap," Owen said, "do I have to, too?"

Sarah smiled, ruffled the boy's hair with

one hand. Over his head, her gaze collided with Wyatt's.

Is it true, Sarah?

"No," she said. "You can stay and look
after Lonesome, or come to the bank with
me."

Owen, apparently concerned about
Ephriam, since his eyes kept straying in
the old man's direction, elected to stay.

Wyatt helped Sarah clear the table.

Ephriam wandered off to his study, on
the other side of the house, and when
Sarah looked in on him, he was asleep
with a newspaper lying across his chest.
She bent next to his chair and planted a
soft kiss on the top of his head.

After that, she and Wyatt left the house
together, walking slowly along the tree-
shaded street.

"Why didn't Langstreet marry you?"
Wyatt asked again, once he was sure no
one would overhear.

"He was already married," Sarah said,
straightening her spine, forcing herself to
look up into Wyatt's face. "I didn't know
that—until it was too late."

She saw one of his fists clench, but he
showed no other reaction. Did he believe

her? she wondered. And why was it so important that he did?

"Wyatt?"

"You needn't explain anything to me, Sarah," he said. "Your past is your own business."

"I don't want Owen to find out," she told him. "He won't understand. He's too young—"

"He'll find out, Sarah," Wyatt interrupted. "Most likely, from another kid in the school yard."

Sarah's stomach jumped at the notion. If Fiona had guessed the truth, so had everyone else in town. It was only a matter if days, if not hours, before Owen knew, too. "You think I should tell him—before that happens?"

"That's up to you."

"Charles—"

"Damn Charles," Wyatt broke in. "He took advantage of you, Sarah. He brought that boy all the way out here from Pennsylvania and left him with strangers. What kind of man does a thing like that?"

Sarah pondered, a little stung. Wyatt had been calm before, in the kitchen, even gentle. Now, she knew he was angry. Now, or one day soon, he *would* walk away. Sure, he'd bought the Henson place, and like as not he'd settle down at Stone Creek. In six months or a year, he'd take a wife—some woman with no book of lies in her pocket—and given the size of the community, Sarah wouldn't be able to avoid seeing them together. Seeing the woman's belly swelling with Wyatt's child. They'd join the church, too, because married folks always did, and every single Sunday for the rest of her natural life, she'd be up there playing the organ while Wyatt and the missus sat close together in a pew, each holding the other's hand.

It was unbearable even to contemplate. How much harder would it be to endure the incessant reality?

"If I tell Owen I'm his mother," Sarah reasoned tonelessly, like someone talking in her sleep, "Charles will be furious. He'll never let me see my son again."

"Then you ought to get a lawyer."

"That would be a waste of time and money. I'm not on any official record as Owen's mother. Marjory Langstreet is."

"The one who calls him a bastard?" Wyatt asked tightly.

Sarah felt sick. What other abuses and humiliation had Owen suffered at that woman's hand? And how could Sarah bear sending him back to such a creature? It was small comfort that he'd be shuffled off to some new boarding school as soon as one could be found. He'd been expelled several times, apparently, but Charles would have no real trouble bribing some other headmaster, in some other town.

"What would you suggest I do, Wyatt?" she inquired, angry herself now, though not with Wyatt. No, she was furious with Charles and Marjory and all the bullies and coldhearted headmasters Owen had already encountered in his short life, and would again, if she didn't do something.

"Get married. Go before a judge and tell him the truth. With a husband, you might be able to keep Owen."

Sarah's heart, fluttering before, nearly quit. Her feet certainly did. She stepped in front of Wyatt, right there on the sidewalk, and stopped, staring up at him. "Get *married?* Where am I supposed to find a man willing to cooperate?"

"Right here, Sarah," Wyatt said gravely.

"That man is standing right here, in front of you."

Heat suffused Sarah's face, while hope flooded her heart. "You'd *marry* me, just so I could get Owen back?"

"I'd planned on doing that anyhow, at some point," he said.

Sarah blinked. Although he'd said he meant to court her, she hadn't taken him seriously. "But we've only known each other for a few days—"

"Sometimes, a few days is all it takes to know you want to spend the rest of your life with somebody. When I saw you sitting up there in the bed of Brother Hickey's buckboard, playing 'What a Friend We Have in Jesus' on that old organ for all you were worth, I knew, Sarah. I knew."

Sarah couldn't speak at all for a few moments.

Wyatt took hold of her shoulders, grinned down at her, though his eyes were serious. "I figured on being able to support you in a fitting manner before I put a ring on your finger, though. I don't own anything, Sarah, except a worn-out old horse and this six-gun on my hip. I served hard time. I've got twenty-six dollars and thirty-four cents in my pocket, and the promise of a job out at Stone Creek Ranch once Sam O'Ballivan gets back, but it might fall through, so I'm not counting on it and you shouldn't, either."

"Is this a proposal?" Sarah asked, ruefully amused and oddly dizzy.

"I guess it is," Wyatt allowed. "Nothing ever goes the way I plan it to. I was going to save up, buy you a ring, gather up some flowers, and get down on one knee to ask you to be my wife. Instead, here we stand on the street, with folks going by in buggies and wondering what we're up to."

Sarah hadn't noticed the buggies. The world had seemed empty of all sound, save her own voice and Wyatt's. It was jarring to come back to the normal stir and noise of Stone Creek.

"Don't you think we ought to talk to Judge Harvey, first?" she asked. "What if we get married and then find out we can't keep Owen anyway? We'll be—well—*stuck* with each other."

"I'd get the best of the bargain, if that happened," Wyatt said, a corner of his mouth hitched up in a smile so faint it broke Sarah's heart to see it. "You'd be the one who lost out."

"This is insane," Sarah said, staggered to realize how much she wanted to take Wyatt Yarbro by the hand, drag him before a preacher, and become his wife.

"Folks get married for crazier reasons," Wyatt said.

"I suppose they do," Sarah agreed, blushing again. "Mama and Papa's marriage was arranged, and they were happy together."

"My ma and pa got married because Ma was expecting me," Wyatt told her. "I can't exactly say they were happy, but I can't say they weren't, either. They had six kids together, and as much as Pappy was away from home, Ma always ran to meet him with her hems flying as soon as she recognized his horse coming down the road."

"I guess being happy isn't everything," Sarah said.

Wyatt arched an eyebrow. "What else is there?"

Sarah didn't have an answer, so she didn't address the question. "I can't cook very well. I just got lucky with supper the other night."

He laughed. "You're hard on pots and pans, I'll say that."

"It doesn't bother you that I'm—I'm not—pure?"

"Not if it doesn't bother *you* that I mean to have you every chance I get."

"Wyatt Yarbro!" she whispered, giving him a little push with both hands. But a thrill sang through her at the prospect of making love with him. She couldn't help imagining lying naked on a bed they shared while he kissed and caressed her. . . .

"Shouldn't we get on about our business before folks start stopping to join in the conversation?" Wyatt's words were sobering.

Sarah drew in a sharp breath, almost a gasp, as embarrassed as if he'd seen directly into her mind and read her thoughts.

Maybe, if the way his eyes danced meant anything, he had.

In any case, Stone Creek, a mere misty void only moments before, solidified around them. Streets. Houses. Trees. The everyday sounds of a small community.

"I've got some horse-counting to do," Wyatt said, walking again. Sarah hurried to keep up. "But I mean to go back out to my place tonight after supper. Put away my tools and inspect the lumber I bought. If you want to go along, I could hire a buggy from the livery stable."

"That," Sarah said, the banker in her surging to the fore, "would be an unnecessary expense. I do ride, you know."

"You'll go?" Wyatt asked. At her nod, he looked less enthusiastic than before.

"Unless you'd rather I didn't, of course."

He glanced down at her. "It's a shack, Sarah. Even after I rebuild the roof and the floor, it's still going to be a shack."

Sarah wanted to say that if they got married, they could live in her father's house for as long as necessary, but she sensed that Wyatt would get his back up if she did. She decided to broach the subject after the wedding.

If indeed there *was* a wedding. Sarah still couldn't believe it would actually happen. This was all a daydream, wasn't it? She'd come out of it at any moment, find herself at the bank, mooning at her father's desk.

"Why are you willing to do this?" she asked, keeping her voice down because they'd reached Main Street by then, and there were more people around. "When Kitty asked you to marry her in Kansas City, you refused."

"You're not Kitty," Wyatt said simply. He escorted her as far as the front door of the Stockman's Bank, tugged at his hat brim, and said he'd see her at supper.

THERE WERE TOO MANY HORSES in front of the Spit Bucket, so Wyatt went inside to look around. Things seemed peaceable enough, at least on the surface, and there was no one he recognized, beyond Kitty and one or two of the other soiled doves. Ever since he'd run into Carl Justice, in some part of his mind, he'd been on the lookout for Billy.

The quiver in the pit of his stomach, one of anticipation rather than fear, told him the outlaw would show himself in or around Stone Creek, sooner rather than later.

In the meantime, he'd be watchful.

Kitty, standing at the bar, chumming up to a cowpoke, saw him and came his way, hips swaying. She was under some strain—he could see that in her face.

"Buy you a drink?" she asked, running

a painted fingernail from the base of his throat to his belt buckle.

Wyatt shook his head. "I'm just making the rounds," he said.

"I heard Rowdy and Sam were on their way back," Kitty observed, after executing a fetching little pout when he didn't respond to the finger stroke. If Sarah had done that, he thought ruefully, he'd have given himself up to lust.

"That's right," Wyatt said, turning to leave.

Kitty caught his arm. "I still need a husband," she said. "Bad."

"I can't help you," he answered.

"It's Sarah, isn't it?" she asked, something jaded rising in her face, behind the paint and the weariness. "Sarah, with her banker father and her fine house and her fancy ways."

"She's made some poor choices when it comes to friends," Wyatt said, removing Kitty's hand from his arm. "I'd hate to have to tell her that."

"She won't know what to do in bed."

"I reckon I'll have to show her, then."

Kitty's face tightened.

Wyatt turned and walked out of the

saloon. It gouged him, deep, to know Sarah trusted Kitty, and Fiona, too. Neither one of them would spit on her if she caught fire.

He progressed to the jailhouse, found the charred beams still warm to the touch. Shook his head. Jody Wexler had raised a solid question the day before—if he *did* manage, by some miracle, to round up Paddy Paudeen and his bunch, where would he put them?

As soon as tomorrow, when the train came in, Paudeen would cease to be his problem. Still, it stuck under his hide like a nettle dug in deep that they'd gotten away with dynamiting the jailhouse.

And had he actually proposed to Sarah Tamlin on the street? Just flat out offered to marry her, without a ring or flowers, never mind a bended knee?

She hadn't said yes.

But she hadn't said no, either.

Basically, she'd said, "if."

If she had a chance of keeping Owen.

So maybe she'd marry him, but maybe not.

Wyatt braced one foot on a blackened beam and contemplated his situation. He *craved* Sarah the way some men craved whiskey. Her shapely body wasn't the least of it, or the most, either. Same with her mind.

Just the sound of her voice was something to celebrate.

The touch of her hand awakened everything inside him.

But did he love her?

He didn't know. He'd never been in love before, had no frame of reference for it, beyond what he'd seen of Rowdy and Lark and a few others like them.

Unable to stand still, with no hard work readily at hand to distract him, he visited all the other saloons in town. In each one, he was offered a drink, and in most of them, a woman, too.

He was passing the mercantile when Doc came out, carrying his medical kit in one hand and looking a little peaky.

"I'm wanting a drink something fierce," Doc told him.

"I'm wanting to keep moving," Wyatt replied. "You just walk along beside me and we'll steer clear of the bottle."

Doc smiled, but his eyes looked haunted.

Wyatt remembered Sarah's concern for

Ephriam, earlier in the day. He related this to Doc.

"Best take a gander at the old coot," Doc said. "And I could use a cup of Sarah's coffee."

"She's at the bank," Wyatt said, "but I know how to make coffee."

They headed for the Tamlin house.

"What's troubling you, Doc?" Wyatt asked, as they approached the kitchen door, after entering by the side gate. "That you'd be wanting whiskey after staying dry so long, I mean?"

Doc stopped, sighed, wiped his forehead with a wadded handkerchief. "There're days when I feel older than dirt," he said. "Older than God and the devil put together."

"Trying times lately," Wyatt said, referring to the shooting and the fire at the jail.

Instead of going inside, Doc sat down heavily on the top step of the little porch. Wyatt perched beside him.

He could hear Owen inside the kitchen, carrying on a one-sided conversation with the dog. It made him smile, though sadly. Charles Langstreet had *something* in mind—he wouldn't have brought the boy all that way if he hadn't wanted to get under Sarah's skin—but he wasn't likely to hand Owen over to be raised by Sarah and her train-robbing husband out of the goodness of his heart.

The boy was a pawn to Langstreet, part of some strategy.

Wyatt's opinion of the man, already low, took a significant dip.

"My little girl would have been sixteen today," Doc said, bringing Wyatt back to the matter at hand. "We always made a big fuss over her birthday, the wife and I. Spoiled her year-round."

It was his dead daughter's birthday. No wonder the old man felt melancholy enough to take a drink.

"I reckon if she could ask for a present this year," Wyatt ventured, "it would be that you stay on the wagon."

Doc's sigh was heavy with sorrow, and probably regret. He leaned back, rested the elbows of his sweaty suit coat on the floor of the porch. "I stay around here because Ephriam is the oldest friend I have in the world, and Sarah's dear to me, too. But sometimes I'd like to head off to some big city and live out the rest of my life wandering among strangers."

"A man can be just as lonely in a city as in a little town like Stone Creek," Wyatt said. "And folks around here need you, Doc."

"They've got Hon Sing," Doc said. "He's a fine doctor—knows twice what I do about medicine. Took a bullet out of your little brother last year and treated the wound with some concoction. The boy was up and around in no time at all. If I'd been the one to take care of young Gideon, he'd probably be lying in yonder graveyard, next to your pa."

Wyatt barely knew Gideon, but something in him seized at the thought of him gunned down, lying helpless on the ground or some floor, fighting for his life. He made up his mind to find out more about his kid brother, before the boy took off for college. "You're being a mite hard on yourself, I'd say," he told Doc.

"The only folks who come to me for care are bigots who don't want a China-man in their sickroom."

"Ephriam's not a bigot, at least as far as I can tell," Wyatt said. "He trusts you."

"That's because he thinks I saved his life. We were both young then. Soldiers, fighting a holy war. It was pure luck I didn't kill him, ignorant as I was. Back then, medicine was more like butchery. Nobody knew about sepsis—we operated with horse shit on our boots and other people's blood on our hands. There was never enough ether, let alone morphine." Doc paused. "Sometimes I can still hear those men screaming."

Wyatt laid a hand to the doctor's back. "You did the best you could with what you knew and what you had," he said, though he doubted the words were any comfort to Doc. He'd heard stories about the war from various old-timers who'd served on both sides of the conflict. Every one of them remembered the gore more than the glory, the horror more than the honor, and dealt with it as they were able.

A shudder went through Doc. "I lived to have a beautiful wife and a lovely daughter," he said, gathering himself to rise, go into the house, and examine Ephriam Tamlin one more time.

Wyatt rose, too, and just as he did, the door sprang open behind them.

Owen stood white-faced in the chasm. "Something's wrong with Mr. Tamlin," he said. "His eyes are open, but he won't talk to me!"

CHAPTER THIRTEEN

"R<small>UN AND FETCH</small> Sarah from the bank," Wyatt told Owen, before following Doc toward the front of the house.

Owen nodded and left on a barefoot run.

Doc had his stethoscope on, the horn-shaped end pressed to Ephriam's chest, by the time Wyatt located the old man's study.

"Is he . . . ?" Wyatt began.

Ephriam's eyes were open wide behind his glasses, just as Owen had said, and his mouth looked distorted somehow, and slack.

"He's alive," Doc said, listening earnestly to Tamlin's heartbeat. "I'd say he's had a stroke. Soon as I'm sure he can be moved, we'll carry him up to bed."

Wyatt nodded, feeling as helpless as Lonesome, now sitting on the floor beside him, whimpering low and deep in his gullet. "Should I fetch water or something?" Wyatt asked.

Doc shook his head, removed the earpieces of the stethoscope, and patted a too-still Ephriam on one shoulder. "You're going to be all right, old friend," he said gruffly. "You're going to be all right."

Ephriam Tamlin didn't look all right to Wyatt. The blue eyes, looming watery and wide behind their smudged spectacles, shifted slowly in his direction, and Wyatt thought he saw a fierce, proud plea in them.

He approached, crouched beside the old man's chair. "I'll take care of Sarah," he said.

"Owen." Ephriam labored to say the name; it was drawn out and garbled.

Wyatt nodded again. He had no more legal rights than Sarah did, where the boy was concerned, but he'd do his best for

Owen, and he wanted Ephriam to rest easy in the knowledge.

Doc and Wyatt waited for five or ten minutes, then Doc took Ephriam's feet, and Wyatt gripped the old man under the shoulders, and they carried him upstairs to his room.

Sarah flew in, hair coming loose from its pins, eyes half-wild with alarm, while they were making the old man comfortable. Owen popped up right behind her, stone quiet and half again as scared as Sarah.

"He's just sleeping, Sarah," Doc said quietly. "He's had a stroke, and there's no knowing, just yet, how serious it is. He could linger for years, or pass over today."

Sarah bit her lip, nodded. Hurried to her father's bedside.

Watching her, Wyatt figured he'd have done just about anything to make things better for her right about then. Changed places with Ephriam, gone forward at an altar call, anything.

Owen huddled close beside him; Wyatt put a hand on the boy's shoulder.

Doc caught Wyatt's eye, indicated the door. Wyatt, Doc and Owen left the room, descended the rear stairway to the kitchen, leaving Sarah alone with her stricken father.

For something to do, Wyatt brewed up a pot of coffee.

Doc and Owen sat numbly at the table, while Lonesome curled up at the boy's feet, with a heavy sigh of dog despondency.

"Is he going to die?" Owen asked, after working up his courage for a while.

Doc sighed, as sorrowfully as the dog had moments before. "I don't know," he said, and caught Wyatt's eye. "I mean to ask Hon Sing's opinion. Might be something he can do."

Wyatt nodded. Doc's despair was palpable. It was easy to see that he felt overwhelmed by his friend's illness, and hoped the Chinese doctor would have a solution. "I'll find him for you, if you want," he said, wishing there'd been some way to keep from treading on Doc's professional pride.

"He'll be over at the old Porter place," Doc said, and gave directions.

Wyatt didn't like leaving the house, lest Sarah need him for some reason, but he went off to fetch Hon Sing.

Wyatt found the Chinese doctor at home.

The man was ridiculously small, but there was a profound dignity in his bearing that made Wyatt like him immediately. He fetched a satchel and accompanied Wyatt back to the Tamlin house without questions or comment.

Sarah had come downstairs to sit staring, numbly, at the table.

Someone had given her a cup of coffee, or she'd poured it herself, but it sat, untouched and still steaming, before her.

Doc and Hon Sing went up the back stairs, conferring quietly as they climbed. Owen was on the floor with Lonesome, his head resting on the dog's back.

Wyatt, watching Sarah the whole time, helped himself to a cup of coffee and eased a chair back at the table. He longed to comfort Sarah somehow, but there were no words for it, at least none that came to mind. He sensed that the best thing was to let her be, but for his own sake, as much as hers, he couldn't bring himself to leave her.

Presently, her eyes found his, caught.

He nodded toward her coffee cup.

She picked it up in both hands and took a sip. Seemed to hearten a little, color rising in her cheeks, some fight in her eyes, though she still didn't speak. She drank more coffee, though, and seemed less like a saint staring at a death vision. Gradually, to Wyatt's profound relief, she rejoined the living, became more present somehow.

"Owen," she said, surprising everyone. "Come and sit here with us, at the table."

Owen got up off the floor and did as he was asked.

"I have something to tell you," Sarah said. She'd rallied that quickly, and was ready to undertake delicate work. Wyatt felt a surge of admiration, and something harder to identify.

Knowing what was coming, he slid his chair back quietly, meaning to make himself scarce.

"Stay," Sarah said. "Please."

Wyatt stayed. He couldn't have refused her anything, then or any other time, no matter how rocky a trail she was traveling.

Owen sat straight-shouldered in his chair, his gaze pinned to Sarah. And she told the story of his birth, the true one, and in great detail, but Wyatt noticed, if Owen didn't, that she took care not to lay any blame at all on Charles or Marjory Langstreet. Again, Wyatt marveled at her.

The boy listened with a sort of stiff stoicism—no tears, no interruptions, no questions. When Sarah finished, he got up out of his chair, strode across the kitchen, wrenched open the door and ran.

He'd run and run and run, Wyatt supposed, trying to use up the energy that had surged up inside him as Sarah spoke. Once, when Wyatt was just seven years old, his mother had given birth to a baby girl. The child, much wanted, was stillborn. And he'd run, just as Owen did now, until he couldn't run anymore, his feet pounding a rocky country road.

"Should I go after him?" Wyatt asked, when a few moments had passed.

Sarah shook her head. "He'll come back when he's ready," she said, sounding spent.

"That was a brave thing you did, Sarah. Telling him the truth, I mean."

She gave a tiny grimace. "My father is upstairs, probably dying," she said. "That makes the truth an urgent thing, don't you think?"

"I think you're a remarkable woman," Wyatt said.

A tear slipped down Sarah's cheek, and it was all Wyatt could do not to lean in and wipe it away. He didn't because, with all she had to endure, she had a right to any tears she needed to shed. "You don't know me," she said. "You don't know how many lies I've told. How many mistakes I've made."

"When it comes to lies and mistakes, Miss Sarah, you'd need to go a far piece to beat *my* record."

She chuckled at that, though with no amusement. Then, without another word, she got up, wandered toward the front of the house. Wyatt stayed behind, and in a few minutes, he heard the first soft strains of the piano. The song Sarah played was "Lorena," a Civil War favorite, mournful and poignantly sweet.

She was serenading her father, the old soldier.

Reaching out to him in the only way she could.

Wyatt was glad he and Lonesome were the only ones in that kitchen, because tears smarted in his eyes.

He hadn't wept since the baby girl died. Not even when he got word of his ma's death, or when his first horse, Whispers, succumbed to the colic and had to be shot, or when he lay down on a filthy cot to sleep his way through his first night in prison.

But Sarah's music, and the love she poured into it, tore a jagged rip in the fabric of his soul.

KITTY STEEL PRESENTED HERSELF at Sarah's door bright and early the next day, wearing a modest calico dress and carrying a valise. She'd colored her bright red hair brown, and pinned it up in a bun at the nape of her neck. The transformation was so complete that Sarah almost didn't recognize her.

"I've come to attend to your father," she told Sarah. "I've had some experience minding the sick."

Sarah, numb-brained after a mostly sleepless night—though he'd eventually come home, and refused supper, Owen wasn't speaking to her, and Ephriam's condition hadn't changed—stared at the woman, struck speechless.

"I don't need any pay," Kitty said, stepping past Sarah into the house. "Just a room and a meal once a day."

Sarah finally managed to wrap her distracted brain around what was happening. Kitty wasn't there out of the goodness of her heart, though she did have a kindly side to her nature. Her daughter, Davina, was due to roll in on the train any day now, and when she arrived, she'd find her mother working as an invalid's nurse, not a prostitute.

"Kitty—"

"I've quit the Spit Bucket," Kitty broke in, with dignity, though her eyes were desperate with hope. "There were hard words spoken and I can't go back there. If you won't take me in, I'll have no choice but to leave town before Davina gets here."

Sarah sighed. She loved her father with her whole heart, but tending to him in the intimate ways that would be required would be too painful for both of them. She needed Kitty's help, whatever the other woman's true motivation might be.

"All right," she said. "But the whole town can't be expected to lie for you, Kitty. Davina will hear about your . . . former employment."

"I know," Kitty said. "This way, though, she might not turn her back on me before

I get a chance to explain things. And I *am* a capable nurse. I took good care of my mother until she passed, and I had a husband and two babies then."

"You can have the room next to mine," Sarah said, and started up the main staircase to show Kitty the way. Kitty put her valise on the floor beside the bureau, took in the simple furnishings—a narrow bed with an iron headboard and foot rail, the one dresser, and a washstand with a bowl and pitcher on top.

"This will do nicely," Kitty said.

"Papa is across the hall," Sarah told her.

Kitty nodded. "Go on over to the bank," she told Sarah.

Sarah opened her father's door, stood just inside the room, watched as Kitty approached the bed.

Ephriam was sleeping.

Kitty adjusted the sheet covering him very gently—it was too hot for blankets or quilts—and drew a rocking chair up beside the bed to keep the vigil. The white lace curtains on the window behind her billowed in a blessed breeze.

Sarah watched for a few moments,

swallowed, and then went out, closing the door behind her.

Owen, Wyatt and Lonesome had gathered in the kitchen. All three were eating fried eggs and toasted bread—Wyatt's handiwork, Sarah supposed—and a place had been set for her.

"If you're my mother," Owen said, as she sat down to eat, surprised by the ferocity of her hunger, "then Mr. Tamlin is my grandfather."

"That's right," Sarah replied carefully, smoothing a cloth napkin across her lap. She was conscious of Wyatt watching her.

"Who was at the door?" he asked, after an interval.

"Kitty Steel," Sarah said, stealing a glance at him out of the corner of her eye. "She's going to look after Papa, for the time being, at least."

"Why didn't you bring me back to Stone Creek with you?" Owen asked, having mulled over the fact that the man lying upstairs, hovering somewhere between life and death, was his grandfather. "When I was a baby, I mean?"

"Your father wouldn't have allowed that," Sarah said.

"Why not? He didn't want me. Neither did Mother. Didn't *you* want me, even a little?"

Sarah's throat constricted, but she managed to speak in a fairly normal tone. "I wanted you a whole lot," she said. "But we don't always *get* what we want in this life, Owen. Mostly, it's a matter of making the best of things."

"Amen to that," Wyatt said, then looked as though he wished he hadn't spoken.

"I don't want to go back to Pennsylvania," Owen announced. "I want to stay here in Stone Creek, with you and Wyatt and Grandfather and Lonesome, even if I have to go to school."

"You definitely have to go to school," Sarah said. "In fact, it starts on Monday morning. I read it in the newspaper."

Owen digested all this. "When Father comes back, he'll take me away with him when he leaves."

The prospect made Sarah's sore throat worse. Was she coming down with something? It wasn't an unfounded fear; she knew, from working with Doc, that people could take sick in the morning and be dead by nightfall. She'd seen diphtheria kill that fast, and milk fever, too.

"I'm sure he loves you," she managed to say. "Charles *is* your father, Owen."

"I wish Wyatt was," Owen said. "Father doesn't love anybody but himself. That's what Mother says."

Sarah offered no comment.

Wyatt shifted in his chair, rose. "I've got things to do," he said. "Walk you to the bank, Sarah?"

She nodded and stood, finished with her breakfast. She'd been so hungry at first, but the conversation with Owen had turned her stomach into a churning knot.

"I'm coming, too," Owen said. "Once I've got Lonesome settled down for his nap, anyhow." Then, quite unnecessarily, he added, "The medicine makes him sleep."

Recalling the ruffians who'd come into the Stockman's Bank, intending to rob it at gunpoint if Wyatt's suspicions were founded, Sarah felt a stab of dread. "You'd be bored at the bank," she said. The word *medicine* had reminded her of the mixture of herbs Hon Sing had left. She was supposed to make a tea from them, and give it to her father three times a day. She would brew a cup before she left for the bank, and pass the instructions on to Kitty.

"You can make rounds with me," Wyatt told Owen.

Owen brightened instantly. "Do I get to go inside *saloons* and everything?"

"No," Wyatt said. "I won't be going in myself unless I have reason to believe there's trouble. If that happens, you'll have to come back here, pronto."

Owen sagged. *"All right,"* he said tragically.

Sarah found the little sachets Hon Sing had given her, put one into a cup, and poured in water from the kettle. Owen was clearing the table when she started up the stairs, and Wyatt was putting on his hat beside the door.

Kitty took the tea from Sarah's hands, her grip reassuringly steady, where Sarah had made the cup rattle in its saucer, and listened carefully to the instructions Hon Sing had left.

Ephriam was half-awake, pillows propped behind him, and there was a book open on the sheet, within reach of Kitty's chair. Evidently, she'd been reading to him.

Sarah watched as Kitty gave Ephriam the tea, holding the cup to his lips, encouraging him, soft-voiced and patient, to drink.

She was so intent on the scene that she didn't hear Doc coming up the back stairs. He was beside her before she knew he was in the house, and she started.

"What have we here?" he asked, seeing Kitty in the role of devoted nurse. Going by the look on his face, he, like Sarah, hadn't recognized the woman for a few moments.

"Kitty will explain," Sarah said. "I'm due at the bank."

With that, she left the house.

WYATT WAS WAITING on the spanking new platform at the depot when the train rolled in at midmorning. Folks leaving, folks coming in. Owen, who'd stayed behind at the house when he and Sarah left, sprang up like a bean shoot at his side.

"Guess you must have seen to Lonesome," Wyatt said easily.

"Yep," Owen confirmed cheerfully.

"How'd you track me here?"

"Most everybody comes to meet the train," Owen said, shouting to be heard over the rattling, screeching din of the arriving locomotive, pulling no less than ten cars behind it. "I figured you'd be no different."

Wyatt chuckled, even though he was both dreading Rowdy's return and eagerly awaiting it. If his brother didn't get off this train, he was going to be mightily disappointed, and about equally relieved. "Good thinking," he said. He recalled the boy saying he wished Wyatt was his father, back in Sarah's kitchen, and felt a little choked up. He ruffled the boy's hair just to have something to do.

The train stopped, huffing steam, and folks dragged their bags and trunks up close, anxious to board. It was one of the curiosities of folks who rode such conveyances, to Wyatt's mind, that they never wanted to wait and let the other people off first, so there'd be room for them.

The conductor got off first, but Rowdy was right behind him, and then Sam. There was no sign of the women and babies, or Gideon, either.

Wyatt drew a deep breath and waited to see what places things fell into.

Owen stared up at the two men, big-eyed with admiration.

Rowdy's expression was unreadable, and so was Sam's.

They both nodded to Wyatt, then went

to see to unloading their horses from a freight car down the line a ways. If they had trunks or valises, they must have meant to have them delivered or come back for them, because they didn't slow their pace.

"Was that the *real* marshal?" Owen asked, breathless.

Wyatt felt a little jealous, what with Owen being so clearly taken with Rowdy. "Yes," he said. "That's the *real* marshal. He isn't wearing a badge, so how did you know who he was?"

"He's famous," Owen said. "I read all about him in a dime novel. There was a picture of him in the front."

So now Rowdy wasn't just married to a beautiful woman who clearly adored him, wasn't just the father of a handsome baby boy and the marshal of Stone Creek. He was *famous.*

"You can't believe everything you read," Wyatt said. "Especially in those books."

"Are you in any of them?"

"Not to my knowledge," Wyatt said. The comparisons just kept on coming, and he fell short in every one of them. Not that he wanted to be immortalized in a dime novel, because he surely didn't. Most of them belonged in outhouses, not libraries, along with last year's mail-order catalog.

He crossed the platform, descended the stairs at the side, and went to look on as Rowdy and Sam led their horses, already saddled, down a ramp from the freight car.

When Rowdy finally broke down and spared a grin, Wyatt remembered how glad he was to see his brother.

"What the hell happened to the jail?" Rowdy asked, affably enough.

Wyatt explained how he'd locked up Paddy Paudeen's gun, along with those of his cohorts, and they'd dynamited the place to get them back.

Sam, already mounted, actually laughed. "Damn fools," he said.

"Where's Lark?" Wyatt asked Rowdy.

"She and Maddie are visiting friends in Phoenix for a day or so," Rowdy said. "Gideon stayed to buy some duds for college. He'll be along tomorrow, with Pardner."

"You still want work on my place?" Sam asked Wyatt.

Apparently, they hadn't found Billy

Justice, or heard that Wyatt had been a part of the gang, however briefly.

"Yes, sir," Wyatt said. "I do."

"Ride out, when you're ready, and I'll show you around. And don't call me 'sir' again. Name's Sam."

Wyatt nodded, so relieved he couldn't speak. He still had a job, a way to earn his keep, and Sarah's, too, if she chose to marry him, until he had his own place ready. Like as not, she'd be reluctant, with her father so sick and the bank to run and the whole situation with Owen.

He'd wait. Wait a thousand years if he had to.

Sam said he'd better get on home and see if the place was still standing, and rode out.

Rowdy led his horse, so he could walk alongside Wyatt and a still-gaping Owen.

Wyatt introduced the boy.

Rowdy grinned and they exchanged a handshake. "You mind taking my horse over to the livery stable for me?" he asked Owen. Most likely, he thought the barn had gone up in the blaze, too, being so close. He didn't seem concerned about the house, though. Someone else, probably Doc, must have wired a little more information than Wyatt had given. "They'll know what to do with him."

Owen was eager to comply. "Can I ride him?"

Wyatt frowned. "Do you know how?" he asked.

"Sure," Owen said, proving his point by mounting Rowdy's gelding. "I was on the polo team at one of my schools."

"I'll be damned," Wyatt muttered. "And here I thought you'd be more inclined to croquet."

"That's a *girl's* game," Owen scoffed, from the saddle.

Then he clicked his tongue and he and the gelding took off for the livery stable at a handsome trot.

"Who is that kid?" Rowdy asked, amused. "He sure is a hand with a horse."

"He's visiting Sarah Tamlin and her father," Wyatt said. The news of Owen's real relationship to the Tamlins wasn't his to spread. "I've—" he stopped, cleared his throat. "I've been boarding over there, since the jail blew up."

Rowdy's light blue eyes twinkled. "Is that so? Guess you meant what you said about courting Sarah."

"I meant it," Wyatt affirmed seriously. "I bought a place, Rowdy. It used to belong to some folks named Henson."

Rowdy looked surprised, but pleased, too. "Hell of a wreck," he said. "You'll need some help fixing it up."

"I'll be hard up for time, once I go to work for Sam O'Ballivan, which I mean to do, right away."

"I was hoping you'd stay," Rowdy said, as they walked, heading by tacit agreement for what was left of the jailhouse. "If things went sour between you and Sarah, though, I figured you'd take to the trail. Now that you've bought land, well, that puts a different light on the matter."

"Did you catch up to those vigilantes?" Wyatt asked, then held his breath while he waited for his brother's answer.

Rowdy nodded. "Sam and I hauled them across from the Mexican side. They're in jail in Tombstone. Lots of folks would just as soon see them turned loose, given that they hanged two members of the Justice

gang and some saw that as a public ser-
vice, but the law's the law. Men can't be
taking it into their own hands."

"There was a gunfight here, Rowdy,"
Wyatt said. "Three men died, and one of
them was Carl Justice. I figure his older
brother Billy will be along one of these
days."

"Doc sent me a telegram right after it
happened," Rowdy said, confirming Wyatt's
earlier suspicion. Then his expression
turned thoughtful. "You knew one of the
Justice boys?" he asked.

It was uncertain ground. Wyatt trod it
carefully. "I was on the wrong side of the
law most of my life, Rowdy," he said. "I
know a lot of outlaws."

"I was, too," Rowdy reminded him. "But I
never crossed paths with Billy Justice and
his bunch. You think Billy will be drawn to
Stone Creek because his brother died
here?"

"No doubt in my mind," Wyatt said
grimly.

They'd reached the jailhouse now.
Rowdy surveyed the ruins and gave a low
whistle of exclamation.

"I guess I shouldn't have locked up those guns," Wyatt said.

"I would have done the same thing," Rowdy told him, raising his eyes to the little house behind the burned-out jail. "At least the house and barn didn't go. Lark would be plenty riled if she lost that big-city bathtub of hers."

Wyatt chuckled. "It's a fine piece of equipment," he said. "I used it once." That was the extent of his confiding; he wasn't about to add that Sarah had bathed there, too. She'd already laundered the dress she'd borrowed from Lark, and Wyatt had returned it to its place in the wardrobe.

"You're welcome to the tub, Wyatt," Rowdy said.

"I owe you for groceries," Wyatt answered. "You going after Paudeen and the others? Because I'll go with you if you do."

Rowdy shook his head. "If they come back on their own, we'll deal with them. If they stay clear, so much the better."

They went inside the house, Rowdy in the lead. Rowdy hung his hat on a peg next to the door, and Wyatt followed suit.

"If I could have the use of Sugarfoot until I get another horse," he said, "I'd be obliged."

Rowdy nodded, took the coffeepot off the stove, and carried it to the sink to rinse and fill. After adding ground beans to the basket, he set the works on the stove and built a fire under it.

They left the door open, on account of the heat.

"Tell me what you know about the Justice boys," Rowdy said.

"Not much," Wyatt answered, and that was true as far as it went. He'd ridden with them for less than a month, helped them set up the rustling of those five hundred cattle, but neither he nor Billy were the sort to exchange confidences around a campfire. "They've done some rustling, and Billy's got a reputation for being hotheaded and vengeful as a wildcat caught in a swarm of bees." He paused, cleared his throat again. "Rowdy, if a man was with somebody when they were fixing to steal cattle, but hadn't gotten around to doing it yet, would he be guilty of a crime?"

Rowdy, busy with his coffee-brewing before, stopped and looked so deep into Wyatt that he'd have sworn he felt his brother's gaze clear to his backbone. "I guess that depends on whether or not the cattle in question were still on the land where they belonged, and if anybody got shot trying to stop the rustlers."

Wyatt said nothing. He was dizzy with relief. They'd rounded up the cattle on an apparently deserted ranch owned by a family named Donagher. No one had come forward to prevent the rustling, and as far as he knew, nobody had been hurt, either.

"But what if a man *intended* to steal cattle?"

"There's no law against intending to do something," Rowdy said. Wyatt could almost see wheels turning behind those Yarbro-blue eyes. "It's the following through that matters."

Wyatt let out his breath.

"Are you telling me that you were with the Justice gang when they went after the Donagher herd and riled up the neighboring ranchers?"

"What if I am?"

"If you are, Billy Justice probably *will*

come after you. I'll stand with you if he does."

"He'll come," Wyatt said.

"We'll be ready," Rowdy replied.

Wyatt unpinned his badge, laid it on the table. He was surprised by the regret he felt, letting it go. For a little while, he'd stood for the same values as the nickel-plated star, much as he'd botched things.

"Thanks," he said. And he wasn't just talking about his brief stint as a deputy.

Rowdy nodded. "I guess you'll be heading out to Sam's now."

"Yep," Wyatt said, walking to the door, taking his hat down off the peg.

The coffee was beginning to perk, but he was too restless to stay around swilling the stuff. He wanted a look at Stone Creek Ranch, needed to map out his duties in his mind.

Owen was still at the livery stable when he went to claim Sugarfoot. He'd finagled himself a quarter's worth of work by offering to muck out stalls.

"I'm going to buy a couple of dime novels with this money," he told Wyatt proudly.

Wyatt grinned as he went into Sugarfoot's stall and set about saddling him up.

"Seems like a waste to me," he said, "but I guess it's better than rock candy to rot your teeth."

Some of the shine had gone off Owen when he realized what Wyatt was doing. "You leavin'?" he asked. He was already picking up the Western vernacular, for better or worse, dropping his *g's* and shortening sentences to pertinent words. "For good?"

Wyatt swung up into the saddle. "No," he said.

"Where's your badge?"

"Gave it back to Rowdy."

Owen sagged a little. "Oh."

Wyatt rode past the kid, out into the sunlight.

"Where you headed?" Owen called after him. "Can I go along?"

Wyatt reined in, turned Sugarfoot, and looked the boy in the eye. "You've got to earn that quarter you told me about," he said. "I'm going to Stone Creek Ranch, to see about a job."

Owen looked relieved. "Can I go some other time?"

"Some other time," Wyatt agreed.

Parts of his heart were light as he turned his horse back in the direction of Sam O'Ballivan's ranch, but parts of it were heavy, too.

CHAPTER FOURTEEN

SAM O'BALLIVAN'S SPREAD WAS something to behold, sprawling across a broad and shallow valley the way it did, with a creek running through so the cattle would have fresh water all year long. There were two houses, both sizable and some distance apart, and one good barn, with what looked like a bunkhouse behind it, and a small cabin beyond that.

Wyatt felt his spirits rise at this reminder of what a man could do, could build and sustain, if he worked hard and played the cards he'd been dealt. He began to see his own hardscrabble little place as it might be, one day.

To the east, he saw Sam's herd, grazing in a high meadow. There must have been a thousand cattle, and he counted five wranglers on horseback, driving strays back to the main bunch.

For the length of a heartbeat, Wyatt was back on the Donagher place, outside Haven, with the storm coming on and the stampede still in his future, and even though the sky was clear and china-blue, he felt the same inexorable sense of dread he had then.

He shook it off. That had been a different time and a different place.

Seeing Sam come out of the barn, Wyatt rode down off the rise toward him.

O'Ballivan, wearing work clothes, with his sleeves rolled up, and manure-caked boots, greeted him with a half smile.

"Only five men tending a herd that big?" Wyatt asked, without meaning to. He swung down off Sugarfoot's sweaty back, and he and Sam shook hands.

"Bunch of yahoos," Sam allowed. "All of them still green as the first corn crop. I don't think one of them is over seventeen. Most of my hands quit on me to go mining for copper down around Bisbee."

The youth, inexperience and limited number of the crew explained, at least partially, why a man like Sam would hire somebody he didn't really know for a fore-man, even on the word of a good friend like Rowdy. Wyatt's own experience with cattle was pretty much limited to stealing them—he'd done that when he was young, given the uncertain pecuniary nature of the train-robbing business—but it was work any halfway competent man could do, long as he had some stamina and could sit a horse.

"I'll show you to your quarters," Sam said, starting off toward the cabin. "You'll take your meals in the bunkhouse, or with Maddie and me if she's of a mind to cook on any given day." He spared another smile at this, gone as quick as it came. Sam O'Ballivan, Wyatt concluded, wasn't the effusive type. "You'll have a string of six horses to choose from, Sundays off unless there's a need to stay on here for some reason, and you'll get extra wages for that. Your job is to ride herd over the cowpokes, more than the cattle. If you can round up any spare help, I'd be glad to hire them on, too. In a month or so, we'll have some culling to do, and we'll drive the critters to the railway, a few miles east of Stone Creek, and load them into cattle cars. They'll be sold in Phoenix, and after that, you can take a week or two off if you're so inclined. Winter's mostly taken up keeping the bulls and heifers and calves alive. The wolves get hungry around that time of year, so we'll be on the lookout for them. Job involves some ice-breaking, too, when the creek freezes, and driving wagonloads of hay out to the pastures. We use dray horses and flatbed sleighs when the snow gets deep. It's cold, hard work, but there's a lot of free time for sitting around the stove, too."

Wyatt took all this in, surprised by none of it. He was thinking of his own little spread, and how he'd spend his Sundays there, driving nails and digging out the well.

A smile touched his mouth. His ma surely wouldn't have approved of his working on the Sabbath Day, but to Wyatt's way of thinking, it would be a holy labor. Where he'd fit Sarah into all this, he didn't know.

They reached the cabin, a sturdy-looking little house, obviously new, with glass and even curtains at the windows. Inside, Wyatt found the accommodations more than satisfactory. There was a sink with a hand-pump, a big freestanding copper bathtub, a stove so new the chrome fenders still gleamed, a table with two chairs, and a wide bed with what looked like a decent mattress. The floor wasn't plain, hard-packed dirt, like it would be in many such places, but smoothly planed planks. There was even a private outhouse, newly built, and a lean-to for firewood. The shelves were stocked with canned goods, should the foreman choose to eat alone, and pots and pans were provided, along with a blue enamel coffeepot and some mismatched cups and plates. Quilts and good sheets lay neatly folded at the foot of the bed.

The place was a palace to a man who'd slept on the ground or on a prison cot so many nights. But Sarah would find it only slightly more habitable than the shack on his land, most probably.

"You can move your gear in tonight, if you'd like, and start work tomorrow morning. There'll be coffee and hot grub in the bunkhouse at five-thirty."

Wyatt nodded, figuring Sam O'Ballivan had probably said more words in the last twenty minutes than in the better part of a year, if he was right in his assessment of the man's character. "What I rightfully own," Wyatt told Sam, "is in my saddlebags. I'll bring it inside and ride out for a look at the herd, if you don't object."

Sam nodded, the matter settled in his mind. He might have been pleased that Wyatt meant to start work immediately, but it was hard to tell. Sam offered to advance a month's wages if Wyatt could use it.

Wyatt refused. He still had most of the money Rowdy had given him, and that chafed at him plenty. What with the mortgage, he owed enough.

Sam went to the doorway, stood in a shaft of sunlight peppered with fine golden dust. "You might have a little trouble with the hands," he said. "They're young, like I said, and most of them are knotheads."

Kids, Wyatt thought. They were the least of his worries.

Sam took his leave, saying he had paperwork to do back at the main house.

Wyatt brought in his saddlebags and put his few belongings in likely places, and they were so few that they hardly changed the look of the place at all. He found a tin of peaches on the shelf, opened it with his pocketknife, and drank the juice before spearing the sweet slices of fruit and devouring them.

Thus restored, he went back outside, mounted Sugarfoot, and rode toward the herd, with his hopes high and that feeling of impending disaster still nettling the pit of his stomach.

WHEN THOMAS RUSHED IN after meeting the morning train, as he always did, Sarah was briefly alarmed, certain he was about to tell her that Charles had returned. With her father so ill, she'd have no hope of convincing him things were fine at the bank, and worse, seeing that Owen had become attached to her and Ephriam, he might take him away immediately. Or send the boy back East alone, while he stayed to destroy Sarah's means of livelihood.

Of course it wasn't the *only* means. She could marry Wyatt, take in boarders—or fill Kitty's place at the Spit Bucket Saloon.

A shiver went through her.

"Rowdy and Sam are back," Thomas announced, instead. He looked so profoundly relieved that Sarah forgot her worrisome prospects and stared at him. "Mother says we could have been murdered in our beds, with a criminal in charge of the town."

Sarah bristled immediately. "A *criminal?*" she repeated. "Are you referring to Wyatt Yarbro?"

Thomas seemed taken aback by her reaction. Maybe he'd expected her to agree—and earlier, before she'd gotten to know Wyatt, she would have. "Well," he said nervously, mopping his broad forehead with an oversize handkerchief, "he freely *admits* that he used to rob trains. Mother said if he'd gone forward at the altar call, when Brother Hickey was here, she'd take a more charitable view of his character."

Thomas's mother, one of those who went forward for a new allotment of salvation every year and kept strict tabs of those who didn't, had probably never taken a charitable view of anyone.

"That's ridiculous," Sarah said. "People

change, Thomas. Rowdy used to be a wanted man, and everyone trusts *him*."

Before Thomas could reply to that, Owen burst through the door behind him, nearly startling the poor teller right into next week. He waved two books with yellow covers over his head.

"I earned the money to buy these!" he crowed. "Mucking out stalls!"

Sarah eyed his manure-stained dungarees. "In your new clothes, Owen?" she asked, but she couldn't bring herself to actually scold him.

"They'll wash," Owen said, beaming, almost breathless with excitement. "Wyatt's in these books! In one, he's a train robber. In the other, he holds up a bank—"

Thomas raised his eyebrows.

Sarah blushed a little.

"I'm going to read them to Grandfather," Owen rushed on.

Sarah took the books from her son's grubby hand and surveyed the lurid covers. Sure enough, the first, entitled, *Wyatt Yarbro, Terror of the Nation's Railways,* showed a rider lying in wait for an unsuspecting train, rifle in hand, bandanna covering his face. The second, *Wyatt Yarbro,*

Robbing the Rich to Save the Poor, depicted a man with blazing six-guns in both hands, and bags of money at his feet. Behind him, a woman cowered, one hand over her mouth.

"Good heavens," Sarah said. "Wyatt ought to sue these people."

"Where there's smoke," Thomas muttered righteously, taking his normal place behind the counter, "there's fire."

Sarah glared at him until he wilted.

Owen, most of the conversation having gone right over his head, waited anxiously for the return of the dime novels. Perhaps, Sarah thought, he'd already read them, since he seemed to know so much about the stories. If so, he was bright for his age; short as the books were, they were geared toward an adult audience.

She returned the pulp-bound volumes, though reluctantly. She was not one to discourage reading, whatever the contents of the books in question. And, because the wild yarns were supposedly about Wyatt, she secretly yearned to read them herself.

"Are you coming home to make us lunch, Aunt Sarah?" Owen's face changed.

"What am I supposed to call you now that I know you're—"

"'Sarah' will be fine for the time being," she broke in hastily, aware of Thomas's renewed and very avid interest. The secret was out, but she didn't want Thomas's mother to be among the first to have it confirmed.

Owen pondered that solemnly, and Sarah wished she hadn't intervened. Did the child think she didn't want him calling her Mother or Mama? The matter would have to be taken up in private.

"I'll be home in an hour," Sarah said.

"Can we have bread and bologna again?"

"I made soup," Sarah answered, smiling. "But you may have bologna if you want."

Owen dashed out of the bank, the two dime novels clutched tightly in his right hand.

"Mother says books like that will destroy civilization as we know it," Thomas pontificated, puffed up like an overfed rooster.

"Thomas," Sarah said crisply, "I have heard enough of your mother's sage opinions for one day. Now, please sort today's receipts if you don't mind."

"Yes, ma'am," Thomas said, red to the ears.

They closed for lunch five minutes earlier than usual. Sarah had already balanced the ledgers, recorded deposits and withdrawals, and cashed Charles's voucher, too.

Although Sarah set a place for Wyatt, he didn't appear for the midday meal. Kitty joined her and Owen, though, while Doc sat with Ephriam upstairs.

Owen ate quickly and went up to ask Doc if he could read the "Wyatt books" to his grandfather. Sarah excused him, keeping her eyes on her bowl of soup. This time, she hadn't scorched it.

"I'm thankful to you, Sarah," Kitty said quietly. "This is a fine chance you're giving me, and I won't disappoint you."

Sarah swallowed, nodded. "When do you suppose Davina will arrive?"

Kitty sighed, laid down her soup spoon. "Probably tomorrow. School takes up on Monday, and she'll need a day or two to settle in."

After Lark married Rowdy and stopped teaching classes, the town council had scraped up the funds to build a small house, hardly larger than Sarah's garden shed, as an abode for future teachers. Fiona had lived there quite happily, or at least without complaint, but now she was heading East to take care of her aunt. It hurt Sarah's feelings that she'd heard about this secondhand; she and Fiona had been friends.

"I guess we'll have to close down the Poker Society, now that you aren't working at the Spit Bucket anymore," Sarah said distractedly.

"We could play right here," Kitty said, with the merest flicker of mischief in her tired eyes, "in your front parlor."

"We could at that," Sarah agreed. They'd have to replace Fiona. Perhaps Davina would be willing to sit in.

"Will you come with me tomorrow, Sarah?" Kitty asked. "To meet Davina's train? Doc said he'd sit with your father."

Sarah nodded. She'd have to leave the bank to accompany Kitty to the depot the next morning, but she knew, for all her circumspection, that her friend could barely wait to lay eyes on the daughter she hadn't seen in so many years.

"Do you know what she looks like?"

"I'll know her," Kitty said, choking up a little. "But I'll be a stranger to her."

Sarah didn't reply.

"Sarah?"

She looked up.

Kitty reached across the table and squeezed Sarah's wrist lightly. "I did something I oughtn't to have done," she said. "I let Wyatt know I'd welcome his attentions—"

Sarah stiffened.

Kitty's smile was forlorn. "He put me right in my place," she went on. "There's a man who knows what he wants. And what he wants, Sarah Tamlin, is you."

Sarah was chagrined at the sense of primitive vindication she felt. She had no reason to mistrust Wyatt—or to trust him, either, for that matter. But she knew if he'd taken Kitty up on her offer, her own heart would have broken.

"Do you love him, Sarah?"

"I don't—I don't know."

"Take my advice—if he proposes, marry him, whether you love him or not."

Sarah wasn't about to confide that Wyatt had *already* proposed, after a manner of speaking. If her father hadn't fallen ill, she might have been planning the wedding already, though she had yet to speak with Judge Harvey about Owen. Franklin Harvey was a kindly man, a friend of her father's, and she'd served him supper at this very table, many a time, right along with Doc and Papa. It was going to be difficult to tell him her story, especially when she thought she knew what he'd say in response.

Charles and Marjory Langstreet were Owen's legal parents, and her claim to be the boy's mother would amount to nothing more than hearsay in a court of law. Marrying Wyatt wouldn't change that.

"Sarah?"

She realized she hadn't replied to Kitty's remark.

Kitty didn't wait for a reply, though. "There aren't many men like Wyatt Yarbro. And it's a hard, cold world out there without one, whatever the fire-eaters say about women's rights."

Doc appeared on the rear stairs before Sarah thought of an answer. He nodded to Kitty, who hastily got up and carried her soup bowl to the sink, smiled at Sarah.

"Owen's regaling Ephriam with wild

tales about Wyatt," Doc said. "I'd swear the old coot is enjoying it. From what little I heard, though, Yarbro would have to be identical quintuplets to get all that done in one lifetime."

Kitty started up the stairs, returning to the sickroom, and Sarah noticed that her arm brushed against Doc's as they passed, and Doc's neck reddened a little.

He drew up a chair, the one Kitty had just left, and Sarah hastened to fetch a bowl and ladle out soup from the kettle on the stove. It was an old pot; she'd had to toss her good one into the rubbish bin when she couldn't get the black globs, hard as coal and sticky as tar, out of the bottom.

"Thank you," Doc said. He glanced toward the stairs, then asked quietly, taking up his soup spoon, "Do you think it's a good idea, letting Kitty board here? I know she means to make a new start, but—"

"There'll be talk?" Sarah finished, raising one eyebrow and smiling wanly. "Doc, there's *already* so much of *that* that bringing a former prostitute into the household to serve as Papa's nurse will be practically superfluous."

The old man chuckled. "I suppose you're right."

"What have you heard, Doc? You know everything that goes on in this town. Tell me—don't hold anything back."

Doc looked uncomfortable. "Well, a few people guessed outright that Owen is your boy. I'm a mite bothered that you never told me, though I had my suspicions. When Ephriam went dashing off to Philadelphia ten years back, with Nancy Anne so sick, I figured there must have been *something* wrong, but Ephriam never said, and I didn't pry." He paused, sighed. "Some say Wyatt is just cozying up to you so he can rob the bank one fine day—even that the reason he was able to turn Paddy Paudeen and those other hoodlums around was because *he's* the leader of the gang."

It was worse than Sarah had thought, if folks were thinking such a thing. And those damnable dime novels wouldn't help matters. She bit her lower lip, pondering, then asked, "What do *you* think, Doc? *Does* Wyatt plan to hold up the Stockman's Bank?"

Doc considered the question, rubbing his beard-stubbled chin with one gnarled hand. Arthritis had begun to bend his fingers, Sarah noticed, and she felt a pang of pure sorrow. "Ephriam was concerned about that, but he underwrote Wyatt's mortgage on the old Henson place, so that would indicate to me that he'd settled the matter in his mind."

"I didn't ask what Papa thought, Doc," Sarah pointed out.

"In my experience, outlaws are generally not the sort to lend a hand with dead bodies or bring a hurt dog to a doctor in a wheelbarrow. I could be wrong, but I'm inclined to believe Wyatt's like Rowdy. We talked, while we were getting those men ready for their coffins, Sarah, and Wyatt told me his mother was a good woman, that she'd be right proud of how Rowdy turned out. They were young, Rowdy and Wyatt and the others, and their pa was as famous as Jesse James. I reckon they followed after him like a bunch of hounds' pups on their first hunt. Like as not, they had prices on their heads before they figured out that they could have chosen a different way."

"I agree with you," Sarah said very quietly. "But what if we're wrong, Doc? What if Wyatt *did* come to Stone Creek to rob the bank?"

Doc's battered old face showed real sympathy. He patted Sarah's hand. "You'll have to trust your own heart, Sarah. That's about all any of us can do." At this, he glanced toward the stairs. "Sometimes, everything in the world seems to be lined up against you. All the evidence says you ought to run the other way. Make the bravest choice, not the safest. It's not the best advice, but it's all I have to offer."

Sarah stood, bent slightly beside Doc's chair, and planted a light kiss on his forehead. Her mind was full, and so was her heart, and it didn't occur to her until much later that Doc might have meant his advice as much for himself as for her.

SAM'S COWPOKES WERE KIDS, all right. Some of them didn't look old enough to shave. Beside them, Jody Wexler and his bunch seemed like seasoned men.

Seeing Wyatt's approach, the riders came toward him, converging from several directions. He waited for them, sitting straight in the saddle, and though he had a strong urge to resettle his hat, he didn't.

If this bunch got the idea that he was nervous about giving orders, they'd be unmanageable.

It would be a while before he could keep their names straight, but he shook hands with each one of them, no one bothering to dismount, and it was clear that they all recognized the name Yarbro.

"Seems we're a mite shorthanded," Wyatt observed. The boys looked as though they hadn't bathed since spring, and it seemed unlikely that they used their free nights to sleep, what with town, and the attractions of whiskey, women and poker so nearby. "Does Sam post a night guard over this herd?"

One of the cowpunchers—his name was Thaddeus if Wyatt recalled correctly—nodded, pushed his hat to the back of his head. He was blond, and put Wyatt in mind of a younger Rowdy, which might or might *not* be a good thing. "We take turns. Three of us ride herd from sundown to sunup, and two of us have the night off."

"Who's riding tonight?"

"Me and Jimmy and ole Robert E. Lee, here," Thaddeus answered.

Robert E. Lee, if that was really his

name, looked to be about fifteen years old. "Bobby-Lee," the boy said. "That's what I like folks to call me."

"Well, Bobby-Lee," Wyatt said amicably, "you can stay in the bunkhouse tonight, after supper. I'll ride with Jimmy and Thaddeus."

This offer, which Wyatt considered to be a generous one, caused some consternation in the ranks.

"You ain't gonna send me packin', are you?" Bobby-Lee asked, while his four companions shifted in their saddles, probably wondering similar things about themselves. "I need this job, and I'm a good cowpoke. Just because a man falls off a horse once in a while—"

The other four hooted at this.

"You damn near got yourself trampled!" one of them said, slugging Bobby-Lee in the shoulder with such force that he had to grip the saddle horn with both hands to hold his seat.

Wyatt suppressed a grin. "If you give me cause, Bobby-Lee," he said, "I'll send you down the road straightaway. Same goes for the rest of you. For right now, though, I'm just trying to get an idea how this setup works." With that, he rode off, made a slow circle around the circumference of the herd.

The cattle themselves looked to be in fine shape, well fed and well watered. The cowboys, on the other hand, couldn't fight off half a dozen spirited old ladies on burros, should said old ladies decide to take up the rustling trade. He'd see what he could do about recruiting some real ranch hands, first thing, though he supposed if Sam O'Ballivan hadn't been successful at it, *he* probably didn't have a chance in hell.

Because he had a few hours before he had to take up the night watch, Wyatt selected a sorrel gelding from the horses Sam had offered him his choice of, switched his saddle from Sugarfoot to the new mount, and headed back toward Stone Creek.

First, he left Sugarfoot at the livery stable.

Second, he rode out to his own place, to make sure his lumber had been delivered, and no outlaws had moved in in his absence.

Everything looked on the up-and-up.

He inspected the lumber, put the tools away in the ruined house, and hoped it wouldn't rain. With luck, he could spend Sunday working on the roof.

He hauled a few beams out of the house, and worked up a good sweat, and by the time he got back to Stone Creek, it was almost sundown. He drew rein at Sarah's gate, hoping to have a word with her.

She must have seen him through the front windows, because she came out before he'd even dismounted. He saw both a welcome and a stand-back in her eyes.

"You missed lunch," she said.

"I was out at Sam O'Ballivan's."

She shaded her eyes with one hand. "You'll be staying out there from now on?" she asked. He couldn't tell from her voice whether that was a sorry prospect or cause for celebration.

He decided not to get down off the new horse. "Yes," he said. "How's your father?" *How are you?*

"He seems to be holding his own," Sarah said.

After that, they were stuck for conversational fodder, the both of them. Wyatt probably would have tipped his hat and ridden off if Owen hadn't come shooting out through the front door like a live bullet out of a hot stove.

"You're famous, Wyatt!" he whooped. "You're *famous,* just like Rowdy and Sam and Jesse James!"

"What?" Wyatt asked, frowning.

"It seems you're the hero—if it can be called that—of two brand-new dime novels," Sarah said, in a tone that could have been called friendly or cool. Or both.

Owen vaulted over the picket fence and jumped up and down on the sidewalk, waving a couple of cheap volumes that looked more like magazines than books.

"I especially enjoyed the part where you robbed the bank," Sarah said mildly, but with a certain edge to her tone. "You went in with 'two six-guns spitting hot lead' and managed to marry the banker's daughter by the end of the story."

Wyatt scowled, leaned in the saddle. "Let me see those," he said, snatching the books from Owen's upraised hand.

He scanned the covers, read the print on the back.

His stomach churned, although he'd

been looking forward to supper up until a moment ago, given that all he'd had since breakfast was a tin of peaches.

"Did you really *do* all that stuff?" Owen asked, still jumping around. He put Wyatt in mind of something he'd seen once in Mexico—a pod with a worm inside it, trying so mightily to get out that it hopped all over the place.

"I can't say," Wyatt said grimly. After all, he hadn't read the books, and had no way of knowing how much truth they contained, if any. He handed them back down to Owen, though his gaze shifted to Sarah. "I'll tell you this much, though. I never robbed any bank—or married anybody."

"There were a lot of copies over at the mercantile," Owen said helpfully. "You ought to go and get some, before they're all gone. Folks were buying them up fast!"

Wyatt winced, wishing he could find the men who'd written those books and throttle them by the neck until their eyes popped out of their heads. But they probably lived in Chicago or New York or some other Eastern place. Someplace where they'd know *all about* the Wild West.

"I reckon I'll come to call on Sunday

evening," he told Sarah. "If that's all right by you."

"I'll be looking for you," Sarah said moderately, so he couldn't tell if she wanted him to call or hoped he'd stay away.

Wyatt tugged at his hat brim, reined his horse around, and headed for the mercantile.

He got the last two copies, supposed installments in his "life story," paid the princely sum of twenty cents for the both of them, tucked them inside his shirt, and rode back to Stone Creek Ranch, still bemused.

CHAPTER FIFTEEN

It was Thaddeus's turn to cook the bunk-house supper, Wyatt discovered, after putting up the sorrel for the night and choosing another for riding guard on the herd. The rule was, if a cowpoke groused about the food, he had to man the cook-stove when it came time for the next meal. Thaddeus, it seemed, had proclaimed the midday beans were too salty and the cornbread too hard.

Wyatt, being ravenous, consumed the burned hash and stone fritters without comment. He'd speak with Sam about hiring a cook, once there were more hands to feed. As it was, each cowpuncher was bent on making up the worst vittles he could, so as to inspire complaint from one of the others and get himself relieved of mess duty.

To Thaddeus's disappointment, nobody else bitched, either, though the grub was nearly inedible. God only knew what he'd serve up next.

Following the meal, Wyatt and Jimmy rode out to take over for the skeleton crew of three riding to the herd, so they could go back to the bunkhouse and eat. Thaddeus would join them after he'd cleaned up the dishes, also a part of the cook's job.

The dime novels he'd bought in town burned beneath the fabric of Wyatt's shirt, chapping his hide and soaking up sweat, but there was work to be done, and he hadn't had time to read up on himself. He'd be dead on his feet after guarding cattle all night, but he knew he'd crack those books as soon as he got back to the cabin. To escape whatever atrocity Thaddeus had in mind for breakfast, he'd fill up on canned goods instead.

As nightfall came on, the herd quieted,

and a full moon rose over the hills, pure silver and big as a barrel lid. Still, the hairs on the nape of Wyatt's neck prickled, and supper wouldn't settle in his stomach. The latter might have been the result of Thaddeus's hash concoction—he'd sworn his ma had made it just that way and been shouted down from all sides of the table— but it didn't explain the former.

Sam rode out around midnight, mounted on a fine stallion, and surveyed the moon-washed herd, periodically standing in his stirrups to stretch his legs.

"You acquainted with a kid named Jody Wexler?" Wyatt asked Sam. Thaddeus and Jimmy were on the other side of the vast sprawl of cattle.

Sam nodded. "Runs with his own bunch," he said. "His pa's so busy getting married and making babies, he doesn't pay much attention to the boy."

Recalling Wexler's eagerness to be part of a posse, Wyatt figured he might be interested in punching cattle. "If I can get him and his friends to agree, will you hire them on?"

"Surprised I didn't think of that myself," Sam said, with an agreeable nod.

That was the end of the conversation.

At sunup, the relief riders came. Wyatt gave a few orders for the day and rode back toward the main ranch house, stopping to put his horse away in the corral, and carefully avoiding the bunkhouse. From the smell coming through the open doorway as he passed, he concluded that Thaddeus was brewing up a stew of old socks and boot soles.

Behind his own door, which he promptly closed, he built a pot of coffee and opened another tin of peaches. When that didn't satisfy, he consumed some pears, too, smooth as alabaster and swimming in sugar syrup.

With his boots off and a cup of fresh, stout coffee at his elbow, Wyatt settled himself at the table and began to read.

By the time he'd finished *Wyatt Yarbro, Terror of the Nation's Railways,* he was laughing out loud. But *Wyatt Yarbro, Robbing the Rich to Save the Poor* had him hopping mad. If it had been *calculated* to turn Sarah against him for all of time and eternity, it couldn't have been more effective. Damned if the dim-witted heroine didn't fit Sarah to a T, at least physically. Her name was Stella, a wicked coincidence, and she wasn't smart enough by half to buttonhook her own shoes, *but* she ran the bank for her father and even had a fat assistant named Ted.

He needed a few hours' sleep, but Wyatt was too stirred up for that. He paced the cabin for a while, then went through his saddlebags for a scrap of writing paper and a pencil stub. He'd have to buy a nib pen and some ink next time he went to town, since a letter of vociferous protest written in pencil would make him look like a lunatic, but he had to get the words down somehow, or he'd explode.

So he looked up the publisher's address in the front of both books, and found they were one and the same. Wild West Publications, New Haven, Connecticut. Hell, if those yahoos had been working out of Cody, Wyoming, say, or someplace in Colorado, he might have been able to forgive them.

But *New Haven, Connecticut?*

He wrote furiously, venting his spleen, and when he was finished, he kicked off his boots, stretched out on the bed he had yet to make up with the sheets and quilts provided, and fell into a shallow sleep.

He dreamed Billy Justice was standing over him with the barrel of that shotgun of his shoved into the hollow of his throat, and awakened with a start, flailing one arm to knock the weapon aside.

The cabin was empty, but somebody was knocking at the door.

Still breathing hard, and a little shaken, Wyatt rolled off the bed and ambled to the door, grumbling under his breath.

When he pulled open the door, he found Owen standing on the step.

He blinked, thinking he was seeing things. It was a fair distance to town, half an hour on a good horse. Since there was no mode of transportation in sight—he leaned out over Owen's head to look for one—he guessed the boy must have walked all the way, probably following the creek.

Having figured out that much, he finally saw that the kid's face was flushed with exertion and streaked with tears. He stepped backward with a gruff, "Come on in."

"He sent for me!" Owen blurted out, before Wyatt could ask what was wrong. He'd been braced for bad news about Sarah, or Ephriam. But the boy waved a half sheet of yellow paper, obviously a telegram. "He wants me to come back to Philadelphia!"

"Take in some air, boy," Wyatt said, indicating that Owen ought to sit down at the table.

"I'm not going!" Owen shouted, though he did take a chair. His feet were bare and grubby with creek mud, and his overalls, probably bought new for the start of school, were ripped at one knee. "I'll run away— I'll—"

"Hold on," Wyatt interrupted, pumping some water into a tin mug and handing it to the boy. "Drink that down—slow—and talk sense."

"Read it for yourself!" Owen cried, but he took the mug, and he drank.

Wyatt scanned the telegram. *Sarah— Marjory gravely ill. Send Owen at once. Charles.*

"This is addressed to Sarah," he said quietly. "How did you come to have it?"

"She went to the train depot with Miss Steel," Owen sniffled, a little calmer than before, but not much. "I was at home with Grandfather when a man brought it."

"You oughtn't to read other people's telegrams, Owen."

"It's about me!"

"Be that as it may, your father sent this to Sarah, not you. Has she seen it?"

Owen shook his head. Dust flew from his fair hair, damp with sweat from covering all that ground under a hot September sun. "Can't I be *your* boy, now?" he asked plaintively. "He doesn't want me, none of them do!"

Wyatt's heart cracked down the middle. He sat down in the remaining chair and drew it up to face Owen's, so their knees were touching. "Listen to me," he said. "I'd like nothing better than to call you my son. But the fact is, your pa is Charles Langstreet. And aren't you even a little bit worried that he said your mother is sick?"

Owen gulped. Tears made little pale channels on his cheeks. "She's *not* my mother. Sarah is."

"Still, Owen, she's evidently under the weather. Don't you want to see her?"

"No! I hate her!"

"Drink some more water," Wyatt sighed, checking his watch. He might have slept another two hours or so, but with a crisis afoot, that was out the window. "I'll go saddle a horse," he said, as gently as he knew how. "We'll go to town together and see what Sarah has to say about this."

"I won't go back!"

"We still need to show Sarah this telegram."

Owen bit his lower lip, nodded miserably.

Wyatt ruffled the boy's hair. "Wait here while I saddle up," he said.

KITTY HUDDLED CLOSE against Sarah's side, there on the crowded platform—the new schoolmarm's arrival was an event— watching as the train came in. She wore one of Sarah's primmest dresses, and a bonnet, too, tied under her chin in a big, loopy bow. With her face scrubbed, she looked like any ranch wife come to town to bid welcome to an important personage.

Davina was instantly recognizable, since she was the only unescorted woman to disembark from the passenger car. Delicately feminine, she sported a simple black bombazine traveling ensemble and carried a parasol as well as a small beaded handbag. Her hair, visible in fringes around her heart-shaped face, was golden, and her enormous eyes were a remarkable greenish-blue.

Kitty stared at her, stricken speechless, and Sarah had to grip the other woman's arm to keep her from backing right off the platform and falling five feet to the rocky ground.

The young lady smiled a warm but shyly tentative smile as members of the school board and town council greeted her, though Fiona was noticeably absent from the eager throng. All the while, though, the marvelous eyes roamed, searching for a face Davina probably remembered only dimly, if at all.

"Speak to her!" Sarah whispered, giving Kitty a little shove forward.

Kitty stumbled ever so slightly, righted herself, and stood straight as a fence post driven deep into hard ground.

There was nothing to do, Sarah decided, but take matters firmly in hand. She approached Davina, introduced herself, and said, "There's someone here who's been waiting to see you."

Both trepidation and relief filled the girl's flawless face. Sarah hoped the school board wasn't naive enough to believe she'd be teaching for long. With her looks, Davina would be snatched up for a wife before the first snowfall.

Elbowing her way through the greeting committee, Sarah presented Davina before Kitty.

Kitty's mouth moved, but no words came out.

"Mother?" Davina asked, almost in a whisper.

Kitty still didn't speak, or move, though her whole body seemed to tremble with the need to embrace her daughter.

"Yes," Sarah said quietly. "This is your mother."

Onlookers began to murmur among themselves.

Sarah swept them all up in a warning glare.

Davina squared her small shoulders and put out a tiny, gloved hand in ladylike greeting. Clearly, her adoptive parents, or someone, had schooled her in deport-ment and good manners. All the social graces, probably.

Kitty hesitated, then took it.

For a long moment, the two women,

one world-worn and the other in the first dewy flower of youth, simply stood there, hands clasped.

Thomas's mother, Helga, stepped forward from the little cluster of people making up the school board. "Miss Wynngate," she said, addressing Davina, "we've prepared a welcome tea for you, over at the schoolhouse—"

Sarah met Helga's eyes. "She'll be along in a little while," she said.

Helga retreated a step, swallowing, her jowls red with offense. "But we've brought a wagon for her trunk and—"

"In a little while," Sarah repeated.

Gossiping in affronted words pitched too low to make out, Helga and her contingent of official busybodies departed. Friendlier women smiled in curious goodwill and went their own ways.

At Sarah's urging, Kitty linked arms with Davina, and the two of them set out for the Tamlin house, where they could talk privately.

"Tell her the truth," Sarah had advised, as she and Kitty approached the depot earlier.

But Kitty had shaken her head. "I'm going to say my husband died, and I couldn't run the ranch by myself, and I'm boarding with you to earn my keep taking care of Mr. Tamlin."

Now, watching them go, Sarah held out little hope that Kitty would change her mind. If she *didn't* tell Davina that she'd fallen from grace, and made her home in a room above the Spit Bucket Saloon, Helga and the others would waste no time in rectifying the error.

When Sarah reached the bank, Thomas was busy taking deposits from four men who looked as though they'd just made a long, hard ride from somewhere. One, a small man with bad skin, greeted her with a tip of the hat.

The gesture reminded her of Wyatt; she wondered how he was faring at Stone Creek Ranch and whether or not he'd come to call on Sunday. She'd been quite cool to him last evening, having just read of his alleged exploits as a bank robber and seducer of stupid, simpering women.

She knew such novels were sensationalized; the popular term for them was "yellow journalism." As a young girl, she'd read a few, in complete secret, and thrilled to the adventures of women like Annie Oakley and Calamity Jane Canary.

No human woman could have done all the things attributed to Miss Oakley or Calamity—Sarah had known that even as a starry-eyed adolescent. It was purely logical to assume that the spectacularly implausible feats ascribed to Wyatt Yarbro were tall tales bearing no real relationship to the truth.

Still, the bat-brained banker's daughter had struck a little too close to the bone for Sarah's comfort, and she'd withdrawn from Wyatt, if only slightly, in order to get some perspective.

And he *had* been a train robber, a part of the infamous Yarbro gang.

Doc's words came back to her, for about the hundredth time, as she ducked into her father's office, smoothed her skirts, and sat down to work.

In my experience, outlaws are generally not the sort to lend a hand with dead bodies or bring a hurt dog to a doctor in a wheelbarrow. . . .

Sarah straightened her spine. "Stop thinking about Wyatt and get something accomplished," she told herself aloud.

She'd been balancing ledgers for the better part of an hour, wondering with part of her mind how things were going with Davina and Kitty over at the house, how her father was, and what Wyatt would have to say for himself once he'd read those dime novels—for she was certain he would— when a knock sounded at the office door.

"Come in," she said, after patting her hair. She'd expected a farmer or a merchant looking to make a loan payment, or offer an excuse for *not* making one, so she was at something of a loss when Wyatt came in, steering a sunburned, sullen and filthy Owen by one shoulder.

"Give her the telegram, boy," Wyatt said.

Owen jutted out his chin. He'd been crying, his new overalls were fit for the ragbag, and his lower lip trembled. "I won't go," he said, taking the wired message from his pocket, crossing to the desk, and laying it in front of Sarah.

Her hands trembled as she picked it up. When the words registered, she gasped and put one hand to her throat.

"Everybody take in some air," Wyatt counseled grimly. He held his hat in one hand, and his clothes looked rumpled, though they were in considerably better condition than Owen's.

Sarah couldn't hold back her tears. "Owen," she said, in a ragged voice, and the little boy ran to her, scrambled into her lap, clung to her neck with small, wiry arms.

"Don't make me go," he wailed, wetting her dress with his own tears. "Please, don't make me go back there!"

Sarah looked up at Wyatt. He was a tall blur, standing awkwardly just inside the closed door, like someone on a narrow and rapidly crumbling precipice, poised either to jump into a rocky chasm on one side or treacherous floodwaters on the other.

"I won't," she said, holding Owen tightly. "I won't let you travel all that way by yourself."

By then, Sarah's vision had cleared enough to see Wyatt's jawline tighten.

"I won't," she repeated, this time for Wyatt's benefit. "Owen's only ten years old, and Philadelphia is halfway across the country!"

Wyatt sighed. Owen still clung to Sarah, his sobs beginning to subside, probably from exhaustion rather than a lessening of grief, and heartrending to hear.

"Charles must be *out of his mind* even

to suggest such a thing!" Sarah rushed on, frantic.

"Reckon he's not thinking straight, with his wife so ill and all," Wyatt reasoned calmly. Sarah felt a stab of chagrin, which only made her more impatient with Wyatt. "You could accompany the boy on the trip, Sarah. Or you could just send an answer by telegram, saying you won't allow him to make the journey without someone along to look after him."

Sarah rocked Owen, thinking hard. She couldn't leave her ailing father to escort Owen to Philadelphia, and she knew if she sent a wire protesting Charles's terse instructions, he would simply hire someone, a Pinkerton or a lawyer or a business colleague, to collect her child and put him on an eastbound train.

Still, she had to acknowledge the message in some way. If she didn't, Charles might call out the military, or something equally drastic. With his influence and resources, he could do it.

She took a deep, shaky breath. Used one hand to wipe her cheeks. Then she stood Owen on his feet, gripped his shoulders firmly, and looked into his eyes.

"I don't know what I'm going to do," she told him, "but I am going to do *something.* I promise you that."

Owen sniffled, nodded.

"You go on home, now. Read to your grandfather and look after Lonesome. I'll be along as soon as I can."

Again, the child nodded.

Sarah watched with her heart in shards as Owen left the office without another word, his small back straight.

"It might be a mistake, getting his hopes up like that, Sarah," Wyatt said.

"It might," Sarah agreed stiffly, rising from her chair. She'd leave Thomas in charge of the bank, send Charles an answering telegram, and pay an unexpected call on Judge Harvey.

"Owen came all the way out to Stone Creek Ranch on foot," Wyatt persisted. "He's full of talk about running away, so be real careful how you handle this."

"I'm grateful that you brought him home," Sarah replied, reaching past Wyatt to take hold of the doorknob and go about her business. She couldn't allow herself to think much about all the dangers Owen might have encountered—

wolves and rattlesnakes were only two of the many possible perils—she might lose her composure if she did.

Wyatt waylaid her, his grip light on her arm, but not to be escaped until he deigned to let go. "*Think,* Sarah," he said. "Be careful what you do. What you promise that boy."

"Let me go, Wyatt," Sarah said.

He released her.

And Sarah headed for the telegraph office.

"I'LL BE DAMNED if I know why she's mad at me," Wyatt told Rowdy, fifteen minutes later, as the two of them led Rowdy's horses back from the livery stable to settle them in the barn behind his house, where they belonged. "I brought the boy home, after all."

Rowdy's grin was thoughtful. "Women are complicated creatures," he said. "Once, when Lark was carrying Hank, I told her she wouldn't need a bustle to stay in fashion, and she cried for a week."

"You told her she had a big backside?" Wyatt marveled.

"That's how she interpreted it, anyhow,"

Rowdy admitted. "I *liked* the way she looked, but she damn near peeled off a strip of my hide."

Wyatt laughed, shaking his head. "If you're stupid enough to say something like that," he said, "I guess there's hope for me."

Rowdy slapped him on the back. "If you care about Sarah, and it seems you do, stick with her. She might lose the boy, there's no getting around that. Langstreet has the full weight of the law behind him. She'll need somebody to lean on, and even though she won't take comfort from it now, there'll be other children in time."

The thought of Sarah carrying, bearing and nursing his child filled Wyatt with a yearning so fierce, he ached. But he was fond of little Owen, and no matter how many babies he and Sarah had together, none of them could replace the boy.

Wyatt was silently miserable. He should have stuck to his old policy of not letting himself care too much about anybody. It had been one hell of a lot safer.

"After we put these horses away," Rowdy said, "let's stop by the dining room over at the hotel and put away a couple of specials. It's fried trout on Fridays, caught fresh in Stone Creek and battered as soon as they quit wiggling."

Wyatt's stomach rumbled. He'd long since burned off the pears and peaches he'd had for breakfast, but Sam O'Ballivan had given him a job and he meant to do it.

He was set on riding back to the ranch as soon as he and Rowdy got the horses back home—his own mount was still tethered to the hitching post in front of the bank—so he started to refuse.

Then he felt that prickle at the back of his neck again, keener now, as though somebody was watching him. Staring a hole right into him, hot as a beam of sunlight through a magnifying glass.

He stopped, looked around.

"Something wrong?" Rowdy asked.

Wyatt shook it off again. "Just a peculiar feeling," he said, just as Jody Wexler and his bunch rode around the bend into town and drew up to say howdy.

"I'm looking to hire some ranch hands," Wyatt said, glad of the distraction, and glad he might be able to make this trip to town count for something in Sam O'Ballivan's eyes. He'd sure made a snarl of things with Sarah, and never mind that he'd been trying to help.

She didn't want his help, and he was ninety-nine percent certain she meant to do something rash, if she couldn't reason Charles Langstreet into letting Owen stay with her.

"Be a good thing to get these wasters off the street," Rowdy joked, grinning at the boys. "They've got too much time on their hands."

"Not much money," Wyatt added, "and a whole lot of hard work. If you're willing, head on out to Stone Creek Ranch and pick out a bunk."

Wexler beamed, already reining his horse in that direction.

They took off, racing down Main Street, whooping and hollering like a pack of Apaches on the warpath.

Rowdy shook his head. "If I wasn't so set on eating trout for lunch," he said, "I'd lock the whole pack of them up for reckless behavior on a public thoroughfare."

"You don't have a jail to put them in," Wyatt reminded him.

"There's that," Rowdy agreed, with a nod.

They put the horses away, made sure they had plenty of hay and water, and headed for the hotel. The fish being fried up inside smelled so good that Wyatt relented, went inside with his brother, and ordered himself a special. For all he knew, Thaddeus was still in charge of the stove out at the bunkhouse, and a man had to eat, didn't he?

SARAH PRESSED PEN TO PAPER so hard, writing out her telegram to Charles, that she punctured it and even scarred the counter beneath.

"Guess you're some rattled, Miss Tamlin," observed the telegraph operator, who, like Thomas, lived with his mother and passed on every whit of gossip that came in or went out over the wire. Which, of course, was considerable. "Everything all right? I hear your father isn't well—"

"My father, Elliott," Sarah broke in sharply, "will be just fine."

Elliott reddened. "Yes, ma'am," he said.

"I need a fresh sheet of paper, please," Sarah told him, speaking more moderately, by dint of great effort and forbearance.

Elliott gave her the paper.

She wrote her message, which she'd been rehearsing in her head since she'd stormed out of the bank to send it.

Elliott's eyes widened as he read. Since he was the telegrapher, there was no way to keep the missive private. "That'll be twenty-five cents," he said.

Sarah took the change from her skirt pocket, since she rarely carried a handbag, and plunked down five nickels.

Elliott scooped them up, still blushing. "If there's an answer, shall I bring it to the bank?" he asked.

"The bank closes promptly at three o'clock," Sarah said, keeping her head high and her backbone rigid. "After that, I will be at home."

Elliott went to his desk and began tapping out Morse code on his telegraph key. Sarah listened for a few moments, as if she understood the incomprehensible dots and dashes and clicks and wanted to make sure the message was being sent correctly, then turned on one heel and marched to the door.

"Give your mother my best regards," she said, passing Elliott a level look.

Elliott, blushing fiercely, merely nodded.

Wyatt's horse, Sarah noted abstractly, was still standing in front of the bank, slurping water from the trough. Looking around, she saw Mr. Yarbro walking into the Phoenix Hotel with Rowdy.

Her hackles rose.

She crossed the street briskly, skirt hems fluttering.

Stomped up the steps in front of the hotel and straight into the lobby, then the dining room adjoining it.

Wyatt and Rowdy had already taken seats at a table by the window but, seeing her, they both got to their feet.

Sarah looked briefly at Rowdy, apologetically furious, then turned to Wyatt. If she hadn't been raised as a lady, she would have slapped his face for him, and the worst thing about it was that she didn't have the vaguest idea why she wanted to do that in the first place.

"Join us?" Rowdy asked, grinning slightly and gesturing toward the chair next to Wyatt's. "We've already ordered, but I could go fetch Wong Su from the kitchen."

"No," Sarah said, drawing herself up. "Thank you."

Wyatt raised an eyebrow, and a grin

twitched at one corner of his mouth. He waited, and it galled Sarah to know he was enjoying her discomfiture. She hadn't a glimmer what she was doing there, and that only made the whole experience more mortifying.

"Sarah—" Rowdy began, but he fell silent at a swift glower from Wyatt.

Sarah drew a deep breath, her face flaming, wishing the floor would open wide, like the maw of some great beast, chew her up and swallow her.

Still, Wyatt didn't speak. Still, he grinned that grin.

Sarah looked around, saw that the three of them were alone in the dining room, which was a miracle given the popularity of the fish special, and then faced Wyatt again.

"I telegraphed Charles," Sarah heard herself say, with helpless horror at her own audacity, "and I told him that you and I are going to be married and we want to raise Owen from now on. Are you willing to marry me or not, Wyatt Yarbro?"

Rowdy pressed a napkin to his mouth, probably to stifle a guffaw.

"I don't reckon you've left me much

choice," Wyatt said dryly. All that time not speaking, and *that* was what he had to say?

"Fine," Sarah said. "The wedding is Sunday afternoon."

"Don't we need a license or something?" Wyatt asked.

"I don't know," Sarah admitted, losing some of her steam.

"I can arrange for one," Rowdy put in. By then, he'd sat himself down again, and put the napkin aside, but his eyes were bright with hilarity.

"Well, then," Wyatt said, "I guess it's settled."

I don't reckon you've left me much choice.

Sarah seethed, swamped in humiliation. "Good!" she spouted, then she spun around and marched right out of the Phoenix Hotel, down the sidewalk a ways, and across the street to the bank.

She stomped through the small lobby, Thomas staring openmouthed as she passed, and into her father's office, where she slammed the door behind her, dropped into Ephriam's chair, laid her head down on her arms atop the desk, and cried until her eyes hurt.

CHAPTER SIXTEEN

THERE WAS NO SIGN of Davina when Sarah got home, at five minutes after three that afternoon, and she found Kitty upstairs, sitting with Ephriam, and staring bleakly into space. Except for their respective positions—Kitty in the rocking chair and Ephriam lying on the bed—it would have been difficult for an objective observer to discern between patient and nurse.

"Kitty?" Sarah asked softly, from the doorway. Owen, calmer now, was in the backyard with Lonesome, and the dog's happy yips wafted in through the open window. Lonesome, at least, was on the mend.

Slowly, Kitty turned her head, looked at Sarah without apparent recognition. Said nothing.

"Where is Davina?" Sarah asked carefully, going to her father's bedside to straighten the already-straight sheets and bend to kiss his forehead. His skin felt cool and moist. She didn't look at Kitty at all, during this exchange, giving the woman the privacy to shift from her sad reverie to the everyday world.

"She's gone to the schoolhouse," Kitty said, her voice toneless and, somehow, raw. "She knows, Sarah. She *knows.*"

There was only one chair in the room, and Kitty occupied it, so Sarah perched on the wide sill of the window. "You told her, Kitty? About the Spit Bucket Saloon and—and everything else?"

Kitty shook her head, her gaze fixed on the wall above the headboard of Ephriam's bed, or something well beyond it. Beyond Stone Creek, even, or the distant horizon itself. Perhaps even beyond the day-cloaked stars. "Someone on the train told her," Kitty said. "She—Davina, I mean—was chatting with the person in the next seat, the way people do to pass the time on a long trip, and said her mother was Kitty Steel, married to a rancher named John Steel."

Then, of course, the other passenger had disabused the young schoolmarm of her deception. Sarah closed her eyes for a moment, imagining what a shock that must have been to Davina. At the same time, she had known all along that discovery was inevitable.

"Did you explain?" Sarah asked.

"I tried, but Davina was having none of it. She said if she didn't have a contract to complete a full school term, she'd get right back on the train and head home to Illinois." Kitty paused, swallowed painfully. "She said I wasn't—I wasn't her mother, Alvira Wynngate was, because she and her husband took her and her sister in when I didn't want them."

"But you've been corresponding with Davina and Leona for years," Sarah reasoned gently. "You must have told them you *did* want them, even with all the lies about being married to a rancher."

"Being wanted by an upstanding mother who once fell on hard times is one thing," Kitty said. "Being wanted by one who's a whore and has to fight off the bottle every day of her life is another."

Sarah bit her lower lip. "At least she's staying in Stone Creek until the school term is over," she said. "You have until next summer to establish some kind of understanding."

"That's going to be hard to do," Kitty replied, "given that Davina never wants to see me again, let alone listen to me."

"With time—"

But Kitty shook her head, cut Sarah off with, "No. You didn't see how angry she was, Sarah. You didn't hear the things she said. I've met up with lots of women who wanted to spit in my face, even some who did, but none of them were my own daughter, my own sweet baby."

Sarah stood on shifting sands herself, given that she'd wired Charles of her impending marriage to Wyatt Yarbro, and then corralled Wyatt into agreeing to participate in the ceremony. Her father was desperately ill, and she was almost certain to lose the child she loved more than anything, or anyone, in the world, for a *second* time. And on top of all that, the bank.

Despite it all, her heart went out to Kitty, and to Davina, too. By now, the girl had probably written to her sister, as well as her adoptive parents, and any illusions remaining to Leona would be shattered. Sarah could only hope that Helga and the delegation had kept the young woman too busy celebrating her installation at Stone Creek School to fall into despondency.

She made up her mind to go and talk to Davina at the first opportunity. Perhaps, as a person one step removed from the situation, she could help establish some kind of truce between the two women.

"Why don't you go across the hall and rest for a while, Kitty?" she asked quietly. "I'll sit with Papa."

Kitty hesitated, then nodded, rose from the rocking chair. Moving like a sleep-walker or someone mesmerized, she left the room. Sarah heard the door across the hall open and close.

She sank into the rocking chair.

Ephriam opened his eyes.

"I'm going to marry Wyatt, Papa," Sarah said. "I'm going to be a ranch foreman's wife." The tears that stung her eyes should have been ones of happiness—she was about to be a bride at last—but instead, they were ones of frustrated humiliation.

Ephriam didn't respond, except to gaze at her, his own eyes suspiciously moist. He didn't need to tell Sarah what he was thinking; she knew. *What will become of my girl?*

Presently, he slept. Sarah sat and rocked.

And then Owen appeared in the doorway, red-eyed himself, and pale. He was a boy in summer, wondrously dirty, his hair a-tousle, his clothes speckled with mud and caked with dust.

Sarah's heart wrenched just to look at him.

"There's a lady here to see you," he told Sarah. "She's sitting in the parlor."

Sarah nodded, got out of the chair and adjusted Ephriam's covers again.

Owen took her place in the rocker, bare feet dangling high off the floor.

Hoping to find Davina waiting downstairs, having had a change of heart, Sarah was mildly disappointed, but also encouraged, to see that her caller was Fiona. She was dressed for travel, no doubt planning to board the six-o'clock train to Flagstaff, which stopped in Stone Creek only on Fridays, weekly in spring and summer, every other week in fall, and once a month in winter.

Sarah paused in the doorway of the parlor, at a loss for words; odd, when she and Fiona had exchanged so many confidences over the length of their acquaintance.

Fiona flushed. "I couldn't leave without saying goodbye, Sarah," she said, fiddling awkwardly with her practical handbag. "I—I hope you won't mind if I write."

"I won't mind," Sarah said, but it was more a concession to manners and traditions of hospitality than truth. She remained in the doorway.

"I shouldn't have told Mr. Yarbro what I did," Fiona said.

"No," Sarah agreed. "You shouldn't have. It might be easier to forgive you if you'd spoken to me first. We were friends, Fiona. I trusted you."

Fiona flushed. "No, you didn't," she said, suddenly recovering some of her spirit. "You could have told me about Owen, and your affair with Mr. Langstreet."

"Obviously," Sarah retorted, "I couldn't

have. Instead of coming to me when you heard the rumors, you went directly to Mr. Yarbro and tried to undermine his good opinion."

Fiona seemed to shrink a little, though she kept her head high. "You would have lied to me," she insisted. "You know you would have said Owen wasn't your child, that it was just nasty gossip."

Sarah couldn't deny that. So she didn't speak.

"None of that matters now, anyway," Fiona said. "I took one look at Wyatt Yarbro, that first day at Brother Hickey's revival, and I felt as though I'd stepped in front of a speeding train. I never wanted a man like I wanted him. But he was only interested in you."

Sarah said nothing. It had not occurred to her, in her self-absorption, that someone else might have been affected by Wyatt's charms the same way she had.

"I'm sorry," Fiona told her. "Not for loving Wyatt, because I can't help it, and I think I'll always care for him. But you were my friend, and I shouldn't have tried to turn him against you. I just thought that—well— when Aunt Lavinia passes, God keep her,

I'll be a wealthy woman. I was going to use that to win him over, but he didn't give me a chance. As soon as I said what I did, he turned his back for good."

"Are you sorry you betrayed me, Fiona, or sorry Wyatt didn't take the bait?"

Fiona gave a wobbly, faltering and wholly tragic smile. "I don't know," she said. "If you won't accept my apology, then there's nothing more I can do. But I had to try, Sarah. And I *do* wish you well."

Sarah nodded. "And I you," she said.

"Can you forgive me?"

"Probably," Sarah said. "But it will be a while."

"May I write to you?"

"Yes," Sarah answered, feeling even more bereft than she had earlier, because she *had* liked Fiona, and confided in her as much as she'd been able.

With that, Fiona gave a little nod, crossed the parlor, brushed Sarah's arm as she passed, and left the house.

CHARLES'S TERSE BUT SCATHING answer to Sarah's telegram came the next morning, a Saturday, while she was opening the bank for the customary half day. Thomas was off, and her father was sick, and so she was alone.

She gave Elliott a nickel for delivering the wire and stoutly refrained from opening it until he left. He'd lingered a few moments, waiting to see her reaction to what he knew was inside, but she wouldn't give him that satisfaction. He'd have enough to report to his mother as it was.

Am detained here for foreseeable future. Send the boy immediately or prepare to deal with consequences. C.L.

Sarah crumpled the telegram into a ball, fetched five nickels from the till, and hurried out onto the sidewalk to call Elliott back to dictate her one-word answer.

No.

She'd barely stopped hyperventilating when Davina Wynngate swept in, looking schoolmarm-proper in a modest brown dress, her spun-honey hair modestly but attractively coiffed.

"I've come to open an account," she said, none too cordial now that she knew Sarah and Kitty were friends. "I would have patronized the other bank, but it's closed."

Sarah rustled up a smile. "I'll be glad to help you," she said.

Davina looked around as she crossed the small lobby and stood, straight backed, at the counter, opposite Sarah. "I must say," the girl announced loftily, lifting her chin, "that I had forgotten how rustic the West really is."

Amused, Sarah hid a smile. "We try to behave in a civilized manner," she replied lightly, "but it's a never-ending challenge."

Davina flushed a little.

Sarah gave her a printed form to fill out.

"How safe is this bank?" Miss Wyngate inquired.

"About as safe as any," Sarah said.

Davina ponied up her cash on hand. Fifty dollars, an impressive sum for a girl who hadn't undertaken her first position yet. Undoubtedly, the school board had paid her train fare to Stone Creek. They provided housing, and the teacher could either cook for herself or dine in a rotating series of homes, of which Sarah's was one. This was probably graduation money, or a leaving-home gift from her adoptive parents.

"I suppose 'Mrs. Steel' told you about our—discussion," Davina said.

So, the girl wanted to talk. Sarah was

both surprised and mildly gratified. Perhaps all wasn't lost, as Kitty seemed to think.

"Some of it," Sarah said, proceeding cautiously. The ice was thin on this particular conversational pond.

Angry tears welled in Davina's beautiful eyes. "How can you befriend her?"

"Because I like her?" Sarah ventured.

"Why?"

Clearly raised by strict Victorian standards, which were more stringent in the East than the West, Davina seemed honestly baffled.

"Kitty has her faults," Sarah said, "like all the rest of us. But she's a good person, totally devoted to caring for my invalid father. Any lies she told you were intended to *protect* you and your sister, rather than deceive you."

"But she's not—*respectable!*"

"I don't suppose I am, either," Sarah allowed. By Eastern social standards, she was little better than Kitty, having borne a married man's child out of wedlock. Davina probably hadn't been apprised of this, having arrived so recently, but it was only a matter of time, of course. And not *very much* time, either.

"The day my contract is fulfilled," Davina said, stiffening up again, "I'm leaving Stone Creek for good."

Sarah permitted herself a smile. Before Christmas, some lonely rancher would have wooed and won Davina Wynngate. She might not teach beyond the agreed term, but she wasn't going anywhere.

The insight reminded Sarah of her own wedding, scheduled for—*tomorrow*. If she had any sense at all, she'd call off the ceremony, since Charles would render it moot, anyway, when he either returned to Stone Creek in person or sent some emissary to collect the son he apparently regarded as his alone.

Beneath all Sarah's doubts and trepidation ran a strong, rebellious current of pure, reckless lust. She would not have lain with Wyatt, no matter how much she wanted him, without marrying him first. The pain of what had happened with Charles, all those years ago, would have rendered that kind of vulnerability impossible.

She'd been young then, and naive. Besotted. Now, she was sadder and wiser, and her desire for Wyatt, though nearly overwhelming when she allowed herself to consider it, was another kind of wanting entirely.

"I'm sure we'll all be very sorry to see you go, Davina," Sarah said, in belated response to the young woman's tremulous assertion. "Teachers are rare commodities in Stone Creek. They keep getting married." *Or heading back East to tend wealthy but ailing relatives.* Sarah felt a stab of sorrow to think she might never see Fiona again, whatever their differences might have been. If Fiona kept her promise to write, she decided firmly, she would definitely write back.

"I prefer to be called Miss Wynngate, if you don't mind," Davina said.

Sarah merely smiled. She recorded the account information, gave the girl a receipt, and watched with a peculiar mingling of sympathy and annoyance as Stone Creek's new schoolmarm glided out of the bank like an offended queen departing from a pesthouse.

Sarah managed to keep busy for the rest of the morning, but there were few customers. She closed the bank promptly at noon and started for home, lost in thought.

LINDA LAEL MILLER 429

When she arrived, Lonesome had taken a turn for the worse, and Owen was clearly worried.

"He's wanting Wyatt," the boy told Sarah. "He keeps on crying."

"Go fetch Doc," Sarah said, because she didn't know what else to do. By now, Wyatt had surely gone back to Stone Creek Ranch.

Owen had no more than left the house when Judge Harvey came to the back door. He'd brought a marriage license along, all in good order.

A corpulent, friendly man with red muttonchop whiskers and a handlebar mustache, the judge, as everyone in and around Stone Creek called him, glanced toward the rear stairs.

"I've mainly come to see Ephriam," he said, his wise, gentle eyes fixed on Sarah. "But I'd like a word with you, too, since we seem to be alone. Except for that whimpering dog over there, anyway. What's ailing him?"

"He's homesick," Sarah said, putting on an apron, because when her father's friends visited the house, she was expected to serve them something.

"Poor critter," the judge said. "Sounds like he's dying."

"There's coffee left from lunch," Sarah said, giving Lonesome a pitying glance. He was indeed inconsolable, it appeared.

The judge shook his head. He reminded Sarah of a portly, though benign, lion, but when it came to presiding over Stone Creek's rare trials and rendering verdicts, he took a hard line. Hanging his bowler hat on the peg by the door, he crossed the room to lay the marriage license on the table. It was ornate, with flowers and raised gold lettering.

"Are you sure you want to get hitched to this man?" the judge asked. "Rowdy's brother or not, he's a stranger. What little folks know about his past is hardly commendable."

"I have my reasons," Sarah said, with what dignity she could muster.

"Wedding happens this fast," the judge persisted, "people are bound to mark the calendar and count off the months, keeping an eye on the bride's girth."

Sarah's cheeks burned, but she knew the judge's intentions were kindly ones. She trusted him as much as she trusted

Doc, and almost as much as her father. "I'm not in the family way," she told him.

"Then why the all-fired hurry?"

Why, indeed? Sarah thought dismally. "Because of Owen," she said.

"That boy who's come to stay with you and Ephriam?"

"Yes. He's my son, Judge."

"Thought he looked like somebody. Now I realize it's your mother's people. Used to visit a lot, before they moved to California."

"I want to keep him, and I thought I'd have a better chance if I had a husband." Sarah held her breath, waiting for the judge's response.

The judge drew back a chair at the table and lowered himself heavily to the seat. "Is there an official record of the birth?"

Since most children were born at home, rather than in infirmaries, as Owen had been, very often there were no records, save a notation in somebody's Bible. "Yes," Sarah said. "But you won't find my name on it."

The old man considered this, rubbing his whiskers as he pondered. "Will he fight you? The lad's father, I mean?"

"Absolutely," Sarah replied.

"That's a problem, Sarah."

She nodded, her breath snagged painfully in her throat.

"Still, the courts *will* be a shade more likely to take your side if you're married. Under the present laws, single women actually have more rights—though few enough of them—than married ones. As you surely know, when you become Mrs. Wyatt Yarbro or Mrs. Anybody Else, any property you may own becomes his, at least in the eyes of the law. The one exception is cases like this one."

It was a sore spot with Sarah, and most of the women she knew, that she could work, bear and raise children, teach school or serve as a nurse, work in a field like a dray horse, but the vote was denied her. Just then, though, she was interested only in finding any thread of hope that she might keep Owen and holding on to it with all her strength.

"Your chances to keep the boy will increase with your marriage, Sarah," the judge said solemnly. "But only very slightly. The father, whoever he is, has the stronger claim, especially since he's evidently been the one to raise the child."

"I understand," Sarah said.

The judge regarded her long and hard. "You'll be bound to this man for the rest of your life," he cautioned. "Even if you lose the boy."

Sarah nodded.

"Do you love Yarbro?"

"I—I don't know," Sarah responded. It had been a while, she reflected, the thought oddly out of context, since she'd felt called upon to record anything in her book of lies.

"Sarah."

"Most marriages aren't based on love," she protested. "You know that."

"I do indeed. But love makes the hardships easier to bear. I know you probably think you're getting on in years and you ought to grab a husband before the chance passes you by, but you're still very young, Sarah. You're a beautiful woman with a good mind. Plenty of men, right here in Stone Creek, would come a-courting if you'd just favor them with a smile and a kind word once in a while. Why get hitched to an outlaw?"

Propriety did not permit a straightforward answer, and Sarah didn't offer one.

The unvarnished truth was that she couldn't bear the idea of intimate intercourse with any of the men she knew—except Wyatt. If she didn't marry him, she'd live out her life as a spinster, proud and poor, perhaps even destitute when her father and the bank were gone, but still the mistress of her own body. Once, in her empathy with Kitty, she'd half believed she could do what Kitty had done, and sell her favors to survive. Now, she knew she'd rather starve to death.

"Well," said the judge, rising again, grimly reconciled to the clear fact that Sarah wasn't going to change her mind, "he's a good-looking fellow, that Yarbro. Must run in the family. Trouble is, the good-looking ones are usually rascals, but I don't suppose I need to tell you that. Have a care that he doesn't break your heart, Sarah Tamlin."

Sarah merely nodded.

"Do you want me to perform the ceremony, or will you be asking the preacher to do it?"

She swallowed. "It will be a civil ceremony," she said. "I'd rather have you than Pastor Wells."

There would be a flurry of gossip over that, too, Sarah supposed, since she played the organ for Sunday services, but Wells was a relative newcomer to Stone Creek, not an old friend like the judge. She'd brace herself for the coming storm, and endure it as best she could.

Judge Harvey nodded, started for the stairs. "I understand from Rowdy that tomorrow is the big day," he said. "The usual time is two o'clock. Will that suit?"

"Yes," Sarah said. Her voice echoed strangely in her ears, as though it belonged to someone else, speaking from a distance over a faulty wire.

All Judge Harvey's arguments against the marriage were good ones. Charles would still have most of the advantages, when it came to Owen's going or staying. There was no flinching from this reality, as harsh and unfair as it was.

Still, she felt strong, too. It seemed that another, more determined, more competent and much fiercer Sarah had stepped forward and taken her over for the duration.

After Judge Harvey went upstairs for a brief visit to Ephriam, she concentrated on soothing the dog. Pulled up the kitchen

rocking chair, hoisted the sorrowing creature onto her lap, and rocked him like a
baby until he slept.

And so, utterly spent, emotionally if not
physically, did she.

STEPPING INTO THE Tamlin kitchen, with
Owen and Doc right behind him, Wyatt
was stopped in his tracks by the vision
Sarah made, holding Lonesome in her
arms, the pair of them sound asleep. The
dog's muzzle rested on her shoulder, in
the curve of her neck, his forelegs on
either side of her waist, as though embrac-
ing her.

Something turned over inside Wyatt.
Made his eyes sting.

He put a finger to his lips as Owen and
Doc nudged past him, probably impatient
with the delay.

Doc chuckled, the sound low and dry
and full of avuncular affection. "Well, I'll be
darned," he said. "Isn't that a sight to see?"

Owen stood staring, and it struck Wyatt
that the boy might be envying the dog a
little, much as he seemed willing to hike
the whole territory on Lonesome's behalf.
He'd run Doc down someplace and talked

him into driving him out to Stone Creek Ranch, the boy had, and pulled Wyatt right off the range.

Had Marjory Langstreet ever gathered Owen up the way Sarah had gathered Lonesome, and rocked him to sleep?

The pure yearning in the boy's face stopped Wyatt's breath with the force of a headlong plunge into slushy creek water in the dead of winter. He laid a hand on Owen's shoulder, squeezed.

Sarah, meanwhile, opened her eyes, saw them all standing there, and smiled, though sleepily and with some pink rising to her cheeks.

Lonesome woke up, too, and when he saw Wyatt, he tried to scramble down off Sarah's lap to come to him.

Wyatt moved quickly to take the dog from her, lest he jump and hurt himself all over again. "Fool mutt," he muttered, because he suddenly found it impossible to speak to Sarah, or even look at her, with his heart so full of confusing and contradictory things. "You're half again more trouble than you're worth."

Sarah laughed, and the sound was like the bells of some small, far-off church, hidden in green woods. "I guess you'd better take him out to the ranch with you," she told Wyatt as he straightened, the dog cradled in his arms like a sack of feed. "He'll give us no peace if you leave him."

Wyatt set Lonesome on his feet, glanced back at Doc, who was already climbing the rear stairway, and Owen, who stood rooted to the kitchen floor, his hands tight at his sides. He didn't want to let the dog go, that was plain, but he'd do it, for Lonesome's sake.

I wish you were my boy, Wyatt would have said, if saying it wouldn't have been wrong and even cruel. Owen was Charles Langstreet's son, and that was the fact of things, pure and simple.

"Doc and me," Owen told Sarah, "are fixing to drive Lonesome to Stone Creek Ranch, since he can't go that far on a horse. He's got to be with Wyatt."

At last, Wyatt was able to look at Sarah, and he found her eyes resting tenderly on Owen. There was a flaw in the plan, since the wedding was supposed to take place the next day, and that would mean hauling Lonesome back to town or leaving him alone, but she didn't speak of it. The boy needed a solution, even if it was a temporary one.

Wyatt had told Sam he was getting married, and Sam had congratulated him and told him to take Monday for a honeymoon, but Wyatt did his best, right along, to keep his thoughts from wandering to the other side of the wedding. He'd arranged to borrow a buckboard from Sam, and he still intended to work on his place until it was time to spruce up for the ceremony.

He'd used up most of his money, refusing the offer of a loan from Rowdy, to buy a skinny gold band to put on Sarah's finger, and it pained him to know that was all he had to give her.

Still, other folks had started out with less.

"Go upstairs and wash up for supper," Sarah told Owen.

He obeyed without question. Having ruined his new school clothes and taken two unauthorized trips to Stone Creek Ranch that day, he must have used up a good measure of the defiance on hand.

"Are we doing the right thing, Wyatt?" Sarah asked softly, when they were alone. A little smile curved her mouth—the mouth

Wyatt wanted to kiss and then kiss again. "Judge Harvey says you're good-looking, and therefore, a rascal."

"I'll be a faithful husband, Sarah," Wyatt said. "Right now, that's about all I can promise."

It must have been enough, because Sarah smiled again, a little wistfully, and nodded once more. "Two o'clock," she said. "Don't be late."

CHAPTER SEVENTEEN

PROMPTLY AT TWO O'CLOCK on Sunday afternoon, the wedding party crowded into Ephriam's bedroom, with Doc and Rowdy and Kitty for witnesses, and Owen standing up as Wyatt's best man. Even Lonesome was in attendance, with a bandanna tied at his throat in honor of the festivities.

Of course, Ephriam could not give Sarah away in the traditional fashion, but Kitty and Doc had propped him up in bed, with many pillows at his back, his hair combed and his face scrubbed shiny, and while he wasn't able to speak, he seemed alert. Just before Judge Harvey began the ceremony, Sarah took her father's hand, and felt his palm press against hers. Her eyes welled when she realized he'd given her his own wedding band, so she'd have one for Wyatt.

She wore her mother's dress, with no veil, and held a bouquet of the last of Maddie O'Ballivan's wild climbing roses, sent to town with Wyatt and Lonesome as a marriage gift from Sam. There'd been a message, too, scrawled in Sam's strong hand, addressed to Sarah alone.

Maddie and Lark will be riled up something considerable when they find out they've missed this shindig. Enjoy it anyway. I think you've chosen well. S.O'B.

Wyatt looked breathtakingly handsome, if a bit strangled by the collar of the white shirt he'd probably borrowed from Rowdy. He wore plain trousers of a lightweight woolen, suspenders, but no coat, due to the heat, and his boots were spitshined. Sarah knew he'd been out at the "new" place since sunup, he and Lonesome, starting on the new roof. Around noon, they'd come to town, and he'd had a bath at Rowdy's.

We don't even know where we're going to live, Sarah thought, joyously fitful, as she took her place beside Wyatt.

The words were a droning blur; Sarah responded when she was supposed to, and Wyatt did the same.

"Mr. Yarbro," the judge said ponderously, "you may kiss your bride."

It was no chaste peck. Indeed, it seemed that Wyatt had barely been able to contain that kiss until the proper moment came. He wrapped one steely arm around Sarah's waist, hoisted her clear off her feet, and kissed her so deeply and so hard that little frissons of excitement erupted inside her, sweet portents of the long, languid night to come. She threw her arms around his neck and kissed him right back, and they might have gone on like that for a good long time if Rowdy hadn't cleared his throat with enough force to get their attention.

They broke apart, Sarah blushing, Wyatt red in the neck and jawline.

There was a cake, made up on short notice over in the hotel kitchen and tilting distinctly to one side, but Sarah didn't care. For his gift, Doc had engaged a photographer, the same oft-drunken saloon rat he'd hired to take the likenesses of the three dead men before they were buried, for purposes of later identification.

Sarah and Wyatt posed together, with the funny dried apple wedding cake listing on the kitchen table in front of them, solemn and unsmiling, for having one's picture made was no light business. In a second pose, Owen stood with them, flouting tradition and grinning wide.

Had Sarah allowed herself to think about her son's hopes to grow up in Stone Creek, with her for a mother and Wyatt for a father, she would have broken down and cried on her own wedding day. So she did her best to stay within the confines of the right now. Right now, she was Mrs. Wyatt Yarbro, and her groom didn't have a penny to his name but she didn't care, and Owen was with them.

The first hint of a disagreement arose over the honeymoon. Sarah had naturally assumed she and Wyatt would spend the night in her room upstairs.

Wyatt clearly had other ideas. He'd brought Sam's buckboard to town for a purpose, he informed her, besides hauling Lonesome in from the ranch and having a way to bring his tools back from the new place. They were honeymooning, he informed Sarah implacably, in his cabin on Stone Creek Ranch. Just the two of them—and, of course, Lonesome. If they left him behind, he'd pine so for Wyatt that the whole household would be disrupted.

Cake was served, and coffee was poured. Hands were shaken, cheeks were kissed.

Kitty smiled at Sarah's reluctant acquiescence and promised to look after Owen, as well as Ephriam, until she and Wyatt decided where the heck they were going to live.

"Here," Sarah insisted. She'd always lived in this house, except while she was away in Philadelphia, of course. The old Henson place wasn't ready to live in, and Wyatt's cabin on the ranch was a long way out of town. Married or not, she still had the bank to run. "We'll live right *here.*"

Kitty took hold of Sarah's arm and pulled her into the pantry for a word. "Sarah Tamlin Yarbro," she said, "don't be a ninny. You can't spend your *wedding night* in the same house with Owen and your papa and me. Wyatt wants to take you to his cabin so he can have you right, with nobody to hear the carrying on!"

Sarah's face burned. "The *carrying on?*"

Kitty looked smug. "Oh, you'll carry on, all right. Fit to raise the roof, probably, once that man of yours gets you out of that corset and everything else under that dress. You're damn lucky, and I'd take your place in a trice if I could. There's no telling what tomorrow will bring, or the day after. Let your hair down, Sarah. Stop being such a—*banker's daughter.* You're married to Wyatt Yarbro in the eyes of God and man. So stop fretting about this and that and the other thing and let him love you."

Sarah put her hands to her cheeks, but they wouldn't cool down. "Kitty!" she whispered, scandalized.

Kitty turned her around and gave her a push toward the pantry door. "The words have been said. The paper's been signed. The cake's been cut. The pictures have been taken. Now, get in the wagon with that man and let him take you wherever he wants, and do whatever he wants."

"Keep your voice down!" Sarah protested, and because she had turned her head to look back at Kitty, she collided hard with Wyatt.

He set his hands on her shoulders to steady her, chuckling under his breath, and even if she'd been suddenly and permanently blinded, she realized with a start, she'd have recognized his touch, his sunlight-and-starch scent, the hard heat and substance of his body.

"I've already loaded up your valise," he told her, his dark eyes at once smoldering and reverent as he gazed down into her upturned and still-flushed face. "Kitty packed it for you earlier." This was said with a nod to the woman standing just behind Sarah. "Are you ready to go home, Mrs. Yarbro?"

Sarah opened her mouth to protest the word *home,* but Kitty gave her a sharp poke from behind, and she held her tongue. "Yes, Mr. Yarbro," she replied. "I think I am."

It was tradition to carry the bride over the threshold of her new home, but Wyatt swept Sarah up into his arms, right then and there, and carried her through the kitchen, where cheers erupted from the few but earnest wedding guests, onto the porch and down the steps.

He hoisted her up into the buckboard seat, Lonesome already installed in back, looking dapper in his wedding bandanna, and then climbed up beside her.

Owen waved from the porch, looking a little forlorn, for all his happy frolic in front of the camera and the two huge pieces of cake he'd consumed. Rowdy stood behind him, laid his hands on the boy's shoulders to reassure him, as well as Sarah.

Wyatt was embarrassingly eager to be away. He climbed up beside Sarah, took the reins, released the brake lever with a hard motion of one foot, and they were rolling.

Sarah felt suddenly shy, as virginal as any bride.

Suppose she'd been wrong about Wyatt? Suppose he wasn't the skilled and gentle lover she'd instinctively believed him to be? All the wedding-night horror stories she'd ever heard, always whispered, always involving blood and pain, came back to her in an overwhelming rush.

Wyatt might have sensed her trepidation, because he shifted the reins to his left hand and took Sarah's in his right.

The drive out to Stone Creek Ranch went too quickly, and not quickly enough. On horseback, it was a half-hour journey. In a buckboard, bouncing over rutted roads that were little more than cattle tracks, a full hour was required. Sarah didn't know whether she wanted to speed up or slow down.

When they reached the top of a rise, Wyatt stopped the wagon and pointed out the cabin, far off in the distance, behind Sam and Maddie's big house and the substantial barn and what was probably the bunkhouse.

Sarah's heart rose into her throat and pounded there. Blood thundered in her ears.

It was still broad daylight, she told herself, in an effort to calm down a little. Surely Wyatt would not expect to make love to her in *broad daylight.*

She breathed a little easier.

Wyatt was grinning, she noticed in a sidelong glance, as he slapped down the reins and whistled to get the two-horse team moving again.

There seemed to be no one around— Sam and whatever other men he employed, besides Wyatt of course, were surely with the herd. Lonesome began to whine, with impatience rather than discomfort, eager to get out of the wagon.

Wyatt stopped the buckboard, sprang down to the ground, and walked around back to lower the tailgate and set Lonesome on his feet in the grass. When that was done, he came to Sarah's side, looked up at her, and extended his arms.

She hesitated for a moment, swallowing her heart. Then she let her bridegroom help her to alight. Instead of setting her on her feet, though, as he'd done with Lonesome, he carried her. Pushed open the door of the cabin with one foot.

Sarah had not known what to expect of the place, had not actually thought about it much at all, since she'd fully expected to spend her wedding night in her own room in town.

Bright pink roses graced the rustic table, charming in their mason-jar vase. The wood floor had been swept, and the bed had been made up with a faded but pretty quilt and serviceable linen sheets. Someone had turned the covers back.

Sarah felt shy again.

"I'll go back to the buckboard for your valise," Wyatt said, sounding shy himself. Only Lonesome, curling up in front of the stove for an afternoon snooze, seemed to feel at home in this strange, small, sturdy place.

Sarah stood in the middle of the room—indeed, the middle of the *house*—and breathed slowly and deeply. She was no frail flower, but just then, she thought if she didn't control her breathing, she would surely get light-headed and swoon.

The door stood open, and through it, Sarah heard Wyatt talking to someone. She turned and saw Jody Wexler climbing up to take the reins of the buckboard and drive it away toward the barn.

She went to the bed, sat down to test the mattress, and immediately sprang up again.

Wyatt had returned just in time to see this, and though he was rimmed in sunlight from the doorway, Sarah knew he was grinning.

"Nervous?" he asked. As he closed the door, she could see his features again—his strong, almost patrician face, his dark, intelligent eyes, his distinctly appealing mouth.

"No," she lied.

He laughed, low and soft. Rubbed his chin. Although he'd surely shaved at Rowdy's, when he bathed, stubble had already appeared.

Sarah sat down on the bed again, because her knees suddenly wouldn't support her.

Wyatt latched the door, watching Sarah the whole time.

She gulped.

"Just in case there's a chivaree planned," Wyatt said.

Sarah nodded, gulped again.

Wyatt crossed the room and sat beside her. This time, the bed springs creaked.

Sarah started a little. Lonesome, dead to the world, didn't even stir. And Wyatt grinned.

"I could leave you alone for a while," he said. "In case you need more time or something."

"Might as well get it over with," Sarah said, and then could have bitten off her tongue.

Wyatt merely laughed and shoved a hand through his hair.

"I didn't mean—"

He turned, cupped her cheeks in his hands, and nuzzled her mouth, just once and very lightly. A hot shiver went through her. If he kissed her, the way he had at the wedding—

He did, but this time there were no witnesses. Rowdy wasn't around to clear his throat. Wyatt's tongue delved deep into Sarah's mouth, and sparred with hers.

Sarah gave a tremulous groan. Put her arms around his neck.

Presently, Wyatt broke off the kiss, stood suddenly, sucked in an audible breath, as though he'd been underwater too long. And, holding Sarah's hand, he brought her right along with him.

Turned her to face him.

"I do believe you're the most beautiful woman I've ever laid eyes on," he said, his voice gruff. And then he began to work the tiny pearl buttons running the full length of her bodice.

"Now?" she whispered. "But Wyatt—it's still light out—there are people around—couldn't we . . . ?"

He chuckled again. Kept right on unbuttoning her dress. "There's one thing you'll need to keep in mind about married life,

Sarah. It doesn't have to be dark outside
for a man to make love to his wife. Fact is,
if you're willing, I'll take you anytime of day,
anywhere that's private enough." He'd
opened all the buttons; now he smoothed
the dress off her shoulders, nibbled at the
long curve of her neck.

Sarah's breath caught at the exquisite
sensation of his lips and his breath moving warm and slow over her skin. Ever
more and more of her skin bared, until the
dress fell in a pool at her feet and she was
left standing there in petticoats, pantaloons, a camisole and the corset Kitty
had teased her about in the pantry.

Wyatt gave a low whistle of exclamation. "I will never understand," he said,
"how you women can tolerate so many
clothes. Especially things with wire and
whalebone in them." He unlaced her
camisole, dispensed with it. Pushed her
petticoats down, so they tumbled, lacy,
on top of the dress. She stood in the swell
of fabric like Venus rising from the sea,
her breasts swelling above the corset-
top, naked without the camisole to cover
them, and Wyatt weighed them gently in
his hands. Chafed the pink nipples with

the sides of his thumbs until they tightened.

Sarah whimpered. Closed her eyes. Swayed slightly.

She wasn't an innocent virgin bride. She'd been with a man—one man—numerous times, and she'd enjoyed the caresses, the holding that came after the hard, moist pounding of Charles's body slamming into hers.

But this was different.

It was as though she were some infinitely precious instrument, rare and perfectly designed, and Wyatt meant to play every string, play every chord, and coax from her soft and tender notes at first, but building, building, until the gentle strains soared into a concerto, thunderous and mighty.

Muttering a little, he freed her from the corset, flung it away. She knew, just by the motion, that if he had his way, she would never wear it again.

He bent his head to her breasts then, tasting one, then the other.

Sarah entwined her fingers in his hair and held him to her, wanting more, and then more still.

He suckled until she was breathless, one of his hands splayed across the small of her back, the other sliding down into her pantaloons, finding and parting her. Plying her.

A thin shimmer of perspiration broke out all over Sarah's body. She felt wet everywhere—on her breasts, between her legs, where Wyatt was igniting a fire with a simple swirling motion of his fingers.

It was a relief when he laid her down on the bed, pulled off her pantaloons, her stockings and garters, her slippers. She watched, dazed, as Wyatt stood watching her, devouring her with his eyes, all the while shedding his own clothes—boots first, then the shirt, then his trousers.

His manhood stood erect, reminding Sarah of stallions in the field, preparing to mount a mare. As primitive as the image was, it made her blood burn and her body strain.

She wanted him inside her, deep inside her.

But he turned her sideways on the bed and knelt between her legs.

She groaned. Now he'd take her. At last, at last, he'd take her.

Instead, he stunned her with a pleasure so unexpected, and so fiercely keen, that she wasn't sure she could endure it. He buried his face in her, took her into his mouth.

She began to rock and writhe on the bed.

He feasted on her, alternately sucking and laving her to madness with the very tip of his tongue. He stroked the insides of her thighs, inciting rather than soothing, keeping her knees apart. And when she arched her back, caught up in the throes of something she had never imagined could happen, he drew on her harder still, and reached up to cover her mouth lightly with one hand.

If he hadn't, the wail she gave would have been heard on every corner of Stone Creek Ranch. The release was utter, shattering, an unhinging of soul from body. Sarah buckled wildly under Wyatt's mouth, howling against his palm. Again and again, she felt that catching deep inside her, the thing she thought she'd experienced before, but never had.

At last, spent, she fell, gasping, to the mattress. Wyatt still knelt between her legs, his head resting on her quivering abdomen.

"I didn't know—" she managed.

"Shhh," he said.

Presently, he turned her again, so that she lay properly on the bed. And he lowered himself onto her.

"Sarah," he told her, looking into her eyes, "the wedding was a prelude. So was what we just did. But when this next thing happens, there'll be no going back. If you've got any doubts, you'd best say so right now."

Sarah knew, though only dimly, what he meant. The marriage could still be annulled, even with the marriage license signed, and her still trembling from the unspeakable satisfaction he'd evoked in her only moments before. But once their bodies had been joined, the die would be cast. She would truly be his wife then, and he would be her husband.

She put her hands on either side of his face, rough now, needing to be shaved, and drew his head down for her kiss. Felt the wetness of her pleasure on his mouth.

What she couldn't say in words, her body said for her.

With a low moan, Wyatt eased inside her.

The sheer size of him made her eyes widen and her breath catch.

"Easy," he said. Ever so slowly, he began to move within her.

The friction was delicious at first, then as necessary as her next breath, her next heartbeat. Sarah clutched and clawed at Wyatt, trying to take him in still deeper, trying to hurry him.

But he would not be hurried.

His thrusts were deliberate and controlled. He murmured senseless words into Sarah's neck, raised his head to look into her eyes.

She began to buck beneath him again, like a wild mare in springtime. And when she cried out, lost in pleasure, flung into it to whirl in breathless spirals toward heaven itself, he covered her mouth with his own.

When she climaxed, he swallowed her fevered shouts.

And when he let himself go, when he thrust back his head and gave a low shout of surrender, spilling his warmth into her, Sarah realized she'd never made love before that day. She'd given herself, yes. She'd even had soft, sweet releases.

But she had never known passion. She had never soared, never been ravished, never felt the stirring, silent music of her own body, expertly rendered by a man who cared as much for her pleasure as his own.

She began to cry.

Wyatt, lying beside her, kissed her temple. Wrapped her in his arms and held her close against him, not minding her tears. She clung to him, their legs entwined. And, eventually, she slept.

When she awakened, the cabin was shadowy with twilight. Lying on her stomach, she stretched, made a little crooning sound of sheer contentment. Wyatt stirred next to her, shifted.

She felt herself drawn up onto her hands and knees, with Wyatt behind her. Kissing her backbone, caressing her buttocks with one hand, he arranged himself and slid into her in a single thrust.

Her sated body thrilled, wanting again.

She whispered his name, raggedly, unashamed of her need.

He held her hips, filling her and then withdrawing. Teasing until she pleaded.

And only when she pleaded did he truly take her, in the way she craved taking. His lovemaking was like some exotic drug; if he withheld it from her, she would suffer. As it was, she gasped and twisted like a woman in a violent fever, but Wyatt did not deny her. He drove into her, hard, at the precise moment she needed him most, and the resultant explosion consumed her.

She collapsed again, but Wyatt got out of bed, pulled on his trousers, and went outside, Lonesome padding after him. When they returned, Wyatt lit a kerosene lantern and set it on the table, began poking kindling and crumpled newspaper into the belly of the stove.

"What are you doing?" Sarah asked drowsily, still almost too breathless to speak.

He laughed, the sound gruff and somehow as intimate as their lovemaking. "Maybe you can keep up a pace like that, Mrs. Yarbro," he said, "but Lonesome and I, we need some supper."

"Supper?"

"Don't worry," Wyatt told her. "You don't have to cook."

"Good," Sarah said, "because I don't think I can *stand up,* let alone make supper."

But she *would* have to stand up, she realized. She needed to use a chamber pot, wash her hands and face.

"Outhouse is behind the cabin," Wyatt said.

Sarah felt the now-familiar heat suffuse her face. How had he known?

She scrambled out of bed, wrapped herself in the quilt, after untangling it from the top sheet, poked her feet into her wedding slippers, and left the cabin as regally as she could, praying that none of the ranch hands would see her.

It was dark out, though, and lights shone in Sam and Maddie's windows, and from the bunkhouse, too. Sarah felt warmed by them, even comforted.

She used the outhouse, which was newly built and therefore had not acquired an odor, then returned to the cabin. Wyatt had set out a basin of warm water for her, along with a washcloth and a bar of soap still in the wrapper.

"I wish I'd known your mother," Sarah said.

Busy frying something in a skillet, Wyatt looked up. "Why?" he asked.

"Because she raised you right. You cook. You knew I'd need hot water and soap—"

"I'm not sure she'd agree," Wyatt said quietly. "That she raised me right, I mean. She sure didn't rock me at her bosom when I was a baby and say, 'I hope my firstborn grows up to rob trains.'"

Sarah felt a pang, because she'd never know Wyatt's mother, and because she missed her own with a sudden soreness of heart. Both of them should have been at the wedding, Nancy giving Sarah shy last-minute advice, Mrs. Yarbro beaming over her handsome son.

"I didn't get to hold Owen, when he was a baby," Sarah said, without ever intending to say any such thing. "They took him away before I could."

Wyatt pushed the skillet to the back of the stove, came to her, took her in his arms. Kissed the top of her head. And he had the good sense not to say anything at all. He simply allowed her to cry.

"There'll be other children," she said presently. "And I'll love them with my whole being. But if Owen's not there, too—"

"Shhh," Wyatt said. "We'll think of something."

But what? she wanted to ask, but didn't.

Lonesome came over, squeezed himself in between them.

They laughed.

Wyatt let Sarah go, went back to the stove. She rummaged through her valise and found her wrapper. Shed the quilt to put it on.

God bless Kitty Steel, she thought. If it had been left up to her, she'd have had nothing to wear but her mother's wedding dress.

Once decently covered, Sarah gathered her scattered clothes from the floor—the petticoats, the gown, the camisole and pantaloons, the corset.

"You're right," she told Wyatt. "Women wear too many clothes."

He grinned, crossed the room, took the corset out of her hand, and carried it back to the stove. Stuffed it right into the fire and watched it catch.

"Wyatt Yarbro," Sarah protested, some-what after the fact. "I need that corset!"

"No, you don't," he replied. "As far as I'm concerned, the pantaloons could go into the stove, too, since it would save me hav-ing to pull them down, but I reckon you'd feel the breeze on windy days."

Sarah laughed, scandalized, not so much because of the audacity of what he'd said, but because she liked the idea.

Whatever Wyatt was cooking sizzled, and it smelled divine. He grinned at her. Waggled his eyebrows.

"You are not going to go around pulling down my pantaloons," she said.

"Wait and see," he answered. "You liked it when I took you from behind, and what you like, I like. I'll be bending you over things right and left, Mrs. Yarbro, and hav-ing you hard and slow, until you howl like a she-wolf in heat."

Sarah fluttered a hand in front of her face, overheated. It must have been the stove, and the summer night. "I take it back, what I said about your mother rais-ing you right," she told him. "You mustn't *say* such things, Wyatt. It's improper."

"Why not, Sarah?" Wyatt asked, still grinning. "Because it makes you want me to put my—money where my mouth is?"

She did want that, and he knew it, and her temper surged, right along with that insatiable passion he'd awakened in her.

"Shall I prove it, Sarah?"

"No," she said, drawing the belt of her wrapper more tightly around her waist. It really *was* too warm in that cabin. "I'm starved. I'm exhausted. And there will be no more talk about where you put your mouth!"

He laughed out loud at that, throwing back his head.

"Wyatt!"

"If I remember correctly, you liked where I put my mouth."

"Open the door," Sarah blustered, "or a window. It's so hot in here."

"I can't do that, Sarah," Wyatt said reasonably. "It's hard enough keeping you quiet, without the door and the window open so half the county can hear you calling out my name."

"Why, you—"

He pushed the skillet to the back of the stove again.

Sarah backed up a step. "Wyatt Yarbro," she warned.

He came to her, undid the belt and opened her wrapper. Waited smugly for her to protest.

She didn't.

He caressed her breasts, suckled at her nipples.

Sarah groaned, let her head fall back. The wrapper went the way of the wedding dress and the petticoats.

And then Wyatt turned her around, bent her over the table, and took her in a single, hard thrust.

It was a very good thing, Sarah would admit later, that they hadn't opened the window or the door.

CHAPTER EIGHTEEN

MONDAY WAS NOT, despite Sam O'Ballivan's generous offer, set aside for more honeymooning. It was to be Owen's first day at Stone Creek School, after all, and Sarah couldn't, in good conscience, leave the bank for Thomas to manage alone. At the first sign of a scruffy cowhand with a gun on his hip, looking to make a deposit or inquire about a mortgage on some patch of land, he'd probably panic and head for the hills.

So Wyatt hitched up Sam's buckboard and loaded Lonesome and his tools in the back, and he and Sarah went to town.

Her father was resting comfortably, though there had been no significant change in his condition, either for better or for worse. Owen was fully dressed, his hair slicked down and his face washed and his new boots on his feet, chomping at the bit to start school. He'd made his own breakfast, and he'd gathered his tablet and pencil box and other school-going gear before dawn, according to an amused Kitty. It had been all she could do, she reported, to keep him from heading for the schoolhouse before it was even light, he was that anxious for classes to commence.

If Kitty noticed the blush in Sarah's cheeks, the light in her eyes, and the new spring in her step, she had the unusual good grace not to comment.

Owen scrambled into the back of the buckboard, greeted Lonesome, and asked Wyatt not to spare the horses. He had things to learn, he said, and he didn't want to be late.

"Not much danger of that," Wyatt said, after consulting his pocket watch. He hoisted Sarah back up into the wagon seat, having waited outside for her and Owen.

"Like as not, that pretty new schoolmarm hasn't even opened her eyes yet."

Sarah gave him an elbow. "How do you know she's pretty?" she demanded, smiling.

He chuckled. "Word gets around," he replied. "Jody Wexler took one look at her—from across the street—and decided to get himself an honest job and save up for a house. It's odd how a woman can have that effect on a man."

"You're all rascals," Sarah said, quietly merry. "Every single one of you."

"Me, too?" Owen piped up, as though it were an honor of some sort. "Am I a rascal, too?"

"Most definitely," Sarah answered, with another smile, thinking if she loved that child any more than she already did, she'd perish from it.

Although the start of the school day was still an hour away, it turned out that Owen wasn't the first pupil to arrive. A band of boys and girls played some chasing game in the school yard, and Davina Wynngate, clad in another prim brown dress with tidy black piping on the bodice, was on hand to supervise.

"Lord," Wyatt said at the sight of her.

Sarah elbowed him again. "You," she told him, "are a married man."

"I still have eyes," Wyatt answered. Then he laughed and kissed her lightly on the nose.

"Stop spooning," Owen ordered from the back. "Everybody will see."

Davina approached the school yard gate, opened it, and walked toward the wagon as Owen jumped nimbly to the ground. Although she turned a reserved and somewhat chilly glance on Sarah, Davina greeted Owen with a genuine smile.

"Put your tablet and pencil box inside," she told the boy. "And join the other children."

After staring up at her in naked adoration—Davina Wynngate would be Owen's first love, it seemed—he rushed to comply.

"His name is Owen," Sarah said, relieved that whatever Davina's opinion of Sarah herself might be, she clearly didn't intend to hold it against the child.

Davina nodded. Her gaze strayed, measuring, to Wyatt.

He tipped his hat.

Sarah refrained from elbowing him a third time, but barely.

Introductions were made, and Sarah and Wyatt went on to the bank.

"Don't worry, Mrs. Yarbro," Wyatt said, holding Sarah unnecessarily close for a few charged moments after he'd helped her down from the buckboard. "I was just teasing you, back there at the schoolhouse. You're all the woman I'm ever going to need. Maybe even a bit more."

Sarah blushed—she was always blushing, with Wyatt—but she felt relieved, even if she could admit that only to herself. "May I remind you," she purred, "that we are on a public street?"

"More's the pity," Wyatt said. And then he kissed her. Left her trembling, there on the sidewalk as he climbed back up into the buckboard seat to drive off.

Sarah's heart seemed determined to chase after him, scramble right up into the back of that wagon with Lonesome and go wherever Wyatt went.

She turned resolutely, got out her key and opened the door of the Stockman's Bank as if it was any other Monday morning of her life.

It wasn't, of course.

Thomas appeared only long enough to plead sickness and ask for the day off. Since he *did* look a little green around the gills, Sarah told him to go home and get into bed. If she happened to see Doc, she said, she'd send him by, in case the malady was serious.

She'd conducted several transactions when the two cowboys came in. They were familiar, though not local men, but she couldn't place them. When the shorter one leered at her, she recalled his previous visit.

He tugged at the brim of his seedy hat and looked around as though he'd never been in a bank before. There was something about the avidity of his attention, both to Sarah and to the bank itself, that troubled her, but she quickly shook it off. Strangers came in all the time, asking questions, looking to do some sort of ordinary business.

"May I help you, gentlemen?" Sarah asked.

"We're thinking of conducting some banking," the shorter man said.

Sarah produced two forms from under

the counter and set the ink bottle and public pen nearer to hand. "If you'll just enter your names and places of residence, I'll be happy to help you."

There was a pause. The taller man, his clothes as shabby and trail-worn as any Sarah had ever seen, looking as if they could stand up on their own, without him in them, didn't even glance at the form. The other one grinned, showing very bad teeth to accent his pockmarked complexion, took up the pen and wrote, *Wm J. Smith* on his form, printing the letters in a childish script. *Genrall Del., Stone Crek, Arizona Terrtary.*

He was barely literate, Sarah concluded. Again, that was not unusual.

"This here's Josh," William J. Smith said, cocking a thumb at his sidekick. "He don't write. Just makes an X when it's required."

"That's fine," Sarah said, mildly disturbed by something in his stance or manner, but unable to put her finger on just what it was.

"We might be dealing in large sums," Smith went on, after laying the pen aside. "So if it wouldn't be too much trouble, we'd appreciate it if you'd let us have a look at your safe. Can't be too careful, these days."

A vague, prickling alarm danced in the pit of Sarah's stomach. She told herself she was being silly. It was perfectly reasonable for someone planning on making a sizable deposit to ask to see the safe.

"You'll find it sound," she assured them. Then she crossed the room and opened the door beside the one leading into her father's office. The safe was inside, the finest to be had, standing almost six feet high and taking up most of the space. The door was solid iron, seven inches thick, and only Sarah and her father knew the combination, which changed weekly. Delivering and installing the monstrosity had required the help of four strong men, several mules, and a variety of pulleys and ramps.

At the same moment Mr. Smith approached to take a closer look, the door of the bank opened and Rowdy came in, the picture of affable goodwill.

"Morning, boys," he said to Mr. Smith and the other man. "I haven't seen you around here before, so I thought I'd stop in and say howdy."

The man called Josh reddened slightly around the jowls, and his right hand twitched, as though it wanted to rise to the handle of his pistol.

"I reckon the safe is sturdy enough," Mr. Smith said, not as ruffled as his partner, but watchful.

Sarah, after closing the door to the closet containing the safe, introduced the men to Rowdy. Nods were exchanged, but no more words.

Mr. Smith and Josh left the bank.

Rowdy lingered, standing at the counter now, his head turned to watch the two men through the broad window. They mounted their horses and reined them away, rode off at a trot.

"Where's Wyatt?" Rowdy asked when he finally spoke, and his eyes were serious as they met and held Sarah's gaze.

"Out at the new place, building a roof," Sarah said. "Why?"

Rowdy's grin was so sudden, it almost dazzled Sarah. "I guess I figured the two of you would still be honeymooning," he said.

"We both have things to do," Sarah said, coloring up.

Rowdy didn't comment. Not on that, at least. "Lark and Gideon and the baby will be coming in on the train today," he said. "Pardner, too. Lark wired me last night, said she hoped you and Wyatt and the boy would join us for supper tonight. Sort of a celebration. She's been wanting a sister-in-law. Told me to tell you that, and that she's glad it turned out to be you."

Sarah was pleased. She'd known Lark Yarbro for some time, of course, and liked her very much. But now they were family, and that made a difference. For so long, she'd had no one but her father. "We'd like that," she said.

"Good," Rowdy replied. "Lark will probably come by the bank before then, to give you her regards in person, if she's not too tired from riding the train all that time and wrangling a fractious baby the whole way."

Sarah nodded.

As quickly as it had come, Rowdy's grin vanished again. "Sarah, you shouldn't be working in this bank all by yourself. I didn't like the looks of those yahoos—Mr. 'Smith' and the other fella. Why did you show them the safe?"

"They asked to see it. It's not uncommon,

Rowdy. I store deeds and other documents in that safe, as well as our cash on hand, and people like to see where their money is being kept. Make sure it's secure."

"Where's Thomas?" Rowdy asked. "Not that he'd be much help if there was trouble."

"He's sick today," Sarah said, mildly affronted. First Wyatt had thought she couldn't protect her own bank, and now Rowdy was echoing his concerns. She drew herself up. "I have a shotgun, and I know how to use it."

Rowdy's grin was wry, a mere twitch at the corner of his mouth. "If 'Smith' and his friend come back, Sarah, call somebody in off the street and send them to fetch me. I'll be around town somewhere, and I'm working out of the house until the new jail gets built."

Sarah nodded. "You keep putting an emphasis on the name 'Smith,'" she said. "Why is that?"

Rowdy sighed. "Well, sister Sarah," he said, "if ever there was a name that gets used for an alias right along, it's 'Smith.' Followed closely by 'Jones.'"

While she was still a little annoyed, Sarah liked being called "sister."

"Remember," Rowdy said, turning to head for the door. "If anybody bothers you, even just makes you feel a little nervous, send for me."

"I will," Sarah said, with no real intention of doing so. If she sent for the marshal every time someone disturbed her nerves, he'd be a permanent fixture in the bank.

They both went on about their normal business.

It wasn't just Lark and Maddie, Gideon and Pardner and the babies who came in on the morning train, unfortunately. Charles Langstreet came, too, wearing a black arm-band on one sleeve of his tailored coat and looking coldly, dangerously furious.

He strode into the bank and scared Miss Tillie Robbins—who was making a fifty-cent deposit to her Christmas fund—so badly that she fled without a receipt.

Sarah simply stood there, stunned. How could Charles have covered the distance between Philadelphia and Stone Creek in such a short time?

But, of course, she realized in the next

dizzying moment, he hadn't *gone* to Philadelphia in the first place. He'd only pretended to make that journey, hoping to catch Sarah off guard perhaps. He'd probably been in Flagstaff, or Phoenix, the whole time. He could have sent the telegrams from there, or routed them through his office back East.

"How dare you flout my orders?" he demanded. His face was white with rage and exhaustion, and as he approached the counter, Sarah actually retreated a step, not entirely certain he wouldn't vault over it and throttle her. *"Owen is my son!"*

"He's my son, too," Sarah managed bravely. "And I won't send him halfway across the continent by himself!"

Charles seemed almost apoplectic, despite his pallor. Was he ill?

Sarah was too alarmed to be sympathetic.

"Where is he?" he demanded, his voice a venomous hiss.

"In school," Sarah said. "Where he belongs." Her gaze strayed to the armband. "Is someone—did someone—?"

"Die?" Charles rasped. "Yes. Marjory did."

"I'm sorry," Sarah said, and she was.

"You married that outlaw," Charles accused, startling Sarah again.

She raised her chin, straightened her spine. "Yes," she answered.

"Divorce him," Charles said.

Sarah's mouth dropped open. She closed it firmly.

"Divorce him and marry me, Sarah. That's the only way—the *only way* you're going to raise Owen. We'll go back to Philadelphia, together. The three of us. Start over—"

Sarah clung to the edge of the counter, her knuckles white with the effort. "Charles, have you gone insane? I wouldn't marry you even if I were free to do it!"

"I'll take him away, Sarah. Owen, I mean. Send him to school in Europe, and you'll never see him again. I'll fill his head so full of stories about you that he wouldn't stoop to spit on you."

She knew he meant it. Knew he would carry out the threat. A terrible dread rose up inside her, fairly shutting down her breath and stopping her heart. *"Why?"* she whispered. "Why are you doing this?"

Charles, his hands braced against the

counter, used them to straighten up. His face was ghastly, ugly and twisted with hatred. "That bitch," he breathed. "I'd dance on her grave if I could. I wanted to marry you, Sarah. I *loved* you. But Marjory wouldn't give me a divorce. She's made my life hell since the day she found out about you. I am *glad*—so *goddammed glad*—she finally had the decency to die!"

Sarah did not know what to say. She felt sick, even faint.

The door of the bank opened again.

Let it be Wyatt, Sarah prayed silently.

But it wasn't Wyatt, or even Rowdy.

The newcomer was Doc.

"You have twenty-four hours, Sarah," Charles said evenly. "Twenty-four hours. I'll be at the hotel, awaiting your decision. Oh, and by the way, I have all the evidence I need to shut this bank down. And I will."

With that, Charles left, not even glancing at Doc as he passed him.

"Sarah?" Doc said. His voice came from far away, and it echoed, as though he were calling to her from the other end of a long culvert, far underground. "Sarah?"

She couldn't answer. The room went

dark, and she collapsed, sinking, sinking, into nothing at all.

"I'M FINE," Sarah said, but she looked like her own ghost to Wyatt, lying there on her bed at the Tamlin house. Doc and Rowdy had brought her there, and then Rowdy had ridden out to fetch him. He'd been so desperate to get to her that he'd left the dog and the buckboard for his brother to manage and streaked into town on Rowdy's horse.

He sat on the edge of the mattress, holding one of her cold hands in both of his. "What happened?" he asked, though he had an idea of what had gone on, thanks to Doc, who'd been waiting here at the house when he rode in.

"Charles is back," Sarah told him. Tears welled in her eyes. "If I marry him, I can raise Owen."

"Sarah," Wyatt said, his throat thick. "You're married to me."

"But we don't love each other, do we?"

"I don't know," Wyatt answered, as windless as if he'd been sucker punched in the belly. "I sure as hell feel *something,* and it's powerful."

She turned her head to one side. A tear slid down onto the pillow. "Owen is my child, Wyatt. My baby."

"I won't let you do this, Sarah. Not even for the boy."

"You can't stop me," she replied, with mourning in her voice. "If I tell Judge Harvey we didn't—we didn't consummate the marriage, he'll believe me. He'll annul it. Tear up the license. And I can marry Charles."

"*No.* We *did* consummate the marriage. For all we know, you're already carrying a child—*our* child—"

She turned her head, looked at him. The depth of her sorrow wounded him. "I don't love you, Wyatt," she said, with no inflection at all. Doc had dosed her with something, she'd been so upset after her fainting spell, but her words were cold and matter-of-fact, as if she'd been rehearsing them in her mind. "You're an outlaw—nothing but a ranch hand. Charles is rich. He can arrange for Papa to have the best possible care. None of us will ever lack for anything."

Wyatt's throat thickened, and his eyes burned. He leaned down, kissed Sarah once on the forehead, and got up to leave the room, moving like a man in a trance. He knew she'd made the only choice she could, but that didn't lessen his grief.

If he'd looked back, he'd have seen Sarah reach for that little book of hers, and scribble something into it with a pencil before collapsing back onto her pillows, her face wet with tears.

SHE'D GET OVER Wyatt Yarbro, Sarah told herself when she'd recovered her composure. She loved him, she knew that for sure, but she loved Owen, too, with the deep and elemental passion of a mother. She could not turn her back on the boy, not again.

Owen would be helpless in Charles's care, neglected and perhaps even abused.

Wyatt was a grown man, the strongest she'd ever known. He would brood a while, and then he'd marry someone like Davina Wynngate, and get on with his life.

Sarah would have to tear her heart in two—one part for Owen, one part forever in Wyatt's keeping. If that left her with nothing, well, it was the lot of women. Had been since time immemorial.

Still rummy from the sedative Doc had given her, she rose from her bed, washed her face at the basin, tidied her hair and slipped Wyatt's thin gold wedding band off her finger, placing it in a little china box on top of her bureau.

Doc and Kitty were sitting in the kitchen when she went downstairs, both of them looking as glum as if they'd just lost their last friend.

"I'm going back to the bank," Sarah told them. "It can't be closed in the middle of the day like this. People will think we're insolvent, and there'll be a run of with-drawals."

Kitty simply stared at her.

Doc rose from his chair. "Sarah, you're in no state to go anywhere. I must insist that you lie down again."

She shook her head. "I have work to do," she said. "Everything has to be in order before Charles and Owen and Papa and I leave for Philadelphia."

"Before you do *what?*"

"Charles loves me. We're getting mar-ried. Raising Owen together." Even in Sarah's own ears, the words sounded impossible, but there was no going back now. She'd said cruel things to Wyatt, out of stark necessity. Sent him away. Written in her book of lies, *Today I told the greatest lie of all. I told Wyatt I didn't love him, didn't want to be his wife.*

"So *that's* why Wyatt left here looking like somebody ran over him with a hay wagon," Kitty marveled. "My God, Sarah, what have you done?"

"The only thing I could do," Sarah said, wondering even then how she'd bear Charles's touch, after what she and Wyatt had shared. How she'd survive the days and weeks and months and years ahead, never looking into those dark eyes and reading secrets there. Never laughing with Wyatt, never feeling his hands on her.

But survive she would. Because of— and for—Owen.

She walked out of the house then, and neither Doc nor Kitty tried to stop her. Maybe they knew she would shatter into pieces if they touched her, and never be able to put herself back together again.

"WYATT?"

He ignored Rowdy. Climbed up into the buckboard, parked in front of the livery stable. Lonesome, the poor old critter, was still sitting in the back.

Slapping down the reins, Wyatt drove the buckboard team hard back to the place he'd hoped to call home, someday. Poor old Lonesome had no choice but to go along, sitting in the back of the wagon like he was, enduring the axle-breaking pace.

He'd have burned the shack to the ground if he'd had the wherewithal to do it, but he didn't. He should have stopped at the mercantile, bought some matches and some kerosene.

Since he hadn't had the foresight to do that, in the shape he was in, he just sat there, staring at the ruins of some long-gone settler's dreams—and of his own. He could protest the dissolution of his marriage to Judge Harvey, say he and Sarah had made love, not once, but half a dozen times. But it would be his word against Sarah's, and the judge would believe her—or pretend he did.

Wyatt had been aware all along that Rowdy had mounted his horse and followed him out from town. Now, his brother rode up alongside the wagon.

"Wyatt," he said, "what the hell happened?"

"It's too hard to say," Wyatt told him. He couldn't look right at Rowdy, but he could see him out of the corner of his eye, and as broken up as he was, he was glad of his presence.

"Sarah?" Rowdy asked, very quietly, shifting in the saddle, resettling his hat, pretending an interest in the far horizon.

"She's come to her senses," Wyatt said, after a very long time.

Rowdy swung down off the horse. Rescued Lonesome from the back of the buckboard. The two of them walked around in the deep grass littered with old wagon wheels, barrel staves, and empty bottles. Lonesome lifted his hind leg against the corner of what had once been a barn.

"How's that?" Rowdy asked, at considerable length. "How, exactly, has Sarah 'come to her senses'?"

"You were right in the beginning, Rowdy." Wyatt's voice came out sounding hoarse. His eyes felt as though he'd splashed them with handfuls of acid, and his throat hurt like sin. Maybe he'd contracted the diphtheria. Maybe he'd die.

He sure as hell *felt* like dying.

"When I said you were an outlaw and she was a lady and you ought to leave her alone?"

Wyatt merely nodded.

"I was wrong about that, Wyatt," Rowdy said.

"There ought to be a parade," Wyatt croaked. "One of Payton Yarbro's sons just admitted he was wrong about something."

Rowdy gave a hoarse laugh. "What's really happening here, Wyatt?" he asked. "Sarah loves you. She glows with it, like she swallowed a lamp with the wick lit."

"She wants the boy," Wyatt said. "And this is the only way to get him."

Rowdy absorbed that. Waited a few moments. "I think I saw Billy Justice today," he said.

If he'd thrown a bucket of cold creek water all over Wyatt, he couldn't have brought him out of his sorry melancholy the way those words did.

Wyatt let go of his deathgrip on the reins, looked down at Rowdy, who was standing by the buckboard now, with his hat pushed to the back of his head. "What?"

Rowdy described the man he'd seen that morning, in the bank.

It had to be Billy.

And he'd been alone within killing distance of Sarah, even persuaded her to show him the safe.

Reflecting on that, Wyatt's whole perspective shifted. He set aside thoughts of Charles Langstreet, and Owen, and how Sarah had run him off. How she'd tried to run him off, that was.

"You going to fight for her, Wyatt?" Rowdy asked quietly, mounting up again. "Fight for the boy?"

Wyatt nodded, released the brake lever, his jaw set so tight that it threatened to snap in two. "Hold on, Lonesome," he told the dog. "There's a rough ride ahead."

WHEN OWEN CAME OUT of the schoolhouse, a stack of new books under one arm, Sarah was waiting for him on the other side of the picket fence. Grinning and shoving with the other boys as they flowed out into the yard, he spotted Sarah and looked delighted at first, then, as he read her face, frightened.

He hurried toward her, through the open gate. "Is something wrong with my grandfather?" he asked.

Sarah shook her head. "No, sweetheart," she said. It was the first time she'd dared to address him with an endearment. "Your—your father is back. And he has something to tell you—"

"What?" Owen fairly spat the word. His face took on an obstinate flush, and he ignored his friends as they went by, casting worried, curious glances in his direction.

"Owen, Mar—your mother—"

"*You* are my mother!"

Some of the children stopped, turned around at Owen's shout, and Davina appeared on the porch of the schoolhouse, looking troubled.

"Yes," Sarah said, putting her hands on his shoulders. "Yes, I'm your mother. But Mrs. Langstreet—"

"She's dead, isn't she?" Owen said woodenly.

"I'm sorry. Yes, Owen. She's gone."

"Good."

"Owen!"

"I don't care! She locked me in closets— she called me a bastard!"

Sarah's heart, already broken over Wyatt, dissolved within her. "Oh, Owen, it's wrong to say such terrible things, no matter what she did or said. And now your father is back in Stone Creek, and he and I are going to be married, and we'll all go back to Philadelphia with him—"

Owen's freckles seemed to stand out from his face as he first reddened, then went pale again. "You can't marry him! You're married to Wyatt—"

Sarah couldn't speak. She simply shook her head.

"I *hate* you!" Owen screamed. "I hate you just like I hated her!" And with that, he ran from her, dropping his books and his tablet and running harder still.

"Mrs. Yarbro?"

Sarah stiffened at the name. Turned and looked at Davina, now standing just on the other side of the fence, watching her. "Please," Sarah whispered, "don't call me that."

"I'm very worried about Owen," Davina said.

"Do you think I'm *not?*" Sarah snapped.

Davina put a hand on her arm. It seemed a mature gesture, for one so young and so sheltered. Full of dignity and tenderness. "Of course you are," Davina said. "Is there anything I can do to help? Either you or Owen?"

"I wish there were," Sarah said, regretting the way she'd spoken to the young woman earlier. She just didn't seem to have the strength to apologize. "I wish there were."

"If you think of anything, will you tell me?" Davina asked. "Please?"

Sarah nodded. Thanked the new schoolmarm and started slowly for home.

Owen would be there when she arrived. She'd find a way to reason with him, a way to make him understand.

He'd forget Wyatt.

He'd forget Lonesome.

They'd be happy together, he'd see.

But Owen wasn't at home when Sarah got there.

She searched the whole house, and the yard, and even the garden shed and the outhouse.

No Owen.

She was standing in the kitchen, barely managing to hold herself together, when she heard the buckboard drive up outside.

Wyatt.

That was it! Owen had gone to Wyatt, and Wyatt had brought him home.

She hurried to the window.

Wyatt was by himself, except for Lonesome.

"Sarah," he began, a few moments later, letting himself in through the back door without knocking, the dog plodding wearily past him to collapse onto the folded quilt still lying next to the stove. "We need to talk."

All Sarah's panic erupted in that one moment, and hysteria wasn't far behind. The rational part of her brain counseled her to be calm, even reasonable, but she couldn't. Too much had happened. Too much was wrong. Too much was at stake.

"I can't find Owen!" she blurted out. "Wyatt, I don't know where Owen is!"

Wyatt said nothing for a long moment. Then a muscle bunched in his jaw. "We'll find him, Sarah," he said. He extended a hand to her, and she went to him, and flung herself into his arms, sobbing. "We'll find him," he repeated.

CHAPTER NINETEEN

ONCE HE'D MADE SENSE of Sarah's disjointed account of what had happened between her and Owen, in front of the schoolhouse, Wyatt knew exactly where the boy had gone. To Charles. The poor kid probably thought he could reason with his father, make him understand how much he wanted to grow up in Stone Creek, with Sarah.

From what Wyatt had gathered, though, reasoning with Langstreet would be like reasoning with a cornered rattlesnake.

So he headed the buckboard straight for the only hotel in town.

Sarah moved to climb down when he drew in the reins and set the brakes, but Wyatt froze her to the wagon seat with a look.

"Let me handle this," he said.

She swallowed visibly, nodded. Wyatt knew it was despair, not docility, that made her comply. She was emotionally spent, overwhelmed, and while her strength and her spirit would return, because she was that kind of woman right down to the marrow of her bones, for a little while, anyhow, she was willing to obey.

It wasn't hard to find Langstreet's room. It was the biggest one, directly at the top of the stairs, and Owen was in there yelling like a rebel soldier charging the whole Union army all by himself.

Wyatt took the stairs two at a time, ignoring the ineffectual protests of a desk clerk, and entered the room without bothering to knock.

Langstreet sat in a chair near the window, his face a mask.

Owen stood directly in front of his father, his little fists clenched. He stopped in midsentence when he realized Wyatt was there, turned his head and looked at him with such desperation in his eyes that Wyatt had to shore himself up a little before he dared to speak.

"Ah, the outlaw-lover," Langstreet drawled. "I knew you'd come."

"Owen," Wyatt said quietly, "your mama is out in front of the hotel, in Sam's wagon. Go and look after her. She's been mighty worried about you."

Owen hesitated, reddened and then nodded. After hurling one last look of pure hatred at Charles, he left the room.

Wyatt closed the door. He hadn't wanted the boy to hear what he knew would be said here.

"At least you had one night with her," Langstreet said. "She's quite the little wild-cat in bed, isn't she?"

Wyatt had never despised a man, not Billy Justice and his ilk, not even the cruelest guards in prison, the way he despised Charles Langstreet in that moment. "I won't discuss that with you," he said evenly, surprised at the dull, painful calm thudding inside him like a second heart.

"It ought to be quite interesting—not to mention diverting—to woo Sarah back to my bed."

"You don't want Sarah. You don't even want the boy. What you want is to make everybody around you as miserable as you are. It'll be a hard life, living with a woman and a boy who hate you half again as much as God hates the devil."

Langstreet sighed. Crossed his legs in that effeminate way of so many men of his class. "The boy will be troublesome, all right. But that will be easily remedied. After a few months, when Sarah's had a chance to get used to being my wife, I'll send him off to school in Europe. Do him good. He's turned wild, even in the short time he's been out here. Dresses like a ruffian. And if he'd been big enough, he'd have taken his fists to me few minutes ago."

"I wouldn't mind doing that myself, right about now," Wyatt said, taking in the black armband of mourning on Langstreet's sleeve. "Sarah is *my* wife. And I'll kill you before I let you take her back East, use her like a whore and throw her to the wolves. You *know* your fancy friends aren't going to accept her."

Langstreet shrugged. "They were *Marjory's* 'fancy friends,' not mine. I've never quite met with their approval. Marjory was the one with the genteel pedigree, you see. Philadelphia Main Line, all the way. But I had the money, only son of a filthy upstart industrialist that I am. Do you think I give a damn what they say? I can ruin most of them with a stroke of a pen."

"And you enjoy that, don't you? Ruining people?"

"It's—amusing. Very interesting, really. Take you, for instance. You're never going to get over Sarah's going away. And I've been keeping a close eye on things at the bank, from a discreet distance, of course. Thomas proved an able and willing spy. I can call your loan, Mr. Yarbro, and pull that little ranch right out from under you."

"You can take that 'little ranch,' Mr. Langstreet, and shove it up your dandified ass."

Langstreet chuckled, framing one side of his face with a thumb and forefinger as he regarded Wyatt. "Do yourself a favor, *Wyatt*. Steal a horse and ride out before I crush you like the cheap hoodlum you are."

"And miss seeing you try to 'crush' me? Not on your life, *Charlie*."

Langstreet's gaze strayed languidly to the gun on Wyatt's hip. "Are you challenging me to a gunfight?" he asked, his voice silky with disdain. "You'd probably win. I would be dead, fodder for those wretched hacks churning out dime novels. And *you,* Mr. Yarbro, would go straight back to prison. Even hang. Where would Sarah and Owen be then? Who would take care of them, with Ephriam lying like a slavering hulk in his sickbed?"

"Sarah would," Wyatt said, knowing it was true. "She'd take care of herself and Owen. She doesn't need me any more than she needs you. But here's the difference, Langstreet—she *wants* me. If she marries you, it will only be because she can't bear being separated from Owen. You wouldn't understand, but unlike you, and unlike your dead wife, Sarah *loves* that boy. He's not an inconvenience to her, not an embarrassment. She loves him enough to forfeit her own happiness to keep him safe."

"Love," Langstreet muttered. "I loved her once, you know. In time, I'll learn to love her again. I'll make her happy."

"If you loved her so much, why did you

desert her? Take her child away? Go back to your wife?"

"Marjory and I had an agreement when we married—a formal one, written down and duly witnessed. I would have had to sign over half of what I owned if I'd divorced her. So I waited for her to die. She certainly took her excruciating time doing it, though."

Bile scalded the back of Wyatt's throat. "If you want to take Sarah, or the boy, you're going to have to come through me to do it. Sure, I'll go to prison if I gun you down, and probably hang, but here's the thing, Langstreet. Without Sarah and Owen, I've got nothing to lose. Nothing at all. Rowdy will look after my dog and my horse. Sarah will mourn a while—not for you, thoroughly dead and six feet under, but for me—and then she'll marry some lucky bastard and make a life for herself and for Owen."

For the first time, Langstreet looked uncertain. "You'd actually do it, wouldn't you? Challenge me to a gunfight. Put a bullet through my heart. All for Sarah and Owen."

"All for Sarah and Owen," Wyatt said.

Langstreet arched an eyebrow. "High

noon tomorrow?" he taunted. "In the middle of Main Street?"

"The place of your choosing. One way or the other, Sarah and Owen aren't going anyplace."

"A word to your brother the marshal, the famed Rowdy Yarbro, and you'll be behind bars before you get the chance to draw on me."

Wyatt smiled. "I guess you didn't hear," he said. "The jailhouse blew up a few days ago. Dynamite. And Rowdy might be marshal, and a fast gun, but he's still my little brother, and he'd need a bigger posse than he could gather on short notice to round me up. Anyhow, blood is blood. More likely, he'd take my part."

He had the satisfaction of watching the color drain from Langstreet's face.

Wyatt tugged at the brim of his hat. Turned to reach for the doorknob. "I'll be seeing you," he said. "Where and when? That's your say, not mine."

"He'll hate you forever, the boy will, if you shoot me," Langstreet said. "Whatever differences Owen and I have, it's as you said. Blood is blood. And I'm his father."

"Maybe he will," Wyatt said with an ease

he didn't feel, "but he'll be with Sarah, and whatever happens to you or me, Owen will grow up to be a fine man, because she'll see to that. Goodbye, Mr. Langstreet. It's been—nice talking to you."

With that, Wyatt left.

He went downstairs, climbed up into the wagon seat beside Sarah, and took up the reins. He felt the boy's gaze burning into his back.

"What happened in there?" Sarah asked.

"Mr. Langstreet and I came to an understanding," Wyatt replied. Then he took Owen and Sarah to the safest place he knew. Sam O'Ballivan's ranch. He installed them in his cabin, told them both to stay put and saddled up a horse. When Langstreet came to terms with the situation, Wyatt meant to be ready.

As MUCH AS Sarah didn't want to believe it, she knew instinctively what was about to happen. Charles Langstreet had money and power. Wyatt had a gun and a reputation. A deadly confrontation was inevitable.

Wyatt would win, if that confrontation

involved pistols, Sarah had no doubt whatsoever of that. But such duels were illegal. In the end, everyone would lose—Charles, herself and Owen, and especially Wyatt. Rowdy, sworn to uphold the law and dead serious about it, would arrest Wyatt. He'd be tried, convicted, and either spend the rest of his life in prison, or be hanged.

Sarah's stomach rolled. She had to stop this somehow.

Get to Rowdy, that was it. Tell him what she suspected.

But what about Owen? She couldn't take him to town. He worshipped Wyatt, and as angry as he was with Charles, the man was *his father.* Dear God, he might even be caught in the cross fire.

"Stay here," she told Owen, with only half a hope that he'd obey. She ran for the bunkhouse, found Jody Wexler there, stirring a pot of beans at the stove. Babbled out her story, begged him to keep Owen on Stone Creek Ranch until she returned, no matter what.

In Sam's barn she chose a likely looking horse, saddled it up, and rode hard for town. She knew by the peaceful quiet surrounding the main house that no one was at home, or she'd have stopped just long enough to ask for Sam's help.

By the time she reached Stone Creek—a strange, frightening silence had fallen over the whole place, and there was no one in sight—she was covered in dust from head to foot, and her hair had long since fallen from its pins, bouncing around her waist as she drew rein in front of Rowdy's house.

Lark came out of the cottage, the baby on her hip, her smile of welcome fading when she got a good look at Sarah.

"Where," Sarah demanded breathlessly, "is Rowdy?"

"I don't know," Lark answered. "He left in a hurry. Said something about having to find Wyatt before all hell broke loose. Sarah, what's—"

Sarah prayed Rowdy had been successful, found Wyatt, talked some sense into him. Maybe they'd gone out to the new place; Wyatt had been working out there.

She reined the horse in that direction and nudged her lathered horse into a run.

Wyatt wasn't at the ranch, and neither was Rowdy.

And it was getting dark.

Dismayed, not knowing where else to look, Sarah rode slowly back to Stone Creek to wait. She couldn't bring herself to go home, so she went to the bank. Locked the door behind her, lit the lamp in her father's office.

Wyatt, her heart cried. *Where are you?*

If he'd only come back. They could leave town, she and Wyatt and Owen—why hadn't she thought of that before? Start over, in some faraway place, with new names. And when things settled down, she could send for her father. Get Doc to bring him to wherever they were—

She sighed, pacing the floor of the office.

Wyatt wouldn't run. He'd done enough of that in his life, and Sarah knew he'd had his fill of it.

Scuffling sounds under the floor stopped Sarah in her tracks. She thought she heard voices, muffled and hurried.

She was losing her mind.

She began pacing again.

Somebody knocked hard at the front door of the bank.

Wyatt.

Sarah rushed to open it, and found not Wyatt, but Owen. And William Smith was right behind him, holding him by the collar with one hand and jamming the barrel of a pistol into the nape of his neck with the other.

Sarah swayed, and a scream surged up into her throat.

"One sound," Smith said, "and I'll blow this kid's brains all over your skirts."

"I'm sorry," Owen croaked, looking up at Sarah with terrified, pleading eyes. "I should have stayed with Jody, but I—"

The armed man shoved Owen over the threshold. Came in and shut the door quietly behind him.

"Ain't it peculiar," Smith said, as Sarah pulled Owen away from him, into her arms. "How things work themselves out? If there's one man I hate in all creation, it's Wyatt Yarbro. He sold us out to the vigilantes. He got Carl killed dead. Now how am I going to tell my poor mama that her Carl's dead and buried?"

Sarah held Owen close, afraid to speak. The rustling sounds under the floor grew louder.

"That's Paddy and the boys," Smith

said, pleased. "They're laying dynamite down there. In a few minutes, this place will blow like the jailhouse did, and money will be raining down from the sky. Pity you and the boy will go up with it."

"Let Owen leave," Sarah said, willing to beg if she had to. "He's a child."

Smith shoved the pistol barrel hard into the hollow of her throat. "That just makes it all the better. It paid off, hiding out around town for a few days, finding out what Wyatt Yarbro is willing to die for. You and the boy, it turns out. But I'm going to be *charitable* about this. I'm going to let ole Wyatt live. Live to mourn his woman and this boy the way Ma and me are mournin' Carl."

Sarah saw a movement behind Smith's shoulder, and he caught the shift of her gaze.

Charles Langstreet stepped into the bank. "Sarah, I saw the light and—" Seeing Smith with a gun to Sarah's throat, he stopped.

Smith turned with a slow, lethal grace and shot him.

Owen screamed, while Sarah stood, frozen in horror.

"Too damn much noise," Smith complained fretfully. Then he turned around again, backhanded Owen so hard that he fell and struck his head against the counter.

Sarah tried to go to him, but Smith slammed her in the temple with his pistol butt, a vicious blow that blinded her, sent her sprawling on top of Owen's motionless body.

"Don't you worry now, little lady," she heard Smith say. "It'll all be over in a couple of minutes."

Sarah was aware of noise outside, men's voices, shooting. She was bleeding, and though she did try to rise, she couldn't move.

The door crashed open with such noise that Sarah thought the dynamite under the floor had been detonated.

Then she heard a familiar voice. Dimly, through a pounding haze of pain and fear.

"Get him out of here!" Wyatt yelled, probably referring to Charles.

Sarah felt herself dragged up from the floor by her waist. "Owen," she whispered. "Owen—"

"I've got him," she heard Wyatt say. Her eyes were blurred with blood from her aching temple; she couldn't see him. "I've got him, Sarah."

She felt cool air next, and hands reaching for her.

Voices, calling her name, calling Owen's.

And then the world exploded with a roar. There was a flash of terrible heat, and more shouting.

Sarah opened her eyes, cleared them. She was lying on the sidewalk, on the opposite side of the street. Mr. Smith had been right, she thought dizzily. Money rained down from the sky.

But Owen was beside her, sitting up, clutching her hand.

Owen was alive, and that, for the moment, was all that mattered.

THE NEXT TIME SHE CAME AROUND, Sarah found herself lying on the examining table in Doc's office. Wyatt bent over her, his face sooty, like the night the jailhouse blew up and burned. He held one of her hands in both of his.

"Am I dead?" she asked.

He chuckled, but his eyes glistened with tears. "No," he said. "Thank God."

"Owen?"

"Upstairs with Doc. Had to give that boy a dose of medicine, just like Lonesome, to keep him down."

"How did—how did you know—?"

"One of the girls at the Spit Bucket heard some bragging about how the bank was about to be robbed, and she told Rowdy. He came and found me, then we both went hunting for Sam. Soon as we got back to town, Lark told me you'd been by, asking for Rowdy. I thought about where you'd go, and figured you'd head for the Stockman's Bank to wait." He leaned in, kissed her forehead. "Damn, Sarah, when I realized you and Owen were in there—"

"Charles—that man shot Charles—"

Sorrow moved in Wyatt's eyes. "He didn't make it, Sarah," he said. "Doc tried to pull him through, but the bullet nicked his heart."

"Owen saw it," Sarah whispered brokenly. "Owen saw his father die. What will that do to him?"

"We'll get him through it, Sarah. You and me."

Her heart warmed and sweetened, as though a thin stream of honey flowed into it. Charles was dead, and as much as Owen had wanted to stay in Stone Creek with her and with Wyatt, with Lonesome and the grandfather he loved, he would mourn the father he *wished* Charles had been, perhaps always.

"Would you have shot Charles yourself, Wyatt?" The answer would be painful to hear, something to grapple with, inside herself, for a long time. But she had to know.

"If it had come to that," Wyatt replied, "yes."

Sarah closed her eyes. Opened them again. "Mr. Smith, and the other robbers—?"

"Got them all," Wyatt said. "Sam and Rowdy and me, and a few of the townsmen. They're all tied up and stowed in a back room, over at Jolene Bell's. Did you know she had a meat locker?"

"No," Sarah said drowsily. "I don't frequent Jolene Bell's Saloon."

Wyatt laughed. "Only because she hasn't got a ladies' poker game running," he said. "Sarah Yarbro, do you really smoke cigars?"

"Once," she admitted. The pain in her

head was receding, but so was waking consciousness. "It made me throw up."

"Rest now, Sarah."

"You won't leave me?"

"Hell itself and a whole crew of demons couldn't make me do that."

"I love you, Wyatt Yarbro," she murmured, going under. Owen wasn't the only one Doc had medicated.

"And I love you," she heard Wyatt say before the darkness surrounded her, lowered her into blessed oblivion.

EPILOGUE

Three months later

SNOW DRIFTED PAST the kitchen windows as Sarah sat at the table, reading her book of lies. She wasn't going to need it, ever again, she thought, smiling, remembering the woman she had been before. Before Wyatt, before Owen's arrival in Stone Creek, before her father's illness.

Doc came down the kitchen stairway, and he was holding Kitty's hand. She blushed like a debutante about to dance at her first cotillion.

Sarah studied them, smiled. She'd had her suspicions, of course. Her father had been rapidly improving over the past few weeks—he was confined to an invalid's chair, but he could say a few words and even play halting games of checkers with Owen or Wyatt. Still, Doc had spent a lot of time in that sickroom, and it didn't take a genius to figure out that it wasn't just Ephriam he'd come to see. It was Kitty.

Sarah got up from her chair, carried her book of lies to the stove, and shoved it into the hot winter fire. Wyatt had gone to Flagstaff with Rowdy on some sort of business, but it was Friday. He'd be back on the evening train. Owen had begged a day out of school and gone with them.

Turning to face Doc and Kitty, Sarah set her hands on her hips and tilted her head to one side. Lonesome, lying on his quilt and all mended now, looked up at her curiously.

"All right," she said, "what's going on here?"

Doc flushed. "Kitty and I—"

"We're in love," Kitty finished for him, her scrubbed face shining. She'd heartened, lately, and she and Davina, though still not a doting mother and daughter, had established the bare beginnings of a truce. Davina, as Sarah had predicted, was engaged. Jody Wexler was the lucky man.

Sarah laughed for joy. Hugged Kitty, hugged Doc.

"I can still sit with Ephriam every day," Kitty said, teary-eyed. "But as soon as Judge Harvey hitches us up proper, I'll be moving out."

Sarah nodded, teary-eyed herself.

Outside, familiar voices carried through the crisp winter night.

Wyatt was back, and Owen.

"Stay for supper," Sarah said to Doc. "I've made stew—"

"I'm taking my future bride to the hotel dining room for an engagement supper," Doc said, with a shake of his head. He took Kitty's plain woolen cloak down from the peg next to the door and draped it gently over her shoulders just as Wyatt and Owen came in, stomping snow off their boots, their faces glowing.

Lonesome gave a yelp of joy and rushed to greet them.

Doc and Kitty slipped out.

"Wyatt's rich now!" Owen piped, peeling himself out of scarf and coat and mittens.

"Not rich," Wyatt said, ruffling the boy's

hair, then bending to do the same with the dog's ears. He'd been working out at Sam's, and coming back to the house at night, because Owen needed to go to school and Sarah, without the bank to occupy her time, had been developing her homemaking skills.

"What is all this talk about being rich?" Sarah asked, turning to stir the stew. She wanted to fling herself into Wyatt's arms, but that would have been unseemly, in front of a child. Besides, there would be plenty of time for holding each other later, when they were alone in their room.

"There was a reward on Billy Justice's head," Wyatt answered. "Fifteen hundred dollars. It's enough to pay off that mortgage, fix the house and barn, even buy a few head of cattle, come spring."

He drew her into his arms, kissed her lightly on the mouth. A thrill went through her.

"Wyatt bought us all presents," Owen said. "Even Lonesome."

Sarah noticed the bundle, wrapped in brown paper and string, resting snow-dampened just inside the door.

"Presents? It's not even Christmas," Sarah said.

"It will be," Owen pointed out. "Next week. We don't have to wait to get our presents, do we, Wyatt?"

Wyatt laughed. "No, boy," he said. "You don't have to wait. But we'd better be rustling ourselves up a tree, if you want Saint Nick to pay you a visit."

Owen beamed. "There isn't any Saint Nick. Just you and Mama."

Mama. Sarah loved the sound of that word.

Somewhat shyly, Wyatt fetched the bundle, set it in the middle of the table, and carefully untied the string. There was a blush in his neck as he worked, and Sarah felt her already fathomless love for him deepen.

Lonesome got a bone, fresh from a Flagstaff butcher shop.

Owen received a book, finely bound, with gold lettering. *The Adventures of Huckleberry Finn.*

There was a fine wooden pipe and tobacco for Ephriam.

And, lastly, a little box for Sarah.

Wyatt's hand trembled, ever so slightly, as he offered it to her.

She opened it.

A golden locket lay inside, gleaming in the light of a warm, sturdy home on a snowy winter's night.

Fumbling a little, Wyatt removed the locket, opened the little catch. There were two tiny pictures inside, one of her and Wyatt on their wedding day, and one of Owen with his arms spread as wide as his smile, cavorting in front of the marriage cake.

"Oh," Sarah whispered. "Oh, Wyatt."

He moved behind her, to clasp the delicate chain at the back of her neck. Kissed her nape, with just the barest touch of his tongue.

Sarah turned in his embrace, smiled tearfully up into his eyes.

"Jupiter and spit," Owen said to Lonesome, with mock disgust. He considered this swearing. Sarah considered it better than a lot of other words he'd probably learned on the school grounds. "Now they're going to start *spooning* again."

"Get used to it," Wyatt said, without breaking the hold of Sarah's gaze.

"I'll *never* get used to it," Owen replied.

"Hard luck for you," Wyatt answered. "Go work on your arithmetic or something."

"You just want to get rid of me. So you and Mama can *spoon.*"

"Smart kid," Wyatt said. "Go."

Owen went, taking Lonesome with him. A few moments later, he began to pound industriously on the keys of Sarah's piano. He had no musical talent whatsoever.

"I have a present for you, too, Wyatt Yarbro," Sarah said, holding on to Wyatt's shoulders so she wouldn't tumble right into his eyes.

He chuckled. "I can hardly wait," he said.

Sarah blushed. "Besides that," she told him.

He looked puzzled then, even a little concerned. "What?"

With one finger, Sarah smoothed the crease in his forehead. "You're going to be a father," she said, very softly.

He was in the process of adopting Owen, with help from Judge Harvey. "I'm already—" Then the realization struck him. His face transformed in an instant, full of disbelief and joy. "A baby, Sarah? We're having a *baby?* When?"

She stood on tiptoe and kissed the cleft in his chin. How she adored that cleft, and everything else about him. His strength, his integrity, his lovemaking, by turns passionate and tender, and the soft words he spoke afterward, when he held her very close.

She beamed. "About nine months and ten minutes from the day we were married," she replied.

He threw back his head and laughed with joy.

And Sarah loved that, too.

December 22, 1896

LIZZIE MCKETTRICK LEANED slightly forward in her seat, as if to do so would make the train go faster. Home. She was going home, at long last, to the Triple M Ranch, to her large rowdy family. After more than two years away, first attending Miss Ridgely's Institute of Deportment and Refinement for Young Women, then normal school, Lizzie was returning for good to the place and the people she loved. She would arrive a day before she was expected, too, and surprise them all—her papa, her stepmother, Lorelei, her little brothers, John Henry, Gabriel and Doss.

She had presents for everyone, most sent ahead from San Francisco weeks ago, but a few especially precious ones secreted away in one of her three huge travel trunks.

Only her grandfather, Angus McKettrick, the patriarch of the sprawling clan, knew she'd be there that very evening. He'd be waiting, Lizzie thought happily, at the small train station in Indian Rock, probably at the reins of one of the big flatbed sleighs used to carry feed to snowbound cattle on the range. She'd warned him, in her most recent letter, that she'd be bringing all her belongings with her, for this homecoming was permanent—not just a brief visit, like the past couple of Christmases.

Lizzie smiled a mischievous little smile. Even Angus, her closest confidant except for her parents, didn't know *all* the facts.

She glanced sideways at Whitley Carson, slumped against the sooty window in the seat next to hers, huddled under a blanket, sound asleep. His breath fogged the glass, and every so often he stirred fitfully, grumbled something.

Alas, for all his sundry charms, Whitley

was not an enthusiastic traveler. His complaints over the three days since they'd boarded the first train in San Francisco had been numerous.

The train was filthy.

There was no dining car.

The cigar smoke roiling overhead made him cough.

He was never going to be warm again.

And *what* in God's green earth had possessed the woman three rows behind them to undertake a journey of any significant distance with two rascally children and a fussy infant in tow?

Now the baby let out a pitiable squall.

Lizzie, used to babies because there were so many on the Triple M, was unruffled. Whitley's obvious annoyance troubled her. Although she planned to teach, married or not, she hoped for a houseful of children of her own someday—healthy, noisy, rambunctious ones, raised to be confident adults and freethinkers.

It was hard, in the moment, to square the Whitley she was seeing now with the kind of father she had hoped he would be.

The man across the aisle from her laid down his newspaper, stood and stretched.

He'd boarded the train several hours earlier, in Phoenix, carrying what looked like a doctor's bag, its leather sides cracked and scratched. His waistcoat was clean but threadbare, and he wore neither a hat nor a sidearm, the absence of both unusual in the still-wild Arizona Territory.

Although Lizzie expected Whitley to propose once they were home with her family, she'd been stealing glances at the stranger ever since he entered the railroad car. There was something about him, beyond his patrician good looks, that constantly drew her attention. His hair was dark, and rather too long, his eyes brown and intense, bespeaking formidable intelligence. Although he probably wasn't a great deal older than Lizzie, who would turn twenty on her next birthday, there was a maturity in his manner and countenance that intrigued her. It was as though he'd lived many other lives, in other times and places, and extracted wisdom from them all . . . .